"Has the 'wow!' factor in spades...Well-developed and wonderfully imaginative, *Finders Keepers* has 'exceptional merit' written all over it." —*Heartstrings Reviews*

"*Finders Keepers* is a great ride from start to finish. . . . A delight to read...Sinclair delivers a story balanced nicely between space opera adventure and emotion-centered romance—not the easiest thing to find anymore. Thanks, Linnea!" —*Speculative Romance Online*

"Five blue ribbons...A wonderful book...not to be missed...Takes romantic sci-fi to an all-new level." —RomanceJunkies.com

PRAISE FOR
GABRIEL'S GHOST

Winner of the 2006 RITA® Award for Best Paranormal Romance
2003 Prism Award, 2nd place (tie with *An Accidental Goddess*), for Best Futuristic Romance
Winner of the 2002 *Affaire de Coeur* Award for Best Futuristic Romance
2002 Sapphire Award, 2nd place (tie with *An Accidental Goddess*), for Best Speculative Romance Novel
***Romance Reviews Today* Perfect 10 Award**

"Five stars! Captures your interest with nonstop action and suspense and keeps it as the tension mounts...A must buy." —*CataRomance Reviews*

"Both an exciting sci-fi adventure and a warm romance, with deep characterization and meaningful relationships. Highly recommended." —*Romance Reviews Today*

"There isn't a shadow of a doubt in this reviewer's mind that Bantam has a bonafide, interstellar star in this author. Prepare to be star-struck, dear reader." —*Heartstrings Reviews*

"With the vision and texture of a poet, the heart of a warrior, and the skill of a master, Sinclair creates a world of psychic gifts and shape shifters, of dangers beyond imagination and love beyond question.... A tale so entrancing, so mesmerizing that readers will be absolutely blown away." —*Midwest Book Review*

"How can a review do justice to a book that sweeps you away from the very first page?... Sinclair has managed to mix religion, politics, adventure, science fiction and romance into one of the best reads of the year. A true winner!" —*Interludes Magazine*

PRAISE FOR
an accidental GODDESS

**Finalist for the 2005 RIO Award for Best
Sci-Fi/Fantasy Romance
Winner of the 2003 RWA® Windy City Choice Award
for Best FF&P Romance
2002 PEARL Award Honorable Mention for
Best Science Fiction Novel
Romantic Times BookClub magazine's
2002 Gold Medal Top Pick Award
Finalist for the *CataRomance* Single Titles Reviewers'
Choice Award**

"Sinclair's fertile imagination scores another winner.... Well written and riveting ... make a place for it on your keeper shelf." —*Romance Reviews Today*

"Entirely entertaining." —*Contra Costa Times*

"Proves once again why Sinclair is one of the reigning queens of science fiction romances...This is a book [with] bright, attractive characters, an interesting plot, action, adventure, humor and romance." —*Starlog*

"A quirky, humorous, fast-paced saga of deception, passion, trust, and risk...Linnea Sinclair's innovative and entertaining story will captivate the reader and provide hours of laughter, suspense, and adventure." —*Fantasy Book Spot*

"A star in the making." —SFCrowsnest.com

PRAISE FOR GAMES OF COMMAND

Winner of the 2007 PEARL Award for Best Science Fiction and Fantasy Romance
2008 RITA® Finalist for Best Paranormal Romance
Finalist for the 2008 Fantasm Award for Best Space Opera Romance
AllAboutRomance.com Top Ten SF/Fantasy & Futuristic Romances
Top Ten in Supernatural Romance Novels from Helium.com

"Linnea Sinclair just gets better and better! *Games of Command* is not to be missed!"
—Mary Jo Putney, author of *A Distant Magic*

"*Games of Command* is a wonderful book. Linnea Sinclair has written a unique and utterly intriguing hero in Kel-Paten. Sexy, complex and devoted, he's a man to fall in love with." —Nalini Singh, author of *Hostage to Pleasure*

"Desert Island Keeper . . . A flat-out terrific story of thrilling action and tender romance." —AllAboutRomance.com

"When it comes to high flying adventure, political intrigue and dark romance, Sinclair has it aced! This surprising tale is filled with shifting loyalties, deception and jaw-dropping flying maneuvers. . . . 4½ stars."
—*Romantic Times Book Review*

"Doesn't disappoint for a single nanosecond. As rich, complex and intriguing as ever, Sinclair's fictional universe is an exciting, mysterious and dangerous place to live and love. . . . Lots of action, lots of fantasy, and lots of romance equals scores of well-pleased readers."
—*Heartstrings Reviews*

PRAISE FOR THE DOWN HOME ZOMBIE BLUES

Honorable Mention for the 2007 PEARL Award for Best Futuristic Romance
Nominated for the 2007 *Romantic Times* Reviewer's Choice Awards for Best Futuristic/Fantasy Romance

PRAISE FOR
SHADES OF DARK

Winner of the CTRR Award for April 2008 by Coffee Time Romance
Romance Reviews Today Perfect 10 Award
Nominated for 2008 *Romantic Times* Reviewer's Choice Award for Best Futuristic/Fantasy Romance

"A rip-roaring tale of danger, passion, and hard choices. No one blends romance and science fiction like Linnea Sinclair, and *Shades of Dark* is another sizzling page-turner!" —Mary Jo Putney, author of *A Distant Magic*

"A masterpiece . . . Not to be missed . . . Linnea Sinclair is always an author you can count on for amazing stories and is one of the best in the business. *Shades of Dark* is going down as one of my favorite books of all time and well deserves RRT'S Perfect 10 award for excellence!" —*Romance Reviews Today*

"The singularly impressive Sinclair thrusts her dynamic lovers into a maelstrom of trouble. The first-person, high-octane action is exhilarating. When it comes to futuristic romance, it doesn't get better than Sinclair! 4½ stars." —*Romantic Times*

"*Shades of Dark* is one of those rare entities; a sequel that is as good, if not better, than the original. . . . This story is a compelling page-turner and a novel that firmly places Linnea Sinclair in my select group of must-have authors. Five cups." —CoffeeTime Romance.com

"I have read books that I couldn't put down before, but nothing has compared to the experience of reading *Shades of Dark*. I found myself hurtling through space, experiencing every twist, every emotion, every betrayal and every victory.... This book should win every literary award on the planet, and then some." —*PNR Reviews*

HOPE'S FOLLY

LINNEA SINCLAIR

BANTAM BOOKS

HOPE'S FOLLY
A Bantam Book / March 2009

Published by
Bantam Dell
A Division of Random House, Inc.
New York, New York

Bantam Books and the rooster colophon are registered trademarks of
Random House, Inc.

ISBN 978-0-553-59218-4

Printed in the United States of America
Published simultaneously in Canada

www.bantamdell.com

OPM 10 9 8 7 6 5 4 3 2 1

acknowledgments

I'm deeply indebted to M. L. Helfstein, USNR (Ret.), for his time, patience, good humor, and the plethora of information he provided me about shipboard protocol and problems. If there was a medal of honor for critique partners/author's helpers, Mikey would take the biggest and best. I'm also indebted to Lynette, his wife, for loaning me her warrior. Her patience goes above and beyond the call of duty.

I'm grateful for the assistance of author Candace Irvin, former U.S. Navy Lieutenant, and Milton Grasle, whose "Writing Fighting" classes are a joy.

However, please note that neither the Alliance Fleet nor the Imperial Fleet is a copy of the U.S. Navy or any one branch of military service currently existing. I have taken literary license, and the militaries presented in this and other books in the Dock Five series are unique unto themselves.

My character Rya Bennton's motto of "Polite, Professional, and Prepared to Kill" is one used by many branches of the armed services and law enforcement today. I honor their bravery, their selflessness, their dedication to protect and to serve. I'd hope you'd find Sub-Lieutenant Bennton a worthy teammate.

Thanks to author Isabo Kelly, for letting me incorporate her sexy swagger as Rya's own.

And thanks to my critique partners and beta readers, who are simply the best: author Stacey (Kade) Klemstein and readers Lynne Welch, Patty Vasquez, Donna Kuhn, and Michelle Williamson. Their creativity and friendship warm my heart.

As always, to Rob, who after almost thirty years still finds me amusing, and to my furry assistants, Daq and Miss Doozy. And to Captain Folly's body double, Fat Tammy the Slut, who crossed the Rainbow Bridge several years ago but still reigns as one of the most memorable and ornery of felines.

AUTHOR'S PLAYLIST

"The Return of the Deji"—DJ Lithium
"Trifecta"—d.a.v.e.//
"Compjacent"—d.a.v.e.//
The above can be found at www.blacktigerrecordings.com

"Toca's Miracle/Toca Me"—Fragma

HOPE'S
FOLLY

1

IMEPRIAL SECURITY BULLETIN 71984-X5Y:
Encryption Level Aldan 1/Top Secret
Immediate Action Required:
Previous reports of the death of former Imperial Admiral Philip Guthrie in Baris sector appear to be in error per new information from one of our operatives in deep cover in the Alliance. Guthrie's capture and/or termination now top priority for all Baris and Calth sector operatives. The Farosians must not be allowed access to Guthrie. The so-called rebel "Alliance" must not be allowed to benefit from this traitor's expertise or financial resources. All restrictions on civilian casualties lifted as per Command Prime. Failure is not an option. This bulletin self-destructs in thirty seconds.

Alliance Admiral Philip Guthrie leaned his forearms on the back of the black padded chair and—heart sinking—studied the silvery image slowly revolving through the holovid suspended above the ready room's table. He hoped—*prayed*—he was wrong, but he knew he wasn't. It took all his training not to let emotions of any kind show on his face.

But, damn, the ship was an ugly, ungainly 850-ton beast, with her billiard-ball bridge and dual bulging cylindrical drive nacelles aft—as bad as he remembered when he'd served aboard her twenty years ago under the command of Captain Cory Bennton. Bennton had been the *Alric Stockwell*'s only saving grace. The *Stockwell* was the last of the Imperial Fleet's Stryker-class heavy cruisers, finally decommissioned—if memory served him—about six years past, though Bennton had moved on to better ships long before that.

And now that ungainly 850-ton beast of a ship was to be Philip's.

"What do you think?" Jodey Bralford, the *Krista Nowicki*'s stocky dark-haired captain, leaned back in his chair at the head of the long table and, chin slightly raised, looked expectantly at Philip. Acquiring the *Stockwell* was the first—some could say desperate—shot at building a workable fleet. But one lone Maven-class 500-ton cruiser, four P-class patrol ships, two fifty-ton Ratch fighters, and two well-armed luxury yachts did not a defense make for the newly formed Alliance of Independent Republics.

But the *Stockwell*?

Bad luck is better than no luck at all, sounded in Philip's mind. He bit back a snort of self-derision. *Beggars—rebels, in this case—can't be choosers*, he reminded that sarcastic part of himself that, lately, he had trouble keeping in check. And had ever since the Imperial Fleet was gutted by one megalomaniac fanatic named Darius Tage, the former first barrister to the ineffectual Emperor Prewitt III. Now, with Prew's mental and emotional collapse, Tage was the self-proclaimed god of all he could get his greedy fingers on.

And executioner of all those who stood in his way—including some of Philip's best captains. He pushed that anger and heartache away and concentrated on the problem—and solution—slowly spinning in front of him in the column of pale-blue light.

"How in hell did you find her?" That question could be interpreted in any number of ways. Jodey was a good friend and Philip hated to sound less than appreciative, but, damn. The *Stockwell*?

"I'd like to impress you with my incisive detective work and infallible contacts, but the truth is we raided her about ten months ago out at the C–D. She was heading out-system from Port January."

The Calth–Dafir border had been an issue for the Imperial Fleet for over a decade, ever since supporters of Sheldon Blaine—Tage's rival for the position as god of the Empire—declared Tos Faros in Dafir as their base of operations. And ten months ago, Jodey and Philip were still part of the Imperial Fleet. Then, Blaine and his Farosian followers were their only serious problem.

"I knew immediately what she was," Jodey continued, pointing to the ship's image between them. "It made no sense for a Stryker-class cruiser to be operating under a passenger-transport registration. Cargo, sure. But not passenger. Obviously, her docs were bogus. She was running arms for the Farosians. They'd acquired her through a series of illegal trades after her original decommission, so we seized her. She was sold about four months later to a Umoran citrus exporter who, with all the problems in Grover's City, was willing to let her go last week for a good price."

"You paid *money* for her?" The words were out before Philip could stop them. He quickly raised his hand, halting whatever was about to come out of

Jodey's mouth in protestation. "Sorry. I didn't mean it quite like it sounded." *Like hell I didn't.* "It's just that other than what we've been able to raise from donations"—much of which had come from his investments—"the Alliance isn't exactly awash in spare funds at the moment." At least, not until he could access the rest of his accounts. He *was* a Guthrie, and he'd be damned if the likes of Tage was going to keep him from retrieving what was rightfully his by hard work and inheritance.

Of course, retrieving the balance of those funds might give Tage a hint that former Imperial Fleet Admiral Philip Guthrie was alive and kicking. And active in trying to take down the old Empire.

But moving assets untraceably was a minor problem, according to a man named Gabriel Sullivan, who had not only faked his own death rather successfully a few years ago but who was also an accomplished mercenary, renowned pirate, heir to his own exorbitant fortune—and a powerful telepathic-energy-wielding half human, half demon. Who was currently married to Captain Chaz Bergren, Philip's ex-wife. There was a lot to be said for family.

"A *good* price," Jodey repeated. He tugged up the sleeves of his gray uniform shirt before reaching for the mug of coffee in front of him. "All the Alliance had to do was to pay three months' back dockage fees to the Kirro dockmaster, clearing the export company of the debt. We still have a good chunk left over."

Philip did a quick tally. Thousands, then, not millions. And low thousands at that. That *was* an incredibly good deal. "That's it?" he asked, not without suspicion, as Jodey sipped his coffee.

Jodey put the mug back on the table and shrugged. "We also had to agree to keep her name."

"What does a fruit shipper care about *Alric Stockwell*?" Stockwell had been some minor senator from some equally minor district. Philip didn't even remember what sector. Baris? Aldan?

"Nothing. She's not the *Stockwell*. She's *Hope's Folly*."

What in hell's fat ass kind of name was that? "You're asking me to lead the Alliance battle group with a flagship called *Hope's Folly?* Bralford, tell me you're not serious."

Jodey leaned his forearms against the table's dull-gray top, his dark brows lowering, his demeanor suddenly somber. "Four months ago, twenty-three innocent people died in Grover's City when Tage released a cargo hold full of jukors at the spaceport. Three children were among the dead. And I know you know all this."

Philip could still see the gruesome images on the news vids. It was the incident that had thrown Prew over the edge, collapsing what little control the emperor had left. It put Tage in charge of the Empire. That had all but gotten Philip killed in an ambush by Tage's private squad of Imperial Security assassins at Raft Thirty at the A–B. He'd risked his life to warn the rest of his captains and his officers. In the case of Cory Bennton, his former CO and longtime friend, and Captain Gemma Junot, he'd been too late.

"Go on."

"A mother and two small children were killed in the first wave. Then, hours later, another mother and her child who'd been in hiding came out, thinking things were safe. The little girl was four, five years old, I think. She was Pavyer's—the grove owner's—only child. Her name was Hope."

Philip shut his eyes briefly, his heart clenching even

though he had no children of his own. But he had three brothers and roomfuls of nieces and nephews, as holiday dinners at his parents' lavish estate proved. Being ripped to shreds by a jukor's powerful jaws was not a death anyone wanted for their child.

"But *folly*?" he asked. "That means mistake, foolishness."

"Folly was the name of the little girl's pet. Pavyer and his wife wanted the name to be *Hope and Folly,* but the girl insisted on *Hope's Folly.* He doesn't know why and he can't ask her now."

Philip wiped one hand down his face. At forty-five and career military, he should be inured to death. But he wasn't—especially when the life taken was that of a child.

"Okay." He straightened and rolled his shoulders, catching his trademark movement only after he completed it. "*Hope's Folly.* Where is she?"

"Shipyards off Seth," Jodey said, naming Umoran's moon. "Basic refit is all we can do right now, given the current situation."

Which was the Empire at war with itself and Tage putting blockades on the major jumpgates in Aldan and Baris in an effort to starve the rebel movement growing beyond those points. A movement under the direction of former Dafir-One senator Mason Falkner, now provisional consul of the Alliance of Independent Republics. Tage had the Imperial Fleet—including Philip's former Galaxy-class flagship, the *Morgan Loviti*—edging into Calth. Which was why the Alliance's new admiral needed more than one lone cruiser.

And he got the *Stockwell. Hope's Folly.* The *Loviti* could probably take her out with half her weaponry off-line. Speaking of which . . .

"Does she have any defenses at all?" The negatives of the situation unfolded in Philip's mind. A former Fleet cruiser turned fruit hauler sitting at Seth's, likely stripped down when decommissioned. And sitting at a commercial yard, not a military one.

"Unfortunately, just the usual allowable package for any commercial vessel. No ion cannons, no torpedoes. She has laser banks, of course, and, oddly, two extremely powerful tow fields. Commercial uses, I guess, but she was decommissioned at Ferrin's before the exporter bought her, and some of her may still be there," Jodey added as Philip nodded. "First bit of good news, if you could call it that."

He could. Ferrin's, on the ass end of Baris, was a combination civilian starport and military repair facility, with strong ties to the Umoran colonies. When the empire split, Ferrin's dockmaster and inhabitants, including the captain and crew of the P-40 based there, wasted no time in allying with Consul Falkner's leadership and his Independent Admirals' Council.

Ferrin's would also have spare parts for a Stryker and, since the decommission had been in their yards, the original command data source codes for the ship. Add in data Philip had brought back from his stay on Sullivan's *Boru Karn*—old trader routes and long-forgotten jumpgates, already programmed in on the *Nowicki*—and the Alliance would have one more ship that could circumvent many of the Imperial blockades.

"You'll need to get her to Ferrin's to finish the refit," Jodey said, echoing Philip's thoughts—not unusual, considering the years they'd served together. "With luck, they'll have what you need either in original stock or from military surplus."

Luck would be nice. It was something they hadn't had in abundance lately.

Nor time. It would be at least six shipdays' travel from Seth to Ferrin's, if the C-6 jumpgate was still operational. Ten days or longer if he had to go a more circuitous route or use one of the older jumpgates the *Karn's* data supplied. In essentially a civilian ship, with laser banks—and his wits—as his only defense.

Luck, indeed.

Jodey seemed to hear his unspoken thoughts. "You know I'm not happy with your taking on this mission, Philip. You're the highest-ranking former Fleet officer we have on our side. If something happens to you, we'll be hard-pressed to replace you. And I'd miss the hell out of our billiards games. But you said to find you a ship. We have."

Philip pushed away from the chair, then hesitated, wincing, as his right leg lodged a formal protest. His shattered leg and hip were a memento of his recent battle out in the Five-Oh-One, not only against Tage's flunky Hayden Burke—now an Alliance prisoner—but against an enemy from within: a Stolorth *Kyi-Ragkiril.* A half demon, like Sullivan. But not of the human variety. And not, like Sullivan, a friend.

He glanced down quickly, grabbed the hated silver metal cane, and walked with far less than his usual grace to the ready room's large viewport. The big, wide darkness beyond looked peaceful, benign.

It was anything but. And now that the Stol Dynasty and Sheldon Blaine's Farosians were each making preliminary moves to grab parts of the Empire as their own, it would only get worse.

"Tell me about my crew," he said as he absently studied the starfield.

He heard Jodey's sigh of exasperation. "Basic command staff, you have. We're still working on the crew. There are some serious security concerns."

He expected that answer. Though in many minds the Alliance was formed the day Tage disbanded the old Admirals' Council—which had governed with the emperor for centuries—in reality the Alliance of Independent Republics was officially born less than two months ago, when Falkner took formal oath in the new capital city of Nascent on Dafir One. Dissenters from Fleet and the various planetary ground services were still coming out of the proverbial woodwork.

So were spies, opportunists, con artists, and thrill seekers.

Culling those problems took time and personnel, and Philip knew they had neither right now.

"I have five officers cleared to go with you," Jodey said. "From your *Loviti,* there's Lieutenant Welford."

No surprise, that. Constantine "Tin Man" Welford, about ten years Philip's junior, was a top helmsman and computer-systems wizard who hadn't hesitated to follow his admiral over to the rebel's camp. Next to Jodey, Con Welford was probably his most trusted officer. He was long overdue for a promotion—something Philip intended to rectify when the Alliance Fleet became a working reality.

"From my ship," Jodey continued, "you're getting Commander Dina Adney and Lieutenant Burnaby Mather. Mather's COMTAC."

Philip had meet Adney and Mather but didn't know either as well as he knew Welford. But a good COMTAC—communications and tactical officer—was always appreciated. And Mather's friendly, always-wanting-to-help attitude had impressed Philip over the past few weeks.

Jodey hesitated. "And Drew Sparkington said he's willing to come out of retirement if you want him."

That name got Philip's attention. "Sparks?"

"Chaz got in touch with him. You know how fond he is of her."

And Jodey still wondered if Philip was more than fond of Captain Chasidah Bergren. Philip could tell by the man's hesitation in mentioning her and the way he wouldn't directly meet Philip's gaze.

Philip and Chaz had been shipmates and friends for over ten years, married for eight, and divorced for three. He'd admired her, loved her, toyed with disliking her—but never quite could—and now...Now he could honestly say they were close friends, probably closer than before they married. For some reason, most people had a hard time accepting the fact that he could feel that way.

Especially Jodey, who'd been through the worst of it with him: the end of the marriage, the few blessedly rare drunken stupors Philip had indulged in, and the hard emotional armor he'd donned through Chaz's orchestrated arrest and trial—one of the first salvos in Tage's plan to discredit Fleet and the Admirals' Council, almost a year ago.

But that was before Chaz and Sullivan had plucked Philip and his faltering pinnace out of the big wide darkness and out of the sights of Tage's fighters gunning for him. And before he witnessed what Chaz and Sullivan had together, which was incredibly strong and incredibly rare.

It was a love Philip could never offer her. He didn't think he could offer it to any woman.

So Chaz was happy, and Philip was happy for her. And content that he would have a ship of his own under his boots shortly, with Commander Drew Sparkington as chief engineer.

"Sparks would be a blessing," he told Jodey. Sparks had been his ex-wife's engineer for four years on the

Meritorious—a P-40 patrol ship known more for speed than power. He'd taken early retirement when Chaz had been falsely court-martialed. Maybe the ruddy-faced man had seen something coming no one else had at the time, Philip thought grimly. "Does he have experience with Strykers?"

"A six-month stint. Not long, but I don't see it as a huge problem. You know the man never met a ship he couldn't fix."

"Agreed. But you said five command staff."

"Sub-Lieutenant Corvang."

Philip thought a moment, hearing Jodey's guttural pronunciation and lack of first name. "Takan?"

"Takan. He's young but whip-smart and tireless. He's third-shift nav here on the *Nowicki* right now. But he's studied everything the Great Guthrie has ever written and has every combat-training holo you've ever done. I fear that if I don't assign him to you, he'll stow away."

"The Great Guthrie, eh?" Philip snorted.

"He has your shoulder roll down pat."

On an eight-foot-tall, fur-covered Takan in the Alliance's standard-issue gray fatigues, that should be a sight to see.

"I have all their service records here." Jodey tapped the screen slanting out of the desktop. "Why don't you sit and review them?"

Because when you were six-foot-two and had a bum leg and shattered hip held together with plastic and metal, sitting was difficult in deck-locked chairs that couldn't move backward. "Just tilt the screen. I'll stand."

"Sit," Jodey repeated. "You've been standing for over an hour. Doc Galan told you that leg is not going to heal any faster if you don't stay off it."

"Ah. The insubordination surfaces because I'm no longer an admiral of the Fleet." Philip plucked at the patch above his shirt pocket. It bore only his last name. Rank pins were an unnecessary luxury at the moment.

It was Jodey's turn to snort. "Admiral Guthrie, sir. Please sit down. I have these records ready for your perusal."

"That's more like it." Philip limped over to the closest chair, sat awkwardly, then took a moment to smack Jodey on the arm with the head of his cane. Jodey had been his first officer for five years on the *Morgan Loviti,* but they'd been friends for longer than that.

"You're still an admiral of the Fleet," Jodey said with a wry grin. "We just don't quite have a fleet— yet."

No. They had a lone Maven-class cruiser, and a handful of patrol ships, Ratch fighters, and luxury yachts. And now an old, ungodly Stryker-class bucket turned fruit hauler that it was Philip's job to shape into a Fleet-worthy heavy cruiser again.

Before Darius Tage decided Calth and Dafir sectors were his for the taking and anyone allying with the rebels was his to destroy.

"I can't believe you're just leaving like this." Matthew Crowley's face—and a pretty one it was—was creased in anger, his voice tinged with bitterness. Rya had never noticed—well, actually, she had a few times but ignored them—how Matt's voice rose to an almost feminine falsetto when he was pissed off. It made his prettiness . . . petulant.

"I'm not leaving *just* like this," she told him, rummaging through the wooden dresser's top drawer for one more pair of heavy socks. Old Stryker-class cruisers were known for inconsistent enviro. Heat in the crew's quarters was spotty at best. She remembered her father's stories about blanket raids and card games where a pair of socks trumped all.

"I'm leaving," she continued without a glance at the naked man in her bed, "exactly when I told you I would: 0600. I have a shuttle to catch."

"It's four-fucking-thirty in the morning! Seeing this is our last night together, I thought, for once, you might want to spend a little more time with me."

Rya stuffed the socks in her dark-blue canvas duffel and turned. God, she was tired of arguing with him. It was all they seemed to have done the past week. "Factually correct, Barrister Crowley. It's 0430, and we have been fucking for the better part of the past few hours."

"We've been fucking," Matt's voice rose again, "for the better part of the past two goddamned years! Two years, Rya. Evidently all that time has meant nothing. Thanks for the great sex, Matt, I'm leaving, goodbye."

She zipped the duffel shut. They'd been over this. She didn't know why he was bringing it up again. Certainly his language—which she'd deliberately thrown back at him in her answer—wasn't exactly endearing. It was almost as if he wanted to part on bad terms. "I have to do this. And, yes, it goes beyond our friendship and our sexual relationship. You know that." She shot him a hard glance in the room's dim lighting.

Matt sat up, the white bedsheet pooling around his waist. He thrust his hands through his shoulder-length blond hair, his demeanor shifting. "I'm sorry about your father, but it's not going to bring him back. And you could get yourself killed."

Rya's throat tightened, not just at the unexpected

concern in Matt's voice but for the grief she still held inside over her father's death. It was raw, angry, ripping. And this was the only way she could assuage it.

She found her dark-blue Imperial Fleet Security Forces beret on the dresser and held it tightly in one hand for a moment before she shoved it into the duffel's side pocket, which already held her now-useless ImpSec badge and ID. Another loss, though not as devastating. Her four-and-a-half-year career with the Empire had ceased when Calth Starport 9 had allied with Consul Falkner's new government after the massacre at Raft Thirty. She'd worked, as everyone in her unit had, as a "striper"—station security—since then, waiting, hoping for a rebirth of a version of ImpSec under the Alliance. It was coming, according to the new Independent Admirals' Council, but Rya couldn't wait any longer. She'd resigned, turning in her temporary striper's badge and service weapon. A Carver-10. Damn, she'd miss that gun. More than she'd miss Matt Crowley.

"Getting myself killed is what I've done for as long as you've known me," she said when she found her voice. And her personal Stinger laser pistol, a gift from her father, along with her L7 pocket laser. She might not be ImpSec anymore, but she was still licensed to carry. The Stinger went into her shoulder holster under her brown leather spacer jacket, the L7 into a paddle holster tucked discreetly in the small of her back.

She already had a sonic knife in each boot.

She still believed in the Imperial Fleet Security Forces Special Protection Service motto: *Polite, Professional, and Prepared to Kill.*

"Being a cop on Calth Nine is not the same thing as running off to join some slagging fleet!"

No, it wasn't. And that was exactly why she had to

leave. After four and a half years working undercover and security ops with ImpSec, spending her shift as a cop corralling bored station brats made her ass pucker, and breaking up bar brawls was becoming a mindless routine. But even before Tage's takeover, Rya's career with ImpSec hadn't been enough to qualify her for a Fleet shipboard posting. Which was what she'd always wanted: to serve on the same ship as her father. She, chief of security. And he...

But he was dead.

And this was the only chance she'd have to do something about that.

"I'll try to drop you some transmits if I can," she said, "but I'm sure security will be tight."

Matt grunted and looked away. "Don't bother. You simply want out of this relationship, and this is as good an excuse as any."

For a moment, her eyes narrowed, and the hair stood up on the back of her neck. He was definitely looking to pick a fight. Her right hand fisted with an overwhelming urge to punch Matthew Crowley's pretty face. Then she relaxed. His words weren't that far from the truth. Matt was a fun, interesting diversion. He was handsome and intelligent. But he was also shallow, petty, self-absorbed, and, honestly, not *that* good in bed.

Like she said, she'd miss her Carver-10 more.

And she did want out of this relationship. But if his ego needed to believe that he was the one breaking it off, fine. No skin off her ass.

"I told Lyza she could have my apartment as of tomorrow. The landlord has the signed docs. Drop the keypad on Lyza's desk when you leave."

"When you come crawling back here in three, four months, I'm going to be with someone else, Rya. Don't think I'm going to wait for you. There are a lot of women on this starport who'd love to have me in bed."

Ah. Now his petulance made sense. Rya stopped in the bedroom doorway and almost pointed out that she was well aware he'd already tried out several of them, as recently as two months ago. But that was her fault as much as his. It was the usual JFFS: Just For Fun Sex. No strings, no promises—she'd told him that when they'd fallen into bed almost two years ago. She'd been twenty-seven and had just received her first promotion with ImpSec. He'd been twenty-eight and a junior barrister with the prosecutor's office in Calth Judicial District 1. Calth Starport 9 was just a temporary stop for her—six years by regulation—on her way to a posting on one of Fleet's top ships.

But Fleet as she knew it was gone. So was Captain Cory Bennton.

And the only thing left for Rya Taylor Bennton was to catch the 0600 Starford flight to Kirro and then the local shuttle to Seth, where her father's Stryker-class cruiser was waiting for her.

As for Matt Crowley, he could do or believe whatever he wanted. It no longer mattered to her.

Rya turned and softly pulled the door shut behind her.

He didn't have much to pack, Philip realized wryly, tossing the heavy-duty black duffel on the narrow bed in his cabin on the *Krista Nowicki*. Two sets of fatigues, one gray and one black, and two pairs of gray coveralls from his short stay on Sullivan's well-armored 200-ton luxury yacht, the *Boru Karn*. A couple of thermal shirts. The repaired remnants of his Imperial Fleet dress uniform—God only knew why he was keeping that. All his other personal effects had been left on the *Morgan Loviti*. God also only knew where those things were now.

After three shipdays of travel, the *Nowicki* was an hour out from Kirro Station, where Philip would catch the shuttle to the Seth shipyards. Adney, Welford, Mather, and Corvang had gone ahead, leaving two shipdays ago in a shuttle that would become the *Folly*'s, loaded with what supplies Jodey could spare. Philip was supposed to be on board that shuttle, but Doc Galan had put her foot down. So they'd compromised, with his command staff going in first—not at all unusual. He'd follow once Christine Galan, CMO, granted him medical clearance.

But with the shuttle gone, the *Nowicki* had to deliver Philip. The large docks at the shipyards were full—little surprise, that. No room for a Maven-class cruiser, which was fine with Philip. He had no taste for big send-offs and had even waved away Jodey's offer of his personal pinnace. The *Nowicki* had work to do. Ferrying *Hope's Folly*'s new captain to his ship's berth wasn't of primary importance when he could get to the shipyards just fine on his own.

More so because—as he'd told Jodey, and his former first officer reluctantly agreed—security was a constant worry. Kirro Station was fairly well protected by the locals and busy enough that even a Maven-class cruiser could blend in among the tankers and luggers. But an officer's sleek pinnace headed for Seth was a blaring target and, as he'd learned off Raft Thirty, far less defensible.

He realized he was standing there with a pair of socks balled up in his hand while his thoughts twisted and turned. He aimed; pitched them. *He shoots, he scores!* Memories of his brothers washed over him with an unaccustomed sentimentality. He didn't have time for such thoughts—*impending doom must make me self-indulgent*—but the images surfaced anyway: the basketball court adjacent to the large pool on his parents' Port Palmero estate, a spring afternoon just warm enough to tug him outside, where Trippy—Jonathan Macy Guthrie III, his oldest nephew—was home from his university and was shooting baskets along with Trip's twelve-year-old brother, Max. Then Philip's youngest brother showed up, and it was Uncle Philip and Trip against Uncle Devin and Max. The score didn't matter. The sense of belonging did.

That was eight months ago. He hadn't seen them since. And he didn't know when he would again. He didn't even know if they knew he was alive.

He limped back to the room's small dresser, images of the *Loviti*'s well-appointed gym replacing his parents' spacious grounds. His officers and crew, laughing, scuffling in a friendly handball competition...

Eleven of his people—two officers and nine crew—had deserted the Imperial Fleet just after he had, escaping Tage's clutches. Five were on the *Nowicki*, including Con Welford, the only one who would be coming to *Hope's Folly* with him. All had wanted to go to the *Folly*, but Philip needed people he could trust on every ship. It did him no good to have the best of the best, as he thought of them, staring at him around his ready-room table.

So the rest were assigned to the patrol ships that comprised the Alliance's meager defense force. Another twenty or fifty of his people from the *Loviti* were still AWOL. Numbers varied, depending on which reports coming out of the Imperial news feeds you believed. He felt strongly that the numbers were higher, but many could be dead.

That would always haunt him. The captain was supposed to stay with his ship until the end, but he'd been on Raft Thirty when the proverbial shit hit the proverbial fan. His attempts to get back to the *Loviti* had been expertly thwarted. Tage was not about to lose a top Galaxy-class destroyer. But Tage had lost the *Nowicki,* two P-40s, and two P-75s, all from Philip's command.

More personnel and more ships would come; Philip felt sure of it. Fleet and the Admirals' Council were one and the same to a large extent. But time . . . it all came back to time.

For now, the smaller planetary and station defenses allied with the Alliance were holding their own and providing needed support, but they had limited range. They could only confront a threat at their doorstep, not break a blockade hours—if not shipdays—away. Tage's fleet could move in insidious increments, and by the time the local security forces realized what was happening, it would be too late.

Philip tossed a thermal shirt into the duffel, turned too quickly, and had to grit his teeth at the pain. At least two weeks, maybe a month yet, Doc Galan told him, before the bone regen devices would complete their work. This was the worst of it, she'd assured him a few hours ago as she made the final adjustments to the damned things implanted in his hip and leg. Most of her patients with his severity of damage would still be in rehab. *He* should still be in rehab.

"Not possible," he'd told her.

She'd huffed out a sigh he'd come to recognize as *don't disobey your CMO* and tucked a strand of her short dark hair behind one ear with an irritated motion. "Then stay off your feet as much as possible and get some rest."

"Sure, Doc." *Hell's fat ass chance of that.*

His door sensor chimed. "Open," he called.

Jodey, grinning broadly, his arms laden with things dark and lumpy, pushed his way past the sliding door. He carefully placed his offerings on the bed next to the duffel. Extra clothes, including another set of gray fatigues and a Fleet-issue blue-gray thermal overcoat. A spare Carver-12—Philip's personal one was already on his hip. Six power packs. Two Fleet-issue L7 small hand lasers. And an expertly modified Norlack 473 sniper laser rifle capable of handling illegal wide-load slash charges. A note was tied to the barrel with a piece of white ribbon.

He plucked it off, opening it while Jodey turned away, inspecting God knows what in the tiny cabin. Giving Philip some privacy.

Sully and I thought you might enjoy this, the note read in Chaz's familiar upright script. *Give 'em hell, Guthrie. Love you—Chaz the nugget.*

It had been five shipweeks since Chaz and Sullivan had left on the *Karn.* The human *Kyi* healed much quicker than Philip had, of course. Sullivan's blindness had faded, leaving him with an oversensitivity to light as his remaining physical challenge.

Mentally and emotionally, though, the man had much more to reconcile because of what had happened in the depot in the Five-Oh-One: the challenge by a deposed Stolorth prince thought to be an ally who wanted more than political gain. Prince Regarth Serian Cordell Delkavra wanted Chaz—Sullivan's wife and *ky'sara:* his mental and emotional bondmate. Regarth also wanted to limit Sullivan's *Kyi* powers—a not uncommon demand when two very powerful *Kyi-Ragkirils* are forced to share proximity.

Regarth didn't succeed in enslaving Chaz, but he

did, for a very tense time, expose Sullivan to the darker side of the *Kyi*. An addictive, insidious side. And Sullivan had, in his own words, "done unforgivable things."

Things that still haunted the man. He'd talked to Philip about that when Chaz was busy elsewhere. There are some things you just don't discuss in front of the woman you love.

And Sullivan did love her, very much. That Philip did believe. It lessened his worries somewhat—though it would be a lie to say he didn't miss her.

But Sullivan and Chaz had important work to do for the new Alliance. So did Philip.

Grinning at the way she'd classified herself as a nugget—someone with much yet to learn—he tucked the note into the inside pocket of his tactical vest.

"Adney confirmed they're on the *Folly*," Jodey said. "Welford's started taking the helm computers apart, and Mather's being typical commo and bitching about the antiquated comm pack. Corvang's updating the charts with the data Sullivan gave us. Sparks is due in day after tomorrow. He's bringing three subbies with him. Adney will clear them, but I'm sure they're fine."

If Sparks had handpicked them, Philip was sure they were. "That leaves only one hundred thirty-one more we have to find to launch that bucket." That would be the minimum crew complement. He would have preferred a full crew, but beggars and rebels can't be choosers.

"Adney has over seventy applications in her in-box just from the feelers she and Con Welford put out the past month. This might not be as hard as you think. She's already placed ten on conditional acceptance and she's been on the job only six hours—and, yes, believe me, Adney knows protocol and knows you have final say."

Philip held up one hand in supplication. The other still gripped his damned cane. "Do I look like I'm complaining?"

"You never complain. You just scowl and grunt a lot."

"Works, doesn't it?"

"I've warned Adney. She's as thorough as they come. That should save you some grunting. She'll make you a top-notch exec."

Philip reached over and clasped his hand on Jodey's shoulder. "The best of the best. You all are. I don't think I can ever really express my gratitude."

"Turn that bucket into a mean fighting machine. That will say it all."

He patted Jodey's shoulder again, then, careful of his leg, turned away from the shorter man. He'd heard such sentiments before in Fleet and had taken them in stride. But this wasn't Fleet. This was at best a rogue's gallery—an uncertain and desperate attempt at salvation and justice.

Hope's Folly suddenly sounded all too accurate.

"I'll leave you to finish packing," Jodey said, "then I'll be back in forty to escort you to the tubeway."

"I'm finished," Philip told him. "I'm going to check my transmits, then do a last round with your crew. I'll meet you on the bridge at ten out."

"Looking to rate my docking skills?" Jodey asked from the open doorway.

Philip grunted.

"That's what I thought." Jodey slipped into the corridor.

As the door closed behind the *Nowicki*'s captain, Philip keyed in his codes to the deskscreen in the room and scanned for messages from Chaz or Sullivan. Low price on the Stryker or not, the Alliance needed funds to keep coming in. He recognized the triple-encrypted message from Sullivan immediately. A major Guthrie account had been shaken free, the funds now going through the requisite laundering before they'd reach the Alliance channels in two shipweeks.

He could live with that. He shoved the clothes on top of his meager wardrobe, packed the weapons in the duffel's special compartment, sealed and locked it, then, tossing the overcoat on top, left to say his goodbyes. Thirty minutes later, feeling uncharacteristically sentimental, he caught up with Jodey on the bridge. The *Nowicki* had already received clearance from Kirro Traffic Control.

"Ten days, two weeks at Seth, max," Jodey was saying as they discussed the refit of the *Folly*. "Sparks will probably shave a day or three off that for you. When you get to Ferrin's, you shouldn't need any more than—"

"Captain Bralford, a Priority One scramble from Commander O'Neil," the communications officer announced.

Philip tensed. A Priority One scramble, out here, now, reeked of trouble.

"My console screen," Jodey said, already sliding into the captain's chair. He swung the armrest screen around so Philip could see it.

Kate O'Neil's face appeared on the small screen, framed by the bridge of the P-75 she commanded. Her short silver hair was mussed, her dark-blue eyes narrowed. "Tage moved against Corsau with three ImpSec assault teams," she said grimly after the perfunctory salutation. "Station security is decimated. We had no ships in range. There was nothing we could do, no way we could help." Her mouth tightened. "Tell Admiral Guthrie there were fifteen *Loviti* crew on Corsau. We think Tage's assassins knew that. We think they were gunning for them specifically. None survived. I'm sorry."

She dropped her gaze for a moment, then looked back up, anger clear in her eyes. "There was nothing we could do," she repeated. "We don't have enough ships to protect even those few stations allied with us. We—as soon as I have updates, I'll send them. O'Neil out."

The screen blanked.

All voices on the bridge were silent.

Philip unclenched his jaw, swallowing his rage. It was unproductive, but it would not be forgotten. He turned to Jodey. "Put Ferrin's on high alert. Tell Adney I waive final review on all the crew. I need every live body she can find. The *Folly* departs Seth as soon as Sparks arrives."

2

The passenger docks on Kirro Station were cavernous, dimly lit, and bitingly cold. It didn't escape Rya's notice that someone with a sick sense of humor had painted the walls and bulkheads a distinctly icy shade of pale blue. Forty-five frigid minutes passed before the Starford Spacelines' transport ship regurgitated Rya's duffel out of its cargo holds, along with the rest of the passengers' baggage. By that point, she had already turned up the collar on her brown leather jacket and tucked her hands under her armpits, releasing them only to make a grab for her duffel on the shuddering, rumbling baggage belt. Then she knelt, unzipped the top, and tucked her travel kit inside. She fished her dark-blue Special Protection Service beret out of a side pocket, removed the rank and service pins, then pulled the beret over her perpetually unruly hair. Some people might look twice if they knew what the beret symbolized. This was, after all, a declared Alliance station. Imperial Fleet in all its flavors—including ImpSec, with its somewhat exaggerated reputation as a top-secret agency that trained assassins—was not welcome.

But the overhead lights were weak, and those milling about the baggage-collection area of the passenger terminal appeared as bleary-eyed as she was. The beret could be mistaken for black. The service pins were deep in her pocket, and her scalp was goddamned frostbitten. She was going to wear her beret, for what little good it did.

It was better than nothing. And it, along with the contents of her duffel, was all she owned.

The two-day flight from Calth Starport had been dismal, with crying infants, hacking old men, and one painfully thin woman who snored like a half-ton freightloader grinding gears.

Kirro was an equally dismal station. Umoran had been hit hard with financial failures the past few years, after the grove cankers and lack of support from what was once the Empire. Exports were down. Imports were priced like luxuries. More than half the food kiosks in the passenger terminal were closed. Those still open offered few selections at ridiculous prices— and with no job and her parents' estate seized by the Imperial government, Rya's own funds were as meager as most of those on station.

But she was cold almost to the point of shivering. She overpaid for a half mug of sweet tea from a thin-faced older woman in one of the plasti-walled units. Then, clutching the thick paper container between chilled hands as the duffel's strap dug a furrow into her shoulder, she headed down the long icy-blue corridor to find the waiting room for the shuttle to Seth.

She passed a few stripers, armed and watchful, the pale stripe on the sides of their brown uniform pant legs giving them their nickname. Seven months ago she might have stopped to talk about the job with one or two. She was law enforcement, as were they, although her jurisdiction as an ImpSec officer had been on a much larger scale than station security. Now she played civilian, let her gaze pass over them as if a man or woman armed with a rifle was an interesting curiosity, nothing more. Though she did wonder if any of them were former ImpSec like herself.

Out of habit, she studied their weaponry more than their faces. No Carvers here; not even Stingers. Standard issue Mag-5 pistols, and their rifles were boring Blue Surgers. She'd trained on them, could dismantle them in her sleep, which was, in her opinion, all they were worth. But, yeah, get shot by a Surger and it still hurt like a bitch and could put you flat-out dead if someone's aim was good. Not center mass, as they were taught. That only worked on the good guys, but it wasn't the good guys who needed shooting. It was the bad guys, and they were smart enough to wear body armor. Good luck getting a standard Surger to penetrate that.

Okay, maybe at point-blank.

But at point-blank, the bad guys had already shot you dead with their nice powerful Carver-12s.

No, with a Surger you had to go for the throat or brain. Stop the blood flow, stop the body functions. Even then, some slag-head twilighting on *rafthkra* might still come at you, full bore.

She'd had to assist station cops twice in her short career, taking down gun-wielding twilighters Surgers couldn't stop. Her Carver-10 had.

That's why she liked working for ImpSec. They carried Carver-10s, minimum. Carver-12s on shipside duty. She'd even heard of 15s, when they worked the rim or were assigned to an admiral's personal protection. Totally apex, to quote Lyza, who was by now sleeping in Rya's bed in Rya's apartment, possibly even with Rya's former lover.

And was warm.

After this, a Stryker-class cruiser might seem like a damned tropical vacation.

The shuttle waiting room at the end of the corridor was crowded. Not surprising. According to the schedule board, the room serviced three shuttles: one dirtside to Umoran, one to the moon colony, and one spaceside to the shipyards in orbit around Seth. She wondered how many of those huddled down on the hard bench seats had seen Commander Dina Adney's coded transmit on available crew positions for the new Alliance fleet. A lot, probably, because this was, after all, Calth, and Calth had almost wholly formally withdrawn from the Empire after the dissolution of the Admirals' Council several months ago.

Only the Walker Colonies and Port January were playing coy, but then, Port January had long been an Imperial base of operations.

She spied an empty row of bench seats facing the floor-to-ceiling viewports and headed for them, only to realize why they were empty. They were broken, their seat backs still connected but the seat bottoms stripped out. She turned and walked again past humans hunched into coats, children huddled close in a mother's or father's lap, and a few Takas lounging casually, not bothered by the cold at all, their furred hands and wrists sticking out of lightweight shirts or thermals. Shipyard patches on their chests marked them as returning workers.

The schedule board suspended over the center of the room flashed, catching her eye. A low groan went around the room even before she finished reading the advisory that all shuttles were delayed one hour due to heightened security concerns.

A baby wailed loudly.

Rya completely concurred with the sentiment and tossed her empty tea container into a trash bin.

Movement near the dirtside shuttle tubeway signaled a family vacating several of the benchlike seats—the delay likely meant time for a lavatory stop, or maybe food. Rya was only a row away. She quickened her steps, then slowed, her duffel bumping her hip. An elderly man and woman pulled themselves off the cold decking, tugging two toddlers with them as they ambled for the seats. A pair of hard-body guys did as well. Dockworkers, Rya guessed, noting their stained coveralls made from a heavy-duty tan fabric. Both wore dark high-necked thermals underneath. They were dressed to deal with the cold temperatures on the docks, not the artificially controlled environment on a ship.

She stepped in front of the men, blocking their path, trying to give the people with the small kids a chance to get there first.

The bearded hard-body stared levelly at her as she shifted her stance until she stood bladed to him, gunside away. Ingrained habit. The man was about her age and not much taller than she was, maybe five-ten. But he outweighed her by at least sixty pounds, and Rya was no lightweight—a factor Matt Crowley had found less than appealing.

"I have hips, I have thighs," she'd told him more than once when he'd patted her ample rump with some snippy comment. "Get used to it."

The bearded man's gaze dropped to her chest, as if he'd heard her thoughts.

Okay, so she had an ample chest too.

"Kind of you to let them have the seats," she told him, bringing his gaze back to her face as her right hand found the small laser tucked against her back.

"Yeah, I'm Mr. Wonderful," he drawled with a quick glance to his friend. His hands edged into his pockets.

She palmed the laser, flicking the setting to stun.

"So now I gotta go sit on the floor again," he continued. "It's real cold on your ass, you know. I think you should come and keep me warm."

"I think you'll do just fine by yourself." She put her professional tone in her voice. "Have a good one, gentlemen. Now, move on."

Maybe it was the tone of her voice, or maybe it was that Mr. Wonderful's friend's gaze flicked to her beret and down again, possibly catching the outline of the gun in the shoulder holster that even her womanly charms and leather jacket failed to fully hide. He nudged his friend. "Let's go, Alvie."

"Hey!"

"We're going now." Alvie's friend grabbed Alvie by the arm and steered him in the opposite direction.

Rya tucked away the L7 at the small of her back and didn't miss the low comment when they were a few steps away.

"Striper? Shit."

No, not a striper. ImpSec Special Protection Service. Polite, professional, and prepared to kill.

She sighed, caught the grateful gaze of the elderly woman with the sleeping toddler in her lap, and shrugged her acknowledgment.

The *shuttle delayed* sign still flashed. Rya wandered away from the tubeway hatchlock and finally ended up leaning against the wall—holding up the bulkhead, as her father would say—where the corridor dead-ended into the waiting area. There was a heat vent overhead, the little warmth trickling out a pleasure almost beyond words at this point.

A few more people stood and filed out, tired of waiting or hungry, or both. Or just needing to move. Mr. Wonderful and friend claimed two seats quickly, but she didn't intervene this time, because no one smaller, weaker, or older needed them.

She glanced away from them and watched the corridor instead.

That's when she saw him. A solitary figure in a bluish-gray thermal overcoat that her mind automatically tagged as *Fleet-issue,* moving with a determined but limping gait. He leaned on his cane with every other step, the wide strap of a duffel a dark stripe against the fabric of his coat.

He was too far for her to see his face, but as he moved under the dim overhead lights, his short-cropped silver hair made her immediately tag him as a veteran. Not recent Fleet, then. Probably a casualty from the Boundary Wars twenty years ago.

Officer? Yeah, she tagged that too. It was in the way that he held himself, in spite of the pain and his limp. The set of his shoulders. The lift of his chin. Retired officer, silver-haired, probably in his seventies. Coming here at Commander Adney's call?

God, were they down to that now? Relying on rheumy old men to try to stop Tage's insanity?

An end seat on the long bench bordering the bulkhead became available when a fidgety young man in plain green coveralls pushed himself out of it and loped for the corridor. She slid quickly into it, next to a dozing Takan shipyard worker on her left. She'd give the space to the old man when he passed by, as he'd have to given his current trajectory. Then maybe she'd splurge on another half mug of sweet tea to thaw her insides and her hands. It was only money, and the damned shuttle—

The old man, about fifteen feet from her now, limped under a dangling spotlight, the harsh glow illuminating his face. And Rya, already rising to offer him her seat, was surprised to realize two things.

He was not an old man at all. And he had the most incredible blue eyes she'd seen in years.

"Excuse me, sir," she said, because that's what she'd planned to say. And, old or not, he was still limping. Injured. Weaker than she was.

He hesitated slightly, those marvelous blue eyes narrowing in a face that was masculine in a classic, rugged sort of way that set her body to tingling. *Damn.*

"You want this seat?" she continued, tugging her duffel's strap over her left shoulder. "I was just leaving. The shuttle's delayed and seats are hard to come by in here. And this one's under the heat vent."

He stopped in front of her and leaned on his cane.

Rya looked up. Yeah, *up.* Six-two, three. Stocky, maybe two thirty-five. Fleet thermal coats were a thin fabric. He had wide shoulders, a muscular neck, and a dual shoulder holster. She judged that too.

Something flashed over his face, a wariness, then it was gone.

Her beret. He was Fleet. He knew its significance: ImpSec. And if he'd ever worked out of Aldan Prime, he knew it could also mean *assassin.* But his features had relaxed, and he wasn't reaching for whatever rested snugly in his shoulder holsters. Not Fleet inner circle, then.

A baby wailed somewhere behind her, its cry dissolving into a series of hiccups.

"AWOL," Rya said quietly in explanation of her headgear, because that wasn't all that far from the truth. Then she said a name and watched for his reaction. "Adney."

Confirmation came in the slight lessening of tension around his mouth, an almost imperceptible nod.

"That's pretty much why a lot of us are here," she said, her voice still low. She didn't know why she'd added that information. No, she did. For some reason she couldn't define, but based on her cop's sense she'd honed over the past few years, she trusted this silver-haired man. It wasn't because he was attractive. She appreciated attractive—okay, her body did—but her mind knew attractive could just be a shallow package. This was something more. He was . . . He exuded something. An aura of command, of respect?

Yes, command *and* respect, now that she thought about it.

But more than that, she sensed that Adney's request was why he was here. And she wanted him to know he wasn't alone. Because in addition to the aura of command that ringed him like an impenetrable halo, she also felt a deep loneliness in him. A heavy weight that maybe had something to do with his injury, or maybe not.

But it was there and it was palpable.

And it wasn't just her cop's instincts telling her that but her years as the daughter of Lieutenant then Commander then Captain Cory Bennton.

"Would you like to sit, sir?"

"How long is the delay?" His voice was deep, resonant.

"One hour, max, due to heightened security concerns."

He was shaking his head in dismay.

The Takan on her left rose to his feet and called out to a group exiting toward the corridor. They waved. He headed for them in a long, striding gait.

When Rya turned back, the silver-haired man had

let his duffel drop to the floor next to his boots, its strap still in his fingers. It was heavy, but he wasn't going to let it go or out of his sight.

"This is never a pretty maneuver," he said, and, twisting slightly, angled himself down into the vacant chair.

She sat in the Taka's seat, dropping her duffel to the floor. She caught the tail end of a half smile, half grimace on his face and realized her error. She'd said she was leaving.

"My leg thanks you," he said with a hint of wry humor, "but my ego is severely deflated."

She grinned back, doing another mental tally of him as he wedged his cane into a niche on the benchlike seats, then dragged his duffel between them. Early to mid-forties, perhaps; the silver hair was an anomaly. It was thick and, judging from some still-dark patches, had once been a rich brown about as dark as her own. Odd that he hadn't tinted it. Most people did. No one wanted to be mistaken for old.

Maybe he didn't care what people thought. That piqued her curiosity as much as his injury.

"Accident?" She pointed to his right leg, extending stiffly out.

"Let's just say negotiations with a possible enemy combatant didn't go as planned." He adjusted his coat as he spoke. She glanced at his hands, looking for a wedding ring, then chastised herself at the small warmth she felt on seeing his ringless finger.

She studied his hands again. They were square, strong, the backs dotted with scars.

No mere pretty boy, this former Fleet officer. Engineer, she thought. Or chief of maintenance. Worked with his hands and cared little about gashes and barked knuckles.

"And the loser bought the beer?" she quipped, because part of his mouth was still quirked when he'd answer her question. Not a real combatant, then. Probably a bar fight.

"Something like that."

His expression sobered.

God, when would she learn her flippancy wasn't appreciated by everyone? The guy had probably been respectfully called Chief by dozens of subbies, and here she was making light of his injury.

The schedule board flashed again, halting whatever apology she was hastily throwing together and hushing a good percentage of the conversations around her.

This time there was a definite announcement. A two-hour delay for the shuttle to the moon colony, and a four-hour delay for the shuttle to Seth's shipyards. The shuttle for Umoran, however, would arrive in fifteen minutes. Boarding would commence ten minutes after that.

Sighs of relief mixed with groans.

"God *damn* it." This softly, from the man next to her. Well, he'd tagged her as Fleet as clearly as she had him. What were a few epithets between friends?

He leaned forward as if to stand, then stopped, slumping back slightly, his gaze pinned on the wide viewport across the waiting area as if he could see all the way to Seth. Or the shipyards.

Shipyards, she guessed. No doubt as to that being his destination. He hadn't questioned her use of Commander Adney's name.

His eyes narrowed, his brows furrowed. She'd seen that look on her father's face when he was forced to make decisions he didn't like. Or when decisions he wanted to make weren't possible. The shuttle delay clearly had this man on edge.

"Life's not going to change all that much in the next four hours," she commented, her voice low.

He slanted her a glance. The hard, angry emotions she saw in his eyes startled her and almost had her reaching for her L7. But he looked away, removing the immediacy of the threat. Still, she watched his hands, because she knew he was armed. One fist clenched.

"It already has." He spoke suddenly, his voice as low as hers but harsh. "Tage hit Corsau an hour ago."

She felt her eyes widen. He was looking at her, studying her, not only anger on his face but grief.

"No." She breathed out the denial, her chest tightening. "How bad?"

"Bad."

She motioned to the solitary vidscreen hanging in the far corner, flickering with images of a concert in Port Chalo last year. "There's been nothing—"

"I noticed. I'm guessing the dockmaster doesn't want to deal with a panic situation. Or the news simply hasn't been cleared for the civilian outlets yet."

"Where did you hear about it?" Maybe it was rumor. Maybe it wasn't true.

"From an Alliance captain." Blue eyes studied her again. "I don't have four hours to waste. How many besides yourself are here to see Commander Adney?"

"No direct knowledge, sir. But guessing from dock-worker uniforms, and discounting families, I'd say thirty or forty." She motioned to a group of men and women about her age seated in the first three rows nearest the shuttle tubeway. "My flight out of Calth Nine got in late. They were already here. I haven't talked to them, but they haven't reacted to any shuttle announcements for the moon colony or Umoran."

She shifted her gaze to their right. "Those three males at our two o'clock position. Middle one in the white thermal, two females in black behind him. They all feel like Fleet to me, or maybe one of the dirtside forces."

"How long were you with ImpSec?"

She looked at him. "Four and half years, sir."

"Academy?"

"Yes, sir."

"Last posting?"

"Sub-lieutenant with SPS, Calth Nine, sir."

That rewarded her with a raised eyebrow. Special Protection Service officers were not only polite, professional, and prepared to kill but received additional undercover and high-security operative training. And the old man next to her knew that.

No, not remotely an old man. But the Old Man. He'd known she was ImpSec. He'd known Adney was a commander, even though Rya hadn't volunteered that information. She felt his rank even more strongly from him now, in the tone of his questions, in his demeanor.

"Well, Subbie, we're about to make the passengers wanting to go home to Umoran very unhappy," he said. "Can you handle it?"

"You intend to commandeer the shuttle?"

"I do."

"I can handle that, sir."

"Find out who's here for Commander Adney. Discreetly. Put them on alert. While you do that," and he shoved himself, grimacing, to his feet, "I'm going to enlist the help of the local stripers."

"Whoever's chief probably won't like that. You may have to get clearance from the dockmaster."

"I fully intend to." He lifted his duffel—clearly heavy—effortlessly. "Ten minutes."

"Yes, sir." She fought the urge to salute and instead

watched him head for a striper standing in the corridor, realizing she didn't know his name or rank. Not that it mattered. There was something very familiar about him, something that resonated in a distant yet warm part of her heart. Something that told her she not only trusted him but that she'd follow him into the jaws of hell and out again. And never regret it.

Philip watched the wariness increase in the striper's eyes as he approached. No rank pins dotted the thin man's brown shirt. A rank-and-file officer, then, meaning he'd have to contact his superior, who'd contact *his* superior . . . More delays. Not four hours' worth, however.

One hour Philip could live with. Four or more hours he could not. He'd almost called back the *Nowicki,* but she'd kicked engines hot on departure. Her return at this point might gain him only an hour, hour and a half at best. And it would delay what the *Nowicki* had to do.

No, he needed to commandeer that shuttle scheduled for Umoran. He needed his people on the way to the shipyards now.

"Officer Holbers," he said, reading the name tag as he slowed at a safe and respectful distance from the man with the god-awful Blue Surger across his back. "I need you to contact your chief and your dockmaster immediately."

Holbers's demeanor shifted from bored to very bored. "Them shuttles run late all the time. There's nothing—"

"I'm Admiral Philip Guthrie. I just came in off the Alliance cruiser, the *Nowicki.* You can verify that while you contact your chief."

Holbers's dark eyes bugged out slightly in his thin face.

"*Now,* Officer Holbers."

"You got some ID?"

"I do. Upper right pocket." Philip raised his hand slowly. "I'm also armed. I'd appreciate it if you don't shoot me."

"Uh," Holbers said.

God save me from moronic stripers, Philip pleaded wryly, pulling his ID from his pocket. Not like his strapping young subbie, who'd tagged him as ex-Fleet as easily as he'd tagged her, dark-blue ImpSec beret notwithstanding. There was a keen intelligence in that face, in those hazel eyes that watched, categorized, and quantified everything. She'd already identified those who might be there for Adney and those who were not. That part reminded him of Chaz, but little else did.

Except maybe her quip about the loser buying the beer.

He held his ID out for Holbers's inspection, well aware the man might well have no idea what a real Alliance Fleet ID looked like. They weren't exactly common yet.

But it was enough to get Holbers chattering into his comm link.

"Chief Carmallis is on her way down," Holbers said.

Philip nodded and spent a few minutes watching his subbie move among the rows of people. She carried a nice air of authority for a youngster. Comfortable in her own skin. Which was, the male in him admitted, a rather nice skin.

The admiral in him admonished that he was likely old enough to be her . . . uncle.

Holbers straightened. A short woman with sufficient rank pins on her brown jacket was striding toward them. She was middle-aged, her dark hair worn in rows of tight braids. She identified herself as Chief Carmallis and spent a little longer examining his ID, her dusky face creased in a frown.

"What can I do for you, Admiral?" she finally asked.

"I need the next incoming shuttle to be allocated for my people going to the shipyards, Chief."

"That's scheduled dirtside for Umoran—"

"I know. I'm sorry. But I have a ship in refit at Seth."

"The Seth shuttle will be here in a few hours."

"The Imperial Fleet attacked Corsau."

The practiced, patient smile dropped from her face. "I haven't heard anything about that."

"I don't control the news vids. Commander O'Neil relayed that information to Captain Bralford of the *Nowicki* just before I was dropped off here."

Carmallis nodded. "I'm aware Captain Bralford's cruiser came in."

He knew she would be. "I need the *Nowicki* out there at the jumpgates, not wasting time ferrying me to Seth. Maybe that was a bad decision on my part, but the *Nowicki* was advised that Kirro provides service to the shipyards every two hours. Now the shuttle I was scheduled on is delayed for four hours. That puts me five hours behind, Chief. And puts a crew ready to assume their duties," he inclined his head to the waiting area on his left, "five hours behind."

"I'll have to talk to the dockmaster."

He pinned her with a stern gaze, letting her know "talk" was not sufficient. "I'll have my people assembled at the tubeway, ready to go."

She hesitated, then: "I'll alert the dockmaster."

"Thank you, Chief. Your cooperation will not be forgotten."

He headed back to the waiting area, his right leg feeling a little less stiff than it had an hour ago. Or else he had too much on his mind to worry about it. Thirty, forty uncleared personnel on a shuttle to the shipyards. And him.

But Adney's call had gone out only to select circles through secure channels. Chances were good that at least half were decent, qualified personnel. The other half could well be Farosians or Imperial spies.

He unfastened his overcoat in spite of the chill. He wanted access to his gun if he needed it.

His subbie raised her gaze when he crossed the waiting area's wide threshold. He inclined his head toward the tubeway, then nodded. *We have permission to take the shuttle* was his unspoken message.

She pulled away from the group she was talking to and walked down the center aisle toward him. He noted again that she was as tall as some of the men, and not a weakling. She carried her bulky duffel easily. There was power in her stride but also a litheness. Her ImpSec beret sat on her head at a jaunty angle. Her hair itself was amazing—less than curly, but far more than wavy. It was just short of shoulder length, as springy and bouncy as she was, and a deep rich brown that these days might be natural or might not.

The rest of her, also bouncy, was very natural. But he wasn't supposed to notice that, as he was old enough to be her . . . uncle. And was now her commanding officer.

"Sir," she said, slowing, then waiting as he fell in step with her. "I have verified fifty-three, including myself, who are here in response to Commander Adney's request. However, sir, there is an issue—"

A group of three men and one woman was moving toward him.

"—of your authority in this matter, though everyone understands the need to get to Seth as soon as possible."

Fifty-three. Well, that wasn't a bad number.

"Thank you, Lieutenant. The dockmaster and security chief are aware of our situation. We have clearance. As for my authority, that can be resolved quickly."

The waiting-room population had reorganized, with his fifty-plus possible crew seated in or standing near the first two rows adjacent to the shuttle tubeway on the far right.

"I don't know who you are, sir," his subbie said quickly, with a slight hitch of embarrassment in her voice.

He'd wondered if she'd recognized him, though his face wasn't one of the more familiar ones. He'd not been an admiral for that long—not even a year. Evidently, she hadn't. And yet she trusted him enough to canvass the room on his orders, without question. Either she was very intuitive or extremely stupid.

"Not a problem." He flashed her a conspiratorial smile. "Because I do know who I am."

She looked momentarily startled at his teasing tone, then a small grin curved her lips.

"I just came off the *Nowicki*," he explained. "We sent an advanced team to Seth, but Captain Bralford and I—"

He paused, the group of four suddenly in front of him, the rest of the forty-nine watching.

"Sir, we understand we're to depart for Seth on the next shuttle," a short, round-faced man clad in plain civilian clothing said. He was the oldest of the group, around Chaz's age, mid-thirties. He wore tan pants of a heavy fabric and a dark-brown flight jacket minus any ship's patches. His short-cropped black hair and solid bearing were all Fleet. No salute, but his tone was respectful.

A reasonable move, since the man had no idea who he was.

"I've cleared it with Chief Carmallis and the dockmaster's office," Philip told him, with a slight nod to the others.

"I'm Commander Martoni, formerly with Baris Division Three and, as best as I've been able to ascertain, the highest-ranking officer here. Thirty-seven of the people here are my personal recruits."

"Thank you, Commander. Excellent job."

"I need to request your authority in this matter, sir," Martoni continued.

"You should. Admiral Philip Guthrie, Alliance First Fleet."

The voices around him quieted. Martoni and his three officers stared at him.

Philip wondered if he'd arisen from the dead or perhaps manifested an energy field and levitated around the room. No, those were Sullivan's *Kyi*-based specialties.

"You should also be asking to see my ID," he prompted Martoni.

"I, yes, sir. That is, may I—"

Philip was already handing it to him when he heard his subbie whisper his name, and not as a question.

"Guthrie."

He glanced over at her, taking in her wide-eyed expression. "Apologies, Lieutenant. I thought you'd guessed who I was."

"I did," she said softly. "I mean, that is..." Her voice trailed off.

She was flustered. He had a feeling that was unusual for her. Evidently meeting an admiral was something she hadn't dealt with before. But she was SPS; she must have. He shook off whatever the issue was, because Martoni was handing him back his ID and saluting.

"Admiral Guthrie, sir, we had no idea you'd be here."

"If it makes you feel any better, neither did I." He could thank Doc Galan for that. He pocketed his ID and shifted the weight of the duffel on his shoulder.

"Can I take that for you, sir?" one of the other men, also in civvies, asked. "We're loading gear first."

"Thank you, but I'll handle it. They should announce the schedule change shortly. Let's make sure everyone's ready to go. I want to keep problems to a minimum."

Martoni nodded, then issued quiet but firm orders to the woman and man closest to him. They hurried off, Martoni not far behind, and with a nod or a hand signal from him, groups of young men and women rose from their seats or straightened from their tired slouches.

Heads turned as Philip walked, limping, toward the tubeway, his blue-bereted subbie on his right. Whispers followed him.

"That's Guthrie."

"Admiral Guthrie."

Well, if they hadn't known who he was before, they sure as hell did now.

The shuttle schedule board flashed, declaring the Umoran shuttle's delay and a *Special Shuttle* to Seth departing in half an hour. Groans and cries of dismay echoed around him. Tired faces watched his people queue at the tubeway. A few angry faces boldly stared at him.

I'm trying to keep you all alive was on the tip of his tongue, but he couldn't—*wouldn't*—say it. An admiral doesn't make excuses. An admiral doesn't explain. An admiral acts.

Two stripers standing at the waiting area's edge took a few steps in. Philip raised his chin, gave his head a small, negative shake. A show of weapons right now would be counterproductive. These were families with children, for the most part. Tired, cranky, and, yes, angry. But they didn't need the insult of stripers bearing Blue Surgers added to the injury of yet another delay.

He counted fifty-two in the queue that wove past two wide pylons and wondered where the fifty-third one was. Then he realized she was standing by his side, her duffel now gone.

"Get in line, Lieutenant. Seats will be first come, first served." And the dirtside shuttle would be a small one.

"I'll board when you do, sir."

Any argument he would have made was halted by the arrival of the dirtside shuttle disgorging its passengers in several noisy clusters. They'd been delayed at the spaceport and, judging from the scowls and grumbling, were in no better frame of mind than those in the waiting room.

He counted forty-five departing. Fifty-three, fifty-four with himself, needed to board. It would be tight—though some could go below if the shuttle had a pressurized cargo deck.

Carmallis appeared at his side. "The ship needs ten minutes to refuel and restock."

"Fuel's most important. Then water. Just the basics. We're not expecting luxury." It would be an eight- to ten-hour trip to Seth, depending on the shuttle's speed.

"I'll tell the captain." She bustled off.

He went in search of Martoni and found him in the middle of the queue, half hidden by a wide pylon, and informed him of the short delay and the possibility of tight quarters.

"We have everyone's baggage almost loaded," Martoni said, motioning to Philip's duffel. "Sir, I can take that."

"I'll keep it," he told Martoni, then turned and almost mowed over his subbie, whose name he'd yet to learn.

"Lieutenant," he said, but loud, hard voices halted his intended question.

Two men shouted as they advanced on the tubeway and the shuttle crew at the check-in counter.

"Oh, God." His subbie sounded exasperated. "Mr. Wonderful and his best friend."

He glanced quickly at her.

"I had to ream them a new one earlier when they tried to take seats away from an elderly couple," she explained hurriedly. "I probably should have shot them then." Her hand snaked inside her jacket.

Philip touched her arm. "Leave that pleasure to the locals."

Her answering sigh was filled with regret, but she didn't refasten her jacket.

"But I paid my money!" the bearded man bellowed. "I have my goddamned rights."

His friend pounded the counter. "Yeah. Yeah!"

The two stripers broke into a trot.

Philip looked over his shoulder at Martoni. "Get your people loaded. Now." Once the shuttle was away, the problem would solve itself.

Then a third person rose from one of the back rows of seats. A woman, waving her ticket in the air. "I paid my money too!"

Some people looked away, but a lot watched her

and watched the bearded man and his now red-faced friend too.

Carmallis's voice came over the speakers. "Ladies and gentlemen, this shuttle is a priority military requisition. You will take your seats or you will be removed from the waiting area by security."

"Military?" the woman with the tickets called out. "This ain't no military. It's a lie. Somebody got paid off."

More angry voices rose around her. One of the stripers pulled away from the ticket counter and headed for the woman, his Blue Surger now in his hands.

Damn it, this is wrong. It makes no sense. Something about the agitators' tones and stances seemed staged, forced.

Philip checked the queue. About half were on board. Martoni was still by the hatchlock, next to a decidedly nervous slender woman in the shuttle company's light-green uniform, holding a databoard.

He nudged his subbie without taking his gaze off the commotion. "Go on."

"With all due respect, Admiral, hell, no."

That warranted a narrow-eyed glance. She didn't budge. And she had a Stinger in her hand, partly shielded from view by the pylon in front of her.

Another loud shout brought his gaze up.

"You wanna arrest me? Go right ahead!" The bearded man backed away from the counter, hands held high, but his tone and manner were clearly taunting the striper.

Philip saw Carmallis moving in from the right, her comm link to her mouth. Then something else caught his eye. Movement almost behind him, near the tubeway at the far end of the waiting area. More stripers? No, they would come from—

He dropped his cane, twisting, drawing his Carver smoothly as five dark figures burst through the service doors next to the far hatchlock. The high-pitched whine of lasers filled the air.

"Down! Get down!" Philip shouted, returning fire, very aware he was an open target in those few seconds, but he had no choice. There were children and elderly in the rows to his left.

Ignoring his leg, he dropped to his knees behind the pylon and fired again as people fled, screaming.

Something crashed in front of him. A long bench, upended, then another, forming a low barricade. His subbie scrambled toward him. "Guthrie!"

He launched himself sideways with a pained, grunted epithet, well aware he might not be able to walk after this, then ducked behind the metal barrier she'd created. His subbie had her Stinger out and was laying down a pattern of fire, keeping their attackers momentarily pinned behind the tubeway check-in counter.

He holstered his Carver with one hand and made a desperate grab at his duffel with the other, dragging it closer, his hip throbbing in painful protest. Teeth gritted in pain, he unlocked the duffel in two quick moves, then yanked out the Norlack, took aim, and fired.

The counter exploded.

He fired again, dropping one of the black-clad figures. He swung to his right for another, but that one was already falling from the stream of fire from the Stinger next to him.

"Admiral Guthrie!"

He recognized Martoni's voice. Out of the corner of his eye he saw a line of stripers surging down the corridor.

"I'll cover you. Now!"

He looped the duffel's strap over his shoulder. No way he was leaving his arsenal behind. "Subbie. On three. Ready?"

She was grinning, her eyes bright. She shoved her beret down the front of her shirt. "Ready."

"One...two...three!" He lurched to his feet, fired once more at his attackers, then took off for the hatchway in his best painful-beyond-belief limping run, laser fire whining around him.

Philip shoved his subbie ahead into waiting hands that tugged and pulled both her and him into the safety of the hatchlock. Someone took his duffel and the Norlack, the hatchlock clanging shut behind him. He let them go this time, because pain screamed through his body and he didn't know how he was going to make it the twenty feet down the tubeway to the ship without falling flat on his face.

An arm went around his waist, a mass of curly brown hair brushed against his shoulder, and he leaned on her, damning his leg but, more so, damning his stupidity.

He should have recognized a diversion the moment the bearded man first shouted. He hadn't, and people back on the station—civilians—were likely injured or dead.

So were most of the attackers. He hoped Carmallis figured it out and had the bearded man—Mr. Wonderful—and his friend in custody. And the ticket-waving woman. They were all part of it.

"Admiral Guthrie, are you all right?" Martoni had his other arm now.

"All things considered, yes." Philip grunted. He shoved at Martoni. "We'll need an armed escort. Tell the captain. Find out what armaments this bucket has. And get your best combat pilot on standby!"

Philip doubted that five attackers were the sum total of the operation the Imperials or the Farosians or whoever was behind this planned to throw at him. Someone wanted to make very sure Admiral Philip Guthrie didn't make it to the Seth shipyards.

Martoni nodded, then plunged through the shuttle's airlock.

Seconds later, Philip and his subbie hobbled through. They were just aft of the bridge and faced the shuttle's small galley. The aisle to his right led to rows of seats filled with people jostling into position, anxious faces turning toward him.

He offered a quick salute, then, still leaning on his subbie, turned for the bridge. Martoni was angled over the back of the captain's chair, talking rapidly. The copilot, a human male with a bushy dark mustache, and the navigator, an older Taka, nodded as Philip edged into the narrow open hatchlock. He took in the shuttle's bridge with a practiced eye. A good ship, less than ten years old judging from the screens and equipment blinking at him. From the configuration, he guessed it to be a 200-plus-ton Rouder. Sturdy and serviceable.

"Status, Martoni." His damned voice rasped from the pain.

Martoni straightened. "Station has a P-33 now deploying as escort. Umoran Defense will have another a few minutes behind us. We're breaking dock in..." He glanced at the captain's armrest screen.

"Five minutes," the captain said, twisting in her chair. She was his own age. No, older, mid-fifties, her pale hair pulled back in a long braid shot through with silver, her face carrying that elegance some women gain later in life. Her eyes, more green than hazel, were lightly edged by lines. "I flew planetary defense for Umoran for fifteen years, Admiral. We'll get you to Seth."

He could feel sweat beading at his temples. His leg throbbed.

"Acknowledged. Thanks." That was good news. A P-33 wasn't. An older thirty-three-ton patrol ship, no ion cannon. Lasers and, if they were lucky, maybe one torpedo bay.

Damned shame he couldn't shoot his own leg off. He shoved his thoughts away from the pain again.

"What are we carrying defensively?" he asked Martoni and the captain—who had a name but, as with his subbie, there hadn't been time to engage in pleasantries. Rank would do until all emergencies were handled.

"Standard laser weapons package you'd find on most Rouders," she said, confirming the shuttle's pedigree. Then she grinned slightly, almost impish. "And a highly illegal Gritter, but you didn't hear me admit that."

A Gritter—a GRT-10 plasma cannon. Small, powerful, and one of the more common weapons used by traders, because it was easily disguised as part of an enviro unit or an auxiliary sublight drive. Of course a shuttle like hers would have one.

He could have kissed her, if that small move wouldn't put him flat on the decking.

"Find a seat, strap in," she told him, her demeanor once again focused, serious. "It's going to be ditch and drop," she glanced at her armrest screen, "in two minutes."

His subbie tugged his arm. "This way. I'll clear you a seat."

"Floor," he said tightly, pointing to the open area between the galley and the airlock. "I need that leg straight out." Or he was going to die right then and there from the pain. "Then you get yourself safe in a seat."

"Floor," she agreed.

He leaned against the bulkhead, ship's drives shuddering hard through his body as they kicked to max, and slid clumsily to the decking. He forced his right leg out, teeth clenched, eyes closed, and fought the urge to pound the back of his head against the bulkhead.

At least that would create a pain he could control.

"One minute to departure." The captain's voice sounded calmly over the speakers.

A sudden lack of warmth on his left told him his subbie had disappeared. Probably to strap in to a seat. Finally, she was listening to him!

Then the warmth was back and, as the shuttle and his stomach lurched sideways, a hand came down firmly on his shoulder. Then a brief sting of something very small and very cold.

"What the hell?" he ground out, slitting his eyes open to see her palming a short cylindrical hypo. "Subbie, tell me you didn't do what I think you"—a slow, numbing heat trickled through his body—"just did."

"Quarter dose, Guthrie." Her beret was back on at that jaunty angle. "Courtesy of the shuttle's med kit, so it's probably not all that strong. Just enough to take the edge off. I hate to see grown men cry."

"I don't cry." He wiped the back of his hand over his face. It came back damp. God, were those tears? No. "That's sweat." He glared at her.

Damn, she had a beautiful smile.

Must be the drugs.

The stiffness leached out of his back, and the spasms

lessened in his right leg. It still throbbed, but the pain was down to a dull roar.

"Better?" she asked.

"Wipe that smug look off your face. That's an order."

"Just doing what I'm trained to do."

"Polite, professional, and prepared to puncture?"

She snorted out a laugh.

"We were set up, Subbie. Ambushed back there."

Her smile faded. "I caught on just about when you did. Mr. Wonderful played his part well."

"Tell the captain I need a report from Carmallis on injuries, fatalities, damages. If we left any of the bastards alive, I want them talking. I want to know who they work for."

"Copy the report to the *Nowicki* and Commander Adney?"

She was good, thorough. That would serve her well on the *Folly*. Less so here.

"I'll do that. I don't trust this shuttle's encryptions. Now, shoo. Get busy." He waved her away.

She rose, nodding, then disappeared toward the bridge. No "yes, Admiral" or even a "yes, sir." He'd have to work on that.

Martoni appeared seconds later, squatting down in her place. "Got two P-33s riding us starboard and aft, sir," he said. "So far, no bogies."

"Kirro security probably won't stay with us all the way to Seth." And his bogies, if they had half a brain, would know that.

Martoni nodded. "Captain Ellis advised that Seth's sending out a P-40 to intercept. But we could have a three-hour window where it's just us and the one thirty-three from Umoran."

His bogies doubtlessly knew that too.

"You said you can vouch for your thirty-seven people in the cabin," Philip said, thrusting his chin toward the cabin behind Martoni. "That leaves fourteen possible unknowns."

"I've got my people spread through the seats. No unknowns are seated together. And as you probably noticed, sir, I'm the only one in the group who was armed."

Philip had caught that when only he, his subbie, and Martoni were returning fire.

"That we know of," he reminded Martoni, but the man was good. He'd earned his place on the *Folly*. Hell of a reward, that. "Your people take any injuries?"

"Nothing serious, sir. Few bumps and scrapes. We were lucky."

"Where's my gear?"

Martoni leaned back on his heels and pointed to a familiar duffel along the galley's outer bulkhead.

"Drag it here, will you?"

Martoni did. Philip pulled it open. His Norlack was there. His fingers found a trio of archivers. He plucked one out. "I'm going to need to send a prelim to Captain Bralford," he said, pulling his comm link from his vest's inside pocket and hooking an archiver into it. "I'll have him contact Dina Adney. I don't want any more messages going in and out of this bucket than are absolutely necessary."

"Understood, sir."

"Your first name, Martoni?" He wanted Jodey to place a commendation in the man's file as soon as possible. It didn't escape him that they might not make it to Seth.

"Cory, sir. Cory Harris Martoni."

"Good name. My first CO was Cory. Captain Cory Bennton," he said, the twenty-year-old memory washing over him along with the regret that it had been over five years since he'd made time to sit down and share a beer with the older man. Now that chance was gone. "We lost him at Raft Thirty."

"I've heard of him, sir. All good things. Damned shame to lose him."

Philip nodded, his subbie's painkillers softening more than just his physical pain. "Go make your presence known in the cabin, Commander. Find out what you can on our mystery fourteen. I'll still be here when you get back."

"I have no doubt of that, sir." Martoni grinned, then shoved himself to his feet and headed toward the chatter of voices beyond the interior dividing bulkhead.

Philip keyed on his comm link. His head propped tiredly against the bulkhead, his voice low but clear as he went through the rote opening identifiers and codes. He gave Bralford only the highlights, the absolutely necessary information. This was a preliminary report, just enough to get the Alliance Fleet moving in the right direction. Once he had Carmallis's information—interrogations could take a while—he'd file something more detailed.

He had finished and was rolling the tension out of his shoulders when his subbie reappeared. He held up the archiver. "Send this via the shuttle's most secure link." The encryption filtered in from his comm link should keep the information safe.

She grabbed it with a nod and strode off.

What in hell *had* happened to "yes, sir"? He sighed.

A few minutes later she was back. "Done." She handed the archiver back to him. He slipped it into a vest pocket.

She folded herself down next to him and, he noticed, kept glancing at his duffel.

He arched an eyebrow.

"Is this," she asked hesitantly, "what I think it is?"

"What do you think it is?"

"Norlack 473 sniper, modified to handle wide-load slash ammo." There was a noticeable reverence in her voice.

He pulled the rifle out, hefting it. She had a good eye. Norlacks weren't common. But recognizing it was modified for illegal and highly destructive charges . . . Then again, she'd seen it in action.

"It is," he confirmed, amused now by the expression on her face. It had gone from reverence to almost rapture.

"That is so totally apex." Her voice was hushed. "May I," and she glanced shyly at him, her eyes bright, spots of color on her cheeks, "fondle it?"

He stared at her, not sure he heard her correctly. Then he snorted, laughing. Fondle it, indeed.

He handed it to her.

She took it, cradling it at first, then running her fingers lovingly down its short barrel.

Sweet holy God. He didn't have enough painkillers in him to stop his body's reaction to the smokiness in her eyes, or the way her lips parted slightly, the edge of her tongue slipping out to moisten them, as her hands slid over the weapon.

"Uh, Subbie."

"Beautiful, beautiful job," she said, turning the Norlack over, inspecting its power pack. One short-nailed finger traced the modified trigger panel. "See? The alignment is perfect. No gaps, no stress points. Nothing to fracture when this baby kicks out. I'll bet her impact field is as sweet and tight as a—oh. Sorry, sir."

She quickly lowered the rifle to her lap, her cheeks reddening.

Well, at least he'd gotten a "sir" out of her. He cleared his throat. "Someone taught you a lot about weapons."

She nodded without looking at him. "My father." She pulled out her Stinger. "He gave me this when I graduated from the academy."

Her eyes were soft and sad. He didn't know why, didn't know if he should ask. He was never good with those kinds of emotions. That was one of the reasons he'd lost Chaz.

"It's a fine pistol, reliable. Your father did well."

"I had a Carver-Ten with the service. Had to give it back, though." She sounded wistful.

If he'd had to give back a Carver-10 at her age, he would have sounded wistful too. And, hell, yeah, if he really wanted to be honest, he would have fondled a modified Norlack back then too.

She reholstered her Stinger.

He pulled out his Carver and passed it to her.

She took it, one hand around its grip, the other just under the barrel. She closed her eyes and sighed.

"A Twelve," he said.

"Mmm." The sound of pleasure rumbled in her throat. She didn't open her eyes.

Good thing. He was starting to sweat again.

Another sigh. She opened her eyes, stared in adoration at it for a very long moment, then handed it back to him.

"They fire a bit differently from a Ten," he told her, hoping she thought the roughness in his voice was due to pain. Or drugs.

"And a Ten fires differently from an Eight. They have that slight left-to-right vibration." She folded her hands together, index fingers out, mimicking a pistol. "Except when you use a Garno High Issue power pack, but Fleet never wanted to budget for them."

Well, damn. She did know her weapons. "How in hell do you know that?" Carver-8s were taken out of service almost twenty years ago. The last time he'd had one was when he was on the *Alric Stockwell*. Under the command of Captain Cory Bennton.

His subbie couldn't have been more than a child.

She turned wide hazel eyes on him. "You showed me."

Something was wrong with his hearing. He swore she said he showed her. "Who showed you?"

"You did."

"I . . . ?" He stared at her, really stared at her.

"It was a long time ago, Guthrie. I thought . . . well, for a bit I thought you might have remembered, but I guess you made more of an impression on me than I did on you. I was, I don't know, maybe nine, ten?"

He raked his mind for any kind of children's camp he might have visited as a young Fleet officer doing a marksmanship demonstration. He couldn't remember one—not even when his brother Devin, ten years his junior, was tucked away as usual in some school camp; not even with his handful of nieces and nephews. His parents never approved of anything military around them.

"Don't feel bad," she continued. "I didn't recognize you at first either. Your hair used to be brown."

He'd gone prematurely gray in his early thirties, just as his mother had. It was sort of a family badge of honor.

"I let you fire a Carver?"

"Carver-Eight. The *Stockwell* was in on liberty. You came to our apartment for dinner. My mother was alive then, and we went to the Fleet shooting range after, even though my father said I was misbehaving as usual and didn't deserve to go."

Memories surfaced, flooding him in a surge of surprise and nostalgia. He was suddenly younger, awed by the friendship extended him by *the* Captain Cory Bennton, who didn't give a damn that the young lieutenant was an heir to the Guthrie wealth but saw him only as a kindred spirit. An officer with a passion for weapons.

He had invited Philip to dinner to meet his wife and view his extensive gun collection. And bear up under the onslaught of his young daughter.

Bennton's little girl . . . a downright annoying, definitely pudgy, freckle-faced imp with wildly curly hair gathered on the sides of her head like two exploding reddish pom-poms. She'd bounced in her chair through cocktails, bounced in her chair through dinner, was soundly reprimanded for launching peas at him across the table with her fork, and had weaseled her way into going to the shooting range afterward, because obviously the brat never heard the word *no* in her entire short life.

She was nine, perhaps ten years old. Philip was around twenty-five. Five hours with her left him feeling as if he'd been through a war zone. He'd even given her an appropriate nickname.

Oh, sweet God.

His beautiful, weapon-loving subbie was Rya the Rebel.

She gently put the Norlack back on top of his duffel. "You hated me. I probably shouldn't have told you who I was, but you'd have found out eventually. Plus, you're half tranked." She poked his shoulder where she'd hit him with the hypo. "I figured this was a safe time."

"I...didn't hate you."

She arched an eyebrow.

"Not exactly," he amended.

"Rya the Rebel?" she prodded. "Do you know how my father hung that over my head for years? Every time I acted up, he—" She turned away suddenly, but not before he saw her face crumpling, her eyes screwing tightly shut.

Cory Bennton, her father, was dead.

Oh, sweet God.

He saw the stiffness in her shoulders, her back. Her posture radiated pain—something deeper and more permanent than his leg's shattered bones. Sullivan would know what to do, but Sullivan wasn't here.

He reached carefully, tentatively toward her, let his hand clasp her shoulder. She was vibrating far worse than an old Carver-8, holding back sobs.

Rya the Rebel had been one of the most out-of-control, annoying children he'd ever had the misfortune to meet. But he'd never doubted she adored, she'd *worshipped*, her father.

And he, her.

And now her father was dead.

And it was Philip's fault.

"Subbie," he said softly.

She sucked in a sob and blindly batted his hand away, then shoved herself to her feet and flung herself into the small lavatory next to the galley. The door slammed shut.

Philip let his head thump back against the bulkhead. He scrubbed his face with his hands.

His subbie was Rya the Rebel. Sub-Lieutenant Rya Bennton. Polite, professional, and prepared to kill.

And fully torn to shreds by the death of her father.

And there was not one goddamned thing Admiral Philip Guthrie could do to change that.

Rya braced herself over the lav's small basin as sobs wracked her body.

Goddamned stupid slag-headed idiot!

She'd fractured completely, coming apart in great horrible ugly chunks right in front of Philip Guthrie. Admiral Philip Guthrie. Her CO, if he didn't toss her fat unworthy ass off his ship the minute they hit the Seth shipyards.

Served her right if he did so.

She was ImpSec. SPS. You did not—*did not*—come apart, ever. And never in front of a senior officer.

Especially not when that CO was the one man besides your father who was your always-forever dream hero.

Lieutenant Philip Guthrie. Odd how over the years she'd forgotten his face but not the effect he'd had on her. And not certain details. The way he'd lounged at her parents' dining-room table, a slender-stemmed wineglass in his thick fingers. Strong fingers. Strong enough to hold something so delicate without breaking it. Strong enough to fire those powerful weapons that were her father's passion.

She'd tried so hard to behave that night, but when her father said he was bringing home one of his officers, she'd never thought it would be someone like Philip. She'd met his officers before. Gruff women who pinched her cheeks. Fat men who smelled like cigars.

And then Philip strode in, tall and strong, with those beautiful blue eyes, like a prince from her storyvids. And for the first time in her life she'd fallen in love with a man who wasn't her father.

She could not sit still. She'd wanted to fling her arms around his waist and hug him.

But she was just a child. Fat and freckled with frizzy hair.

Then he'd put his Carver in her hands, talking all the while about the weapon's problems as if she were a grown-up and really understood, and he held her small hands in his large warm ones while she aimed at the target and fired.

She didn't wash her hands for a week after that.

And now she'd just completely unraveled in front of him. Dishonored herself. Dishonored her duty to her father.

Fat slag-headed idiot.

She pulled off her beret, splashed water on her face, then ran damp hands through her hair. She stared at her reflection in the mirror.

Lose thirty pounds and you'd be decent, Rya.

Yeah, and do something with the hair. Cut your legs off at the ankles. You're too damned tall. Thinner waist, thinner thighs. Learn not to snort when you laugh. Stop saying *fuck* so much.

Fuck you.

Get control of your emotions, Subbie. You've an injured officer out there, an admiral who has no time for your hormonal meltdowns, your stupid petty daydreams. Do your fucking job. Make your father proud.

Find Tage and shove his goddamned fucking head up his goddamned fucking ass.

She grabbed her beret, opened the lav door, and steeled herself to face Guthrie's wrath.

But he was gone, only his neatly folded overcoat on the decking proof that he'd ever been there.

Rya followed the deep, cultured tones to the shuttle's large passenger cabin and found Admiral Philip Guthrie perched on the arm of someone's—some woman's—seat, putting in face time with those who were soon to be his ship's crew.

Martoni stood a few seats behind him, one elbow on the back of another seat.

Guthrie was talking about the ship, the Stryker-class cruiser. She remembered the thrill, the *vindication* she felt when her former chief on Calth 9 told her Adney's call for crew was to serve on the old *Stockwell*. It had been her father's ship. She shoved that thought away.

"We're going to have to push her through basic re-fit, fast," Guthrie said. "Head for Ferrin's. Keep in mind she's essentially functioning as a civilian ship, so we'll have minimal weapons until we get there. I'm going to cadge all the favors I can with planetary defenses. A couple of P-40s would help. A P-75 would be outstanding. But we can't count on that."

Martoni saw her, and because he did so did Guthrie, turning slightly as the commander's gaze flicked upward.

Cut a few inches off at the ankles, Rya. And lose thirty pounds.

Shut the hell up.

Something flashed through Guthrie's blue eyes that she couldn't identify.

"Subbie."

She nodded. "Present and accounted for, sir." She quirked her mouth into a smile.

He turned away.

Her heart broke for reasons she couldn't define.

"Questions?" he asked.

There were many. She waited while he fielded them, watched as he gave thoughtful contemplation to each one as if the questioner were a lord of some ministry and not a still-wet-behind-the-ears ensign looking for fame and glory fighting for the Alliance.

Finally he stood and, using the seat backs in place of the cane he'd left behind on Kirro, headed stiffly toward his "command center," as he jokingly referred to the open decking between the shuttle's airlock and the galley.

Rya strode in front of him, hand on her Stinger, watching everyone else's hands, occasionally committing faces to memory. She was back in ImpSec mode. Admiral Guthrie was her charge, her assignment, not her long-lost always-forever dream hero.

A privacy curtain imprinted with the shuttle company's star-and-moon logo separated the front section of the shuttle—bridge and galley—from the passenger cabin. As Martoni drew it closed behind them, voices in the cabin hushed. They'd been in transit for almost two hours. Adrenaline was winding down. Exhaustion was setting in.

Guthrie braced himself against the bulkhead, then slid down to the decking, his right leg out stiffly. The determined, almost heroic mien he'd worn in the passenger cabin shifted to humanly tired. He closed his eyes.

She holstered her Stinger and remained standing, uncertain and extraneous. Then her training kicked in. "Let me get you another short trank, sir. It'll help with the pain."

Those magnificent blue eyes opened. "Take a load off, Subbie. Sit."

Oddly, being in close proximity to him was the last thing she wanted right now. "Tea? Something to eat? When's the last time you ate, sir?"

"Right before Bralford dumped me on Kirro. Four or so hours ago. Sit."

"Sir—"

"We need to talk about your father."

"I'm not one to fall apart. It won't happen again."

"Were you paying attention in there when I talked about the *Folly*?"

"Yes, sir."

"Tell me why you want to serve on that ship, Lieutenant Bennton."

She assumed it would be Commander Adney asking that question. She had her answer prepared: "Because the Empire, under Darius Tage's direction, has become corrupt and dangerous. With the dissolution of the Admirals' Council, our liberties and our lives are at risk. The Alliance is our only hope of staving off disaster."

He studied her for a moment. She cringed internally. Maybe she'd prepared too well. Her answer sounded rote, even to her ears. But she knew they'd be culling the daredevils, the thrill seekers, the misguided heroes. She didn't want to come across like that.

"Your life is at risk fighting *for* the Alliance," he said finally.

"I'm aware of that, sir."

"We're underfunded, understaffed. You'll be serving—quite possibly fighting—under conditions you've never faced before. Being a rebel is not the glamour and glory the vids make it out to be."

"I'm aware of that too, sir."

"The danger doesn't concern you?"

"Danger concerns any good officer. But I'm ImpSec, sir. Special Protection Service."

"Polite, professional, and prepared to kill?"

"Yes, sir."

He nodded slowly. "And if I put you in the same room with the man responsible for the death of your father and handed you a Carver-Twelve, would you be able to press the trigger?"

Did he really doubt that? "Absolutely, sir."

He pulled his Carver out of the right side of his shoulder holster and held it up toward her. The grip of a second Carver—another 12, she thought—curved out of the left side.

She took it, not understanding. Did he mean for her to carry his weapon? A small thrill raced through her. Okay, it wasn't that small. A Carver-12, and his as well. It was still warm from the heat of his body.

"Why haven't you pressed the trigger?" he asked quietly.

"Why would I—" She stopped and stared at him. *If I put you in the same room with the man responsible for the death of your father and handed you a Carver-Twelve* . . .

No, that wasn't possible. He couldn't have—

"Sit, Rya. We need to talk about your father."

Still grasping the Carver, she lowered herself to her knees, her legs suddenly feeling boneless. She'd seen no official reports on her father's death. There *were* no official reports, only bare information that Tage had dissolved the Admirals' Council and then had the emperor's Special Reserve Guard—rumored to be an elite and secretive division in ImpSec—move against those officers he'd deemed traitors. Her father being one of them.

"How did he . . . What happened?"

"A farce," he said after a moment. "A deadly one. You don't convene a High Command strategy session on Raft Thirty, not even an unofficial one. I should have realized that. I should have told my people not to leave their ships until I'd spoken to Tage. If I had . . ." He went silent, shaking his head.

"Tage is—was—first barrister," she said. "The emperor's second in command. How could you know—"

"I knew what he'd done against Sullivan, and against my wife. But I wanted desperately to believe that the man I'd known and admired for decades could still be reasoned with."

Rya barely heard the rest of his sentence. Her mind had latched on to one word and not moved beyond. *Wife.* His wife.

Philip Guthrie was married.

Of course he was, idiot. Not every man wore a wedding ring. He was an admiral. His family was wealthy. He was handsome. Respected.

He had a wife.

She shook herself. This was not about her dreams. This was about what had happened to her father and the Empire she once believed in. And what she was going to do about it.

"I thought this was my chance to make Tage see reason," he was saying. "He said he wanted my input. He said the Empire was coming to a crucial turn. I saw the same thing. So I followed Tage's orders to bring specific captains and officers he'd named to meet with him or the strategy session on Raft Thirty." He stopped, is fist clenching, and when he spoke again, his voice vas low and hard. "It was a massacre."

That much Rya had heard, though not how or why er father came to be on Raft Thirty, other than it was n Tage's orders. But it had been on Philip's orders too.

Pain battered her heart.

"I know it's no consolation," Philip said, "but I illed the man who shot your father. And I will live vith your father's death on my soul's slate to the end of ny days."

"Because you followed orders," she said.

"Some of the best men and women the Empire ever roduced died because of it. Their deaths haunt me, ut that doesn't excuse my failure. Or the fact that I'm live and they're not." He wiped one hand over his ace.

"Which brings me to the reason I need to talk to you. suspect very strongly you're looking to avenge your ather's death and you see the recommission of the *tockwell* as your sign to do so. I know how you feel. *3elieve me,* I know. But you need to take those stars out f your eyes, Lieutenant. This is going to be a tough, lirty mission with a haphazard crew under the command of someone who has made mistakes and will continue to do so. It's going to be against enemies we know, nemies we don't know, and friends who have their own gendas. Right now the only thing we can say for certain is that there is nothing we can say for certain.

"This is not, *cannot,* be all about Rya's revenge. f that's where your focus is, you're going to be disppointed. You might also get yourself and others killed."

She stared at him, hating his words, hating the fact he was so transparent.

"And you don't want revenge?" she asked harshly.

He shook his head. "Revenge is a waste of time. It will never happen the way you want. And whatever does happen won't be enough."

"Then why bother with all this?" She swung one hand out toward the cabin, toward Martoni and the others.

"For victory." He raised his chin slightly. "And now, yes, I think I would like that mug of tea. Take your time making it. Make one for yourself. Think about everything I've said. Because you've already failed your first test. You lied when you said you would be able to shoot the man responsible for the death of your father." He plucked the Carver from her fingers. "Now you need to decide whether you're cut out for this mission."

Rya stood in the utilitarian galley, a few feet away from where Philip Guthrie sat on the decking, and stared at the plastic dispenser full of tea bags on the metal counter, anger mixing with shame. She had been soundly and professionally manipulated. He had read her like a data archiver on max download and then set her up, drawing from her the only answer she could give.

The wrong one.

Damn you, Philip Guthrie!

She closed her fingers around a green plastic mug's handle and ignored Martoni as he walked toward the bridge, then ignored him again when he came out and squatted down next to the admiral. The mug was still empty. The dispenser of tea bags was still full.

A thousand excuses, rejoinders, and rebuttals whirled through her mind. But it all came back to one thing: was she here because of the Alliance or because of her father?

And her answer, she knew, was the wrong one.

But damn it all, did it really matter if revenge was her motivation? Yes. Because it took her focus off whatever mission her CO assigned her, took her focus off her teammates and put it on what she wanted.

She could so very clearly hear her father explaining that to her. And her father had trained Philip Guthrie.

She understood the point of his story, of how and why he was responsible for her father's death. Yes, he'd followed orders, but with his own agenda, his own beliefs in mind. He hadn't seen what Tage intended to do, because he'd wanted the meeting to be something other than what it was, just as he'd wanted Tage to be someone other than what he was.

People had died because, for a few short hours, Admiral Philip Guthrie had lost his focus.

She should hate him, refuse to serve under him. If she thought long enough about it, she probably could muster up some decent ire. And that would give him, she knew, what he wanted: ImpSec Sub-Lieutenant Rya Bennton on the next shuttle back to Calth 9.

But Rya the Rebel would not give him that satisfaction.

She pushed a tea bag into the plastic mug, then shoved it under the hot-water spigot, not even bothering to ask if he liked that particular herbal blend. It was healthy, high in those nutrients that kept your brain working.

He would need those if he thought he was going to put something past her again.

She stepped out of the galley alcove, tea in hand. Martoni was in her spot on the decking, frowning. Guthrie had the transceiver from his comm link ringing his ear. And he was frowning.

She stepped over to him and waited, the musky aroma of the tea wafting under her nose.

He acknowledged her with a slight nod, eyes narrowed, fingers now pressing the transceiver's tiny speaker against his ear. She squatted down and he took the mug from her without comment.

She looked at Martoni.

"Preliminary report from Kirro," he said quietly.

Not good news, then. "You want tea?" she asked Martoni. Might as well make herself useful. Might as well make it clear to Guthrie she was here to stay and work.

"Yeah, thanks."

She returned to the galley, made a cup for Martoni and one for herself, then again lowered herself to the decking at the edge of Guthrie's outstretched boots.

And damned herself because, in spite of all that was going on—the ambush, the firefight, the desperate attempt to get to Seth before someone put a torpedo through the shuttle's hull—she couldn't stop wondering about Guthrie's wife.

Professional curiosity, she told herself. The man was to be her commanding officer. Of that she was very sure. And he'd been a friend of her father's. He'd known her mother. It was only natural to wonder what kind of family he had.

One of her strong points as an ImpSec SPS officer was profiling. Who was this sentient, and why did he do what he did? What might he do? That was all she was doing now as she watched Guthrie pull the unit from around his ear.

She'd always been able to get a quick read on her superiors and use that to make sure she not only did her job well but also fulfilled their expectations. That was also her motivation for studying him.

His damned magnificent blue eyes—and mysterious wife—notwithstanding.

He tucked the transceiver in his vest pocket. "Farosians," he said, without any preliminary. "Doesn't that goddamned beat all?"

"Justice Wardens?" Martoni asked, clearly surprised.

Rya was nodding. "Makes sense. Mr. Wonderful didn't have any aspect of Fleet about him. Had he or his friend been ex-Fleeties with Imperial training, I think I would have known. They backed off when I stood up to them, thinking I was a striper. The friend said as much. They didn't recognize the beret. A Fleetie would have."

She didn't miss the whisper of a smile on Guthrie's lips. That warmed her. She didn't want to think about why.

"What else, Subbie?" Guthrie prompted.

This was another test. She frowned, letting the scenario of the ambush play over in her mind, from Mr. Wonderful's overacting at the ticket counter to the black-clad figures swarming from the crew access door next to the far tubeway.

There was something . . .

She raised one hand. "Give me a moment." She closed her eyes and saw it in detail this time. And listened, hearing what she'd missed because she'd not really been in working mode. And was so distracted by the shock of Philip's identity.

When she opened her eyes, it was to see the admiral's hand, slightly raised. "Don't answer yet. Just tell me this: are you keying on something you saw or something you heard?"

"Heard."

He turned to Martoni. "Commander?"

"The guy's accent, the way he spoke?" Martoni pursed his lips, thinking hard. "Could be fake, that dockworker's rough speech. Not a Farosian accent, but not all of Blaine's followers are from there." He ran one hand down his pant leg, still thinking.

"Subbie?"

"Their weapons were set to stun. Not kill. They wanted you alive."

Martoni stared at her. Philip's smile widened.

"The pitch of a laser pistol on stun is considerably higher," she continued with a nod. "Granted, the waiting area was high-ceilinged and that could affect acoustics. But taking that into account, the pitch was a quarter to a half octave above a laser set to kill." She glanced at Martoni. "The reduction of energy through the baffles creates more resistance in the amplifiers and filters. Especially in Stingers," she added. "Four of them carried Stingers, like mine, though possibly a bit older."

"One had an Aero," Philip said. "New model."

"That was the one going *zeef zeef*?"

"Yeah." Still grinning.

"Never came across one before."

"I've never heard one described as going *zeef*, but that's fairly accurate."

Martoni logged their exchange with a slight back and forth movement of his head.

"So why the different pitch?" she asked.

"Ever see the schematics for the converter?"

"I let my subscription to *Weapons Quarterly* lapse."

"It wasn't in there. It was in a recent issue of *Helfstein's Armaments Review*. Speculation, though, because it's a Stol-produced weapon. Helfstein wasn't quoting sources. Doing so could get him killed. But the data and analysis read true to me."

"Don't suppose you have a copy? Sir," she added

hastily, because of the way Martoni was looking at her. At them.

"I might be able to scare one up when we get to Ferrin's."

When we get to Ferrin's. That meant he wasn't sending her back on the return shuttle.

"I look forward to reading it. Sir," she added again, for good measure.

"Don't pick out your cabin yet, Subbie. I could be sending a copy of that article to Calth Nine via transmit. We still need to have our talk."

"Yes, sir." She wanted to bounce where she sat. She forced herself not to. She'd already chosen her cabin, knowing the layout of the *Stockwell* as she knew the layout of all her father's ships. She'd have the small cabin next to the admiral's, as was befitting his personal bodyguard. After all, he was injured. And she was sure his wife wanted to see him alive again.

"So the question now," Philip said, "is why. Why not kill me? What do they gain by simply stunning me?"

"Kidnap you for interrogation?" Martoni answered quickly.

Damned well he'd better answer, Rya thought. He'd been left behind in the exchange up to this point.

"Valid," Philip agreed.

"You're the highest-ranking officer of the Alliance Fleet," Martoni continued. "They could hamper our momentum by doing so. Plus, they assume you'd know upcoming plans, ship acquisitions."

"But why would they care? We're ostensibly on the same side. We both want Tage out of power."

"But we want to restore the Admirals' Council," Martoni said. "They want Blaine on the throne."

"True. Subbie?"

She turned the mug of tea around in her hands.

Philip had finished his. Hers was cold now, almost as cold as the chill that shot through her when Philip's questions made everything fall into place. "Blaine's on Moabar, under Tage's control. Tage tried to kill you and failed. They want to kidnap you and trade you to Tage for Blaine."

Martoni stared at her. Philip nodded. "Chief Carmallis's interrogators are very skilled. And that's exactly what Mr. Wonderful told them."

Rya's mind kicked into overdrive. "How did they know you'd be on Kirro?" She remembered him saying that hadn't been his original plan.

"Mr. Wonderful didn't know. I can make some guesses, not the least of which being they have someone watching traffic. A former Imperial Maven-class cruiser is easy to spot if you know what you're looking for. On the downside, it could be they have moles in the Alliance. Actually, I expect they do. I expect," and he nodded to Martoni, "we have some on this shuttle."

"I'm working under that assumption as well, Admiral."

"But I wasn't on schedule," Philip continued, as Rya's mind raced through scenarios and options. She always put herself in the other sentient's boots. What did they know, and what would they do with that information in order to get what they wanted?

"And we didn't depart in the expected manner, on the shuttle to Seth," he said. "It looked as if their attack was thrown together with what they had on hand. There were over thirty former Fleet personnel under your command, Martoni, in the area. They put five of their people against us? A shot in the dark, I think."

"Mole," Rya said, still synthesizing what he'd said. "I didn't know who you were. Martoni didn't either. I don't remember anyone who didn't act with surprise when you revealed your identity. You don't exactly—begging the admiral's pardon—look the part."

Philip grunted, then chuckled.

"So someone," Rya said, "overheard. And rushed to act just as we were boarding. A now-or-never operation."

"So which of the fourteen is our mole?" Philip asked. "Or, and I know you don't want to hear this, Martoni, but which of those in your group could work for Blaine?" He sighed. "We need Sullivan."

"Sullivan?" Rya couldn't specifically place the name in this context. The Sullivans she'd heard of were either obscenely wealthy or on the Empire's list of pirates.

Philip looked from her to Martoni and back again. "*Ragkiril.* You know the term?"

"Stolorth?" Martoni asked.

"Mind-fucker." Rya spat out the word. She was ImpSec, had studied ImpSec's and Stol's tactics during the Boundary Wars. *Ragkiril* and all associated epithets were things she knew.

Philip laughed again softly. "Some of my best friends are mind-fuckers. And, no, not Stolorth. Human. A human *Kyi-Ragkiril.* He could walk down that aisle," he nodded toward the cabin, "and know within moments who your mole was. Mission accomplished. But there's no time for me to locate him and ask for a meetpoint. So for now we have to assume we have one or more moles on board. We have to be careful what we say and to whom we say it. And we also have to note who's more than normally interested in what we say."

He turned to Martoni. "I assume you have two, three people you've worked with for years that you trust unequivocally?"

"Yes, sir, I do."

"Take them aside, bring them up to date. Then go

be friendly to everyone. And note who you think might be a problem. I need to know before we make the shipyards."

"Yes, sir."

"I'll take that," Rya said as Martoni pushed himself to his feet, juggling his empty mug of tea in one hand. She detested playing the role of housemaid, but she wanted Martoni to move on. She had to talk to Philip without Martoni hearing.

"Thanks." He handed her the mug and slipped past the curtain into the larger cabin.

"You suspect him," she said, her voice low.

"I suspect everyone, Lieutenant Bennton." His voice was a deep rumble. "I have to, after Raft Thirty."

"If you didn't, I'd tell you to do so."

"Chapter six, subsection ten of the ImpSec training manual?"

"Subsections ten and eleven." She rose, not at all surprised he could quote it to her. "More tea?"

He held up the empty mug. "That was fine for now. Thank you."

She put the mugs in the shuttle's recycler, then returned to the spot at Guthrie's side that Martoni had vacated.

"I can handle this mission, sir," she said when he slanted a glance at her, his eyes half hooded. He might be tired, but she suspected that was simply his thinking mode and that it amused him to have people believe he was resting when in fact his mind was through the jumpgate and out the other side already. She remembered her father saying something to that effect about Lieutenant Guthrie as she was growing up.

The half-hooded eyes showed no change.

"I can also handle my desire for revenge. It's there, but it is tempered through my training."

"All that wisdom in four and a half years?"

"Four and a half on duty, four in the academy, twenty-nine as my father's daughter."

"Twenty-nine?" His voice held a distinctive drawl. "We may have to get you a cane, Subbie."

"Only if it can be modified to handle wide-load slash ammo."

"That would be useful, with enemies coming out of every crevice."

She nodded, thinking. "Once we get to Seth, I'll need to do a personal assessment of the armaments you carry. The Carver's effective but bulky, obvious. An L7—"

"Already carry one."

"Good, because it's easily concealed and is sometimes missed even during pat-downs."

"Are you presuming to inform me not only that you'll be part of this mission but what position you'll be working as well?"

Rya sucked in a short breath. They'd been talking so naturally—and about weapons—that she'd let herself relax. "Not at all, sir. But I know you'd apply your expertise in allocating personnel to positions based on their training and past postings. You'd utilize my ImpSec background to your best advantage."

"You'd be best utilized in a court of law, standing in front of a judge and jury, telling them the man who murdered his five children just happened to be slicing the holiday roast when he sneezed and the knife slipped accidentally. And damned if they wouldn't believe you."

She grinned. "That's because it would be the truth."

He pulled his comm link from his vest pocket and pointed it at her. "I have work to do. Did your gear make it on board or was it left behind at Kirro?"

"I gave it to the shuttle crew when we were first

loading. It's probably stowed below in cargo." At least, she hoped it was, or she'd be spending a lot of time playing cards trying to win socks. And clothes, boots, and underwear. Everything she owned was in that duffel.

"You should go check on it."

She shrugged. "If it didn't make it, there's little I can do about it now."

"Let me make myself clearer, Subbie. Go check on your gear. Then go play nice and chatty to the rest of ship's crew in the cabin. Same thing I told Martoni." He pinned her with a hard look. "I have work to do."

Dense, Rya, really dense. The man wants you out of his face. "Yes, sir. With your permission, I'd like to check that my gear made it, then get to know the crew."

"Excellent idea. Shoo."

She pushed herself to her feet. "But before I—"

"Shoo!"

"Shooing now." She sidled around the curtain and stopped short as several bodies clogged the narrow aisle between the rows of seats. "Oh, sorry!"

"Not a problem," a round-faced woman about her own age, wearing an oversize brown sweater, said. "We'll just be a minute."

Rya glanced back through a break in the curtain to where Philip Guthrie sat. He pulled a small folded slip of paper from his vest pocket, opening it with a flick of his thumb. His gaze focused on it, his mouth curving slightly into a soft smile.

Years and tension dropped briefly from his face.

He closed his eyes, leaning his head back against the bulkhead, the small note still between his fingers.

A note from his wife. It had to be.

Rya tore her gaze away and stared over the heads of the new crew of *Hope's Folly,* an inexplicable tightness in her throat. So the admiral's wife wrote him love notes. What business was that of hers?

None.

Now, where in hell was her goddamned duffel?

Philip tucked Chaz's note away with a sigh. It sure as hell would be easier if he could somehow materialize Chaz and Sullivan on this shuttle and find out who his moles were. He was sure there were at least two, and he'd been honest in what he'd told Rya: he didn't discount Martoni. The efficient, stalwart commander was exactly the kind of officer Fleet traitor Nayla Dalby would have trained.

But he couldn't materialize Sullivan and Chaz right now. He was surprised how much at peace he finally felt because Chaz was happy. At least one little corner of the universe was behaving as it should.

The rest of it...He shook his head. The Farosians were trying to take him hostage to force a swap for Sheldon Blaine. How was that for an unexpected turn of events? But not an unreasonable one. He couldn't honestly say Tage would turn down the opportunity—especially if Tage could somehow turn events around and place the blame on the Alliance.

He plugged in the archiver and keyed on his comm link. Jodey needed an update, as did Dina Adney. One out there behind him, one in front of him.

The Empire is trying to kill us. The Farosians are trying to kidnap us.

Helluva party.

And in the middle of it all sat one Sub-Lieutenant Rya Bennton. He mentioned her existence only briefly to Jodey and only that she was Cory's daughter. Not that the universe seemed a little brighter, a little fresher when she was around. And not that she longed to fondle his Norlack.

He smiled, because that's what was in his mind when he'd pulled out Chaz's note that had come with the Norlack: Rya's hushed tones and rapturous expression.

God give him strength.

If he was ten years younger . . . But he wasn't. *Stow that thought, Guthrie. She's a nice kid. Kid, you fool. Bright, energetic, dedicated. And the daughter of your close friend, who's no longer around to kick your ass all over Calth for thinking lustful thoughts about his only child.*

He had a ship to refit, a fleet to build, and, God willing, a war to win. Let someone else tame Rya the Rebel. *But I'll watch after her, Cap'n Cory. That much I will do. That's a promise.*

He pocketed the comm link and archiver and, glad Rya wasn't there to witness his flailing, shoved himself awkwardly to his feet. He limped for the bridge to borrow Captain Ellis's comm system yet again.

An alarm blared just as he crossed the hatchlock.

Captain Ellis swore harshly, tearing her gaze away from her console just long enough to shoot him a narrow-eyed glance. "Trouble, Guthrie."

He dropped the archiver back into his pocket and leaned on her chair. Three bogies, about thirty-five minutes out, were coming at them from their starboard axis, weapons' ports hot. And one had the distinctive silhouette of an Elarwin Infiltrator—two hundred fifty tons of speed, weapons, and agility.

All they had were the two P-33s. And Ellis's Gritter cannon.

"Shields at combat strength," she intoned. "Engine at max. Escorts acknowledge the bogies." The P-33s were moving into defensive position off the shuttle's starboard side. "That's an Infiltrator," Ellis continued, studying the data as he had. "Jammed my long-range. Or I would have known a while ago the sons of bitches were there."

"Where's Seth's P-40?" he asked.

"Two hours out," the Takan navigator told him without turning around. "Just confirmed ten minutes ago. Sending advisory now." His voice held that gruff Takan growl, making it impossible for Philip to tell if the navigator was nervous or not.

Two hours. They could be dead in two hours, especially against an Infiltrator. Fast and deadly with ion cannons, torpedoes, and lasers—possibly more if this was the Infiltrator Chaz had told him about, the one that had challenged Sullivan's ship four months ago. The one that had Fleet traitor—*careful, Guthrie, you're one of those now*—and Farosian assassin Nayla Dalby in the captain's chair.

But Commander Dalby had been a traitor when Fleet was still an honorable organization. She was also associated with that same Stolorth *Kyi-Ragkiril* prince who had attacked Chaz, shattered Philip's leg, and damned near killed Sullivan, four months ago.

That deposed Stolorth prince might well be the reason this Infiltrator chased them now. He was dead, his and the Farosians' plans thwarted because of Chaz, Philip, and Sullivan. Rya the Rebel might not be the only one with revenge on her mind.

"If they want you alive," Ellis said, "they'll just try to shoot my engines out."

"Force us to the life pods." He was nodding. "But having failed at Kirro, they may no longer care."

"You're sure it's the Farosians?"

He reached over her shoulder and tapped the icon

for the Infiltrator. "You piss off anyone with that kind of firepower lately?"

"Not lately."

"Then it's me, and, yes, it's the Farosians." Tage would have sent a couple of heavy cruisers, or a destroyer or three. He fished the archiver out of his pocket and handed it to her. "Send this, priority, now. We might not get another chance."

"Dargo," she called out, and the Takan navigator turned, neatly catching the archiver she tossed to him, then slotting it into the ship's comm system.

Philip glanced over his shoulder. Rya waited in the bridge's hatchlock; Martoni was behind her but with his back to the bridge, keeping watch on the passenger cabin. Good positioning.

"You heard?" he asked Rya.

"Unfriendlies. Infiltrator and two bogies," she said.

"You ever face combat on a ship before?"

"Sims, sir."

This was going to be nothing like the simulators. They were in a goddamned civilian shuttle. "Life pods are belowdecks here, through cargo," he told her. "Make sure access is clear." The Farosians wanted him, alive or dead. He wasn't sure which he'd prefer, if they intended to trade him to Tage.

Captain Ellis tapped his arm, then passed the archiver back to him. "How many pods?" he asked her. He thought six, but he could be wrong.

"Six plus the bridge pod."

He nodded. "Martoni makes one," he told Rya. "Get five other pod captains, get them down there and familiar with pod operation."

Alarm flashed briefly in her eyes.

C'mon, you're a Bennton. Hang in there for me, Rebel.

Then it was gone. He saw her center herself, drop into working mode.

Good girl. Do Dad and Uncle Philip proud.

Uncle Philip? Maybe not. And this was not the time to argue with his libido over that.

"Yes, sir." She turned, grabbing for Martoni's arm, ducking her head down as she relayed Philip's orders.

"I've got the Gritter. We've got two patrol ships," Ellis reminded him when he glanced down at the flashing icons on her console.

"We also have a ship full of fresh-out-of-the-academy inexperienced kids, for the most part. And this is not an official Fleet transport." He met her gaze levelly. "I have no doubt that someday I'll go out in a blaze of glory, but today's not the day."

"You and me both," she quipped, and Philip decided if they lived through this, he'd buy her a drink. Maybe three. He liked her confidence, her sassy attitude, and, hell, what were a few years or so? She was an attractive woman—who illegally loaded her ship with a Gritter cannon, probably tucked neatly under the decking, disguised as an enviro booster. He liked that.

"My husband would kill me if I died," she added wryly.

Stow that thought.

But it also added one. He'd do everything he could to get her back to her husband. "Send out a broad hail," he said. "Let's see if that Infiltrator has anything to say."

He did not want to become the Farosians' captive and a bargaining chip with Tage. But he didn't want sixty innocent people to die for him either. Enough had already. And he had a promise to Cory to keep.

5

It took three minutes for the Infiltrator to respond to
the shuttle's hail, during which time Philip once more
ran through his options and best strategies. In his
twenty years with Fleet, he'd never been in exactly this
situation: a civilian ship, a military threat.

It was the word *civilian* that forced a great deal of
soul-searching thought. No one on board had yet

pledged to risk their life for some abstract ideal known as the Alliance. Except him.

"Kirro Path Shuttle, this is the Infiltrator. Put Guthrie on."

He recognized the Dafirian drawl of Nayla Dalby's voice immediately. He took the spare comm head-set and slipped it on, twirling the microphone up. "Commander Dalby. Tell me this isn't a meeting we're both going to regret."

A sharp bark of laughter. "Guthrie, you old bastard. I'm so going to enjoy this. How does it feel to be on the losing side?"

"I wouldn't know," he shot back. "You're the one sucking up to Tage."

"Dirty words, rich boy. Traveling in a piece-of-shit shuttle and not an admiral's pinnace. Shame."

"Fuck you," he heard Ellis intone under her breath. He'd surmised the shuttle company and this shuttle were hers. That confirmed it.

He also knew that other than their Star-Ripper—a small but heavily armed 300-ton ship less than half the size of the *Stockwell*—the Infiltrator was one of the Farosians' best ships, courtesy of that late Stolorth prince. But the Farosians had owned the *Stockwell* for a short period of time and lost it, so Dalby had no standing—other than personal—to belittle his method of transportation.

"If we're so unworthy, then why are you dead-eyeing us?" he asked smoothly, leaning against the edge of the communications console because his leg was warning it wanted to collapse again.

"Leveling the score, Guthrie."

That worried him, hinting that Dalby was here for revenge and could kill everyone on board to get to him. But he wouldn't let that happen. Death was final.

Being taken prisoner by Blaine's Tos Faros-based Justice Wardens still left options. "Tage won't be interested in my dead body, if you want Blaine in exchange."

Ellis was watching him closely, her green eyes narrowed. Not happy. Well, neither was he.

"Tage is in no position to defend Moabar," Dalby said, naming the remote, inhospitable world the Empire used as a prison planet. "Whether you're breathing air or sucking vacuum makes no difference to us."

The first Philip judged to be true. The second he knew was a lie, based on what Carmallis had found out from the Farosian agents left alive. Which meant Dalby's personal vendetta notwithstanding, she still had her orders: to get Guthrie.

"Tage is in no position to defend Moabar," Philip said, repeating her assertion back to her, "because we're hampering him. You need to rethink your aggression toward the Alliance."

Ellis jerked her chin to get his attention. He leaned away from the console and glanced at her screens. The two unknown bogies had just been identified as older R-3 thirty-ton Ratch fighters. First bit of good news. Their P-33s should be able to handle them defensively.

That left only the Infiltrator. One clean shot from the Gritter could handle that. But there was no way a captain like Dalby would allow a clean shot. Still, Philip felt marginally better about this encounter than he had five minutes before.

"Surrender your personnel, your ships, to us," Dalby said with a smug tone in her voice. "And we just might do some rethinking."

"Not an option, Dalby." Especially because a new ident had just flashed on Ellis's screen. And Ellis's Takan navigator was grinning widely.

Not Seth's P-40 but a Takan armored freighter answering the shuttle's distress code, thirty minutes out and closing. That meant a few more banks of lasers and, yes, sweet God, a torpedo tube registering hot.

Dalby evidently saw the same information. She cut their comm link, the bridge's speakers going silent with a slight hiss. The Ratch fighters slowed.

"Ha!" Ellis barked out a laugh. "I was hoping Fregmar was out here somewhere. I also wasn't going to play this hand until I had to," she continued, tapping a series of commands on her screen, "but I think now's the time to give those Farosians an even better reason to leave. Arming the Gritter," she announced.

"Wait 'til the Infiltrator sees *that* port go hot on her scans," the mustachioed copilot said.

Hell's fat ass. They just might make it. Philip angled around, looking through the bridge hatchlock for Martoni or Rya. They needed an update. He didn't see either. Martoni, he remembered, had been sent belowdecks to the life pods. Rya was likely with him.

"Things look better," Philip told Ellis as Dalby's Infiltrator abruptly changed course, heading away from them. "I'm going to check in with Commander Martoni."

He lumbered off the bridge, right hand flat against the bulkhead for support as his leg shot insistent jolts of pain with every step. People milled about in the wide center aisle, and many seats were empty. At least five would have been designated life-pod captains.

"Commander Martoni's below?" he asked a young man seated in the second row—the kid couldn't be more than twenty. He'd watched Philip approach, wide-eyed. Philip didn't know whether the kid had never seen an admiral before or an admiral who limped as badly as he did.

"Yes, sir. At least, I believe so, sir." He started to rise. "Would you like me to find him for you, sir?"

Lots of "sirs." His subbie should take note.

"Thanks, but I'll go below. The leg feels better when I move." It did. As long as he had something to hang on to, like the seat backs.

He passed by the rear lavs and a secondary, smaller galley. The lav doors were closed, the galley empty. The stairwell behind that was more of a narrow ladderway. Belatedly, he realized negotiating that with his bad leg was probably not the best idea, but each step was also a handhold. He was halfway down when he realized what was odd. Except for his own grunting, it was silent.

He jerked around, freeing one hand to reach for his Carver, but it was too late. Two laser pistols were aimed at him.

"Don't even think about it, Admiral," a pale-skinned woman in a bulky brown sweater said, eyes narrowed as she pointed her weapon at him.

Philip froze, his gaze immediately taking in and analyzing everything around him, including Martoni's still form, facedown on his right, and three other crew slumped, unconscious or dead, on his left. Relief momentarily flooded him because none of the three was Rya. But there were three crew down, four counting Martoni. He made a quick assessment of his situation as he prayed they were alive.

He was about four rungs from the decking. The woman in the brown sweater was closest to him. A few feet behind her to Philip's left was her other armed accomplice—a tall, dusky-skinned man, head shaved bald. Martoni's people, or two of the mystery fourteen? Philip didn't know.

But they were Farosians, of that he was sure. Tage's people would have killed him.

"I can either stun you and you can fall and break your other leg, or maybe your neck," the woman said as the man advanced toward Philip, "or you can come down easily, let my associate take your weapons, and be in far less pain when we put you in the pod."

Philip eased down the last few rungs. They knew he had the Carvers. They'd probably also find the L7. But he had more than that, and if they thought he was going to willingly be shipped off to Nayla Dalby's Infiltrator, they were wrong.

Not that he'd let them know that just yet.

His good leg hit the decking. He half-turned, leaning against the ladderway's rungs, and slowly raised his hands out to his sides, sizing up the man coming at him. They were about equal height. He could feign weakness, then head-butt the guy in the chest and hope the guy didn't shoot him. That might also give him the guy's body as a shield if the woman took a shot.

But they were going to stun him anyway. He saw that as her grip on the gun shifted, the man holstering his weapon now. Stun him, shove him in the pod, and—

Philip lunged for the guy, low and hard, teeth clenched in pain as he put his full weight on his broken leg. He heard the high whine of the stunner, heard the man groan out something as Philip's head plowed into his gut.

Pain blinded him as he tried to barrel the man to the ground and reach for his Carver at the same time. The guy grabbed him in a headlock. The woman shouted. Philip choked, wrenching, going for the small knife tucked in his belt. His fingers found the hilt, but the guy twisted him sideways. They stumbled, falling, hitting the decking with a bone-grinding crunch.

Philip tasted blood, and his ears rang from pain and the sound of laser fire. He brought his elbow up, smashing it into the guy's nose. His attacker went suddenly—inexplicably—limp, but there was no time to ponder his good fortune. Philip yanked his Carver out, leaned over the guy's body, and took aim at the woman. Before he could push the trigger, she gasped and crumbled to the deck.

"Philip!" Rya's voice, behind him.

He rolled on his back, Carver gripped tightly in both hands, and found his subbie in his sights, hanging upside down through the top of the ladderway, Stinger in hand.

"You okay?" she asked.

He took one more glance at the man and the woman to make sure they weren't a threat, then pushed himself painfully into a sitting position. "Delightful," he rasped out, understanding dawning.

Rya angled up, her head disappearing, then her boots appeared and she was scrambling down the ladderway, Stinger still in her grasp. Other booted feet followed.

"Secure the cabin, the bridge," he ordered, the sound of his voice far less commanding then he wanted it to be but, damn, the pain was coming in ugly, fat waves now. Hitting the deck with a guy his own size landing on him had done some damage. "Check on Martoni and those others."

He tried to push himself up.

Rya repeated his orders, pulling out an L7 and tossing it to a lanky, dark-haired man behind her. He took off back up the ladderway as she holstered her Stinger. Then her hands were on Philip's shoulders as she pushed him back down. "Sit." She knelt in front of him, her hair disheveled from her upside-down position, her eyes dark with concern. Behind her, someone had a medistat in hand and was running it over Martoni's still form.

"Alive. Just stunned," he heard a woman say.

Good news. Goddamn.

Rya took the Carver from his grasp and put it back in his shoulder holster. "You going to pass out on me, Guthrie?" She laid her hand gently against the side of his face.

"Trying not to." He was, really hard. He was in a cold sweat now, and even breathing hurt. Bad. "Status?" he asked as she drew her hand away, then reached into her jacket pocket. "Dalby's ship?"

She pulled out a familiar-looking hypo.

"That's not my main area of concern this second, but I'll find out." She glanced quickly over her shoulder. "Holton! The admiral needs status from Captain Ellis. There should be a comm panel in the galley."

"Don't knock me out. I need to be functioning," he warned as a woman scrambled back up the ladderway at Rya's command. The cold sting of the hypo hit his neck. He was shaking.

"Just a little more than I gave you last time." Rya's voice was soft, reassuring. One arm went tightly around his back, holding him upright. "Hang in there. The trank will kick in in just a bit."

It already was, the numbness welcome this time as it spread through his body. He leaned against her warmth and, for a long, luxuriant moment, let himself close his eyes. He heard and felt her sigh.

Then there was the sound of more boots on the ladderway rungs. He opened his eyes and straightened as best he could.

"Let's get you back against that wall," Rya said, and he didn't argue when she and one of his crewmen grabbed him under the armpits. "Careful of his leg," she added.

The wall was cold and not remotely as pleasant as leaning against his subbie, but it was definitely more advisable.

Goddamned drugs.

The woman—Holton, he remembered, tagging the round, dusky-skinned face, full lips, and short, dark braid with the name—knelt down next to Rya. "Sir, Captain Ellis said the Infiltrator and two Ratches are hanging well back but still shadowing us. They haven't made any aggressive moves since Captain Fregmar— that's the Taken freighter, sir—responded to our hail."

"Dalby's waiting for me to be delivered in a life pod," Philip said. "Though I'm guessing by now she knows that's not going to happen." He glanced around Rya, feeling somewhat as if he moved in slow motion. He thrust his chin to where his attackers lay. "Do they have comm units on them, something they've used to be in touch with Dalby?"

Rya, kneeling, started to rise. He tugged on her sleeve. "Holton, go find out." He wanted Rya here with him. He didn't want to think about why, other than it was the goddamned drugs.

Holton lunged away.

"When Dalby knows that's not going to happen," he told Rya, "she may change tactics again."

"What in hell were you doing on that ladderway in your condition, anyway?" Rya asked, brows drawn down.

His subbie was mad at him.

"Sir," he told her, wrestling with a grin that fought

to take over his mouth, "what in hell were you doing on that ladderway in your condition, *sir.*"

Her pursed mouth shifted to a smirk. "What in hell were you doing on that ladderway in your condition, *sir?*"

"Looking to tell you and Martoni that we had backup from a Takan armored freighter and that it appeared the immediate crisis was passing." Idiot that he was. He should have known better than to underestimate Dalby. Then he frowned, remembering his trek through the passenger area of the cabin. "Where were you, Lieutenant?"

Spots of color dotted her cheeks. "Lav. Sir," she added.

"What were these two doing with Martoni when you left?"

"I wasn't with him. He picked his pod captains, came down here. I didn't think it wise to have both of us belowdecks at once, so I stayed in the cabin to finish my security assessment of those on board. I found out that Holton and Tramer served with my father. They verified a few others, personally. Then I ducked into the lav and, when I came out, I heard some woman threatening to stun you or break your other leg. I grabbed Tramer, Holton went for her friends, and the rest you know."

"Hanging upside down and shooting?"

"When you work on stations, you learn all sorts of techniques for ladderways. Going ass first usually just gets you shot in the ass. Sir."

Holton was back, a round silver object about the size of a large button in the palm of her hand. "The woman had this, sir. And here's her and the other guy's IDs. Probably bogus."

Rya picked up the two thin ID cards that Philip

could immediately tell weren't Fleet but civilian. He took the round transmitter. Short-range burst link. That explained Dalby's shadowing. He pocketed it in his vest. If it beeped or burped, he wanted to know. "I need to get back on the bridge," he said.

Rya was shaking her head. "There's no way you're going up that ladder. You need to stay in sick bay."

"This shuttle doesn't have a sick bay."

She swept one hand at Martoni, who was just starting to twitch, and at the still unconscious forms of his attackers. "It does now."

"I can't—"

"You can and you will." She pinned him with a stern look that had Cory Bennton clearly behind it, in the way her brows slanted down and her eyes narrowed. "Holton, find out if Captain Ellis has a spare intraship pocket comm so the admiral can chatter at her. Update her, while you're at it. And see what that Infiltrator's up to."

"Just about to suggest that myself," Holton said, grinning. She punched Rya playfully on the arm. "She's good, this one, isn't she, sir?"

Philip grunted, Holton headed for the ladderway, and Rya pulled herself out of her kneeling position, then sat, folding her legs in front of her. She studied the ID cards. "Amalia Mirrow and Gilbert Rolf Samling. Issued out of Baris."

"Martoni's people?"

She frowned. "The guy was, I'm pretty sure. She was an unknown, seated up near the front."

"We need to hear everyone's story, when they wake. And I don't want them hearing one another's."

She caught on right away. "Getting shot doesn't mean Martoni wasn't part of it. They only stunned him."

"Agreed. Or they may have intended to send him and the others along with me."

"Commander Adney needs to know what's going on. Do you still have your archiver?"

Philip nodded, patting his vest pockets. He found it and pulled it out, Chaz's note coming with it, fluttering to the decking. Something odd played over his subbie's face when she handed the slip of paper to him, but it wasn't something he understood or could place. She looked . . . hurt.

Goddamned drugs.

"I'll let you work in peace," she said, shoving herself to her feet. She headed for Martoni before Philip could reply, before he could ask what was bothering her more than their getting ambushed and threatened or shot. Because he felt it was something more than that.

He grunted at his own ruminations, then slipped the archiver to his comm link and went through the requisite codes. "Adney, Guthrie again. We've got more problems. I don't know what you're figuring on as the minimum crew complement for that damned bucket Bralford bought us, but you'd better cut it in half. Right now I don't think we're going to have enough crew to even get us to Ferrin's."

Rya didn't want to believe Commander Martoni worked for the Farosians. Not because she liked—or disliked—the dark-haired man but because she knew Philip needed every live, trustworthy body he could find if they were going to create an Alliance Fleet. And trustworthy was starting to be a serious problem.

Sachi Holton and Willym Tramer she trusted. Mostly. They'd recognized her name when she introduced herself and provided the right answers to the right questions, so she felt sure that, yes, they'd served with her father. Holton's name she even remembered. But she'd verify everything as soon as they got to Seth.

She glanced down at Martoni's vitals on the medistat's screen. He was climbing back to consciousness with no permanent damage. She followed the med-tech as he screened the others, including Mirrow and Samling again. Out of the corner of her eye she kept watch on Philip. When she saw him disengage the archiver, she nudged the med-tech and sent him over to run a full scan on Philip.

Then Holton came down the ladderway. Rya caught up with her.

"Pocket comm," Holton said, palming the unit. "Captain Ellis offered to come down and see the admiral, but I thought it best if she stayed on the bridge with Tramer watching her back, until we're really sure who's who."

"We might not know until we hit Seth," Rya said grimly.

"Five more hours," Sachi said. "But at least this ship's got weapons if someone comes at us again."

Rya had heard Ellis mention the Gritter cannon. She knew immediately what it was—every first-year rook in ImpSec was trained to search and spot illegal weapons on board pirate vessels, and the easily disguised GRT-10 cannon was one of the most common. Instinctively, she swept the cargo bay with an appraising glance. Gritters were more often tucked in between enviro converters, but she'd seen one or two tucked nicely in a cargo bay's utility power station.

Not on this ship, though. Enviro, then.

"I'll give this to the admiral," Sachi said, and stepped away to hand the pocket comm to Philip.

Rya stayed by the ladderway, alternately damning

herself and calling herself an idiot. She now had a ridiculous, full-blown crush going on Admiral Philip Guthrie, and every time she thought she'd managed to get hold of her emotions and shake some sense into her head, he'd lean against her or look at her with those damned magnificent eyes, and her toes would curl and she was lost. Again.

This was just so very much not like Rya Taylor Bennton. She did not get crushes on guys—not since she was ten years old, anyway. Rya Taylor Bennton found hard-bodies who amused her and bedded them. Sex was fun, great exercise, super stress relief. Nothing more.

Then Philip had walked—well, limped—back into her life, amid guns blazing and punches flying. And in two, three short hours her life changed.

She'd just managed to get her head and heart back on straight when she heard Mirrow threaten him. And when she came down that ladderway to find him on the decking, all her hard work was for naught. Because she knew if he died, she'd be devastated beyond words. And if Mirrow had put him in that life pod and sent him to the Infiltrator, Rya would have grabbed another one for herself and tried to follow.

This was crazy. She was crazy. Guthrie was her father's friend. He was an admiral. He had a wife. Rya was just "Subbie" to him, one of his crew. He'd never be interested in her. But if he was . . . No. Rya wouldn't want to be the reason he cheated on his wife.

Liar. Oh, hell, yeah, she would. She never had before. It was something—for all her sexual liaisons with her hard-body boys—that she swore she'd never do: break up a marriage. But for Philip Guthrie . . .

She slanted a glance his way. He was watching her, something unreadable on his face, which was sweat-streaked and bruised. Tired. Determined. Her heart sped up, her breath hitched, her toes curled. And she knew if she didn't get up that ladderway *right now,* she was going to drop to her knees at his side, take that beautifully rugged face in her hands, and kiss him— and do whatever else he wanted in as many ways as he wanted—until they hit the docks at Seth. The rest of the crew and his mysterious wife be damned.

She pulled herself up the ladderway, not once looking back.

"Infiltrator's off my grids now," Rya heard Captain Ellis say, then saw her repeat it through the pocket link the shuttle's captain shared with the admiral. Rya had been standing near the galley behind the bridge, talking to Tramer and watching the passenger cabin, for about fifteen minutes, reminding herself all the while that *he* was the admiral. Admiral Guthrie. Not Guthrie. And definitely not Philip. Admiral, admiral, admiral.

So when her brain told her Ellis was sharing the good news with *the admiral,* she felt pleased on both counts. Dalby was going away, and Rya hadn't thought of the admiral as Philip.

"We'll lose Kirro's P-33 shortly," Tramer said, with a nod toward the bridge. "But it sounds like that freighter is heading to Seth. And we should pick up Seth's P-40 in about an hour."

"Why am I not ready to relax yet?" she drawled.

Tramer snorted. He was an average-looking guy, maybe four or five years older than she was. About her height, but thinner than she found attractive. Built kind of lanky. And his eyes were small, giving him a haughty look.

"You could put a squadron of P-40s out there and none of us would relax, not after today," he admitted. Then he grinned.

Okay, he had a somewhat nice grin. She'd watched him flirt earlier with a couple of the female crew. They seemed to find him worthy.

Of course, he hadn't stared at their chests the way his gaze kept dropping to hers.

He was talking about P-40s. She half-listened, trying to hear what Ellis was telling Phil—the admiral. Updates on their freighter escort and, yeah, the P-40 from Seth would be picking them up earlier than anticipated. They'd put a push on after the shuttle's first distress call.

"I worked relief shift for two weeks on a P-40 with Guthrie's wife," Tramer said.

Rya's brain froze. All the sounds in the shuttle shut down except for Tramer's voice. She thought he said . . .

"You worked with the admiral before?" she asked, trying not to stammer. She knew her question was false because Phil—the admiral hadn't recognized Tramer. But she had to get clarification. He couldn't have said he'd worked with—

"No, his wife. Captain Bergren. She ran the *Meritorious* in Calth, sometimes Baris. I think Guthrie said Sparkington, the engineer, will be chief engineer for us on the *Folly*."

"Captain Bergren is Guthrie's wife?" Rya tried very hard to keep her voice low and level. It took her a few moments, while Tramer was rattling on about someone named Sparkington, to place the name. Captain Chasidah Bergren. Court-martialed about a year ago, a big mess about a dozen or so crew members dying because she'd failed to follow orders.

But Rya remembered that, right before her father was killed, he mentioned in passing that the whole thing had been staged and Chasidah Bergren was set up by Tage. He'd never mentioned that Bergren was Philip Guthrie's wife, though. Or maybe he had but Rya hadn't been listening. Considering everything else that had been going on, that was very possible.

Guthrie and Bergren had just been names then, familiar but distant.

Now they were real.

"Captain Bergren never mentioned it, not to me," Tramer was saying, "but Sparks said something one day. I don't think a lot of people knew. They wanted their privacy. Considering their positions in Fleet, and Guthrie's family, that's understandable."

"Bergren." The name surfaced with another bit of information. "Didn't a Commander Bergren die recently?"

"Her brother, I think."

And Tage had something to do with that. Rya couldn't place the few mentions in the news vids, but she could suddenly remember Captain Chasidah Bergren's face. A very pretty woman, probably prettier than her official Fleet image, because those images were always so stilted. But very pretty. Gorgeous, silky auburn hair. Long. Even in her uniform she looked slender. And younger than Phil—the admiral.

She turned away from Tramer before the hurt and dismay on her own face betrayed her.

"She's a damned fine captain," Tramer said. "Never believed those charges against her, which turned out to be all pure slag. I'd serve on a ship with her again in a minute."

"Why isn't she with the Alliance?" Maybe the beautiful Captain Bergren supported Tage. Or the Farosians.

Then it wouldn't be cheating. And Rya could comfort Philip over the loss of his wife.

"She *is* with the Alliance. Maybe she's coming in with Sparks. That would make sense. They worked together for a long time."

Philip's wife was meeting him at the *Folly*. God, that *would* make sense. *And that would make Philip happy, so get over it, Rya. Get over him. It's a useless, stupid little crush. He's too old for you, anyway. And with that admiral-always-in-command mentality, he wouldn't be any fun. Right?*

Right. She straightened her shoulders, giving them a little roll to release tension.

Poof! You're gone, Philip. Out of my mind, out of my heart.

Tramer was smiling at her chest again.

"So, Willym," she said, "what do you usually carry? Stinger? Carver Ten?"

The Infiltrator was now officially off the scanners, and Ellis had just confirmed Seth's P-40 coming alongside. Philip leaned his head back against the bulkhead wall. Four more hours to survive. A lot could happen in four hours, but, God, please. No more. What was it Chaz liked to say? He was over quota on trouble this week.

He had two Farosian operatives sedated and locked in separate-life-pods-turned-holding-cells. He had Commander Martoni, angry and chagrined at not knowing that one of his own people was a Farosian Justice Warden—or lying convincingly that he didn't know. But Martoni and the others stunned in the attack had recovered sufficiently to return to the passenger cabin above.

So it was just Philip, his pocket link to Ellis, and the

two Farosians in this makeshift sick bay, except when Sachi Holton came down to bring him a blanket, then a pillow and a bottle of water, and, later, another larger bottle of water.

His subbie was conspicuously absent. He'd almost asked Holton to find her but held back. She'd rescued him twice since he'd set foot on Kirro. No doubt she was tired of babysitting a weakling, injured admiral. Plus, keeping Ellis alive and everyone else away from the bridge was far more important.

Still, every time he heard boots coming down the ladderway, he did two things: unholstered his Carver, and wished his visitor was Rya the Rebel.

He finished the bottle of water, pressure reminding him that what goes in must come out. Damn. He glanced around the cargo area and spotted the door for a crew lav to his right. At least there was no one around to witness him flail, hop, hobble, and limp to the lav.

He exited the lav and was halfway back to his blanket and pillow when boots again thumped against the rungs.

Fuck. He leaned awkwardly against the wall and pulled out his Carver. Then he recognized the boots, the thighs, that lovely curvy ass, and a very familiar scowl that told him his subbie was mad at him.

Again.

"What are you doing? Sir," she added, hands on hips.

He grinned as he holstered his gun. "Taking a piss, if you must know. In the lav," he added hurriedly, seeing her eyes widen. Hell, he was leaning against the wall. What did she think, he was writing his name?

Oh, those damned drugs.

He motioned to the crew lav behind him and almost fell over.

"Damn you, Guthrie!" she said, moving quickly, putting her shoulder against his and her arm around his waist, holding him up.

"Getting tired of the Old Man falling at your feet, Rebel?"

She lifted her chin just as he looked down at her, her brows lifting out of their frown, her eyes softening, widening slightly. Lips parting . . .

No, Guthrie. Bad idea. Very bad idea.

He could feel her breath feathering against his face, knew his own brushed hers. They were that close, which was far too close.

She's Cory's daughter.

"I'm fine now. Just turned too quickly." His voice was gruff. He looked away from her, staring at the blanket on the floor as if he could will his body there without her help. He needed to sit down and he needed, desperately, for the heat of her body against his to go away.

"Of course, sir." She pulled her arm away, just steadying him with her hand under his elbow.

Thank you, Rya, for stopping me from making a complete fool of myself.

He limped toward the blanket, then did his usual brace-and-slide down the wall, her hand on his arm guiding him down.

"Holton's fault," he said, because she was standing there far too quietly. "She kept bringing me these." He pointed to the empty water bottles.

"Can I get you anything else, sir?"

Got any spare sanity? "No, thanks. We're, what? Two hours out?"

"Hour and a half, sir."

He grunted. "Still time for someone to throw a few torpedoes at us."

"They want you alive, sir."

He looked up at her. She was damned near standing at parade rest. "You're doing good, Subbie. Those 'sirs' are rolling right off the tongue now."

He waited for a grin, a snort, something rebellious.

"Yes, sir."

Hell. "Sorry, Rya. Those painkillers you pumped into me have loosed my sarcastic side. Just ignore me. It's only another hour and a half."

"Yes, sir." But that "yes, sir" sounded nervous. So was the way she chewed on her lip. "Hour and a half. And then...well, I guess you'll be glad to see her, won't you?"

"Hell, yeah. I mean, she's only a Stryker-class, but after what we've been through—"

Emotions shifted across her face. "The *Folly*? No, I didn't mean the ship. I meant..." She halted, pursing her lips. "It's none of my business. Really."

"Rya." He pinned her with what Chaz used to call his steely-eyed captain's glare. Except he was an admiral now. "Would you please sit? I'm getting a crick in my neck *and* in my brain trying to understand what you're talking about."

For a few long seconds she didn't move, then she lowered herself to her knees and sat back stiffly on her heels.

"It's none of my business," she said again.

"What is?"

"Your wife. Sir."

"My?" He frowned. She was watching him closely. "My wife?"

"Captain Bergren."

"Chaz? What about Chaz?" For a moment, panic struck. Had something happened to Chaz and Sullivan?

"I thought she might be meeting you on the *Folly*," she said, her voice sounding unusually small and lost. "With Sparks. And you'd be glad to see your wife—"

"Chaz isn't my wife."

Rya was staring at him as if he was gibbering in some alien tongue.

"We're divorced. She's married to Sullivan. Who told you they're coming in with Sparks?"

"They're . . . I don't know. I thought . . ." Rya leaned to one side, collapsing down on her right hip. "You're not married?"

"No." He thought he'd already said that, several times. "Who told you Chaz and Sullivan are coming in to Seth?" That would be great news and would certainly solve his hidden-Farosian problems.

"No, no. God, Philip, I'm sorry." She ran one hand over her face. "I misunderstood something Tramer said. He pulled a relief shift on the *Meritorious* years ago." She stopped. "That was her ship?"

"The *Meritorious*? Yes. Tramer knew Chaz?" He still wasn't sure what was going on in this conversation.

"And Sparks, the engineer. Tramer told me he thought if Sparks was coming to Seth, your wife was too. Except that she's not your wife."

And that pronouncement, Philip noticed, seemed oddly to make Rya happy.

She'd also stopped calling him "sir."

"So Tramer just got his story wrong," she continued. "I'm sorry."

She didn't look sorry. She was smiling.

He didn't understand any of this. It must be the drugs.

The shuttle's lower deck was packed and noisy, the influx starting shortly after Rya had come below to pepper him with her strange line of questions and increasing the closer they got to the shipyards. Their arrival added the *Folly*'s officers to the mix.

Now Commander Dina Adney—a slender, dusky-skinned woman with short, tightly curled black hair—was calling orders to her people working with Seth stripers. They were locking sonicuffs on the wrists of the two Farosian agents, who were looking alternately glum and sullen or defiant and sullen. Sub-Lieutenant Sachi Holton was directing three crew acting as baggage handlers, dispersing the duffels to small anti-grav pallets for transport to the *Folly*. Commander Martoni, head bowed, was listening intently to something Captain Ellis was saying. Philip hadn't realized how short Ellis was until he saw her standing next to Martoni. Sitting in her captain's chair, grinning gleefully as she brought her GRT-10 cannon online, had made her seem taller.

Of course, the nearly eight-foot-tall Takan, Dargo,

standing behind her didn't help his perspective on her height. But he doubted Ellis was much over five foot.

Not like his strapping subbie, who was...there, yes, talking to Willym Tramer and Con Welford, standing at an angle to them both. She did that a lot, Philip noticed, gun hand free and clear.

Shouldering his duffel with its much-coveted Norlack, he leaned on the cane Burnaby Mather—one of Jodey's people—had brought him and limped toward Rya.

No, not Jodey's people. Burnaby Mather was one of his people now, just like Holton, Welford, Tramer, and more names he had yet to commit to his drug-hazed memory, including—unless his instincts were widely wrong—Martoni.

Rya, well...Every instinct Philip had told him to get her on the next shuttle back to Kirro or Calth 9. But he couldn't do that, because, in order to do so, he'd have to provide some logical instance where she'd failed in performance of her duties. He couldn't. The reasons he wanted her on the next shuttle out were purely personal.

And he was not about to put something like that in writing.

He was stuck with Sub-Lieutenant Rya Bennton, and there wasn't a damned thing he could do about it. So he might as well torture himself a bit longer and go stand next to her in the chilly cargo bay, so that her smile could warm him, so that the touch of her hand on his arm would heat him. And so that Con Welford and Will Tramer would stop staring at his subbie's chest.

Goddamned Fleeties. They were all animals. He should know.

"Let me take that, Admiral Guthrie, sir." A tall—

well, they were all tall—young Takan stepped up to him, pointing to Philip's duffel. *Corvang,* the tag on his gray coveralls read, but Philip could have guessed that anyway from the almost devoted, wide-eyed expression on the young male's face.

Another subbie.

"I have a number of valuable weapons in there, Lieutenant," Philip said. "This doesn't leave your sight until you put it in my quarters on the *Folly.*"

"It won't leave my *side.* Promise, sir. Admiral, sir."

Philip grabbed the duffel's wide strap and passed it to Corvang's eager hands. Honestly, other than Rya, Corvang was the only one he'd trust with his duffel. Rya because she shared his passion for the weapons. Corvang because, once a Takan took hold of something, it was damned near impossible to get it away.

"Thanks, Lieutenant. Good to have you here. Captain Bralford spoke very highly of you."

"Yes, sir. You have no idea, sir. The pleasure is all mine." Corvang's long face bobbed, sharp teeth bared in a typical Taken exuberant grin. "With your permission, sir." With one more nod, he loped away toward the airlock.

Things—people, baggage—were progressing in small, chaotically organized clumps out the shuttle's airlock and toward the *Folly,* berthed two levels down. Prospective crew and their baggage first, to be cleared by those crew already on board who'd been cleared by Adney. After that, Philip and his key people, which, yes, now meant Martoni, Holton, Tramer, and Rya.

Speaking of the latter, Con Welford was holding her hand. Philip put a little more force behind his limp and joined the group quickly, restraining himself from knocking Con on the knuckles with his cane.

She was *his subbie*, but she wasn't *his. Get your libido in line, mister.*

But Con wasn't for her either. He was, what, thirty-seven, thirty-eight? Okay, built solidly, with a face Philip knew woman found "ruggedly attractive." All Philip saw was a broken nose and scar on the man's chin, but that wasn't his area of expertise.

Con was almost ten years her senior.

And Philip had been ten years older than Chaz and was sixteen years older than Rya.

Stow it, Guthrie.

But he had his silent promise to Cory to look after her. He'd fail if she fell into Con's clutches.

"Admiral." Con acknowledged his presence with a grin and released Rya's hand.

Good. Won't have to make your knuckles bleed. "Welford," Philip said. "I hear helm's computers are a nightmare."

"She's Stryker class."

Well, yes. That said it all.

"But I have some ideas," Con continued.

"Report on my desk in the morning?"

"Already there."

Not surprising. He'd been as efficient on the *Loviti.*

"Ready to leave this bucket?" Philip asked Rya. He hadn't originally intended to have her accompany him. He was fully aware he needed a breather from her, until the drugs were out of his body and he was more in control. But he wasn't going to let Con Welford or Tramer escort his subbie to the *Folly,* and with the operation here on the shuttle winding down, the options for escorts were dwindling. At least if she went with him, he knew she'd be safe.

He caught that train of thought. Safe? Most people would need protection from *her.* She was ImpSec and had two laser weapons he knew of on her body. God only knew what else she had, and where. Though Philip would love to—

Down, boy.

"Ready," she said, her face and her beret decidedly jaunty.

"If we're lucky," he said as she fell into step with him, "no one will shoot at us between here and the *Folly.*"

They were lucky.

The adrenaline rush that had kept Rya almost supercharged and hyperfocused since Kirro suddenly flagged as she stood in her cabin. Part of it was relief, and part of it was exhaustion. But a lot of it was reality.

She'd won, yet she'd failed.

She'd won because she was on the *Folly,* her father's old ship, having been through two hours of processing, identity clearance, and the typical military datalogging.

She'd failed because her cabin was not next to Philip's, not even on his deck. She knew the *Stockwell's*—the *Folly's* layout intimately from hours of sitting at her father's desk, or in his lap, as he explained his ship's schematics to her. She was in Crew 3—crew's quarters, Deck 3 of the *Folly's* six decks. One deck below the captain's—now admiral's—quarters and private office, as well as the first officer's quarters, where the private executive mess and two auxiliary cabins were located, on Deck 2 Forward. Either one of those auxiliary cabins would have suited Sub-Lieutenant Rya Bennton just fine. Philip was injured. He needed protection. He needed her.

But she was in Crew 3, Cabin 8—a small bedroom with a two-cushion brown couch in the sitting area and a workstation with the ubiquitous deck-locked swivel chair. And a tall, narrow rectangular viewport, where she perched now—jacket still on because Crew Deck 3 was like a fucking ice cube—watching Seth's moon blot out the twinkling of lights peppering the big, wide darkness.

She sniffed.

Oranges. The scent came and went, stronger in some areas of the ship than in others. Though she'd not been through the entire ship yet.

"Cannot find them anywhere," Con Welford had told her as she followed him to her new quarters, her duffel slung over her shoulder. "Commander Adney and I searched the whole damned ship, day one. We can smell 'em. But we can't find 'em."

She closed her eyes for a moment, leaning her head against the viewport's frame. It had been one fucking hell of a day. She was bone-tired, should be stripping down to get some sleep.

She couldn't.

Philip wasn't married. He had been, but he wasn't, and his ex was happily married to someone else.

Rya knew it was ridiculous for her to even care about such things.

But she did.

Maybe come shipmorning she might not. Maybe this insane crush that had blossomed full bore on Kirro—somewhere between "My leg thanks you, but my ego is severely deflated" and "Subbie, on three, ready?"—was just a temporary aberration. It would settle down to good old-fashioned respect for a charismatic senior officer. Admiration for the man who was going to set things right, punish those who killed her father.

Right now, though, it didn't feel like it.

She pushed herself away from the viewport, the cabin's chill closing around her as she peeled off her jacket and headed for the lav. A hot shower and a few hours' sleep were what she needed to clear her head.

Her heart she'd deal with later.

Philip had no idea how long he'd been awake or when he'd last slept. First was two and a half hours with Adney while the prospective crew that came in on the Kirro shuttle were processed, accepted, or rejected, and while station stripers vied with Alliance Legal over custody and interrogation rights of the two Farosian agents. The attack had been made on an Alliance officer but on a civilian ship.

Then another hour and a half at the shipyard's sick bay—the very tall Corvang and the short and rotund Mather his escorts—while the doctors there swapped charts and his med-stats with Doc Galan on the *Nowicki* through a top-priority deep-space transmit link. There was a lot of frowning, head shaking, and grunting. Though he couldn't hear her, he could well imagine the usually mild-mannered Christine Galan swearing. He'd managed to undo most of her best work.

Then back to the *Folly*, where Adney met him with the news that they had a working and cleared crew complement of seventy-four, not including Sparks and his three subbies arriving soon. Tomorrow. Today. Whenever.

And he hadn't even yet officially read himself on board, taking legal command of the *Folly* via formal ceremony in front of Adney and the crew. There hadn't been time.

A Stryker-class heavy cruiser usually shipped out with a crew of one hundred forty. One twenty, maybe one fifteen if times were desperate.

Times were desperate. He had seventy-eight plus himself.

"I'm still waiting for some callbacks," Adney said, sitting in one of two low-backed black chairs across from his desk. Like most of the *Folly*'s officers and crew, she was in gray fatigues, pants tucked into dark boots secured by cross-straps. Her sleeves were rolled up and, as she spoke to him, she absently ran long fingers through her thick dark curls. "Another ten, maybe fifteen. As for the rest, well, there's always Ferrin's. It's a much larger station and, after what happened on Corsau, more people may rise to the call."

"Or run away." Tage might be a despot, but he was a known despot in a sector with jobs, security, and Philip sniffed—clean air. "You really can't find the oranges?"

Adney sighed. "It comes and goes. I think it's that we're sitting still. Once we get moving, systems working, air-recyc and all . . ." She shrugged.

"It could be worse," she added, biting back a grin, giving her face an almost impish quality that made her look younger than the forty-two years he knew she was. "They could have been hauling manure."

He couldn't stop himself. "No shit."

"Captain Bralford said you were bad."

Philip grunted.

"That too," Adney said.

He tapped his deskscreen. "Welford has the helm computers cooperating now."

"Mather still has problems with encryption on

outgoing priority communications, so I'd work through archivers until he tells us otherwise."

"Saw that too." He rubbed one hand over his face.

"Get some downtime, Admiral. We're not leaving until Sparks gets here, and that's not for," she turned her wrist, glancing at the square black metal watch, "eight, ten hours yet."

Philip frowned. "Did I lose a day?"

"One of his subbies freed up early." She shoved herself to her feet, her movement showing both grace and power. Not unlike his rebel. "With your permission, I'm ordering you to bed. Most of your recruits have tucked in. We'll all get a fresh start in a few hours and have your formal change-of-command once Sparks get here."

"Permission granted." He rose too, grabbing his cane. Adney slipped out into the corridor. Her cabin was on the other side. Philip hit the palm pad for the door leading to his quarters. His office shared a wall with his main salon, smaller than he'd had on the *Loviti* but not dissimilar in layout. On the left, a couch and matching padded chair. On the right, a dining table with four chairs framed by the large double viewport. At the eleven o'clock position, a short hallway, then the door to his bedroom and private lav.

"Lights," he said, entering the dark bedroom. The small viewport, of course, offered no illumination. Decklights and overheads flickered on, revealing his duffel where he'd had Corvang leave it on the edge of his bed. Still locked, secure.

But that wasn't what had Philip frowning, mouth opening slightly in surprise.

It was what else was in the middle of his bed.

He slapped intraship, knowing Adney couldn't be far. "Guthrie to Adney. My quarters, now!"

Seconds later his door chimed. He opened it remotely.

"Sir?"

"Here!"

"Sir?" she said again, stepping into his bedroom. "Is there a problem?"

"Damned straight there's a problem. What in hell's fat ass is a cat doing sleeping in my bed?"

The cat—and a damned ugly thing it was, lumpy and white, except for one black ear and a black tail—chose that moment to raise its large head, open one golden eye, yawn, and put its head back on its paws again.

"Apologies, sir. I had no idea. That's Folly, sir."

"Folly?" He took his gaze off the cat and stared at Dina Adney.

"Folly. Hope's Folly. The little girl, Hope. Her cat's name is Folly."

"But she's"—and he hesitated, aware the cat's eyes were now open—"dead," he said softly. Maybe the beast didn't know.

Guthrie. It's a damned cat. It doesn't care.

Adney looked troubled. "He's part of the deal Bralford made with Pavyer."

"He?"

"Folly."

"Folly's a he?" Folly was not a name for a male cat, especially not one that looked like that. Damned thing should have been called Bruiser. Or Hellspawn, with its wide face, thick legs, and body that looked like a bag stuffed with old socks.

"Actually, he's Captain Folly. Bralford didn't tell you about him?"

"He did not."

"I guess if you don't want him in here, you can put

him in the corridor. But this," and she hesitated just long enough for Philip to glimpse a nervous smile on her lips, "is the captain's cabin."

"Adney, don't. It's been a long, goddamned miserable day." But he snorted. "Maybe I should be reading my change-of-command orders to him."

That got a laugh out of Adney. She walked over to the bed and clapped her hands. "C'mon, Folly. The admiral doesn't want you in here. Let's go."

The cat turned its face away.

Adney looked at Philip.

"Let me guess," Philip said. "The last time you picked him up, he bit you."

"I dropped him before he could draw blood."

Philip eased himself down on the edge of the bed under the cat's watchful eye. He didn't dislike cats. He just had no desire to share his bed with one. He nudged the cat's ample belly with the head of his cane. "Move, cat."

Folly growled—a low, menacing sound.

"I can get gloves, a towel," Adney offered.

"You're telling me no one's been able to touch this cat since you came on board?"

Adney nodded. "That's about the size of it. And I'm really sorry, Admiral. I had no idea he slept in here. He shows up on the bridge. He has a dish in the main mess, where the ship's previous owner always fed him. When he's not around . . . well, it's not like Welford or Mather or I are much interested in looking for him."

No, he couldn't imagine why anyone would want to spend time with something that ugly and unpleasant.

Philip ran one hand through his hair. It felt gritty. Rolling around on the decking of Kirro Station and then the shuttle's cargo bay hadn't helped. "I need to

shower and sleep. If I make enough noise, he'll probably leave."

"Probably."

"I *will* pay you and Jodey back for not telling me."
He shot her a smirk to take the sting out of his words.
A reprimand from an admiral, even a limping one with
no working fleet, wasn't something someone as by-the-
book as Adney would take lightly. "But you will do me
a favor and, shipmorning, contact Pavyer and have
him come get his daughter's cat before we ship out to
Ferrin's."

She smiled back. "Will do, sir." She saluted him—or
maybe the cat—and left.

He pushed himself up, then opened his duffel. "I'm
taking a shower," he told the beast. "If you want to
make yourself useful, unpack this while I'm in the lav."

He swore the cat grunted at him in answer.

When Philip came out of the shower, towel around
his waist, his duffel wasn't unpacked. And the cat
hadn't moved.

"Not much help, are you?" Philip shoved his few
pieces of clothing in the closet drawers. He was too
tired to care what went where, other than his weapons.
His spare Carver-12, power pack, and an L7 went into
his nightstand. For now, the Norlack and the rest went
into a locked closet. He'd find or build something more
secure over the next few days.

He left his cane by the side of his bed. The room
was small enough that he could use the bulkhead to
keep his balance as he limped around the bed. He
threw back the covers. Sheets and blanket seemed
clean. He almost reconsidered sleeping as he usually
did—naked—as the beast had teeth and, he was sure,
claws. But Folly had edged down toward the bed's

lower corner by then. His toes might suffer, but they'd be shielded by the blanket and sheet.

He told the room monitor to wake him in five hours, told the room's light to shut off, with decklights on low. He pulled the covers up. The pillow was fine except for one thing.

Everything on this goddamned ship smelled like oranges.

Philip woke, as expected, five minutes before his cabin monitor announced the time and started increasing the bedroom illumination. Yellow eyes, inches from his face, stared at him, unblinking.

"Coffee would be nice," Philip said, his voice rough with sleep.

The cat leapt gracefully off the bed and disappeared.

Philip sat up. If the beast brought coffee, he'd rescind his order to Adney.

He grabbed his cane, rifled through the closet drawers for underwear and a pair of gray fatigue pants, and headed for the lav. When he came out, the cabin lights were at full brightness. Shirtless, he limped for the main salon. The cat was sitting on the galley counter. A sliding cabinet door was open and he could see three white mugs decorated with—God help him—images of fruit.

He looked at the cat.

The cat looked at him.

"I'm guessing you take cream," Philip said, reaching for a mug. Then he gave a self-derisive snort. The drugs had to be out of his system by now, but he was having a conversation with a cat. One-sided, admittedly, but a conversation.

The beverage dispenser, an original twenty-year-old

model, was set into the galley wall. He shoved the mug in the opening, selected black coffee, and only then wondered if the thing even worked.

The coffee came out, sputtering and splashing, but it was hot and more than decent. He sipped it gratefully as he found a shallow bowl in the cabinet, then cadged some creamlike substance from the unit.

The cat lapped it up quickly, then jumped down and bounded to the door to the corridor.

"You want out?" Philip hobbled toward him. "Ah, call of nature, is that it?" He realized he had no idea where the cat did his business. Maybe the fragrance of oranges wasn't a bad thing.

But the persistent citrus was gone this morning. He hit the palm pad, the cat snaking through before the door was fully open. Philip peered out the door, sniffing. Nothing. No oranges. No crew. Just the flick of a black tail around the edge of the open stairwell blast door at the end of the corridor.

Philip closed the door. Time to finish getting dressed and get to work.

A few minutes later, he took his second mug of coffee into the office adjoining his quarters, angled himself into the chair behind the desk—with a bit less pain today—and keyed his office door open. His office door was always open when he was on duty. No one ever had to wonder if they could come and talk to the Old Man.

He tapped on his deskscreen, realizing he had no idea if Adney or any of his officers were asleep or working. He brought up ship's shift schedule along with a barely adequate personnel locator, functional only through key deskscreens. Like the beverage dispenser, the systems were older. He felt as if he were in a time warp. The system response was slower, information less complete.

But his brain finally kicked out fifteen-year-old short-cuts and commands, and he was able to ascertain that Adney was on duty, though not where she was. He'd need Sparks and Mather to integrate some kind of personnel signal device to everyone's ship badge or comm link and then synch it to ship's systems.

His to-do list was growing by leaps and bounds. And he hadn't even officially taken command of the *Folly* yet.

He found Adney's personnel list, now sorted by assignments and divisions. A few names were slotted to engineering but noted as pending, waiting for Sparks's approval. Everyone else was confirmed. Including Sub-Lieutenant Rya Taylor Bennton.

He knew there were other service records he should review before hers, but he found himself bringing her folio on-screen anyway.

Her official holos failed to capture her sparkle. And though her overall record was excellent, he didn't miss the few notations from former COs about her *brassy attitude*.

Brassy, indeed. They'd never met Cap'n Cory. The man's under-his-breath running dialogues during boring SOP meetings were legendary.

Interestingly, some of her superiors found Rya's tendency to take initiative problematic. Others saw it as a sign of an intelligent officer able to make the right decisions under pressure. Well, he'd seen her under pressure. At the moment, he'd side with the latter commentators, but he'd keep an eye on her. Being impulsive could be dangerous, and serving on board the *Folly* was likely the most dangerous thing she'd yet to do.

Except, of course, surviving an ambush on Kirro and an attack on a shuttle.

He pulled up her personal data, expecting to find little that surprised him. After all, he'd known Cory for years. But he'd forgotten that Aliandra had died. Damn. That made Philip sit back for a moment. She'd lost two parents unexpectedly in under three years. And...he checked. No, she hadn't gone for counseling.

Well, there were no counselors on the *Folly*. Nor on the *Karn*, Sullivan's ship, and the memory of Chaz collapsing in his arms when she learned of her brother's death washed over him. Chaz was strong, one of the gutsiest women he knew. And she'd sobbed uncontrollably. But then, her life hadn't been easy, and part of that was his fault. Counselors equated divorce right up there with death. And he and Chaz had been through that, along with her father's rejection of her, her sham court-martial, and her imprisonment on Moabar. His ex-wife had been through hell, and much of that had been his fault.

But Chaz had Sullivan and, yeah, she had Philip as her close friend. Those wounds had healed. Rya had no one. He ran down her personal data again. Only child. Parents and grandparents deceased. No close connection with aunts or uncles.

Just Matthew Crowley.

Matthew Crowley?

Two-year personal exclusive relationship, her last chief had noted. Because of Rya's position with ImpSec, all her close associations were also cleared. Crowley was a barrister, a year older than Rya, well-educated, modestly successful. No past or outstanding wants, warrants, or unsavory associations.

Philip tabbed up an image of a smugly handsome man with shoulder-length blond hair.

Rya the Rebel had a lover. So, like Chaz, she'd had a

shoulder to cry on, someone to comfort her on the loss of her parents. Someone very likely Cory had met and approved of.

That should make Philip feel better. But it didn't.

"Admiral Guthrie, good morning."

Philip raised his gaze from the deskscreen and saw Dina Adney in his doorway. "Morning. We working shiptime or stationtime?"

"I thought it best to stay shiptime, but we're not far off from stationtime, so if there's something you need from the yardmaster, I can reach her easily." They were hardlined into Seth through their docking clamps. Ship-to-yard communications were one of the few things that worked.

Philip cleared Rya's file from his screen and leaned back in his chair with a sigh. "I have a long list, but we need to budget and prioritize. I also need this bucket out there and in working order before Tage makes another move." Working order was the big issue. Cutting corners was necessary. But cutting corners could cost lives.

"I've just reviewed your personnel division assignments," he continued. "Everything looks good, considering."

"Considering we're understaffed and more than a third of these people, while cleared, are unknowns?"

"Mind reader. Did Jodey train you or is it a natural talent?"

She smiled, but it was a tense smile. She hit the palm pad to close the door, then took the chair she'd sat in a few hours ago. "It's a song my mind has been singing for the past forty-eight hours."

"I'm familiar with the tune." He paused. "Have you screened any of our new recruits for dual assignments? A nav officer who also has paramedic training? A weapons tech who can also sit helm?" He thought of the way Sullivan worked his people on the *Karn.* "Command staff, especially. Right now, doing may be more important than commanding."

Adney was nodding. "I'll get Martoni running a filter on all the personnel files and pull out the best candidates. It will play hell with the usual shifts." She pulled her hand-held datapad from its sling on her belt and tapped at it.

"I'm thinking split shifts," Philip said. "Nav, weapons, engineering, and enviro being highest priority. Support services are lowest priority. Which means when we hit jump, everyone does their own laundry. Even me."

An edge of her mouth turned up. "I believe our commo, Mather, worked nights while in the academy as a bartender."

And filched popcorn and pretzels from behind the bar, judging from Mather's waistline. "I can cook."

Adney's dark eyes widened.

Dorsie, Sullivan's cook on his ship, hadn't believed him either, at first. "I'm not kidding. My parents loved to throw huge, lavish parties, and I spent my formative years with our chef in the kitchen. The biggest party I handled was one hundred twenty-five. Cooking for seventy, eighty people is not a problem."

"Admiral Guthrie, are you assigning yourself to the galley?"

Philip grinned. "You might never let me back on the bridge."

"We do have basic food dispensers."

"I can't ask my crew to work their asses off and then give them nothing but coffee and soup."

"Actually, that's what we've been living on since we came on board."

Philip tapped his screen, found the file he wanted. "We have enough budget for a bit more than basic foodstuffs. I'll do a walk-through of the galley later, though it's probably not changed from what I remember. Then I'll make a list and get it here, hopefully, by dinner."

Adney sat back. "I'm impressed."

"Save that until after you taste my cooking."

"Now if only you could wave a magic wand and turn laser banks into ion cannons."

"I'm hoping Ferrin's has that magic wand." And he hoped Tage or the Farosians didn't dead-eye the *Folly* before it got there. "What else is top priority this morning?"

Adney glanced at her datapad. "Should be coming to your in-box right about now."

He found it, though the ship's antiquated system still confounded him a bit. That was one of the overall problems along with ship's comm pack and lack of encryption—lack of a functional personnel-locator system. Data could be sent terminal to terminal, or hand-held to terminal, but there was no way to determine who was sitting at that terminal. Forward port laser banks were misbehaving during testing. Aft lift number two overshot Deck 4 several times, but that was more annoying than critical. Sublights and jump-drives were unknown and would have to wait for Sparks.

The only good news was that Corvang had all nav charts loaded—including the old trader data from Sullivan's ship—and responding to the nav comps' commands. And that they had one top-notch pair of tow-field generators.

Philip scrubbed one hand over his face. "So essentially we can't talk to anybody, shoot at anybody, find

anybody, or move crew between decks with any relia-
bility at this point. However, we won't get lost."

"And we smell nice," Adney said.

Philip sniffed again. "Not today."

"Told you. Comes and goes."

"Speaking of going. The cat?"

Adney shifted in her chair with a sigh.

Not good news. "We're stuck with him," Philip
guessed before she could answer.

"Captain Bralford did agree to it," Adney said. "But
more than that, Pavyer is still devastated over losing
his wife and child. I spoke to his cousin who runs the
export business with him. He's afraid if the guy sees
Folly, it'll throw him over the edge. Plus, the cousin
said the family has this belief that the cat is some kind
of good-luck charm for the ship. They want the cat
here when we start shooting at Imperials."

And people said Fleeties were a superstitious bunch.
"For now—"

Overheads flickered and died. Philip's office
plunged into darkness. His right hand went immediately to the Carver on his hip, his senses going on high
alert. Then the green emergency lights kicked on, and
in their dim glow and the pale light from his
deskscreen, he saw Adney rising, her hand also on the
gun on her hip.

"What now?" he asked, hitting the pad for intraship
on his desk. No double-chime sounded. "Intraship's
out too."

"Could be Welford doing something," Adney said,
heading for the door. "Or it could be one more damned
thing."

"Would be nice for Con to let me know before he
goes tinkering like that," Philip said tersely, rising,
reaching for his cane. "Main computer's down." The

screens were powered by the same backups that the emergency lights were.

Adney hit the palm pad. "Doors work."

"Bridge," Philip told her, moving now, every inch of him alert and unhappy. "We secure the bridge, then start asking questions."

The large room plunged into darkness, then slowly glowed green. The moment she could discern the outlines of the furniture around her, Rya lunged from her chair behind a workstation in the divisional offices' section of Deck 2 Aft, Stinger in hand.

"Get people to lock down the tubeway and cargo bay," she called to Martoni, now rising in the green gloom. "I'm on him." Pulse jumping, she sprinted toward the aft stairwell.

There was no reason to define "him." Even though a formal security detail for the admiral's protection had yet to be set, Rya had claimed Philip as her charge. Through a bit of well-timed evasive obfuscation, she'd let Martoni, now functioning as Adney's new assistant, believe that assignment was on Philip's orders.

So she'd made it her business to know where Philip was at all times—not the easiest thing on a ship without functioning security cameras, an ass-backward crew-locator system, and its main working deck—Deck 2—split in two different sections. She knew Adney had gone to the admiral's office on 2 Forward for a briefing and, based on what had just come in via Martoni's deskscreen, was likely still there.

She bolted down the metal stairs two at a time as Martoni yelled "Stations!" sending people scrambling. She hit the landing on Deck 3, then bounded up again for Deck 2 Forward.

She saw two forms in the green-tinged lighting of the corridor as she came through the open blast door on Deck 2 Forward. With relief she recognized Philip's shape and height, as well as the way he leaned on his cane. "Bennton. Security," she called out because he turned, the Carver's power lights glowing tiny dots of red and blue in his hand. "Are you all right, Admiral?"

"Going to secure the bridge, Subbie."

"With you on that, sir." She caught up to him and Adney. "Commander." She nodded, seeing the shape of a laser pistol in Adney's hand as well. "I have point, by your leave."

She didn't wait for Adney's or Philip's leave but stepped in front of them. She glanced repeatedly over her shoulder, watching, listening for anyone or anything from behind as they moved for the forward stairwell.

"Where were you?" Philip asked her.

"Deck Two Aft. We're dark there too. Martoni's securing the tubeway. Got people on all other access points."

She had her handbeam locked on top of her Stinger by the time they hit the stairwell blast doors. She zigzagged the wide beam through the darkness, in full ImpSec protection mode now. The officers behind her were her charges, all personal feelings gone, though her heart rate had sped up. She'd never worked ship security before, but how different could it be from a station?

"Clear." She took the short flight of stairs quickly,

then waited on the landing, listening as Philip and Adney followed.

She cracked Deck 1's blast door open and heard nothing to raise suspicion, so she pushed through, Stinger ready, holding the door ajar with her foot until Adney and Philip were behind her. In the green glow of the corridor, Rya saw that the wide doors to the bridge were open. She soft-footed quickly forward and halted at the opening. She swept the round space with her light. Screens glowed blankly, a muted silver. She heard a grunt, and for a moment all her senses prickled. Then she recognized Con Welford, rising from under a console on the left. An open tool case was on the decking next to him.

"You break my ship?" Philip's voice boomed over Rya's shoulder.

It would be too much, she thought wryly, for her to expect Philip Guthrie to wait until she'd announced the bridge clear and safe.

"Not my doing, sir. I swear." Welford lumbered to his feet.

"Then let's find out who's doing it was."

Rya played her handbeam into the recesses of the bridge and under consoles. Welford was the only one there, and he did not look happy.

"Can I have that?" Welford asked, pointing to her handbeam.

"No."

"Give the man the light, Subbie," Philip said. "He was on the *Loviti* with me. If he wanted to kill me, he's had years to do so."

"Yes, sir." She flicked it off and tossed the handbeam to Welford. He caught it easily, flicking it back on and playing it over the dark consoles. She stationed herself at the bridge's doors. "You want these locked, Admiral?"

"Leave them open for now. I want to hear anyone coming, and I sincerely doubt anything will get past you." Philip limped around the bridge, poking at screens as he went. One flickered on, databoxes sluggishly appearing. "Knew one of these was hardwired on backup," he said, as she watched the corridor again. "Couldn't remember which one."

Rya glanced at him.

"Let me at it," Welford said, swiveling the chair around in front of the sole working screen, then sitting. He leaned forward, concentrating, poking. "Okay, okay." A moment later, "Oh. Uh-huh."

Noise in the aft stairwell made her look down the corridor, then a quick glance behind. "Admiral, Commander, please stay out of the direct line."

She turned back to the corridor, Stinger raised, knowing Adney would comply, knowing as well that Philip would grumble something under his breath, which he did.

"Holton, Mather, and Tramer." Sachi Holton's voice rang out as the blast door clanged.

"Bennton," Rya replied, damning the fact they'd yet to set up security codes or phrases. "Proceed." She didn't lower her weapon.

Three forms emerged. Holton, Mather—about the same height—and, trailing behind and taller, Tramer. No one else, no more noise in the stairwell.

"Tubeway, cargo access secured," Lieutenant Burnaby Mather said, plodding toward her. The short man was about Philip's age, she guessed, his broad form and thick arms hinting at a muscular past. "Lifts are working, enviro's on except for engineering and sick bay. All personnel cleared out of there."

Rya didn't lower her Stinger. "Hands."

"Bennton, it's us," Mather said, a clear note of exasperation.

"Hands," Rya repeated. Martoni had trusted his people too.

Sachi extended her hands, empty. After a sigh, so did Mather.

"Tramer, show me your hands."

"For God's sake, Rya—"

"Hands." Philip's voice sounded behind her, somewhere in the middle of the bridge, she guessed.

Damn it, Guthrie, get out of the line of fire.

"Yes, sir. Sorry, sir." Tramer's empty hands came out. "We're just trying to help."

"We don't know what's going on," Philip said. "Until we do, anything other than immediate cooperation is viewed as a problem."

"Welford there?" Mather asked.

"Three up," Welford said.

"Two down, one up," Mather answered.

"Commo and his friends are fine, Admiral Guthrie," Welford said.

"*Nowicki* codes?" Philip asked, but Rya already knew, even before she heard Welford's affirmative. They had to set up ship's codes today. Now. But, damn, clearances on the crew were still marginal, as far as she was concerned. Her ImpSec chief would be spitting fire over who was on board and walking around unchecked.

"We need to do those," Rya told him.

"We do," Mather agreed. He patted her shoulder as he walked by. "Good job, Bennton. Sorry we gave you a start."

Tramer said nothing, frowning. Sachi grinned at her. "You can be one scary woman, you know that?"

"My job, Sach." Rya braced herself against the doorjamb again and shot Sachi a quick grin. She liked

Sachi Holton. But she trusted no one completely, except Philip. And she didn't holster her Stinger.

"Hey, Tin Man," Mather said, "let me and Tramer take a look at what you've got."

"Only one working deskscreen is what we got, Commo. Need to reconfigure backup, but for now . . ." Welford's voice trailed off. Mather grunted. Tramer cleared his throat. Then there were more "ohs" and "okays" and "uh-huhs" floating in the dim lighting.

"Can you get me intraship yet?" Philip asked. He leaned on the captain's chair and swiveled up the console screen.

"Not yet, sir," Mather answered.

"Holton and I will go below, check on Martoni." Adney pulled her laser pistol out and motioned to Sachi, who'd taken position across from Rya in the bridge doorway.

"Wait," Mather said, straightening. "I think . . . Yes. It looks like we might have juice to the auxiliary bridge on Five. If I can't get it working, I'll be back up." He edged past Rya with a nod. "You're two up, two down," he told her, under his breath.

"Two up, two down," she repeated quietly.

He hurried after Adney and Sachi.

Two up, two down. Mather was two down, one up. Welford, three up. She'd grant Mather and Welford her trust because Philip did. For now, it would have to do.

Tramer and Welford were talking—well, swearing— softly, hunched over the console. Movement behind her told her Philip had walked over to them.

"Sabotage?" she heard him ask.

"Yeah, the ship hates us," Welford answered with a snort.

"I can deal with that. But you damned well better be sure that's all it is."

"I'm not ready yet to rule anything out," Welford answered.

"What about this?" Tramer asked.

Rya didn't know what "this" was. She watched the corridor, with only occasional brief glances over her shoulder to make sure that, yes, Welford and Tramer were continuing to be trustworthy.

But even her brief glances wouldn't show her what was on the screen on the other side of the bridge.

"Yeah, okay." Welford. More grunts. A few "mm-hmms."

She listened to the men's voices but, more than that, she listened to the ship. At the moment, docked at the yard, it wasn't that different from another part of a station. It clanged and pinged. Things echoed. Enviro whooshed, but it was softer than she remembered. Temperature was warmer too. It might be that Deck 3 was perversely frigid, as she remembered her father saying. Or it might be that enviro, too, was on backup and not at full power.

A shipweek from now she'd know more, and every little ping wouldn't have her mind seeking its source. But right now, every ping mattered. Philip was on the bridge.

Then, between pings, whooshes, and terse male epithets, came uneven footsteps. Philip, coming her way.

Her heart, dreamer that it was, sped up slightly.

"Subbie." His deep voice was soft and just off her left ear. Then she could feel the heat of his body behind her. Every inch of her felt doubly alive.

You're certifiably insane, Rya. Matt would be laughing his ass off at you right now, just about melting at this man's feet.

She forced herself not to look at him.

"It's probably just mechanical error," he said.

"And a Stinger is just a monochromatic beam of

coherent amplified light," she said, her voice as low as his. "Still hurts like a bitch when it puts a hole in you."

That earned her the snort she'd hoped for. She feared that once he assumed the responsibilities of his position and this ship, the easy—though, granted, brief—camaraderie they'd shared on Kirro and then on the shuttle would disappear. She needed to know she could still make him laugh.

"If this was a deliberate action, wouldn't it just be easier to blow up the ship?"

"Not if they want you alive."

He grunted an acknowledgment. Then: "They'd still have to get through shipyard security, which is a lot nastier than Kirro's, then get on board. Then find me. Do they think at that point I wouldn't know they were coming?"

"Amateurs wouldn't, but they're not amateurs. Not the Farosians, and not the Imperials. You fuc—pardon." *God, Rya, watch that mouth!* "You messed up their timetable. You weren't supposed to be on Kirro. Then you left earlier than scheduled. They were slapping things together there in a desperate attempt not to let an opportunity to get you slip by.

"But this ship," and she chanced quick glance at him. His eyes were narrowed in concentration. "I'm sure they know when Commander Adney came in. That's the shuttle you were supposed to be on. Now they need you responding to their timetable. I'm also sure they know how far along this ship is in refit. This," and she jerked her head to where Welford and Tramer were working, "*if* it's from an outside source, is to delay you. Yeah, I'm worried that someone could take advantage of it and storm the ship. I'll be more worried if suddenly everything works perfectly. It would almost be like they're saying, 'We're ready for you now. Come to Mama.' "

She waited for his counterargument. When none came, she turned her face slightly.

"Holton's right," he said quietly. "You are scary."

She wasn't quite sure how to view his comment, and in the dim green lighting, she couldn't read his face, his eyes. "Just doing my job, sir."

"Hey." He shook his head slightly, his expression softening. His mouth quirked slightly. "You—"

Noise in the stairwell halted his comment. Lots of noise. She straightened, motioning for Philip to move back against the console behind her.

Not surprisingly, he waved his Carver in response, its power lights glinting. "Stow it, Subbie."

Then the blast doors opened and in the dim light she saw Mather, Adney, and four other people she didn't know, all in military fatigues, pants tucked into strapped boots.

"Bennton, security," she called out.

"Mather, two down, one up."

"Two up, two down," she answered, lowering her Stinger. Then Philip brushed by her, holstering his gun.

"Sparks!"

A balding older man stepped in front of Mather, grinning, hand out.

Sparks. Commander Drew Sparkington, Philip's ex-wife's former engineer. And new chief engineer of the *Folly*.

"You arrange this disaster just for me, Skipper?" Sparks grabbed Philip's hand and shook it vigorously.

Late fifties, maybe even early sixties, Rya judged, even in the lighting. Five-seven or so, one-seventy, some of which was in an ample belly that strained the front of his gray fatigue shirt. Sparks had a round face, pug nose, and bushy eyebrows.

"Have to make you earn your keep somehow," Philip was saying.

"And what's this?" Sparks pointed to Philip's cane. They headed for the bridge doors. "Fall off your barstool again?"

Rya stepped back to let them pass.

Philip stopped, touching Sparks's arm. "Commander Sparkington, Sub-Lieutenant Rya Bennton."

"Subbie," Sparks said, nodding, his gaze politely holding hers for a moment. Then he stopped, his expression shifting. "Rya *Bennton*?" He glanced up at Philip.

A short nod.

Sparks looked back at her, laying one hand lightly on her arm. "Cory's little girl?"

"Yes, sir."

"God and stars above." He patted her arm. "My heartfelt condolences, child. I have some stories you might like to hear, when there's time."

She didn't know Sparks had known her father, but that didn't surprise her. "I'd like that, sir." She meant that. There was something very solid, very real about the short, balding man.

Then they were moving by her, along with Mather and a woman and two men who were obviously part of Sparks's team. She logged her overall impressions as they hurried past: the woman and the shorter man were dusky like Sachi and Adney. The woman was almost as tall as Rya, long-legged, curly red-gold chin-length hair tucked behind her ears. Her position blocked Rya's view of the shorter man, but he looked to be about five-eight or -nine, maybe one-thirty.

The last newcomer lagged a bit behind. He was taller than the two in front, his complexion pale. He had a strong nose and dark hair pulled back in a tail that reached just below his shoulders. Wide shoulders, narrow waist. Nice ass in black fatigues that fit very well. Great thighs.

Down, girl.

Just because she had a galactic-size crush on Philip didn't mean she was blind.

She watched the corridor again and listened to the chatter of voices behind her. Sparks's drawl, Philip's deep tones, Welford's "yeah, uh-huhs." The woman's voice was nasal, her questions soft.

Mather swore a few times, then headed for the corridor, his shoulders hunched as he brushed by her without comment.

The "yeah, uh-huhs" started up again.

"Auxiliary bridge on five?" Sparks asked.

"Lieutenant Mather's heading down there now," Philip said.

"Children, that's where we need to be." Sparks again. "Kagdan, Vange "

"I can do more up here," a man's voice said.

Rya shot a glance over her shoulder to see who the voice—an interesting low growl, with an accent she couldn't quite place—belonged to. Ah, Mr. Nice Ass.

"Welford," Sparks said, "Dillon knows his stuff. But more than that, he knows how I work."

"I'm fine with that, Commander," Welford said with a nod.

So Mr. Nice Ass was Dillon. Vange and Kagdan were the other man and woman.

Sparks hustled Vange and Kagdan back to the corridor, offering a small fingers-to-temple salute to Rya.

She returned it, made sure they were safely clambering down the stairs, then turned to find Dillon watching her. No, he had to be watching Sparks leave. There was no reason he'd be watching her.

Part of her job had always been to watch the watchers. She held his gaze disinterestedly for a moment, then glanced around the bridge before turning to the corridor. Always meet someone's glance, but always take control.

In the next twenty minutes, Martoni came up bearing two hand-held datapads, which he gave to Welford. He left, crossing with Commander Adney in the corridor. Adney spoke with Philip in hushed tones, ushering him into the ready room through the single door on the bridge. The ready room's double doors to the corridor were closed. Ten minutes later, Adney strode back on the bridge.

"Yes, sir. Will do," she called over her shoulder, then nodded to Rya as she moved into the corridor.

Philip ambled out, glancing only briefly at the cluster of men at the console before stopping in front of her. "Mechanical failure, plain and simple," he said. "Sparks pinned it down. I'm no engineer, but in layman's language, previous repairs used ittle-doos. And they didn't do."

It took her a moment, and then she smiled. Ittle-doos. *It'll do,* as in it'll be just enough to fix whatever the problem is, for now. She hadn't heard that expression in a while. *Don't tell me it'll do,* her father used to warn. *Do it right. Ittle-doos eventually fail.*

"We should be up and running," Philip said, "in about—"

Lights flickered overhead, startling Rya. She blinked at the unexpected brightness.

"—now."

Bridge stations pinged and hummed to life. Tramer applauded.

"Thank you, Commander Sparks!" Welford said heartily, even though Sparks couldn't hear him. He pushed himself out of his chair and moved to the next station, tapping and poking. "Okay, that's much better. Tramer. Dillon. I need resets."

Both men moved to other consoles.

"Crisis averted," Philip said, half under his breath, a wry grin on his face.

"Better here at dock than out there."

"Out there will have troubles of its own." His smile faded slightly, concern written in his eyes, in the slight droop of his shoulders. Was he worried about what waited for them, or was he going to try, again, to convince her she didn't belong on board?

"Every shift on Calth Nine, when I strapped on my gun, put on my beret and my badge, every shift held that same promise, that same threat," she told him, meeting his gaze levelly.

Concern on his face changed to . . . She didn't know. Only that emotions shifted, then disappeared, his demeanor suddenly blank but professional. He turned away from her just as Welford called out her name.

"Bennton, if you don't have to kill anyone in the next five minutes, you think you can give me a hand?"

"What do you need, Con?" Philip answered instead, heading for Welford at the far console.

"Not you crawling underneath things, Admiral. No offense." Welford held out the datapad Adney had given him. "You know how to greenpoint this to a deskscreen?" he asked Rya.

"Of course." Greenpoint transceiver protocol was used by every division in Fleet. She stepped around Philip and took the datapad from Welford.

"Ready room." Welford pointed behind her. "Keep in mind these deskscreens are old. You're going to have to hard reset the base unit first. That's under the table in the center. Three buttons. Hard reset is the top one. Hold it in and holler when you're doing so."

"No access codes?" The ease with which the units could be reset surprised her. That was very lax security.

"These are *old*, Bennton. They're from twenty years ago. Or more. Ancient times."

Philip grunted something.

Welford chuckled. "People age better than equipment. Anyway, once you do that," he said, angling around as he tapped an icon on the deskscreen behind him, "you're going to have to find the hand-held's ID of four-six-one and manually tell it to link. Got that?"

"Got it, Lieutenant."

"Good, because there's no other way right now to get those units synched in. Dillon, you there yet?"

"Still working," Mr. Nice Ass answered.

"I'm on," Tramer called out.

"Go," Welford said. "By the time you get the reset done, Dillon should have his units on. But if you need help, ask."

"Will do, sir." Rya hefted the datapad and headed for the ready room.

"Twenty years ago," she heard Philip say, "is not ancient times."

She put the datapad on the ready-room table, unlocked the chairs on her left and right, and slid them out of the way. She hunkered down, peering under the table. She'd have to crawl underneath to get at the base—there was definitely no way Philip was going to do that. But it would really help if—

She angled up. "Lieutenant Welford, may I have my handbeam, please?"

"Sorry," he called back to her. "Should have thought of that. Don't shoot me, okay?"

Philip grabbed it from Welford's hand. "I'm useless

around here otherwise," he grumbled, but she could see a grin quirking across his mouth again. He limped into the ready room, coming around the table to sit— still carefully, she noted—in one of the chairs she'd pushed aside. He held out the handbeam.

"Kind of you, sir."

"I come from a good family, Subbie. My mother taught me to be useful."

No wonder her father and Philip had gotten along well, Rya thought, slipping under the table. He had a comeback for everything.

"Anything interesting under there?" his voice asked, as she played the beam around the base of the table. "Like oranges?"

"You smelled that yesterday too?"

"And last night. Adney says it comes and goes."

She rolled on her side, finding the series of buttons. "No oranges. Some dust. A broken lightpen. Okay." She raised her voice. "Welford, got the buttons. Holding in the reset now!" She pushed.

"Got the reset button," she heard Philip call out. She grinned. He really was trying to be useful. It had to grate on him, being injured and unable to help. He hadn't struck her as a man who was afraid to get his hands dirty. Or his knuckles skinned. She remembered that was her first impression of him.

"Few more seconds," she heard Welford say. "Okay. Release."

She released.

"Get those greenpoints going, Bennton!"

She wriggled out from under the table, ass first. God. Nothing like showing Philip her worst feature. She angled sideways, dropping down on her left hip, bringing her feet under her.

Philip leaned toward her, hand out. "Need help?"

Oh, please don't. Grasping her hand would mean nothing to him. But it would get her galactic-size crush going universal, just like when he'd leaned on her on the shuttle. She did not want to feel his warm, rough skin against her own right now.

She passed him the handbeam instead, pulled herself onto her knees, then grabbed the table's edge and levered up.

Philip was eyeing her. "More than a little dust."

She looked down, saw the long smudges on her thigh. She brushed at that, then brushed at another smudge on her arm. "Oh, hell." She sat, pulling the datapad to her, and tapped the recessed release for the deskscreen. It slid up . . . slowly. Too slowly. Something else likely clogged with dust.

Philip sighed as if he knew her thoughts.

She brought up the sniffer program, waited a few seconds, then a few more while it searched and logged compatible units. Numbers appeared, finally. She saw the hand-held's ID, linked them. "Got one," she called out.

"Got it," Welford answered. "Next!"

Philip—being useful—had the screen already up in front of him. She leaned over him, tapping the icon on the screen.

The ship shuddered, hard. She stumbled, adrenaline spiking as she braced herself against the table. Philip's hands grabbed her waist, his cane thudding to the decking. Then the room plunged into darkness. Again. And she heard the *screech-thud, screech-thud* of the blast doors slamming shut as the emergency lights trickled on.

"What the hell?" She straightened, drawing her Stinger, aware of Philip's hand on the small of her back. Aware of everything else too, her senses all but prickling. Two power failures?

"Don't know, but I don't like it." He flicked on the

handbeam, playing it quickly across the bulkheads, left and right.

"Stay there," she told him, moving behind his chair. But he ignored her command and rose, moving with her. Admirals didn't have to follow orders, evidently.

"This one first," he said, aiming the beam at the double doors to the corridor.

The palm-pad lights were out. She hit the pad with her left hand anyway, expecting no response and getting none. And not seeing any manual override. But there had to be one.

She sprinted to the single door to the bridge, the small circle of light pacing her. Those, too, were locked.

She faced Philip in the dimness. "Where are the manual releases?"

He came up next to her, holding the beam of light on the panel, frowning. "I honestly have no idea. These aren't the original door pads. Hopefully Welford or Sparks—"

"Admiral?" Welford's muffled voice came through the door.

Philip leaned against the door. "You break my ship again, Constantine?"

"It's not my doing, sir. I swear!"

"Can you reach Sparks or Adney?"

"We're locked in. Everything's out again. Datapads too."

Rya knew that. It was one of the first things she looked at after Philip grabbed her. "Whatever went *thump* triggered the blast doors," Rya guessed out loud.

Philip said something bitter under his breath in frustration. "Get back to that one console that's hardwired in. If you need us to do something with the units in here, tell us. And get Tramer or Dillon working on the corridor doors. I do not like being held hostage on my own ship, *by* my own ship."

"Yes, sir," Welford said, his voice fading, but not before Rya heard, "Goddamned Stryker-class bucket."

"Let's pray that's all this is," Philip said, his voice hard. He turned the handbeam around, held it toward her. "See what you can find in here that will help us take these palm pads apart."

She found several things, including the broken light-pen, which Philip used to pry the faceplates off the palm pads. But no manual door overrides lurked beneath. And their fingers could find no release mechanisms on the doors or doorjambs or decking.

Small thumps and grunts from the bridge told her Tramer and Dillon weren't having any better luck.

"Serious design flaw," Philip grumbled.

Rya folded herself down on the decking, her back against the door to the bridge. "This is incredibly annoying." She didn't do useless or helpless any better than Philip did.

He slid down next to her with a grunt, which, seconds later, was followed by a self-derisive snort. "You know, if I was ten years younger and this mission wasn't so damned critical..."

She glanced at him as his voice trailed off. His face was inches from hers, and she was seconds from blurting out that ten years didn't matter one bit to her. But she knew she might be reading what she wanted into his words. And his face.

And it would be just her luck that if she gave in to what her body was screaming for her to do—kiss him, right here, right now—the damned blast doors would open, sending them both flat on their backs and embarrassingly so in front of Welford, Tramer, and Mr. Nice Ass.

Get over it, Rya.

But he's not married.

He's an admiral. Your commanding officer. Want to be accused of sleeping your way to the top?

No, she didn't. But God damn if it might not be well worth the risk.

He was still watching her. Her arm ached from fighting the desire to reach up and touch his face. But that would give everything away and, if she was misreading him, would also give him just cause for booting her back to Calth 9. *Unwanted and inappropriate sexual advances,* or however the regulation read. Usually she could quote them word for word. But not now.

Because something else slithered into her mind. Something she'd heard before and would hear again: *Of all the women a man like Philip Guthrie could get, why in hell would he want you?*

Why in hell, indeed? She couldn't think of one reason.

But Matt had wanted her, and before him there'd been Jason. In the past seven years, she'd not had trouble finding men for JFFS, as her friends put it. Just For Fun Sex. It was what a lot of her friends her age did, especially when careers were beginning to build and transfers could happen at any moment. Your JFFS buddy kept you from being lonely, gave you something to focus on other than the day's aggravations. You made each other feel good.

Then you moved on.

But Philip Guthrie wasn't like Matt or Jason.

She turned her face away with a restrained sigh.

Then a not so restrained one. Then a real deep breath.

"They're back," she said, darting a glance his way.

He nodded. "I know. Goddamned oranges." He angled himself up. "Let's try that other door again."

It took fifteen minutes for the lights to come back on this time and for the blast doors to unlock. Fifteen minutes during which Philip Guthrie questioned his sanity, his morals, and his definitely skewed sense of priority, all the while trying to get the damned ready-room doors open.

He was worried about his ship and his crew. Images of people trapped in cabins and bays with no one knowing where they were—because there was no goddamned functional crew locator and no working central ship comm-link system yet—kept playing in his mind.

Whenever every inch of him wasn't aware of the presence of Rya Bennton.

He was certifiably insane. He was sure of it. These past few months, the physical damage his body had taken, the stresses of losing one command and gaining another, the deaths of friends and crew—it had all taken a toll. That was the only explanation he could come up with as to why he was so emotionally vulnerable to—and fixated on—Cory Bennton's twenty-nine-year-old daughter.

This had to stop. But when the lights had failed again and he'd almost found her in his lap, and then when all means to escape the ready room were exhausted and she was again those few tantalizing inches away from him, and he had the damned stupidity to make the flippant comment that if he'd been ten years younger . . .

Hell's fat ass. He was certifiably insane.

She was twenty-nine. She was Cory's daughter. She had some young buck named Matt hot for her back on Calth 9. She was not for Philip Guthrie, divorced, jaded, and limping around like some ancient—yeah, Welford had deemed him so—relic.

Plus, he had a ship to refit and a war to get under way.

But when he was around Rya . . . he just wanted to keep being around Rya.

This was not good.

So he'd sent her to check the perimeters and recesses of the blast door to the corridor once more for hidden release mechanisms, because he knew if he sat that close to her any longer he was going to do something stupid.

Like ask her if she ever dated older men.

Then the lights flickered on, the palm pads activated, and Rya let out a surprised whoop.

He was on the floor at that point, trying to pry up a section of the decking. He struggled to his feet, glad she was focused on getting the door open and a chair shoved in that same opening in case things went out again and not watching him do his best flailing-invalid imitation.

Definitely the way to catch the eye of a woman sixteen years your junior.

When she turned, he was standing, sweating, and

swearing because the blast doors to the bridge had also opened. "Welford, get me status! I need to know what in hell's going on here."

Deskscreens lit up, consoles flashed. The datapad on the ready-room desk pinged. Rya reached it before he did. "Commander Adney's on her way up."

Adney arrived, then Sparks, then this team and that organized by Adney and Sparks. Philip sat at the head of the ready-room table, deskscreen up and active, datapad blinking and downloading, headache starting to kick in as his officers came and went with data, reports, small successes, and more problems.

All because of mechanical failure. Basic, unimaginative mechanical failure on a ship past its prime, cobbled together with low-cost ittle-doos that—for reasons known only to God and the Fates—all decided to reach critical mass today. Just for him.

Time to start fighting back.

"I want the locks disengaged on the bridge and ready-room corridor doors," he told Sparks. "Also my quarters and my office corridor door."

Sparks puffed his cheeks out in exasperation. "I don't recommend that, Skipper. Ready room, okay. The bridge, well, it's defensible. But your quarters, especially when you're off duty, sleeping—"

"Disengaged, Sparks."

"I agree with Commander Sparks." Rya appeared in the open ready-room doorway on his right. He shot her a narrow-eyed glance, because she'd left the bridge an hour ago with Sachi Holton, and Philip had just calmed his brain and body down where she was concerned.

She shot him a similar glance back. "I'm not one hundred percent sure this isn't sabotage utilizing already known mechanical flaws. You know there hasn't been sufficient time to do a thorough assessment."

"Sir," he prompted her.

"Sir," she said, but he could tell by the way her hazel eyes flashed at him she hated his decision.

Sparks coughed.

Philip realized he and Rya were staring at each other. Or, rather, he was trapped by the intensity of her gaze, which held a distinct similarity to the way she'd looked at him just before she'd launched a forkful of peas at him from across her parents' dining table twenty years ago.

"Disengage those locks," he said, looking abruptly away from her and back at Sparks, perched on the edge of the table. "Discussion on this subject is now officially closed."

"I'll get to it within the hour," Sparks said.

Rya ducked back into the corridor. Sparks followed her.

Adney strode in.

"I know you wanted to head out for Ferrin's in two, three shipdays," she said. "I'm just not confident, even with Sparks working on everything now, that we can do that."

She handed him her datapad, and he spent the next ten minutes reading the various reports in grim silence while Adney went to the bridge and came back again. He could have blamed Jodey. He could have blamed Pavyer, the fruit exporter. But the reality was that a good portion of the ship had been inoperative for years because it had functioned strictly for cargo, even when the Farosians had it. Now it was full of live bodies, and those live bodies—living, breathing, eating, showering, and flushing—put stress on long-unused systems.

Or else—and Rya's warnings echoed in his head—

the two systems failures were designed to look that way.

"I need to know how close we can get," he told Adney, synching her datapad to his deskscreen and downloading yet more reports. "Tell Sparks to concentrate on what needs to be done in dock. If there are less-critical repairs we can make under way, push those back." He wanted to move on his timetable, not dance like a puppet for the Imperials or the Farosians.

He handed her the datapad, his mind still processing the data as Adney turned toward the bridge.

"Commander," he said, calling her back from the double doorway. "One more thing." He motioned her over. He lowered his voice. "For security reasons, Sparks, you, and I are the only ones who will know our exact departure time until thirty minutes before departure."

"Mather . . . ?"

"I know you worked with him, and I know you trust him, but I'm not willing to discount anything at this point. The three of us, Dina. That's it. If anyone else asks, tell them we're still working on it. Half hour's notice is all I'm going to give anyone. Fifteen minutes would be preferable."

"You think Samling and Mirrow weren't the only moles." It wasn't a question.

"I don't discount anything," he repeated.

He could tell by the stiff set of her shoulders that Dina Adney wasn't happy as she headed back to the bridge, again. But happy no longer was an option. Doing everything he could to guarantee the safety of everyone on board was.

Even the moles.

In spite of Rya's assertion that neither the Imperials nor the Farosians were amateurs, there was always a chance that individual agents might panic, or at least try something stupid if things went awry. He needed to force them out into the open, now.

The *Folly*'s shakedown cruise was going to be a shakedown in more ways than one.

He grabbed Con Welford about an hour later and walked each deck on an unofficial inspection tour of the ship, limping a bit less noticeably, he hoped. The *Folly* was eighty-five percent the old *Stockwell,* but there had been changes, including new temporary walls in cargo bays and a couple of new access tunnels. Much of the ship's intraship system had been disconnected. Cargo haulers carried less crew than a military heavy cruiser. Some of the equipment, he suspected, had been stripped out and sold to raise funds. Farosian or fruit, he didn't know.

Rya popped in and out of his peripheral vision—and other senses—during the trek. He assumed they were simply on a complementary orbit, but he didn't discount that Adney had assigned him a bodyguard. But he didn't need a bodyguard, and especially not one so distracting. He'd have to talk to Adney about that—after he cleared the other three hundred critical things off his plate first.

Like dinner. Somehow lunch had slipped by him. He realized that as he stood in the general mess hall on Deck 3 and watched Con try to cadge a protein tube out of a recalcitrant dispenser. Philip had told Adney he'd help with galley duties before he'd realized the *Folly*'s menu was the least of her problems.

But now . . . Actually, there was little else for him to be doing. He'd read all the reports, authorized what needed to be done. He'd met with Adney and his command staff. There might be three hundred critical things to finish yet, but at least two hundred eighty-eight of them were under way. The other dozen he couldn't do one damned thing about.

He hadn't read himself on board. Without a working intraship system, it didn't seem right. But if he gathered most everyone in the mess hall for dinner... A plan formed.

Philip Guthrie felt useful again.

He grabbed Con's wrist, stopping the man from shoving something brown, tubular, and disgusting in his mouth. "Don't do that."

"Sir?"

He tugged the lieutenant toward the galley doors. "I put an order through for supplies a few hours ago. Let's see what's come in."

Quite a bit. Three crew were unpacking, shelving, and securing. They straightened, saluting. He returned the gesture, then poked through the open dull-gray plastic duro-hards. He checked perishables. Not bad, he thought, picking up a large yellow roasting pepper and sniffing it. Though if he had access to those incoming funds Sullivan had snagged for him...but they were two shipweeks away yet. A gala dinner, then, when they arrived.

Con was eyeing him strangely.

Philip put down the pepper and smiled. "Do me a favor," he asked, pointing to a workstation against the wall. "Find out from the personnel rosters who's admitted to a talent for cooking, and if they're not critical elsewhere, get four or five down here in the next half hour." He plucked a few boxes and bags from a duro-hard. "We're going to have ourselves a decent dinner."

"Finally," Martoni said. "This should be the last one."

Rya saw the reflections of the conveyor freight-loader's flashing red lights as they strobed the wide cargo passageway. She stepped closer to the cargo bay's airlock, where Martoni leaned against a pylon, one of the coveted working datapads in hand. With intraship and comm links still not functioning reliably, the datapads were the only way officers could communicate with one another when they weren't at a deskscreen.

Martoni tilted the pad's screen toward her. "All the supplies Commander Sparkington ordered are here. Eight duro-hards. Same routine as the others."

"Not a problem." She, Martoni, and four other crew had spent the past two hours clearing incoming supplies. Nothing got on the ship unless it was thoroughly inspected, counted, and verified.

He handed her the pad. "Log everything here, then patch it to a workstation to upload the data to Commander Adney's files." He hesitated. "Sorry I can't give you the comm-link codes for it, but this is Commander Adney's."

That meant she was locked out of all the pad's functions except for data input and transmittal.

"I'll either be in Adney's office or in divisionals," he continued. "You can leave it with the commander when you're done."

She waved him on. She and Martoni had been running from one assignment to the next the entire day. Now he was off again for another meeting. She'd finish up here.

She met the loader's driver at the base of the cargo ramp, synched the loader's manifest datapad with hers, and, by the impatient tapping of the stocky woman's boot, could tell she was taking far longer than the driver liked in double-checking everything. Too bad.

"Heard you had some mechanical problems on board," the woman said.

Rya's scrutiny hesitated, but only for a second.

There was no way the *Folly*'s problems should have made it to dock. "Just came on shift," she lied. "Woke up late." She yawned, then grinned self-consciously. "Did I miss something exciting?"

"Something about a lift dropping four decks, crashing in one of your shuttle bays, I think." The woman shrugged.

"You serious? Anyone get hurt?"

"Not that I heard."

"Well, damn!" Rya disengaged the two units, her mind parsing the woman's story while she continued her role as cargohand. "Everything looks perfect. You people make my job easier. I appreciate that, you know?"

Another shrug, but the woman was smiling now, thawing a bit. Which was what Rya wanted. *Trust me. Talk to me.* There hadn'd been any lift crashes, or she'd have heard. Problems with the lights, yes. Blast doors, yes. Maybe it was an error in the story, or maybe not. If something was supposed to have happened to the lifts, she wanted to know.

"No problem," the woman said in response to Rya's appreciative words. "We're all in this together, right? I'll get the belt going."

Rya watched the belt extend up the ramp. Then the first gray duro-hard appeared, a good ten feet in length and half that in width.

"So I guess I should avoid the lifts," Rya said as she walked toward the driver. "This is my first shipboard assignment." She put a nervous tone in her voice. "My boyfriend talked me into it."

"It was probably just jumpjockey talk." The woman patted Rya's arm. "The two guys I overheard talking about it, they didn't seem real worried. They said your guy was just glad the supply depot had the parts he needed."

"A crew member from here?" Rya knew that was impossible. The ship was under security lockdown since the Kirro and shuttle incidents. No leaves had been authorized. All communications to the shipyard had been through Adney's office. No one should be off ship getting supplies, and especially not without a security bodyguard.

The woman shook her head. "Don't know if your guy in the depot was officer or crew. The ones talking about him were yardworkers. Tugs, 'cause one had the black and gold wings." She touched the space above her right pocket where the double-S of her Seth Shipyard insignia was. "You know those tuggies love to gossip. And not a one ever sets foot in a ship. I've been in more than they have!"

"The red-haired tuggy with a beard that was here earlier?" Rya lied again.

"Don't know that one. This one's pale, had dark hair pulled in a tail. He was tall. The other was shorter, pale too. But he had a cap on."

"Well, they haven't come to cargo or I'd have seen them. So you're probably right. Just talk."

The woman pointed her pad at the large duro-hard. "That's the last one. You doing the verifications too?"

"I am," Rya said, suddenly wishing Martoni were here, suddenly wishing she wasn't doing verifications. She wanted to find the tall tuggy with the dark hair pulled back, and his shorter friend, and find out just what they knew about what purportedly happened on the *Folly*. And who they talked to in the supply depot.

She headed back up the ramp and with a start saw Mr. Nice Ass standing near the top, watching her, arms folded across his chest. *Dillon,* she reminded herself. She didn't even know his rank or first name.

He nodded as she approached. "This is for Sparks, yes?" His voice held that light accent.

"Looks like it. Martoni send you?"

"Sparks did." He curved part of his mouth in a grin. A sexy grin. "Old man likes his toys, you know?"

"I'm not releasing anything until I've done verifications." That came out sharper than she intended, but something about Mr. Nice Ass rankled her. Because he was Mr. Nice Ass? Another good-looking hard-body, like Matt? Amazing how they could be so enjoyable and annoying at the same time.

She broke the security seals on the first container, angled the datapad to read the embedded datapeg, then did a visual.

"I can help," Dillon offered.

"This won't take long." The second read as clean as the first. The third container wasn't as cooperative. Dozens of small parts.

"Here." Dillon pulled a portable reader from his tool belt.

"Where'd you get that?"

"My job." The grin widened, then he leaned over and whispered in her ear. "The old man isn't the only one who likes his toys."

His tone was playful, suggestive. Definitely enjoyable and annoying. And not her problem at the moment.

She synched the pad to his reader, verifying the data as he sent it to her. This was going faster than she expected. That might give her time to get up to Adney's office, tell her what the driver said. Get permission to—

"That's it?"

She looked up from the pad. Dillion looked at her, one dark eyebrow raised. She glanced at the pad again. "That's it. Eight. Everything looks good." She turned and trotted to the middle of the ramp. "I'll sign off on the shipment," she told the driver.

"Your boyfriend's not bad at all," the driver said as Rya tapped in her code on the pad. "Understand why you followed him on the ship."

Boyfriend? She shot a glance over her shoulder, seeing only Dillon. He grinned. "He's not—"

But the driver was already trudging down the ramp toward the chugging loader.

Rya shrugged it off and hurried back to the cargo bay. "Spare servopallets are there," she told Dillon, pointing to a wide locker in the bulkhead as she walked past him. "Thanks for your help." She keyed in the locking codes, closing the bay doors behind her. Damn it all! If only she had her own datapad or a comm link. She had to talk to Adney. Or Welford, if Adney wasn't around. Philip trusted Con Welford.

Dillon caught up with her. "Leaving?"

"Things to do. Thanks," she said again.

He was still trotting next to her. "You play cards?"

She slowed, his question catching her unaware. "Sure, but—"

"When all this craziness dies down, a couple of us, we thought we'd get a game going. Get to know one another a little better. Yes?"

"Look, Dillon—"

"Alek." He ducked his head shyly for a moment.

Shyly? Well, fancy that. "Look, Alek, I have no idea when this craziness is going to stop. But sure, at some point, if you've got a card game going, I'm interested. Okay?"

"That's really good. Yes."

She nodded, suddenly feeling awkward with the way he was looking at her. She was rarely awkward around men, but Dillon was looking at her as if her answer really mattered. "I have to find Commander Adney."

His hand on her arm stopped her. "Lieutenant Bennton?"

"Yes?"

"I don't... What's your first name?"

She was on a ship with no functional crew locator, insufficient datapads, and no name tags for their nonexistent uniforms. First names were definitely a problem. "Rya."

"Rya." His voice dropped to a rumble. "I look forward to seeing you again, Rya."

Well, fancy that. She felt like she was back in the pubs on Calth 9 with Lyza, flirting with the hardbodies. Why had she assumed shipboard would be any different?

She found a functioning workstation about twenty feet from the cargo-hold exterior hatchlock and linked the datapad in, sending a ping to Commander Adney with the data: *Cargo complete. I have some information that might be important. Would like to discuss. Lt. R. Bennton.*

She waited about thirty seconds with no answer, then decided she might as well start climbing. She was on the *Folly*'s lowest deck, Deck 6. At the very least Adney would be on Deck 3, the largest deck, encompassing most of the crew's quarters as well as the general mess. More likely, Adney was in one of the divisional offices in Deck 2 Aft or on the bridge.

Rya wasn't about to chance the lifts.

The stairwell between Deck 5 and Deck 4 amidships was the longest on board—more like three flights than one—and Rya was sucking wind by the time she pushed through the doors to the corridor. She found a workstation and patched in again.

My office, Adney's reply said.

Only two more flights. Oh, joy.

Commander Adney leaned back in her office chair, fingertips resting lightly on the edge of her dull-gray metal desk. "That's very vague information, Bennton."

"Yes, ma'am, I agree. Any other circumstance, any other ship, I'd discount it. Or if the driver said the blast doors were stuck, then we'd know someone on the ship said something they shouldn't. But this specifically was a lift-crash problem, something that hasn't happened. Unless it has and I haven't heard about."

"We had one that wouldn't stop at Deck Four, but that was minor, and definitely not a crash."

Rya hesitated. "I recommend shutting down all lifts and making a thorough mechanical inspection."

"I understand your concern. But the fact is, we're severely shorthanded. The admiral has made it very clear that our first priorities are systems that are essential to the operation of this ship and the crew. A rumor about a lift malfunction is hardly life-threatening. A mention of someone buying supplies for this ship is misleading. I am in touch with the yardmaster's office and we are purchasing supplies through her. But that doesn't mean *Folly* crew are on the docks." She pinned Rya with a hard look. "I suggest you concentrate on doing what you're asked to do."

Rya could think of a dozen scenarios where it would be life-threatening, especially if malfunctioning lifts kept security from reaching Philip if another attempt was made to kidnap him. And if there were Imperial or

Justice Warden operatives on the dock waiting to receive his unconscious body. She opened her mouth, then closed it, biting back disappointment and frustration. But she couldn't give up. "Requesting permission to track down the source of the information, Commander."

"The tuggies on the shipyards?" Adney shook her head slowly. "Request denied. No personnel are permitted to leave this ship, given what happened on Kirro. You should understand that better than anyone."

"Yes, ma'am, I do. But I'm concerned—"

Adney held up one hand, then pointed to her deskscreen. "See these files, Bennton? These are all my concerns. Dozens of them. If a malfunctioning lift was the worst thing on my list, I'd be a very happy woman."

"Yes, ma'am." *Damn, damn.*

"Let me give you a word of advice, Bennton. I've reviewed your personnel file thoroughly. I've talked to your superiors, and others, on Calth Nine. It's time you realized you're not ImpSec anymore. I'm not going to authorize sending you out on the docks on some kind of mission. The civilians out there don't need to see that kind of demonstration. We will solve this problem my way. By *thinking*, Bennton. Not with fear."

Rya was shocked by the vehemence in Adney's tone, but she didn't permit herself to show it. She might not be ImpSec anymore, but she couldn't remove their training. Nor did she want to, and, somehow, she knew Adney suspected that. "Yes, ma'am."

"If that's all, then you're dismissed, Lieutenant."

"That's all. Thank you, ma'am." Rya saluted, then turned and headed back to the corridor, mouth grim. She didn't know who Adney had talked to on Calth 9 or why the commander's opinion of her would be so negative. Her performance reports were always excellent. Sure, a few times she'd pushed beyond mission guidelines, but she'd *succeeded*. And maybe she could be a bit overzealous, but her instincts had never failed her.

And her instincts said something bad was going to happen. Again.

She found an empty—and working—deskscreen at the far end of divisionals. A lot of the stations were empty. She glanced at the time stamp, her stomach agreeing with the information. It was main shift dinnertime. Just as well. Less people around to ask what she was doing.

She brought up the security logs she and Martoni were constructing, looking for any shipments brought in by tugs since Adney and her team had arrived. There was no way for her to check what happened before that—or was there? She made a mental note to hunt down Welford if she dead-ended here.

There were long lists of supplies incoming. Some of the procurement codes were ones she'd become familiar with on Calth 9. Others she'd never seen. With a fully functional data system, she could have the whole list decoded in seconds.

Now it could take hours and there would still be gaps.

Forty-five minutes later she narrowed down two shipments that possibly had to do with lift mechanisms, antigrav pods, or guidance rails. But AG pods were also used to move cargo. Smaller ones even had medical uses.

Hell, she was security, not an engineer. And this still didn't tell her if someone had snuck off the ship.

For a moment she considered tracking down Alek

Dillon. He was one of Spark's techies and knew much more than she did about things like this. But he'd start asking questions, and she wasn't yet ready to answer them. Sparks, maybe, because Philip trusted him. But Dillon? No.

It was her damned gut again.

Plus, Adney had already said she'd handle it. By researching data, Rya was going against Adney's orders, and she'd already landed on the commander's bad side. Adney inhaled the regs and exhaled procedure and obviously hated ImpSec. Rya knew if she sought out Sparks or Welford and Adney found out, she'd really be in a world of shit.

She put her head in her hands and scrubbed at her face in frustration.

She had to chance talking to Welford and somehow convince him not to mention her name to Adney. Or she might find herself on a shuttle back to Calth.

Philip's change-of-command orders were short and, being similarly worded to ones he'd said before in the Imperial Fleet, not unfamiliar. Except this time they started with, "By the command of the Consul of the Alliance of Independent Republics, Mason Falkner, and under the authority of the Independent Admirals' Council." Words he hoped would be said several more times over the next few months as the fleet continued to grow.

Of course, he had to get this bucket to Ferrin's before most of that would happen.

"Admiral Guthrie." Commander Adney, standing next to him in the crowded mess on Deck 3 Aft, nodded. "You have the command."

"Commander Adney, I accept the responsibilities of

command," he answered perfunctorily and, as he returned Adney's salute, saw Rya slip in through the doors at the back of the room, her holstered Stinger peeking out from the edge of her leather jacket. He'd been watching for her and had been a little disappointed she hadn't shown up for dinner.

Maybe more than a little, but he couldn't think about that at the moment, because there was applause and then Adney shaking his hand, then Con, then Sparks, and he lost sight of her again as his crew—*his* crew—stood as one, glasses raised.

He'd cooked one damned fine dinner.

"You mean, I didn't have to listen to anything you said up until now?" Con laughed, clasping him on the arm.

There were more well-wishes and thanks to Dina Adney for running the show so well to this point.

Sparks touched his arm. "Mather has a live link to Captain Bralford. Commander Adney's office."

He made some quick excuses, then followed the shorter man out the doors, down the corridor to the lifts, then up one deck to the divisional offices, enduring his fair share of good-natured ribbing that his official insignia should bear a cook's apron.

"Chaz used to tell me of your prowess with a frying pan," Sparks said as they exited the lift. "Now I believe her."

"Casseroles are easy." Philip shrugged off the compliment, though he was, in truth, rather proud of what he'd been able to do on such short notice. In two shipweeks, when his funds arrived, he'd do even better. "If we'd had the time and resources for a pastry-crusted stuffed roast, we—"

"Congratulations, sir." Mather, waiting in the corridor, saluted.

"You get to eat, Commo?"

"Yes, sir. It was excellent." He stepped aside to let Philip into the office, then he and Sparks followed.

Philip lowered himself into Adney's chair and nodded at the familiar face on the deskscreen. The image was decent but a bit grainy. "Captain Bralford. You missed dinner."

Jodey laughed. "Then you owe me one. Congratulations, Philip. Though from what Mather's been telling me, it should be condolences as well." His smile faded. "Damn, I had no idea she needed so much work. The reports Pavyer supplied us indicated no such problems."

"Plague of the ittle-doos," Philip said. "It will slow us down a bit. But at least when she's finally running, we can trust everything's been done right."

Sparks turned and tapped Mather on the shoulder, motioning to the corridor. They ducked out of the office together—Sparks palming the door shut on his way out. Then it was just Philip with Jodey on the screen.

Philip leaned back in the chair. "Bring me up to date."

"I'm sending the complete reports now," Jodey said, "but the key points are we have reason to believe the Empire is moving to blockade the two primary jumpgates between Baris and Calth: B–C-Three and B–C-Seven."

Philip knew why immediately. "They want to secure Calth Prime and the Walker Colonies."

Jodey pursed his mouth, nodding. "They have a considerable investment in Port January and Rawton."

They did. Port January was a sprawling, prosperous city and the baronial seat on Calth Prime. Rawton, outside Port January, was the largest contained prison compound in the Empire, excluding the prison world of Moabar. The Empire wouldn't want either in Alliance hands.

"Is there someone in Rawton they have a particular interest in, or do you think it's just resources overall?"

"I'd never discount resources," Jodey said, "but we're checking into the 'special prisoner' angle. It's not Blaine. He's still on Moabar—something else they may try to secure because of him."

"I'm still surprised the Farosians haven't tried to spring Blaine. We know they have a Star-Ripper, the Infiltrator, and probably a few other ships we haven't found out about yet."

"You know what Moabar is like. Finding Blaine dirtside would entail a considerable operation—if they could even get access to the planet. Plus, Tage moved the *Vidovik Lu* and a squadron of P-75s out there. Kidnapping you is easier, I guess," Jodey said.

The *Lu* was a well-armed and deadly battleship. Add in the P-75s and, yes, the Farosians had nothing to match that.

Philip turned his mind back to Tage and the Empire again. "The Walker Colonies also give Tage entry into Dafir."

"No one ever said Tage was stupid."

No, sadly, the man whom Philip at one time considered a friend wasn't stupid. Crafty, cunning, and lately diabolical. But not stupid.

"The consul's people have been making the preliminary political noises to the Empire," Jodey continued. "But word coming down from our Admirals' Council is we may need to make a show of force. You'll be getting all this direct once you get the *Folly* online."

Philip sighed. "I've been told we'll have communications and encryption up and running fully tomorrow. Day after, the latest."

"Would be nice if the Admirals' Council and the counsul's people could talk directly to the admiral."

"Just as well they haven't been able to today. My vocabulary hasn't been fit for polite company." Philip glanced at the icon flashing on the corner of his screen. "Reports are in."

"Then I'll leave you to your work. I'm hoping the next time we talk it'll be from your office and you'll have more than just Dina's comm link functioning."

Philip grunted. "Ever the optimist, Bralford. Stay safe, my friend."

"And you stay out of trouble."

That warranted another grunt. "Hell's fat ass chance of that." Philip signed off, the screen fading to black. He snagged the reports Jodey'd sent and shunted them over to his in-box in his office. It was almost 1930 hours, and his day was far from over.

But his officers and crew should be changing shifts, although he knew a lot of them would keep on working, regardless.

Philip shoved himself out of Adney's chair and limped for the door. He grabbed the closest lift down to Deck 3. The goddamned Stryker-class design split Deck 2 in forward and aft sections, with no direct access between the two other than to go down, then up again.

Not one thing about this mission was easy. Not even the ship.

He stepped out of the lift on Deck 3, nodded to crew hustling past, and heard a familiar throaty laugh behind him. He glanced over his shoulder and caught a glimpse of Rya farther down the corridor in the crew's quarters' section. Con Welford had his hand on Rya's shoulder, the two of them mere inches apart.

Then the cabin door opened and Con ushered Rya inside.

Philip stood, staring. Something he couldn't—*didn't*—want to define tightened in his chest. There were a hundred legitimate reasons why Rya Bennton could be in Con's cabin, but only the less-than-legitimate ones seemed to want to surface in his mind. And even those were none of Philip Guthrie's god-damned business.

He turned abruptly, his right leg protesting in pain. He used that pain as the excuse for his foul mood for the next several hours—and as a reminder that life rarely goes as planned. Not even for the Great Guthrie, who had far more-serious considerations than what Cory's daughter was doing with Constantine Welford.

Didn't he?

Rya sat in one of the two dark-blue padded chairs in Con Welford's cabin and watched him study the information she'd sent to his datapad. He was willing to listen to her concerns and look at what she'd found, though he'd not bothered to hide his skepticism.

"Everyone on the docks talks," he'd said when she first told him her findings.

She couldn't disagree. "But it's my job to listen."

So he'd listened, and now he was looking. Unofficially, of course, which was why they were in his cabin and not using one of the workstations in divisionals.

His cabin was slightly larger than hers but, she noted wryly, not any warmer. He'd warned her about that as she followed him down the corridor on Crew 3. She'd countered with her father's gambling-for-socks story, which made him laugh. But the levity was brief. Problems were far too real and far more plentiful than solutions at the moment.

She shifted position in the chair, adjusting her shoulder holster, bringing one leg up underneath her. The edge of her boot knife peeked out. She caught Welford's questioning glance.

"Stinger won't kill them dead enough?" he asked.

"Safety," she told him, tapping the blunt hilt. "Someone gets one weapon away from you, you have options. Stunner." She jerked her thumb over her shoulder, indicating where the L7 rested snug at her waist. "ImpSec issued Carver-Tens. Now, *those* are fun."

"Fun? Necessary, sure. But fun?" Welford just shook his head and perched on the edge of his bed, then secured his datapad on his bedside table.

She stopped herself from launching into one of her father's favorite discussions about fear versus familiarity, whether it be jumpgate transits or speaking in front of an assembly or high-powered laser rifles. They weren't here to talk weapons; they were here to find possible intruders. Far more important than Welford's opinions on her armaments. Her mind went in worried circles, so she studied Welford to keep it busy.

He was not as tall as Philip and had short sandy hair and a somewhat crooked nose. Judging from the scar on his chin and the shape of his nose, she pegged him as a scrapper, someone always in the middle of a bar fight.

His features could make him appear gruff, but he had a wide mouth that smiled easily and often. Rya knew Sachi found Welford attractive.

He was frowning now. She didn't know if that was a good sign or a bad one.

"Anything?" she asked.

"Standard replacement parts, but that's not the problem." He waved her over.

She uncrossed her legs, pulling herself out of the chair, then stepped next to him. Five databoxes dotted his screen.

"This." He pointed to one on the lower right.

"There were two unauthorized accesses through the cargo hatchlocks three hours after we—Commander Adney and the team—arrived," he explained.

Unauthorized accesses? "There were, what, five of you on board at that time?"

"Four. Adney, myself, Corvang, and Mather. All the more reason the ship was in total lockdown at that point. We knew how vulnerable we were. But someone got on board, twice, without setting off any alarms. Without us seeing them." Anger tinged his voice.

A chill scurried up Rya's spine. "Fuck." The crude epithet slipped out before she could stop it. "Sorry, Lieutenant Welford."

Welford snorted. "I agree with the sentiment—though this could be nothing. We were still taking possession of the ship. The owner's people might have made two last trips on board for personal possessions. But it could also be one big fucking problem."

"You can't tell?"

"From this? No. I need to get into the main logs and see if I can't pick up what codes, if any, were used to open the hatchlock. But we've had two system crashes since then. I don't even know if that data is still accessible." He thrust one hand through his short sandy hair. "I guess I know what I'm doing the rest of tonight."

"Can I help?"

"I'll call you if I need you to shoot or stab someone. But until then, no."

"Will you tell Commander Adney?"

"Once I have a better idea of what we have here, yes."

"Adney . . . doesn't give credence to what I say." She almost told Welford about her earlier conversation. About Adney's limited view of ImpSec. But for all she knew, Welford felt the same way. He hadn't seemed comfortable when she'd pointed out her weaponry.

"Don't worry about that. Dina just loves the rule book. But she recognizes and will act on a problem when she sees one."

A weight lifted, somewhat. Welford would find out. Adney would listen to him, a former *Loviti* officer. But would he find out in time? Maybe, as he said, the intrusions were harmless. Just the ship's previous owner retrieving possessions at the last minute.

Maybe it was time to let go of her ImpSec training and mind-set. And maybe not.

"And if it's all nothing, you owe me some socks." He winked. Some of her discomfort with him lessened.

"The warmest pair I have," she told him, turning to leave. She turned back just as she reached for the palm pad. "Con, can you tell if whoever came on board left? Or should I be looking for stowaways?"

The smile faded from his face. "Oh, hell. Yeah, I'll check for that too. Keep that Stinger primed. You might be shooting someone after all."

Rya was officially off duty. She unofficially walked the entire ship, the old *Stockwell*'s schematics coming easily to mind as she fell into covert-mission mode and tried to think like a stowaway. The perfect opportunity for someone to slip on board was that narrow window of the first few hours of the ship's turnover to Commander Adney. With less than a full crew complement, places to hide were plentiful. If she'd known it would have been so easy, she'd not have worried at all about qualifying for an assignment to the *Folly*.

She could have just stowed away and, if she wanted

to, caused all the problems to date. Especially as she
knew the ship's schematics by heart.

Likely so did some of the Farosians who'd crewed
on her. And any number of Imperials.

If she were the infamous Commander Dalby, she
would have tried for Philip at Kirro, tried again in the
space lanes, but have someone already on board as
backup.

For the hundredth time she wanted to go barging
back into Welford's cabin and demand he alert Adney
now, but she knew he wouldn't until he had proof.

She looked in unoccupied cabins for telltale signs of a
stowaway. She stood quietly in stairwells, listening. She
noted crew she knew—though, admittedly, barely—and
studied those she didn't. It was annoying, frustrating,
but it was something to do. If she sat in her cabin or even
went to find a card game—there was bound to be at least
one, and Alek Dillon was likely already there—she'd go
crazy. Crazier than she already was.

She got to know the *Folly* better than she normally
would have with only one day on board, translating
schematics to real time. The ship had six decks, starting from the bridge and ready room on Deck 1, down
to cargo and storage on Deck 6. Shuttle bay, maintenance, and engineering were on 5, just as they had
been when her father sat in command. Sparks was
working—not surprising—but she didn't stop to talk.
She wanted to listen. Deck 4 was crew's quarters, ship's
gym—which already had a few hard-bodies getting
busy—and more storerooms. Deck 3 was more crew's
quarters, general mess hall, and galley. Deck 2 was
split forward and aft, with no way to get from one to
the other without going down one deck—one of the
things her father found annoying. Aft were the divisional offices, including Commander Adney's, and sick

bay. Forward were the admiral's quarters and office, Adney's cabin, and two spare cabins.

The small blue light glowing next to Adney's palm pad showed she wasn't in her office. Rya hoped they were all in Philip's, tracking down whoever had come abroad during those critical first hours.

She started her circuit again.

This time, when she reached Deck 6, she could almost recognize where she was on the ship just by the sounds. Crew movement —the thudding of boots, the high and low pitches of conversations—was more apparent on Decks 3 and 4. Deck 6 was more ship sounds—pinging and whooshing and clanking. Deck 5 was a combination of both: the hard bark of voices from engineering aft, the groaning and pinging of metal forward in the shuttle bays and cargo areas, unoccupied now with the ship so understaffed. Even the machine shop—

She stopped, head tilted. There were footsteps coming from the maintenance shop. No one was assigned to the shop that she knew of, but maybe one of Sparks's people had a project. . . . No; she didn't hear voices.

Hand resting on her Stinger, she padded softly toward the shop. The door was slightly ajar and she could see from its angle that it was out of kilter. She frowned. Did someone force it or was this another inherited problem?

The shop's lighting was scattered. It looked as if most of the overheads were nonworking, but a small light glowed softly over a nearby worktable. A figure moved through her narrow line of vision, and Rya relaxed. Mather. Commo, carrying parts to the low table. Not Sparks's project then, but something Welford put him up to. She remembered the two of them working—and swearing—over the problems on the bridge.

"Hey, Commo," she called, pushing the palm pad. The door edged open.

A crash sounded, a metal box clanking to the floor. Mather spun, eyes wide.

Shit. She was so used to moving soundlessly that she often forgot it startled people. "Sorry. Didn't mean to scare you." She stepped toward him.

Mather crouched quickly, retrieving the box. "That's what I get for not paying attention." He laughed, but it was a shaky one.

"What's Welford got you doing?"

"Welford? No, I just had an idea." He turned, placing the box on the bench and dropping some thin metal rods into it. "Like to be helpful, you know?" he said over his shoulder. "Thought maybe I could find something down here to work into a panel, where at least officers could log in and out of locations." He turned back and shook his head. "It's all junk."

"I can tell you how to modify a Stinger or an L7," Rya said, "but nothing larger than that." She hesitated. "Sparks had a big shipment of tech come in about two hours ago."

"It arrived early? Great!" He tapped off the small work light over the table, then headed for her.

It made sense Mather would know about the parts. From everything she'd heard, he and Welford had been doing nonstop repairs since they set foot on board.

"Martoni, Dillon, and I logged it in."

"First bit of good news I've had. I forgive you for giving me heart failure."

"Hey, Commo, I didn't mean to—"

He punched her lightly on the shoulder. "Just teasing, my dear. I think I'll go inflict myself on our chief engineer. Maybe I can lend a hand."

"Watch the door," she said, following him toward the corridor. "It doesn't close properly."

Mather stared at it for a moment, then shook his head, a wry grin on his lips. "This ship is just ... perfect."

She almost reminded him that wasn't at all the words he and Welford used to describe the *Folly* earlier on the bridge, but he was already trudging toward engineering.

No, the *Folly* wasn't perfect—yet. But at least she had people like Welford and Sparks and Mather—and Philip—doing all they could to rectify that.

She headed for the stairwell, listening, hoping Adney was doing the same.

"Unknown and unauthorized access." Philip's narrow-eyed gaze went from Adney to his deskscreen back to Adney again. Her wide mouth was pursed, her dark eyes as narrow as his. Dina Adney wasn't happy.

Neither was Philip. He hadn't been in the best of moods before Adney walked in. Now the words *unknown and unauthorized access* made his teeth clench, his skin crawl, and his trigger finger itch like crazy.

"Welford said he found it during a routine check and confirmed it two minutes ago. I came up straight-away. He and Martoni, Bennton, Holton, and a few others are on serious spook patrol."

"We have visuals on the intrusion?"

"Cameras aren't working. Something we need to rectify, quickly. We do show an enviro malfunction on Deck Six at that time. I'm guessing now that was a planned error."

Philip swore and wiped his hand over his face.

Adney leaned forward. "I could ask shipyard security—"

"Not yet." Maybe not at all. "I don't want to add more unknown moving parts to the problem."

Adney hesitated, then: "I'll go see what Martoni and Welford have found, if anything," she said, rising.

Philip rose also. "I'll be down in engineering." He had to talk to Sparks. He had to know how soon they could get this bucket to Ferrin's, where a real military shipyard could provide solutions to many of their problems, including a functional crew-locator system and security cameras.

If they lived long enough to get there.

He stopped in his cabin first to get his jacket. The lower decks were cold. "You have fur," he told the sleeping lump in the middle of his bed. Captain Folly had returned.

One yellow eye opened. The tip of the black tail flicked with disdain.

"We also had intruders," he said to the cat. "Mind telling me why you didn't bite them?"

The cat had no answer. Philip grabbed his jacket and limped out to the corridor.

"Welford and Cory's kid told me about the security breach when they searched engineering." Sparks sat hunched over in a chair deck-locked in front of the main console. His sleeves were rolled up and a dark sweater was tossed haphazardly over the chair's back. He held a small analyzer in one hand. It was blinking and beeping softly. "It would take Dillon, Vange, Kagdan, and me at least three full shipdays to get the kind of locator system you want rigged and installed.

Here. On Ferrin's, with their people's help, we'd cut that time in half. Maybe less, because they have parts. Here I'd have to cobble stuff together."

Philip nodded and studied the older man as he spoke. "Helluva first day," he intoned, because the stubble was already apparent on Sparks's chin. Only the cat was in bed, which was where they all should have been hours ago.

And he didn't miss the mention of "Cory's kid." Rya. Rya and Welford.

None of his damned business.

"Day's been a bit more than I expected, but nothing I can't handle," Sparks replied, in typical Sparks fashion. The man loved a challenge. "But I don't think your problem is a stowaway."

Neither did Philip, honestly. "Sabotage or a mole waiting to make the next move."

"The list of people who don't like us is legion."

Philip snorted.

"You want to be in the lanes in forty-eight hours," Sparks continued, glancing down as his analyzer beeped. "It might be a few hours later than that, barring any more unusual crises."

"You start working miracles this early in the mission, I'll expect them at every turn."

"You're going to need them, Skipper." Sparks tapped the analyzer against his palm. "This ship, this crew. Hell, this Alliance. Falkner's a charismatic leader, but Tage is old guard. Crafty. Experienced. And greedy. He won't easily relinquish what he sees as rightfully his."

"If the emperor dies, there'll be a challenge, probably from some of the baronies in Aldan." Philip could think of three or four other "old guard" types who were loyal to Prew and less so to Tage.

"Prew's body is healthy. It's his mind that's gone. Tage can be the emperor's voice for decades yet."

Philip scrubbed his hands over his face, the undeniable truth in Sparks's words grating. The Alliance was not on a firm foundation and faced an enemy that—even with the depletion of Fleet—was certainly more well organized and well financed.

"Chaz sounded good," Sparks said.

Philip gave himself a mental shake at the engineer's abrupt change of subject, but that was also typical Sparks. His conversations, like his mind, jumped back and forth in odd directions.

"Talked to her ten days or so ago," Sparks went on. "Told me how you damned near crash-landed your pinnace in Sullivan's bay. Told me she's happy."

"Sullivan's good for her," Philip admitted, still surprised that he actually meant it. "And he can keep her a lot safer than I can." Not that his ex-wife needed anyone to keep her safe. She'd excelled in his combat-training classes and was top of her class in hand-to-hand. She also wielded a mean Stinger and was no stranger to a modified Norlack.

"You were good for her in your own way."

Philip slanted a glance at the older man. Sparks had been Chaz's chief engineer and probably had spent almost as much time with her as Philip had, given that his and Chaz's careers had kept them apart for lengths at a time. "I tried," Philip said: "But I failed her in a lot of ways. It was more my fault than hers. I could blame my family"—choosing a military career against his parents' expectations had made him try harder, after marrying Chaz, to fit in with the wealthy, entrepreneurial Guthries—"but the reality is, I'm more hard-wired for duty than relationships."

Losing Chaz had cemented that belief.

Sparks was frowning at his analyzer. "This—"

The overhead lights flickered. Philip tensed, one hand automatically grasping the Carver at his hip.

"—is just us, testing," Sparks continued. He swiveled around in his chair and slapped at his console. "That's a go, Kagdan. Let's not scare the locals any more tonight. Secure and shut down."

"Got it, Sparks," said a disembodied female voice through the console speaker.

Philip grabbed his cane, then shoved himself to his feet. "We need to get to Ferrin's."

"There are a few tricks I haven't tried yet. I'll give them a go tomorrow," Sparks promised.

Belatedly, Philip remembered—as he stripped off his clothes, his body craving sleep—that the doors to his quarters and his office no longer locked.

"You're on guard duty," he told the cat nestled at the foot of his bed, one white paw curled over his face in protest of the cabin lights.

Philip put the L7 on his nightstand. And the Carver, safety off, inside the nightstand drawer. As he and Sparks had agreed, he didn't feel the problem was a stowaway. But the thought of moles made him sleep very lightly.

So he was aware two hours later when the cat jumped off the bed and headed for his cabin's main room. That didn't bother him, until he heard footsteps that were distinctly uncatlike.

His breath hitched, then slowed as he segued into defense mode. Someone besides the cat was in his quarters.

He slipped his legs soundlessly from under the covers, his bare feet finding the lightweight drawstring pants he'd left on the floor. One hand pulled the pants to his waist, the other palmed the L7. Whoever this was, it would be close range. A stunner would do.

Plus, he wanted whoever this was alive and talking.

He grabbed his cane—as much for defense as for balance—then stood by his bedroom's open doorway, listening. The short hallway was dark, but his eyes didn't need to adjust. He'd awakened in darkness. And he'd trained in low-light and night combat for years.

He'd even written a manual on the subject.

The noises he thought he heard stopped. He slowed his breath. Could he have been wrong? He wasn't used to sleeping with a domestic pet. He could have misinterpreted the cat's explorations—

No, definitely a footfall. Soft, measured. Had he not written a manual on the subject, he might have missed it.

Someone was well trained. But so was he. Just as softly, he moved into his quarters' short hallway, watching for shifting shadows. He heard only one person. He couldn't discount there could be another standing as motionless as he had been seconds before.

It was a common ploy—one agent to distract, one to act. He didn't believe for a moment the Farosians had given up on kidnapping him. Or killing him. They wanted Sheldon Blaine's freedom badly, and his body was a ticket they could use to ensure that.

He also believed they'd make an attempt before the *Folly* left the shipyards. Logistically, it was easier than attacking the ship in transit. And they probably saw an injured admiral as an easy target.

They were about to learn just how wrong they were.

Noises moved, nothing much more than a shifting of breath, an infinitesimal displacement of air. The cat was the cause of one. Something larger was the other. Philip felt more than saw his intruder near the small galley to his left. But he'd have to swing around the corner of the hallway wall to get a position, and that would mean leaving his back exposed.

He stood silently a few more heartbeats, straining to discern if anyone was waiting to his right—or if that same someone might be behind him when he moved. Nothing. Not that that was a guarantee.

He swung out, muscles tensed, stunner trained on his armed intruder—

"Philip!"

—and almost shot Rya the Rebel.

"Rya? What in hell's fat ass...?" Thumbing the safety back on the stunner, he stepped toward her. "Lights on, galley." The overhead flickered, then glowed, and he could clearly see that what he'd taken for a weapon in her right hand was a small dish. In her other was a cup, likely filled with cream or milk, because the cat was on the counter behind her, waiting, tail thumping softly but insistently.

"Rya," he repeated, because he couldn't think of anything to say that wouldn't involve a healthy dose of epithets. His heart still raced, his trigger finger still itched, and with all his senses on overload he was far too aware that he was damned near naked. And that she was far too close to him, her mouth parted in surprise.

Or as if waiting for a kiss...

Power down, Guthrie.

She tilted her face slightly, which only made the whole kiss scenario flare in his mind and his blood heat again. "You have a cat?"

He tore his gaze from the softness of her mouth and glanced at the beast. "Came with the ship. Lives here because—Rya, what are you doing in my quarters?" He blurted the last part out, because all this inane talk about the cat was just that: inane. And because for reasons he didn't want to explore, the incident reminded him of when Chaz had slipped into his small cabin on the *Karn* months back, awakening him to ask for his help. "You can't be here for the reason I'd like you to be," he'd quipped to his ex-wife.

He'd almost said that to Rya.

Her attention was on the milk she poured for the cat. "I'm security, sir. You disabled the lock. We've had serious security breaches and a few attempts on your life. It seemed advisable."

Philip grunted. "Would have been nice for Commander Adney to inform me so I didn't end up shooting—" Philip stopped again. Rya was scratching the cat's head, and the beast was actually purring. Purring! And leaning into her hand, eyes half closed.

"Martoni and Commander Adney are still working out formal shift schedules," Rya said, obviously unaware she risked life and limb by touching the beast. She glanced briefly over at him, almost shyly, he thought. Except *shy* wasn't an adjective that came to mind when he thought of Rya the Rebel. "I didn't mean to wake you. I'm usually very good at being silent. I was just surprised by your cat."

"He's not my cat," Philip said. "I'm a light sleeper, especially considering current circumstances."

"Yes, sir. That's why I'm here, sir. You could close your bedroom door if my presence disturbs you."

A lot of "sirs" from someone who had a noticeable lack of them a few hours before.

"Your presence..." He did not want Rya here, closed door or not. "I don't need a bodyguard."

"Without a lockable door, yes, you do."

"Are you telling me you and Adney found proof we

have stowaways?" He knew they hadn't. He would have been notified long before now if they had.

"No, but—"

"Get some sleep, Lieutenant." He hefted the small L7 as a reminder he wasn't helpless, then used it to point toward the corridor. "And not here."

Rya glared at him. He stepped toward her and straightened because that let him glare down at her. The extra height didn't help, nor did it get her moving for the door. But the movement did put him that much closer to her, and that was a bad, bad idea. A stray curl had escaped from under the edge of her beret and dangled across one eyebrow. Had he not been holding—*clutching*—the L7, he would already be reaching to brush it away, reaching to touch her face...

Cap'n Cory is really going to kick my ass.

"Out, Rya. Now." His voice was harsher than he wanted it to be, but it did the trick. Something flared in her eyes, then she turned.

"I'll be in your office," she said.

That would put two closed doors between them. He would have to live with that. "That's acceptable."

She disappeared into the dark opening, and seconds later he heard the low squeak of his office chair. He crossed his small living room, then palmed the door to the office shut.

He was at his own bedroom door when he heard the muted whoosh of his office door opening in direct defiance. So he climbed into bed, damning Rya Bennton, damning his malfunctioning body and perversely fully functioning libido, damning the Farosians, the Imperials, Tage, oranges, and cats. And knew there was no way he was going to get to sleep wearing those damned drawstring pants.

Which meant there'd be hell to pay tomorrow.

"Black tea," Philip called from the bedroom, in answer to Rya's question about his morning beverage of choice. "If you can coax some from the damned unit."

She could, because she'd already made one for herself and didn't know whether it was the unit's rhythmic thumping that had awakened Philip or if he was simply an early riser. And it was early—0545—but he was awake, which meant she could officially be off her unofficial duty of guarding Philip. With luck she'd catch a few hours' sleep before she was back on duty. On her official duty. Which, she felt sure, would soon include watching after Philip. As soon as Adney and Martoni finalized duty schedules...

She blinked. Her mind was looping. It had been a while since she'd worked a double shift. Stifling a yawn, she retrieved the cup of hot tea from the dispenser and was putting it on the counter when Philip appeared around the corner of the short hallway to his bedroom. He was half dressed, his hair damp and mussed, his gray uniform shirt hanging open, the zipper pull dangling at the halfway point. A frown creased his forehead, lessening when he reached for the tea.

"Mine?"

"Yours." *All yours,* she amended mentally, then chastised herself. *It's just a crush. It'll fade over time.*

He took a sip of his tea, eyeing her from over the rim of the cup.

She eyed him back. His annoyance of last night had apparently faded. Tousled, some of the hardness was gone from his face. He looked younger, approachable. His open shirt revealed a wide stripe of a well-muscled chest that segued into a flat stomach. Approachable, hell. He was goddamned delicious.

Damn. It had better fade over time.

The large white cat materialized at her feet, then launched himself onto the counter with a flick of his black tail. She'd watched him come and go on soft, silent paws all night and twice caught him skulking away with her beret in his mouth. He viewed it as a toy, she assumed. Or perhaps simply wanted something soft to sleep on.

A corner of Philip's mouth quirked up. "Good morning, Captain."

Startled, Rya shot a glance over her shoulder, belatedly remembering no one on board held the rank of captain. Philip was chuckling when she looked back.

"Guess he didn't introduce himself to you last night. Captain Folly, this is Lieutenant Rya Bennton. Also known as Rebel. Subbie, this is Captain Folly. Also known as He Who Shall Be Obeyed."

Captain Folly emitted a raspy meow, then sauntered over to the cabinets against the wall and, as Rya watched in fascination, pawed open a sliding cabinet door.

"I wondered about that," Rya heard Philip say almost under his breath. He pulled a saucer from the cabinet.

"Someone trained him well." She took the saucer from him and tapped the unit's code for cream.

"Or he trained someone, just as he's now trained you and me," Philip answered as she put the saucer in front of the cat. The cat lapped noisily at the thick white liquid. Philip cradled his tea in one hand and turned away from her.

She knew she was being dismissed even before he said, over his shoulder: "I think I can handle things from here, Subbie." He headed for the short hallway to his bedroom.

No, he couldn't in all good conscience handle things from here, with his unlockable quarters and his bad leg and breaches in security that made the hair on the back of her neck stand up every time she thought about it. But Rya was too tired to point those things out and well aware she had an official duty day to face. She snatched her leather jacket from where she'd left it draped across the back of one of his soft chairs, then hit the palm pad. A mischievous, Rya the Rebel impulse seized her. Very sure Admiral Philip Guthrie couldn't see her, she touched her fingers to her lips and blew him a kiss as she backed out the doorway to the corridor.

She had one arm halfway down the sleeve of her jacket when she realized Con Welford was in the corridor. Frowning.

"Hey, Tin Man," she called, using the nickname that either came from an aberration of his first name—people often pronounced it Con*tin*tine—or from his fascination with things metallic and technical. It looked as if Philip wasn't the only early riser. Welford must have just exited the lift. He couldn't have been in the corridor, because then he might have seen . . . No. She felt her face heat. There was no way. She would have known if Welford was there.

Welford stepped toward her, eyes still slightly narrow. "He awake?"

"And on his first cup of tea, yeah." She realized belatedly that hers was still on the counter. Should have brought it with her. She'd need the warmth in her cabin.

"Lots to do today," Welford said, and then he was past her and she was in front of the lift. She pushed Welford's somewhat indifferent tone from her mind. There *was* a lot to do today. And Rya had only an hour or two to catch some sleep before that "lots to do" became part of her problems as well.

"Admiral Guthrie?"

Philip was stripping off the gray shirt with the broken zipper when Con Welford's voice sounded in his quarters. From the volume and slight echo, Philip guessed the lieutenant was probably standing in the doorway between his office and his main salon. Not bothering to restrain his grunt of aggravation with his uncooperative uniform, Philip grabbed another shirt from his closet, then strode—limped quickly, actually—out of his bedroom, shirt in one hand, damned cane in the other.

Con Welford stood exactly where Philip thought he was. "Tell me some good news, Constantine."

Con adjusted the tool belt around his waist as he answered. "Nothing major malfunctioned and no one attacked us in the past five hours."

"Nothing major?" Philip leaned against the back of the padded chair, propping his cane against the chair's broad arm.

"Glitch in enviro. Deck Three's like a polar ice cap."

"Deck Three's always been a polar ice cap." Philip thrust his left arm into his shirtsleeve. "Rya told me our security breach didn't result in any stowaways. Or has that changed?"

"Unless someone recruited an army of midgets and they're hiding in our ventilation ducts, no." Con's tone was light, but Philip noticed the lieutenant wasn't looking at him when he spoke. His interest seemed to be the cabin's small galley.

Philip zipped up his shirt—this one didn't snag halfway—and grabbed his cane. "You want tea, coffee? Don't mind that dish. Rya's spoiling the damned cat."

Something flickered through Con's eyes when Philip said "Rya." Philip wasn't sure the first time he mentioned her name. He was now.

It's none of your damned business, he reminded himself. But it didn't stop him from noticing Con's reaction, and it didn't stop him from wondering what had gone on behind Con's closed cabin door.

"White tea, if it'll make some," Con was saying,

heading for the galley counter. "Mess hall's won't, but yours might."

"Rank, privileges, and all that crap? Help yourself. I left my cup in the bedroom. I'll meet you in my office."

Philip ambled back to his bedroom for his unfinished tea. It was cold. His leg was bothering him more than usual this morning. He hadn't slept well, far too aware that Rya was in the next room even though he no longer heard noises alerting him to her presence. Far too aware he had a derelict ship and insufficient crew that faced problems—and enemies—that could easily overwhelm both those things.

Far too aware that, for the first time in his life, he could be on the losing side.

That people—*his* people—would die was inevitable. He just had to find a way to stave off the inevitable as long as possible and keep the body count to a minimum when options were exhausted.

Hell's fat ass, you're a grim bastard this morning.

He hadn't been fifteen minutes ago when Rya the Rebel stood at his galley counter, offering him tea, her eyes sparkling with something he couldn't quite name and was more than likely imagining.

But that was fifteen minutes ago, and reality kicked in hard about that time. Con Welford showed up as well. It was the start of Day Two on board *Hope's Folly.*

"Other than enviro on Three, we seem to have most of the system glitches under control," Con said, lounging back in the chair across from Philip's desk while Philip perused third shift's reports on his screen.

"Under control but not fixed?"

"Best we can hope for until we hit Ferrin's."

Hope? Hope's folly, he thought but didn't say, and not just because the cat strolled through his office's open door at that moment. But answers and solutions seemed to be more and more tantalizingly out of reach, always around the next bend, at the next port . . .

This was not, he reminded himself as the cat sidled around the back of Con's chair and disappeared into his quarters, the Imperial Fleet with its resources, financial and otherwise.

"Sparks is sure Seth has nothing we can use?" Philip knew the answer but he had to ask. Sparks had a reputation for finding the unfindable.

"Seth has plenty of parts, but they're all civilian or commercial configuration. That's the root of our problems. The fruit guy—"

"Pavyer," Philip put in, aware of the first whiff of oranges now.

"—bastardized the ship's original systems, forcing incompatible military components to integrate with commercial ones. Just enough to get by and just enough to screw up when systems get one hair over basic functional usage. Sparks just keeps shaking his head, but Mather's throwing fits. I'm learning to stay away from him and let him do what needs to be done."

"Plague of the ittle-dos," Philip intoned, knowing Con was well familiar with Philip's favorite expression denoting substandard work.

"She's not the *Loviti*," Con said, shaking his head.

No, the *Folly* definitely wasn't Philip's pristine former Imperial flagship. Integration wouldn't be a major problem there, because Imperial ship designers had learned a thing or three in the years since the Stryker-class ships had been commissioned. And one of those things was improved replacement-part compatibility. The *Loviti* could filch from the *Nowicki*, if need be. And the *Nowicki* from the *Masling*. Cross-compatibility was now the standard.

"When do we head out for Ferrin's?" Con asked.

Philip rocked back in his chair. "That depends on what Sparks and Dina have to say." It pained him to lie to Con. Damn it all, he trusted the man with his ship, his life . . . well, not with Rya Bennton, but with everything else. But he'd told Adney, and for good reason: *Sparks, you, and I are the only ones who will know our exact departure time.*

And no one included Con Welford.

No, this was not like the *Loviti* at all.

Philip was still reviewing the systems upgrade and repairs report Con left behind when, five minutes later, a noise in the corridor made him raise his gaze from his deskscreen. Dina Adney touched her fingers to her temple in salute.

"You free?" she asked, hesitating in the open doorway.

"No, but my rates are reasonable," he quipped, and when her frown told him his humor was clearly wasted, he motioned to the chair Con had vacated. "Sit. I'm just going over Welford's shopping list."

"Do I have a copy of that?" She was frowning at her datapad now.

"I'll try to send it to you, but in the meantime, feel free to read over my shoulder."

She glanced up, eyes narrowed. Then she sighed, shaking her head.

"Things will be better once we get to Ferrin's," he said, sensing her frustration.

"We need to . . . Admiral, that's something I'd like to discuss with you."

Her tone shifted, tinged with a distant yet distinct formality. Philip could almost feel her physically withdraw.

And there was something else. A hesitancy? Nervousness?

"I spent most of last night thinking about our status and mission," she said.

Well, at least he wasn't the only one who hadn't slept well.

"About this ship," she continued, "our crew situation. The attempts on your life on Kirro and on the shuttle."

"This is war, Dina," he said quietly. "It may not have yet been officially declared so, but it is war."

"We're not prepared for that." Her hands tightened around the datapad's metal casing. "Proceeding now, ill-staffed and ill-equipped as we are, even to Ferrin's, violates every operational rule Fleet—"

"This isn't Fleet."

Something flashed in her dark eyes at his interruption. Anger? Fear? He couldn't tell. He didn't know Dina Adney well enough.

She leaned toward him. "With all due respect, Admiral—"

He definitely didn't like the sound of that.

"—we have uncleared personnel working in sensitive positions and an inadequate physical plant with components Commander Sparkington and Lieutenants Mather and Welford cannot verify. We have no chief medical officer on board. We have no working security cameras. We have no consistent line of communications with other ships in the fleet. We can't even communicate with the crew on *this* ship! And we've yet to have an SOP meeting."

She sat back abruptly.

Standard Operating Procedures? He knew they were necessary, but he hated those policies-and-procedures meetings. He doubted if in this instance having one would greatly solve anything, other than reassuring Adney that they were, indeed, a legitimate fleet.

This was the first time he'd seen Adney so on edge, and he wondered if something had happened third shift that he was yet to become aware of. But then, there were a number of minor crises yesterday, with the systems failures and overly enthusiastic blast doors. Those things kept Adney running.

Last night she'd evidently started thinking, as he had. It sounded as if she wasn't pleased with Philip's first day in command. He—in honest self-appraisal— wasn't either. But he was trying to solve the difficult things first. He'd work on the impossible ones next.

Or so he hoped.

"Suggestions, Commander?" he asked, trying to keep his own frustration out of his voice. Yes, things were worse than either he, Jodey, and obviously Dina Adney had anticipated. But they would not be unsolvable. Eventually.

"Delay departure for Ferrin's until we can fill all critical crew assignments and bring ship's systems up to Fleet standards."

This isn't Fleet, he almost said again but didn't. In Adney's mind, this was still Fleet. A different division, perhaps—a limping, wounded, bedraggled cousin. But Fleet.

He had to remember she'd come off the *Nowicki,* which was already to Fleet standards with crew and captain and equipment. Only allegiances had changed.

The *Folly* . . . A puff of orange-scented air flowed through the vents in silent reminder of what else had changed.

"I understand your concerns," he said, "but Ferrin's is still compiling crew rosters for us. Many, including our CMO, aren't even on station yet. And Seth doesn't have Stryker-class components readily available. You're not dealing with a military shipyard here."

Which raised another problem, more than the fact that this was not a military facility: every day they sat in dock was another day their presence threatened the civilian workers. Philip didn't discount Tage launching a strike force against Seth. Tage could launch one against Ferrin's, but Ferrin's was a military base and it could defend itself far better than Seth could.

"The components at Ferrin's could be shipped here, along with whatever officers and crew *have* been approved for our clearance," Adney insisted. "We could get bids from the long-haulers who work this quadrant. It would mean two, three weeks' delay, but we could use that time to train whatever additional crew we might find on Seth."

"You're talking commercial freighters transporting not only parts but personnel. We'd need at least two P-75s running as security in case Tage or the Farosians decided to intercept. We don't have two P-75s we can pull off Baris jumpgate duty right now, not even with the extra squadrons from Corsau and Dafir filling in the gaps." If Tage pushed an entire phalanx of ships through a critical gate from Baris into Calth, guarding components on their way to Seth would be the least of Philip's problems. The *Folly* wouldn't even be at Seth at that point. She'd be out there, doing whatever she could with whatever she had.

"Umoran Planetary Defense has Ratch fighters and P-33s," Adney countered.

"Which we need here, guarding Seth and this ship. Commander, I hear your concerns," he said, as she opened her mouth for another argument. "Every single one and more paraded through my head last night. I'm looking for answers—and for *better* answers too. You have some good suggestions. I'll consider them. But right now I need to keep Sparks, Welford, and Mather working toward our earliest possible departure for Ferrin's. Unless I see critical reasons not to, that will be in the next thirty-six hours."

He had to get the *Folly* functional and out there before Tage made his next move. If that meant working outside "Fleet-accepted parameters," so be it. He didn't see they had any choice.

And he knew with a sinking feeling, as Adney made her excuses and left his office, hurrying stiff-backed into the corridor, that his second in command didn't share his vision.

His screen pinged. He swiveled, then tapped at the pulsing databox tagged with Seth Security's ID. The communications link opened, and Security Chief Roderiko Hamil's bald-headed image filled part of the screen. The rest held Yardmaster Bahati Delainey's angular face. Both looked troubled, dark eyes narrowed, brows drawn, mouths pinched. Delainey's hands were folded tightly on the tabletop.

Philip's sinking feeling sank even further, plummeting like an overloaded lugger caught helplessly in a sun's gravity well.

"Admiral Guthrie," Chief Hamil said. "Samling just led us to some information that appears to be critical."

Samling. Gilbert Samling, the Farosian agent who, along with Amalia Mirrow, had tried to stuff Philip in a life pod with Nayla Dalby's address on it. Both Mirrow and Samling had been kept in Seth Security custody, as Consul Falkner had yet to authorize an Alliance version of ImpSec or a formal intelligence division to deal with enemy agents. Not that Philip had any personnel to spare for interrogations at the moment.

"I just hope we can react in time," the chief was saying.

"The Farosians intend to move against Seth," Philip guessed grimly.

"Not quite," Hamil said. "The C-Six jumpgate. They know your ship needs to get to Ferrin's to complete a refit. They want you delayed here, if not trapped."

"To attack this ship or kidnap me?"

"Samling's not saying. All we know is it sounds like they've got their Star-Ripper moving in to blow the gate, sometime in the next four hours."

Years of training kept Philip's mouth from dropping open but couldn't stop his body from going rigid. Four *hours*. By hell's fat unholy ass. Even if the *Folly* was fully refitted, bristling with weapons, drives pristine, it would take her two hours to get to the C-6 in time to confront the Farosians. If she didn't, the wrecked jumpgate would load an additional nine shipdays' travel to the *Folly*'s journey to Ferrin's—there was no alternate jumpgate in the old trader data—and disrupt God-only-knew-what incoming supplies to an already battered section of Calth and, from there, into Dafir and Narfial.

Something the Farosians obviously knew. They wanted the *Folly* on the slower route, where they could launch attack after attack on her or draw her into an ambush. And they wanted to hamper any incoming help.

"I need to determine where our closest resources are," Philip said, damning the fact he couldn't raise the *Nowicki* on a simultaneous link. Maybe Jodey had pulled in O'Neil's P-75. Maybe he could get her and a couple of P-40s from Calth 9 out here in time—if that would even be enough firepower. All the *Folly* had at this juncture were her laser banks and two—as Sparks liked to remind him—heavy-duty tow fields. But, as Adney had pointed out, the UPD had ships. "You've alerted Umoran Defense?"

"Lieutenant Kamau is making them aware of the information as I'm talking to you. They have their 33s and Ratch fighters. We have two 33s ready to deploy on your signal. I don't know if that's enough to stop a Star-Ripper, but that's not our only problem." Hamil turned to Yardmaster Delainey with a nod.

"We've been alerted that a hospital ship is on top priority incoming," she said. "They report a serious internal systems' malfunction. If they can't make it to the yards, more than fifty of their critical patients will die—including two of Consul Falkner's top aides, who were on Corsau when the Empire attacked. The ship's scheduled to exit the C-Six. They have no idea they'll be facing a Farosian Star-Ripper when they come through jump. And we have no way to warn them."

An admiral doesn't make excuses. An admiral doesn't explain. An admiral acts.

Sparks was the last to arrive in Philip's office, ruddy face slightly redder than usual. "Damned lifts," he murmured, slightly out of breath as he took the open chair next to Con Welford in front of Philip's desk. Con and Sparks exchanged glances. Con shrugged.

"Seal the door, Subbie," Philip told Rya. He stood behind his desk, fisted hands resting lightly against the top, and didn't miss how Con's glance now flicked to Rya and away again as she pushed off the bulkhead.

Worry about it later. Philip, tight-lipped, let his gaze

wander over Dina Adney, then Con, Sparks, and finally back to Rya, catching a twitch of movement by
her feet. The large white and black cat had ghosted in
from the corridor just before the doors closed. The
beast plodded softly behind her as she returned to her
place against the bulkhead, next to the already closed
door to his quarters.

Adney, Con, Sparks, Bennton: the newly expanded
list of the only four people on board the *Folly* he could
risk trusting with his plans. Each represented a key position: command, helm, engineering, and security. If
need be, he'd handle weapons himself. He knew Adney
trusted Mather at communications, as Jodey had.

"What I'm going to tell you now doesn't leave this
room. This ship breaks dock—*must* break dock—in
forty-five minutes." His voice was low, deep, and allowed for no argument.

Adney, as expected, had one. "With all due respect,
Admiral, forty—"

He cut her off and gave a succinct recap of what
Hamil and Delainey had told him. A Farosian Star-
Ripper. A crippled hospital ship with VIP patients. A
move to hamper Falkner's government; a move to
make the *Folly* and the Alliance Fleet do the Farosians'
bidding on the Farosians' timetable.

He'd be thrice damned if he'd cooperate. There
would be no discussion on the matter. The Star-
Ripper's ETA at the gate's vicinity was in less than
three and a half hours.

They must be moving in forty-five minutes.

"Delainey is going to engineer a power failure at our
docking clamps," he told them as Adney leaned forward and started to speak. He could guess at her question: how could the *Folly*, in her current state of
disrepair, possibly take on a heavily armed Star-

Ripper? He would get to that. But first: "As far as any-one on dock, in the yard, or on this ship is concerned, we're simply relocating to another berth in the yard."

He looked squarely at Adney. "Adney, you're going to have to take the brunt of crew confusion until I give the all-clear. It won't be long. Chief Hamil will have his people on the docks watching for any unusual reac-tion. Once I'm sure no one's hijacking a Ratch fighter and coming after us, I'll issue general orders over intra-ship, providing it's working."

"Mather confirmed it's fixed," Con said.

"Sparks, I'm going to need those sublights cranking to max on very short notice."

"The drives are one of the few things on this ship I have no worries about."

"Constantine, helm will have the only true course coordinates. Can you rig nav to read something else?"

"In forty minutes? No, sir." Con shook his head. "But I can blank their screens temporarily. Just another glitch, you know." He shrugged. "Since we're suppos-edly only going to the other side of the shipyard, it won't worry anyone. At least not until we're hitting the lanes."

"Do it." Philip faced Rya, the member of his im-promptu team who had the least amount of experi-ence, who probably surprised the others by her presence here in the admiral's office. Hell, it surprised him, if he was perfectly honest about it. She was a nugget, a novice, her few years in ImpSec notwith-standing.

But she was ImpSec trained. And she was Cory's daughter. He ... trusted her, beyond any fully rational explanation. He connected with Rya—and he knew he did, even if that admission scared him—on a very dif-ferent level. Looking at her now, her eyes bright and clear, a slight flush on her face, a shine in the haphazard curls tumbling from beneath her dark service beret . . . Looking at her now he was aware of every one of the sixteen years that separated them.

But the moment she moved, spoke, questioned him, challenged him, made him think, made him laugh, those years disappeared and they *connected*.

That almost scared him more than the Farosians and their weapons-laden Star-Ripper.

"Bennton," he said, watching a spark light in her eyes, feeling a corresponding lurch in his own heart. "I have to assume we have moles on board, and I have to assume the ship's movement is going to force their hand. Someone may try to take the bridge. Or someone may try to send a message off ship, warning the Farosians what we're doing. Welford and Commander Adney can try to monitor any outgoing communications. We might not be able to stop it—"

"If I catch it in time, maybe," Con put in.

"—but we will be aware of it. The first problem, though, is all yours."

She nodded, a curl falling into her eyes. She brushed it away with a crisp movement. "First, shut down the lifts. They're malfunctioning, anyway."

Sparks snorted.

"That means anyone coming to take the bridge has to take the forward stairs. We'll hear them coming. Second, shut the blast doors in the crew and mess areas on Three and Four. People aren't going to like being trapped, but it will be for only a short period of time." She angled her head at Con Welford. "Can you or Sparks do that? Another malfunction?"

"A ship runs blast-door safety tests all the time," Con said. "We just announce a test commencing at that specific time, and the crew will kick back and wait it out."

"That will leave only bridge crew and whoever is in divisionals on Two Aft to worry about," she said. "But divisionals would have to go down to Three to come up to the bridge. Not a huge delay, but it buys us a little more secure time."

Adney shifted in her seat. Still not happy, Philip noticed. His executive officer held her datapad in a choking grip. And she was staring at Rya, her expression almost bitter. Did Rya have a run-in with Adney? He made a mental note to ask his XO later.

"I'm concerned about engineering." Rya took a step toward Sparks. "The bridge isn't the only vulnerable area if we have a mole on board who wants to stop us."

"Most of the crew will be contained on Three or Four," Sparks said. "I can run my drives for a short time with only Kagdan, Vauge, and Dillon. And trust me, Lieutenant Bennton. I'm one damned good shot with a Carver. My team will take down anyone I miss."

Philip knew Sparks trusted those three. He wasn't sure right now that was good enough insurance. "Sparks—"

"Hear you loud and clear, Admiral. They know security is tight and why, just like everyone else on this ship does. Kirro Station. And that's all they're going to know until you tell me otherwise."

"Admiral." Adney sat forward stiffly, as if pushed by some invisible force. It was clear she wanted to be heard now, not even giving Philip a chance to respond to Sparks's comment. "I must respectfully voice my dissent. Restricting the crew. Threatening to shoot them." She glanced quickly at Rya. "Then proceeding under such conditions in a ship with no defenses. You can't seriously think we can win in a firefight with a Star-Ripper?"

Philip leaned forward also, bracing his hands on the top of his desk. "We're not going to engage the Farosians in a firefight, Commander Adney. That's exactly what they're expecting us to do. And that's the very reason I have no intention of doing it."

11

At departure-minus-fifteen, Rya tracked Philip down in his office. He hadn't been there five minutes earlier. She'd checked. But he was here now, leaning over his deskscreen, frowning. He straightened as she stepped through the open doorway, one eyebrow arching slightly.

"Lieutenant Bennton?" Her name was both a question and an acknowledgment that the mode was business. "Subbie" had a friendlier tone. And when he called her "Rebel," parts of her positively overheated.

Not the time to think of that now. This was business. Shortly, the *Folly* would be on its way. Step one, as far as Rya was concerned, in the downfall of the Empire.

"I have to assume we could face a challenge before we reach the gate," she said without any preliminaries, because there was no time for them. "I have my Stinger and an L7. I know you carry an L7 and your Carver. But if we have enemy operatives on board or if another ship gains access, I don't want to have them between me up there," she pointed to the bridge deck above, "and that Norlack down here."

For the briefest of moments, the narrowed blue eyes widened, and for the briefest of moments, the mouth that was a tight line quirked slightly. She wondered if Adney had spoken to him, warning him about Lieutenant Bennton's overzealous ImpSec tendencies. But then he nodded. "Agreed," he said, much to her relief. "Come."

She followed him through his quarters' main salon and into his bedroom, forcing herself to halt in the doorway of the small room. It *was* small. Philip was a big man and she was no lightweight. And then there was the bed . . .

She stepped back while he tapped open a locked cabinet.

"Just so you know," he said, hefting the Norlack in one hand, "there's more to me than an L7, the Carver, and this Norlack." He lowered the rifle, thumping the tip of the barrel against his right ankle. "Sonic knife here. Mini-pulser on the other." He was grinning now. Commander Adney and Welford would probably be appalled. "And—"

"Core pulser or a Ninety-seven?"

"Slasher Five. And—"

"Damn!" A Slasher 5 pulser was fine, totally apex. Way beyond her budget. She'd fired one only a few times during a special training session in the academy.

"And . . ." He tossed the Norlack on his bed, then twisted slightly, turning his back to her as he tugged at his shirt. Something thin and silvery glinted at her from above the edge of his belt and waistband. She moved toward him, curious, drawn by the object she couldn't quite recognize, but it just might be—

"Hot holy damn!"

He palmed the octagonal-shaped weapon with a

practiced ease, swiveling back to her. She could have sworn his eyes twinkled. "You've seen one before?"

"A plasma star? Only in vids and tech demos." The star had multiple firing ports segued through a sophisticated targeting sensor. It could be tossed into a room or launched into a crowd of attackers with silent but deadly consequences. And without puncturing ship bulkheads—something a Norlack was prone to do. Hot holy damn, indeed.

"If we ever get a spare moment, I'll train you on the other one. Sparks brought me two." Philip returned the star to the back of his pants and was tucking his shirt in, so he missed the mixture of joy and incredulity that flashed over Rya's face. She felt her cheeks heat and her breath catch in her throat. If they had time, he would, he would . . .

"Oh, God, I'd love that," she managed to choke out.

He faced her. They were inches apart, very small inches in a very small bedroom that was suddenly getting smaller. His grin softened to a smile, and his smile softened to something she couldn't read. The twinkle in his eyes faded, his gaze becoming focused yet searching, almost as if . . .

She closed the short distance between them with a step because the ache in her body told her it was the only answer to the sweet pain that started whenever he was near. She breathed in the warm clean scent of him, a mix of soap and cotton and male tinged with the sharp, familiar tang of gunmetal and the muskier odor of leather from his holster and weapons belt. All this was Philip Guthrie, and she'd known it from the moment he'd leaned on her in the shuttle's rampway and rested against her in the shuttle's passageway. Then on the *Folly* they'd become distant, except for their brief shared captivity in the ready room. She hadn't realized how much she'd missed him. How much she craved him.

Something between a sigh and a groan rumbled in his throat. She knew they had only minutes, if not mere moments, before they were part of a mission on which they all could die far too easily. His gaze seemed to search her face. She wanted to be the answer he was seeking.

"Philip." His name came out on the breath of a whisper.

Surprise flickered over his face, his lips parting, and Rya didn't know which one of them closed that last inch, but someone did. She tilted her face to meet his, felt the warmth of his breath against her skin, then the strong yet gentle pressure of his fingers against her jaw. His touch sent her pulse racing. She leaned into his hand, then edged her body against his, splaying her fingers across his shirtfront. Through half-lowered lashes she watched the most incredible blue eyes darken.

His voice was hoarse. "Rya—"

Footsteps sounded behind her. Then a man called out: "Admiral Guthrie?"

Philip jerked back, leaving Rya chilled and confused, until the fact the Con Welford was coming toward them—*her and Philip, together, in his bedroom*—registered with alarm in the part of her brain that still worked.

She had to make it look like she and Philip were doing anything but what they'd been about to do. She snatched the Norlack from the bed and spun toward the door just as a dark shadow filled the short hallway beyond. Then she was staring at Welford, and Welford was staring at her. Hard. His gaze traveled over her shoulder, his eyes narrowing.

"You looking to raid my weapons stash too, Welford?" Philip's light drawl held none of the breathless excitement it had seconds before. Her own heart still pounded, and she hoped Welford's focus on Philip missed that fact, as well as the flush she still could feel on her face.

"Sorry. Your office door was open. I thought . . . that is . . ." Welford's voice trailed off. He cleared his throat.

"My office door's always open," Philip said easily. "And if this damned bucket had a damned weapons locker in the ready room like it should, I wouldn't be forced to arm this ship's chief of security in my own quarters. Now, if you'll give me a minute to lock this, I'll meet you back in my office so we can deal with the latest crisis at hand before we have to face the Farosians."

Welford nodded stiffly. "Yes, sir." He disappeared back into the hallway, his heavy footsteps quicker this time.

Rya heard the snick of a lock latching into place. She turned, still gripping the Norlack with sweaty hands, her heart still pounding, and found nothing of the man who'd so tenderly touched her face—almost kissed her—in the demeanor of the officer standing stiffly, his right hand resting on his cane.

"Lieutenant Bennton." His voice low and devoid of emotion. "That cannot—*will not*—ever happen again. You have my abject apologies. Now, if you'll excuse me, I have a crisis that demands my attention."

She stepped back as he strode past her, his uneven footsteps fading as Welford's had. Only when her arms started to tremble did she realize that she clutched the Norlack against her chest and that she stood alone in a cold and small bedroom, feeling confused and bereft.

And rejected.

Damn you, don't apologize for wanting me the way I want you! She fought the urge to scream at him, but he was no longer there. Only—

Sweet holy God. Her brain replayed his earlier words.

He'd named her as the *Folly*'s chief of security.

That took some of the sting out of his rejection, but not quite. Especially as she couldn't discount his reasons behind it. Placating her? She could almost hear Matt's voice chiding her: *You're a nice kid, Rya, but not remotely worthy of a man like Admiral Philip Guthrie.*

She looped the Norlack's strap over one shoulder and marched out of his quarters and into the corridor. She might be too tall, too curvy, and have hair that definitely had a mind of its own, but she *was* Rya Taylor Bennton. She would be the best damned chief of security he ever had. And that, she hoped, would count for something with a man like Admiral Philip Guthrie.

It might even allow her a small inroad into his heart.

Philip Guthrie, you are a galactic-class ass. That litany kept surfacing in Philip's mind as he listened to Con outline how he'd worked up a glitch that would temporarily take the bridge's navigational screens off line while he altered the *Folly*'s course for the C-6 jumpgate. That would keep their actions secret and secure— for about four and a half minutes. But only on the bridge.

"I can't get the bridge's computers to accept the glitch program as long as the auxiliary bridge is on standby," Con said. "Since the screens are mirrored to us, it will show nav's controls working off my station. And they shouldn't be."

You are really, really a galactic-class ass. You lost Chaz because every time she breached your emotional wall, you shut down. It was always business, always duty—

"No one should be in auxiliary," Philip replied.

"Unless he's an Imperial or Farosian agent, which is exactly where he'd be if he got wind this ship's on the move. And he or she would know we're not heading to a new berth."

Philip—the galactic-class ass—had no argument for that. Nor could he forgot the hurt that flared in Rya's eyes when he made his brusque apology for wanting to kiss her so badly he was barely able to think straight. He had no idea how he was able to deflect Con's suspicion about what was going on—or was about to go on. From some of the glances his officer had leveled at him since coming into the office, Philip wasn't fully sure he had. "Deck Five's a long way down with the lifts inoperative. To be safe, include it in the blast-door tests. Lock the auxiliary bridge in."

"You're locking Sparks in too if you do that."

Damn, damn! Philip pursed his lips and fought the urge to massage the growing ache between his eyes.

"The only thing I can do," Con continued, "is take the auxiliary bridge completely off line, but that will put us in a world of hurt if we lose the main bridge. We'd have to get someone down there to physically bring systems back up. But I can't control the nav screens any other way."

Philip glanced at the time stamp on his deskscreen. Less than ten minutes until Delainey shut off power to the ship's docking clamps. "Do it. I'll take responsibility if things go wrong."

"Aye, sir." Con rose, glanced over his shoulder as if

to turn for the door, then stopped. "One more thing, sir. Lieutenant Bennton."

Rya. Con had seen or heard something or just had known Philip long enough to recognize when his CO was rattled. And rattled Philip was, not only by his reaction to Rya but by what had caught him fully off guard—her response to him. She'd leaned into his touch, every inch of her pressing against him, sending a message that he didn't have the strength to say no to, that he didn't want to say no to. *She's Cory's daughter* warred in his mind with *but she's also a grown woman.* Definitely grown up in all the right places.

Power down, Guthrie. He blanked his face of any expression. "Yes?"

Con hesitated, choosing his words carefully, Philip guessed. He was still the Old Man, the Great Guthrie. *The galactic-class ass.*

"I didn't know you and Commander Adney had decided to promote her to chief of security."

"It wasn't Adney's decision. It was mine."

Con studied him, something shifting across his features, causing his mouth to tighten ever so slightly. "I understand, sir. But I've been going over personnel assignments with Commander Adney, and she has reservations about Bennton."

"I know she's young. But she's ImpSec trained, Constantine. ImpSec Special Protection Service."

"They're trained as bodyguards and assassins, sir, not ship security."

He knew ImpSec's reputation as well as Con did. In his opinion, it was partly deserved and partly overrated. "In our current situation, that might come in handy. She's also worked undercover and as a cop. She can think on her feet and make decisions under pressure. She can handle just about any weapon you throw at her. And she's a Bennton. She may not have logged a lot of time in the lanes, but it's in her blood." He paused. "I trust her."

"I'm sure you do, sir."

Too many "sirs" now, even from Constantine Welford. "Anything else?"

"No, sir."

"Then I'll see you on the bridge in five."

Con saluted, then ducked through the open door and into the corridor.

Philip stared at his blank deskscreen for a moment, then shoved himself to his feet, grabbing for his cane. If he lived through this—a confrontation with a Farosian Star-Ripper on a ship with limited defenses, the possibility of sabotage by Farosian and Imperial agents on a ship with limited security, and a desperate flight through a jumpgate on a ship with a plethora of non-working systems—if he lived through all this, he might just use his damned cane to beat himself senseless.

But until that time, he had a job to do. And he'd be damned if Adney's fears or Con's suspicions were going to stop him from doing it.

"Blast-door tests commencing in one minute." Lieutenant Burnaby Mather's voice rang out over intraship. "All personnel on Decks Three and Four, stand clear. Repeat, stand clear. Forty seconds to—"

A screech and a hiss sounded through the overheads.

"What the—" Mather rose partly out of his seat at communications on Philip's left and jabbed angrily at his console. "I swear I fixed this. This isn't supposed to . . . Wait. Got something."

He cupped one hand over the comm set ringing his

right ear. "Seth Shipyards for you, Admiral. Yardmaster Delainey. I'll put her through on...Damn it. The only thing working is private channel. I'll put her through to you via that, Admiral."

Philip nodded absently and hooked the small transmitter around his ear. "The yard reports we have power surges coming through the docking clamps," he announced to the bridge after a few moments during which he and Delainey went through their rehearsed ruse. "Seth Yard apologizes, but they've had the same problems with this berth before. They're clearing us to move to"—he hesitated, listening for Delainey's confirmation. Everything appeared to be a go—"Seven Five One C."

Adney was already at the XO's console on Philip's left, tapping out the prearranged information to Sparks. "Commander Sparkington acknowledges. We'll have maneuvering sublight power in about twenty—"

The deck vibrated slightly.

"Make that ten seconds."

"Nav screens are dead, sir!" someone called out.

"I'm on it," Con answered. "It's the surges, frying our signals. Don't worry, boys and girls. The admiral and I can hand-fly this beast. We've done it before."

They had, on the *Loviti*, but that had been with the rest of the crew standing by, ready to help. Right now, it was just Philip and Con—and who knew which one of his crew trying to stop them.

The *Folly* disengaged from her berth with a rumbling shudder. Dina Adney pushed away from her station and paced, frowning, over to engineering on Philip's right. Behind him stood Rya the Rebel, Norlack slung across her back, the safety off her Stinger. He hadn't looked at her in ten minutes, but he could feel her there—a bright, warm glow with dark, angry eyes. They hadn't exchanged any words since he came on the bridge; they'd barely exchanged glances. But he knew without a doubt that although she probably itched to smack him across the back of his head for his abrupt dismissal of her in his quarters, she was watching his back and would put herself between him and any attacker.

He wondered who would protect his heart.

"Communications coming back online," Mather announced. "Must have been that faulty interface." He shook his head, clearly still perplexed, not knowing Welford's tampering was behind it all.

"Plague of the ittle-doos," Philip intoned, watching Con edge the *Folly* away from shipyards in orbit above Seth and toward the lanes. He checked traffic in the lanes. Delainey had cleared them a path. Good.

"Nav screens are still out."

"Countering for that interference," Con said, his concentration on his screens, his fingers rapidly tapping course adjustments on his console. And more.

At the four-minute mark, Philip knew it was time. "Mr. Mather, open intraship."

"Not sure it's operational yet, sir."

"It is. Trust me."

Mather shot him a puzzled glance over his right shoulder. Then the lights on Philip's console flashed to life. He adjusted the comm set around his ear, then keyed the microphone. "All hands, this is Admiral Guthrie. We are not, as you will shortly surmise, on our way to another berth at the shipyards. We are under way to our first mission as part of the Alliance Fleet..."

He swiveled his chair a quarter turn as he continued with the short briefing. Rya stood in the bridge's wide doorway, her back to engineering, her narrowed gaze sweeping the various stations on the bridge, then back to the corridor.

If they—whoever they were—were going to make a move, it would start now.

He glanced at his console. Blast doors still sealed off Decks 3 and 4. He'd have to release the crew soon, but he needed a few more minutes of safety, of certainty. Of, if nothing else, a narrowing down of numbers.

If one of his bridge staff was an enemy agent, his next announcement could well force him or her to act.

"A Farosian Star-Ripper intends to shut down the jumpgate at the C-Six to prevent us from reaching Ferrin's. This act, if accomplished, will also doom a hospital ship in transit—a ship with key Alliance government personnel on board. It's our job to make sure that doesn't happen.

"This is our first test, ladies and gentleman. It's one we cannot fail. Guthrie out."

Ship's systems flickered to life, those screens that worked flashing on. Somewhere two decks below Rya's boots, the blast doors rumbled open—though she couldn't hear them. She glanced at Con Welford, glanced at Philip when she thought he wouldn't catch her doing so, and saw identical patterns of movement on their two consoles. Philip and Welford had been in total control of the ship but were releasing that control, system by system, deck by deck.

They were now fifteen minutes out from station, fully in the lanes, with the sublights cranked to max, if the thrumming under her boots told her anything. The forward viewscreens told her two P-33s were running escort port and starboard.

Rya raked the bridge with a quick but thorough

appraisal again, ears alert to any noises behind her. A range of expressions played over the features of the gray-uniformed bridge crew she could see: excitement, curiosity, concern. Others whose faces she couldn't see betrayed themselves with a quick tapping of one foot or a nervous jostling of a knee.

Dina Adney stood stick-straight at her console, mouth pursed as if tasting something unpleasant. *If I nudged her, she'd snap in half,* Rya thought absently. Then a low whining noise behind her jerked her attention from Adney.

Rya spun around just as a low thud reverberated through the bulkheads. The ship lurched, hard. She fell to one knee, left hand bracing her fall. Her pulse rate spiked. Her right hand yanked out her Stinger. Pain lanced her wrist and leg as her mind grabbed for answers. An explosion? Had they hit something?

"Damage control, status!" Philip's voice boomed behind her, over the grunts and cries of surprise on the bridge. Lights flickered as Rya pulled herself to her feet. With a quick motion, she tapped on her handbeam, letting it dangle from her weapons belt. Insurance. She did not want to face an intruder in the dim green glow of the emergency lights.

She swept the corridor with her Stinger. Empty. She turned back to the bridge, bracing herself against the nonfunctioning security console on her right, the Norlack digging into her back, as the ship shuddered again. She had no way of providing answers with no security sensors to relay data and no security cams to provide an immediate visual report.

Philip was still in the command chair, his screen alive with data. Adney was pulling herself off the floor, as were several other crew. Welford clutched his console, tapping in commands with a focused fury.

"Hull secure," Adney called out. She leaned over her console, her uniform shirt slightly twisted. One screen scrolled with data, one blinked on and off. Two others were dark. "Shields at full. Enviro working on all decks."

Rya sniffed, her throat catching. Her gut seized. She knew that smell. She whipped around, saw the first tendrils of gray haze sliding through the lift doors at the end of the corridor. "Fire! Lift bays one and two. Engage fire systems, now!"

She raced for the emergency-gear locker in the corridor. The suppression systems should have kicked on automatically, just like they always had on every station she'd worked on. The fact that she was seeing and smelling smoke—and hearing no alarms—told her they hadn't.

She holstered her Stinger and slammed open the locker as Philip's voice called, "Battle stations!" over intraship. An alarm wailed loudly, accompanied by Adney's voice detailing the location of the fire. Eyes stinging, Rya pulled out a compressed-air breather mask and shoved it over her face. Hands appeared at her side—two crew from navigation. She pushed containers of breathers into their arms. "Go! Guthrie first." Her voice sounded eerily hollow through the respirator.

A third crew member pounded by her, squat fire extinguisher in her hands. A temporary measure at best. Why in hell hadn't the fire systems kicked on?

"Seal the bridge!" someone shouted.

They couldn't do that. The blast doors wouldn't work on this level or the one below. Philip had ordered Sparks to disconnect them—an argument Rya had lost. Now they could well lose their lives.

She sprinted the short distance back to the bridge, a quick glance confirming that everyone hunched over consoles or hefting emergency gear—including Philip—had a wide, clear mask covering eyes, nose, and mouth. Philip was no longer in the command chair but stood at engineering, cane on his left. Adney stood on his right. Damage-control screens flashed images and data.

He angled around as she came up behind him.

"Suppression systems?" she asked, because the smoke was thicker and it shouldn't be.

"Malfunctioning." Determination and something else mixed in his eyes, shielded by the mask. "By accident or design, we don't know yet. Damage control is on it. You have permission to tell me you told me so about the blast doors. Later."

She stared at him, only half-hearing his grim attempt at levity. Suppression-system malfunctioning. Something her father had shown her on the schematics, something about the goddamned design of a Stryker—

She grabbed Philip's arm. "There's an override in the maintenance tunnel in the forward stairwell. It's a clean-out that doubles back through the fire-suppression lines. It drove my father crazy because it bypassed the main computers and had to be manually—"

"Welford!" Philip's voice bellowed out through his mask. "Rya says there's a manual override right here. Get with her. Tell Sparks!"

But Rya was already moving back to the corridor, her father's words echoing in her head. She could see the schematics on his home deskscreen, the ship's sections he wanted redesigned highlighted in yellow. But he had moved on to better ships before those changes were made.

She knew exactly where they were, exactly what she

needed to do. Into the maintenance tunnel from a panel in the ready room and then down. But the tunnel bordered the lift shaft and the fire. It would be hugely risky getting in.

It could be fatal if she couldn't get out.

12

Philip had never hated his damaged leg, his rank of admiral, and his goddamned understaffed and antiquated ship more than he did at that moment, as Rya disappeared into the thickening gray haze. "Go with her!" he ordered Con, who was already rising from his seat. "I'll sit helm." And handle everything else he and Con did on this goddamned understaffed and antiquated ship.

He had no idea what Rya was going to do—no, he did, and that scared the life out of him—but every inch of him wanted to be by her side when she did it. He couldn't be. His injuries notwithstanding, he couldn't leave his post. Frustration threatened to choke him.

She was Cory's daughter. Risking her just after losing Cory set his teeth on edge. But more than that, she was Rya. If anything happened to her, it would affect him in ways he didn't want to contemplate and couldn't rationally explain.

He lunged back to the command chair and hit intra-ship's icon for engineering. "Sparks, keep us moving."

He had an Alliance hospital ship on a collision course with a Farosian Star-Ripper and a fire on board.

God-fucking-damn it all!

"Adney, damage report!"

"I'm trying!" Her voice was shrill. Or maybe it was the damned breather mask. He angled around to face her as she continued: "The fire seems to be contained between Decks One and Two Forward, but comp systems aren't responding on Deck Four crew's quarters. I can't . . . There's no data. I—damn it!"

He concurred. They were damned, indeed. "Where's Martoni?"

"Divisionals. I think," she said, without looking up from her console.

"Dina, don't waste time trying to pinpoint him." A beep from Philip's screen drew his attention. He adjusted course, saw a minor shield fluctuation, countered for that. The fire was his immediate concern, but that Star-Ripper was less than three hours away. "Get on intraship. Get Martoni down to Crew Four, find out what's going on."

She raised her face. "But security procedures state—"

"*Now*, Dina!"

She hunched back over her console, then seconds later her voice sounded on intraship, ordering Martoni to take a team to Crew 4.

A damage-control team, including that ponytailed officer Sparks had brought on board, swarmed onto the bridge through the ready room just as the blast doors slid shut behind them.

"Sparks reactivated the blast doors here, sir," the officer told him, a light, clipped accent obvious in his words. *Dillon*, Philip remembered. "If we can't get the fire under control, he wants to try blowing holes at the top of the shafts. We're worried about the effects of the decompression on these two decks. The shafts aren't sealed like a bay. Sir."

Space was an airless vacuum. It would extinguish a fire that fed on oxygen, but they could lose not only the lifts but the forward stairwells, the corridors, the maintenance tunnels behind the bulkheads where even now...

"Rya—Bennton and Welford are in the tunnel, working on the fire system's manual overrides." Philip rose out of his chair, grasping his cane. "Do not, I repeat, do *not* try anything until we're very sure they're out of harm's way."

"Sparks recommends evacuating the bridge as a precaution," Dillon said. "The auxiliary bridge—"

"Is off line," Philip replied grimly. He was standing. He never liked sitting in the command chair. It left him feeling trapped, helpless. And he'd never felt quite as helpless as he did right now.

"Off line?" Dillon echoed.

"On my orders. Welford needs to manually reset all the codes." But Con was with Rya, somewhere between here and Deck 2 Forward. No crew-locator system. No security cameras.

"Who else is authorized to reset the codes?"

"I am. But getting down there with this leg and no working lifts will take me a good ten minutes. Another ten to reset." He didn't have Con's skill; his own specialty was always more with weapons and military strategy. And he and Jodey had agreed not to trust anyone other than Con Welford with something as critical as the *Folly*'s primaries until they reached Ferrin's and the requisite fail-safes could be installed.

That included Dina Adney and Burnaby Mather, but he had no choice now. He glanced through the haze and frenzied movement on the bridge. He couldn't spot Mather's burly form at communications. But Adney was at the XO's console as if glued there.

He called her name twice before she turned, and when she did, he didn't like at all what he saw in her eyes. Panic. Wild panic.

Hell's fat ass, don't freeze up on me now, Dina. He motioned her over with a short jerk of his hand.

"Systems aren't responding." Her voice shook even through the breather mask. "I can't raise Creston at Aldan HQ."

He stared at her, hard. Aldan HQ was the Imperial Fleet's central command. And Creston—Admiral Maura Creston—was dead, a casualty of another of Tage's purges. He knew Dina knew that. Or had. "We don't need Aldan," he said carefully. "We need to bring the auxiliary bridge online."

"Online? Isn't it—"

"Welford took it off line on my orders."

"But that's a violation—"

"Damn it, listen to me. Get down there, now, with Dillon." He grabbed a small datapad from Dillon's outstretched hand and typed as he talked. "These are the ship's primaries. You need to do a manual reset, you understand? We need to evacuate the bridge, run the ship from down there until the fire is contained. You need to get those systems online."

"But systems aren't responding! Creston won't answer me. Aldan HQ isn't responding!"

He stared at her for one, two seconds, the hard, ugly reality that his executive officer was in the midst of a mental and emotional collapse hitting him like the back-thrust from a hidden Gritter-10 cannon. And just as much of a surprise. He had no time to deal with this.

And now he had one less officer he could rely on.

"Return to your post, Commander." He didn't want

her there; he didn't want her anywhere near ship's systems. But he had neither time nor the means to get her to sick bay, where the two med-techs on his roster could sedate her. He needed everyone with damage-control experience at a post now. Except—Mather. He could spare the commo long enough to get Adney, his former crewmate, to sick bay. Mather—

Philip glanced quickly around. The communications console was vacant. That would have puzzled him more except for the amount of movement on the bridge. Everyone was trying to help. Then a familiar face flashed in his peripheral vision, somewhat skewed by the edges of the mask. "Holton!" He knew Rya trusted her.

Sachi Holton turned, her own mask glinting under the bridge lights, made harsher by the smoky haze. "Sir?"

"Commander Adney . . . must be relieved of duty, due to medical issues. I don't think she'll try to do anything. Get her to sick bay. She's convinced she needs to contact Admiral Creston—the *late* Admiral Creston." Hell's fat ass, he couldn't believe he was issuing this order. Not here. Not now. And where in hell was Rya?

Holton's dark eyes widened slightly, then she nodded. "Understand, sir. I'll do everything I can to keep her and this ship safe." She hurried over to Adney.

One down, a thousand crises to go.

Where in hell was Rya?

Another bit of movement snagged his attention amid all the bodies coursing about the bridge. A large bit of movement. "Corvang!" he called out. If he had to trust someone, the Takan navigator wasn't a bad candidate. Sparks trusted Dillon, but Corvang carried Jodey's seal of approval. Philip pushed away the thought that Jodey had approved Adney as well. Corvang had delivered Philip's arsenal unscathed and had been exemplary in all other areas since coming on board.

"Sir!"

He thrust the datapad into Corvang's large furred hands. "The auxiliary bridge needs a manual reset. I can't get down there to input ship's primaries. You understand the importance of the data you now hold?"

A quick nod of a long face partly covered by a breather mask. "I will forfeit my life first, sir."

Corvang would. Philip knew that. "Go with Dillon. I need that bridge operational in five minutes. Make it in four and I'll buy you a pot of honeylace at the next port. My treat."

That bribe was answered with a toothy grin. Corvang knew the cost of honeylace as well as he did. "Yes, sir!"

"Secure all stations," Philip called out as Corvang moved away in a blur, with Dillon on his heels. The smoke was thicker, and the crew from damage control didn't seem to be making significant headway. There were lives at risk, more than just Rya's and Con Welford's. He didn't like it, but he had to consider that fact. "Prepare to evacuate the bridge."

There was a moment of tense silence, then a surge of action. Console lights blinked as they accepted commands, then went dark in shutdown.

Corvang earned his honeylace. It was a little over four but less than five minutes when the auxiliary bridge came back online, databoxes winking the connection hot on the two bridge screens still operational: Welford's and Philip's.

One of the last remaining bridge crew came up to Philip as he stood by the command chair.

"Sir, do you need assistance?"

The smoke was so thick Philip couldn't read the man's makeshift name tag.

"Get down to Deck Five. You have work to do."

"Sir?"

"That is an order."

Where in hell was Rya?

Where in hell's that shutoff valve? Rya played her handbeam over the tangle of pipes and conduit secured to the walls of the narrow maintenance tunnel. It was fifteen minutes since she'd dashed off the bridge, and Con Welford had helped her remove a large section of the ready-room bulkhead. Welford was now a dozen feet if not more behind her. He couldn't fit in this tunnel, his broad shoulders threatening to rip the conduit and feed lines from the walls. She barely could and, crawling on all fours, had snagged her pants and belt on more things than she cared to count as she'd scooched, wiggled, and shoved her way toward her goal.

The heat from the fire in the lift shafts had her sweating, rivulets running into her eyes, making them sting. She blinked rapidly—all she could do with the mask over her face. Her shirt lay against her skin like a hot, damp blanket.

She had to find the override valves. That thought made her push on past the pain, past the fear. It wasn't just saving lives. It wasn't just the mission. It was everything. Philip was right when he'd cautioned her on the shuttle about knowing her priorities. Anything that hampered the *Folly* hampered the Alliance. And only the Alliance could take on the Empire and take down Tage.

If not for Tage, her father would still be alive.

Light flashed dimly in front of her. Two bursts of light from a handbeam. A prearranged signal to get her attention. Then, Welford's voice: "You okay, Bennton?"

She lifted her mask quickly. "Delightful," she shouted back. "Having a wonderful time. Wish you were here." She pulled the mask down, the taste of the smoke acrid against her tongue, and shoved away the thought that Welford couldn't get in here if she needed help. She had to find that—

There. Had to be. A clear box of what was probably durocrylic covered a series of flip-tab valves. She'd seen similar configurations in the maintenance shafts of Calth 9. She pulled on the cover. It was stuck.

Shit. She angled her mask up. "Think I found it!"

Mask in place again, she propped her handbeam against a wide pipe, then fished in her utility belt for her small tool kit. She needed something to dig under the edge of the cover.

She opted for a manual screwdriver, not a sonic one. She couldn't chance what the vibrations would do to the valves. She lay on her side in the tunnel's narrow confines and shoved the screwdriver against one edge. Her hands were slick with sweat. Twice she lost her grip, the screwdriver spinning out of her fingers. She groped for it against the rapidly heating decking beneath her.

And she swore, volubly, with every expression she'd ever heard in her almost thirty years.

"Rya!"

A man's voice—Welford's? It sounded different now, probably because of his mask—interrupted her litany of maledictions. She nearly had the box pried off. She gritted her teeth, closing her eyes for a moment. What did he want? She was doing all she could, and it was so slagging hot in here, hell would seem downright frigid after this.

"Almost there!" she shouted back, not bothering to lift her mask. She didn't want to let go of the pressure she had on the screwdriver.

"Rya, get out. Now! Bridge is evacuated!"

Fuck. That meant the fire had spread, bad. Something she could have guessed from the blistering heat around her. She yanked on the screwdriver. "Few more seconds!"

She had no idea if he heard her through the mask. It didn't matter. She could feel the cover giving way, cracking, splintering—

The lower half sheared off with a hard snap. Her screwdriver flew from her fingers, disappearing somewhere in the tunnel. She didn't know, she didn't care. She shoved her hand under the broken cover, scraping her knuckles raw, and shoved the valve tabs down, one by one. That had to release the fire-suppression system. That had to flood the lifts with chemical foam from one system and possibly—she couldn't remember—water or some other nontoxic suppressant from the other.

There was a sprinkler outlet just over her head. She cupped her hand around it, waiting for the burst of whatever would come out, praying it wouldn't peel the clothes off her body or the skin off her bones.

Nothing. Nothing happened.

Her heart pounded. Her teeth ached from clenching them. She wanted to scream. The *Folly* was going to lose the bridge, maybe Deck 2 Forward.

The Alliance would lose a ship. No one would stop the Farosians. And Tage—

"Rya, damn you, now!"

Fuck.

She shoved her handbeam back into her belt, then skittered backward, suddenly aware she could see barely inches in front of her face. Heat closed around her. It felt as if her skin glowed. She pushed and shoved like a sand crawler in full reverse, but pipe outcroppings and metal flanges snatched her pants and belt, gouged her shoulders and elbows.

Then strong hands closed around her ankles, and with an "oof!" she found herself flat on her stomach and being dragged, feetfirst, out the darkness of the narrow tunnel and into the equally dark but larger one.

"Damn it, Welford!"

She braced herself for a fall, but he grabbed the waistband of her pants. She was again dragged backward, pushing with the flat of her hands to keep up lest the damned man pull her pants right off.

Then they were out of the tunnel, the thick hazy light in the ready room making her blink and sway on her feet. She staggered against the edge of the open bulkhead panel, turned—

—and was met by a hissing deluge from above. Water, sheets of water, spraying forcefully through the round sprinkler heads, coating her mask, all but blinding her. It soaked her hair, drenched her shirt, slid with a welcome chill down her thighs.

She ripped off her mask, let out a whoop...and found herself crushed, hard, against Philip Guthrie's sopping-wet chest. One arm locked around her waist, the other across her shoulder, his fingers threading up into her hair. Blinking water out of her eyes, she looked up at him. His mask was shoved up over his hair, which was darker now, as wet as her own. She glimpsed a younger Lieutenant Philip Guthrie in the face of Admiral Philip Guthrie. Both looked intensely angry. And she wasn't even launching peas at him.

She released her grasp on her mask. It fell with a thump into the seat of a nearby chair. She curled her hands over his shoulders, just tight enough to let him know that if he let go, she wouldn't.

For three very long, wet seconds they stared at each other, the hissing of the sprinklers and the rapid staccato of the water hitting the table and the decking the only sounds. Then he kissed her. Not gently, not tentatively, not at all the kiss she'd expected in his quarters earlier. There was nothing tender or hesitant in the way his mouth covered hers, expertly parting her lips, which were already opening, already demanding a taste of him. This was a rough kiss, a desperate kiss, a kiss with an almost frenzied passion that made her heart pound, her knees go liquid, and pulsing sensations flare between her thighs.

His tongue stroked, teased hers as he held her tightly against him. She angled her face, bruising his lips as he bruised hers, and shoved her fingers into the short hair at the nape of his neck, wanting more of this exquisite punishment. Not letting him escape if he wanted to.

He broke the kiss, then nuzzled the side of her face. Cold water splattered against her neck, doing little to cool the heat in her body.

His lips touched her ear. "Subbie. We need to talk." His voice went tight, serious.

She could feel the rapid rise and fall of his chest. He was breathing hard. So was she.

He stepped back slightly. She straightened, her wet hands sliding to his equally as wet shoulders.

Subbie. He was putting distance between them, and

not just physically. But she wasn't yet ready to let him go.

"This is the damnably worst timing," he said, beads of water dotting his eyebrows and dark lashes, streaking down his face. "I have no right to—"

"How bad is the damage?" She cut him off, heart pounding now for a different reason. She didn't want to hear about his rights. She definitely didn't want to hear his apologies.

"To my sanity? That's shredded." He barked out a short, mirthless laugh and took another step back. Her hands fell from his shoulders.

"Damage to the bridge?" he continued, twisting slightly. He reached for his cane, which lay in a growing puddle on the ready-room table. "The fire was confined to Decks One and Two. For once, the damned layout of this bucket worked in our favor. I don't know if we've lost any main bridge systems, though. I probably should be checking that right now." He ran one hand over his face, and for a moment she was sure he was going to turn for the corridor, head to the bridge. Instead, he studied her through the cascading water for a heartbeat. Two.

"But there's something about impending doom that makes me self-indulgent." He surprised her by stepping closer, raising one hand to her face. Hesitantly, his fingertips skimmed the wet line of her jaw, then pulled away. "We need to talk about this. But—"

"I know." She cut him off in the same way she shut down her hopes. She could hear what was coming in the firmer tone of his voice, in the way his touch disappeared as quickly as it had appeared. "You have a crisis that demands your attention. Mine too." But she did not want her crisis to be one of the heart.

They had enough problems with the cleanup of the bridge and getting the ship functional again. Then stopping the Farosian Star-Ripper, getting to the jump-gate. Getting to Ferrin's. A huge task.

But the first step in retaliation on the Empire.

Think about that, she told herself. *Not about being some man's self-indulgence, even if he is your long-lost always-forever dream hero.*

The volume of water cascading down suddenly reduced, the hiss of liquid through the sprinklers quieting. Instead of sheets, it was a lively trickle. She realized the wailing of the alarms had stopped several minutes ago. The fire had to be out.

She spied the dark shape of the Norlack on the seat where she'd left it, under Welford's care. She snagged the weapon. "Where's Welford?" She looped the Norlack's strap over her left shoulder.

Some of the tension slipped from Philip's face. As did the last of the passion. The intensity with which he watched her minutes before was gone. The admiral was fully back in command. "Auxiliary bridge. I gave the order to evacuate."

"The situation was that bad?"

"Worse." His lips tightened. "Commander Adney—"

"Admiral Guthrie?" Footsteps, lots of them, sounded in the corridor, splashing and thudding.

Rya recognized Con Welford's voice.

"Ready room," Philip called out, leaning on his cane as he turned away from her.

Welford strode in, Sachi and Corvang behind him.

Welford's glance—unreadable—raked her.

"We need a basic cleanup here and on the bridge, quickly," Philip said. "I assume you and Sparks have kept us moving toward the C-Six. I need to know what systems aren't working. We can worry about fixing the lifts and any bulkhead damage once we hit jump."

"We have more than that to worry about," Welford said. He jerked his chin toward the tall Takan standing at his side. "Someone made an attempt to take control of this ship using the auxiliary bridge before Corvang got there. Systems were already coming online when he and Dillon arrived."

Rya sucked in a breath, her senses focusing. An Imperial agent on board. Or a Farosian one. After Kirro, she'd expected something, but this was proof.

Philip stiffened noticeably. "Maybe Sparks—"

"No, sir. Dillon checked. Corvang checked. And I double-checked them both. Someone used that fire and a diversion on Deck Four to gain access to the auxiliary bridge. Access *and* entry into this ship's computer systems. Which means that same someone is in possession of this ship's primaries." Welford hesitated, then jerked his chin toward Rya. "Bennton may fulfill her wish to kill someone yet."

The closed-door meeting in Philip's office this time was without Dina Adney. It did include, however, one very wet, very surly cat. Judging from the paw prints on his dining table and now on his office desk, Captain Folly was in Philip's quarters when the sprinklers kicked on in there—though not in Philip's dry office, which was either in a different fire zone or else the sprinklers had malfunctioned. A smart move on the cat's part; the admiral's quarters were double-insulated, shielded, and had a very noisy emergency air recycler, which still groaned and churned through the overhead ducts, removing the acrid tang of smoke that still hung in the air of his office. The drenching was by far the worst thing the cat had suffered.

A smarter move than Philip's maneuver in the maintenance tunnels. He was no longer drenched—he'd changed quickly into a pair of black coveralls before convening this meeting—but his hip ached and his leg throbbed, sending twinges of pain that could easily make him as surly as the cat.

But they'd run out of time to deal with the fire. Sparks had wanted to blow a hole in the hull. Philip had to get Rya out before her impulsive tendencies— he now had some sympathy for the supervisor who had noted that in her personnel file—got them both killed.

Then he made the damned fool mistake of standing far too close to her, feeling the heat of her body, watching the sparkle of success glint in her eyes, watching the cascading water sculpt her uniform to her breasts and thighs. Something primal in him surfaced. He had to brand her, taste her, kiss her. He could write it off as the result of stress, of relief that she was alive and unharmed, but the truth was that kissing her was something he'd wanted to do ever since he saw her on Kirro. Because he knew he shouldn't? That wasn't like him. Because he knew he'd lost Chaz, and this Alliance was poised for failure—and something inside him was grasping for a reason to go on?

Inane logic. It was nothing that convoluted or deep. He was happy for Chaz, and he was far too busy to ponder the politics of the Alliance. It was . . . He had no idea. And he had to worry about that later. Because the next stage of the current crisis came with the realization that there was an enemy agent on board. Because of that, he should keep the crew locked down on 3 and 4. But the fire proved how vulnerable and shorthanded they were. So the ship was on open access but under a Code 2 battle stations order—no one went anywhere alone. Preliminary investigations were already being conducted in the forward lifts and the auxiliary bridge. Maybe there was something about the fire that would lead them to the enemy agent. Maybe some telltale clue to his or her identity would be found in the auxiliary bridge. But until they had answers, the bridge and officer quarters required tighter security. Rya stationed Sachi Holton—armed with Rya's L7—at the end of the corridor on Deck 2 Forward. Corvang and Mather guarded the bridge. It was an impromptu setup but might well function as permanent until they hit Ferrin's.

An attempt had been made to take control of his ship. Philip didn't think it was going to stop there. He doubted it would stop even when they hit Ferrin's. If they hit Ferrin's.

One hour ten minutes to the C-6.

Captain Folly stretched, arched his back, then flattened his considerable furry white girth across the right corner of Philip's desktop, black tail dangling over the edge, tapping to a rhythm only the beast could hear.

Philip swiveled his chair slightly and angled away from the cat. "Commander Adney's sedated, resting," he told Con, Sparks, Martoni, and Rya. They'd already been briefed on Adney's emotional collapse. "It doesn't appear she'll be returning to duty. Likely she'll transfer to medical when we hit Ferrin's. That leaves me without an exec, without someone to function as my second in command." He looked at Con. Martoni outranked Con, but Philip didn't know Martoni. And Con was long overdue for a promotion. "Lieutenant Welford, are you prepared to assume the duties of executive officer of the *Folly*?"

"I am, sir." Welford seemed slightly surprised. "Thank you for your faith in me."

"I have to consider a number of parameters here, not the least of which is familiarity with the way I operate. I don't have time to do a thorough analysis of all qualified candidates. The current situation doesn't allow that luxury. But be very sure, all of you here, that I don't make these decisions lightly, even if there are times you think I do," Philip said, not mentioning Rya. But he had a feeling his point was made. "This will add to your workload—to all our workloads," he continued, singling out Martoni, then Rya, with a nod. "Commander Martoni, I want you to work closely with Welford. Sparks, you said Dillon has helm experience. If you can spare him, at least until we clear the gate, we need him on the bridge."

"Dillon's never flown a Stryker," Sparks said, "but few of the kids on board have any direct experience with this class ship. Dillon's a quick learner. Vange, Kagdan, and I can hold down engineering with the rest of the team."

"Lieutenant Bennton." Philip brought his gaze up to hers. Up because he was seated and she was at her usual place on his right, back against the bulkhead that separated his office from his quarters, one hand resting lightly on her Stinger. The Norlack dangled at her side. Judging from her mismatched uniform—half Alliance gray, half ImpSec dark blue—she'd thrown on dry clothes as quickly as he had. The cat, he noticed, was watching her as well. "Who do you recommend assigning to your security team besides Holton?"

"Corvang excelled in SECTAC in the academy," she

said, and Philip remembered Jodey's comment about the rangy Takan: *He's studied everything the Great Guthrie has ever written...every combat-training holo you've ever done.* That included two manuals Philip had authored for Security and Tactics: SECTAC.

"He can still sit nav," Rya added, "but he can sit armed. Having him on the bridge is extra insurance and frees up me or Holton to patrol lower decks, if need be."

"I agree with the choice of Corvang, but I want no solo patrols." Philip leaned back in his chair, ignoring the zingers of pain racing up his leg. "We have an enemy agent on board. The only way we're going to make it to the C-Six, let alone Ferrin's, is by putting this ship under Code Two battle stations, including the auxiliary bridge."

Martoni's eyes widened, but Rya, Philip noted, was nodding. Con and Sparks showed no reaction. They knew emergency procedures as well as he did.

"The main bridge and engineering will be the most heavily guarded. Until we hit Ferrin's, command and bridge staff will eat, live, and sleep here on Deck Two Forward or the bridge. Same for engineering. All other personnel will be either in their cabins or at their stations. No one—I repeat, *no one*—works any station alone.

"Martoni, Sparks's people are going to need bedding and food. Take who you can trust to get supplies down there. You have ten minutes to do so. Then report back up here, because I'm sure Lieutenant Welford will have a long list of things he wants done."

"Sir," Martoni said, rising.

Philip waved him away with one hand, a movement that had the cat opening one eye in annoyance. "Dismissed. You and Sparks get going."

When his office door slid closed behind the two men, Philip focused on Con. "This isn't going to be pretty, Constantine."

"I'll trade pretty for functional any day."

"I'm not even sure we're functional. Get back to the bridge, light a fire—sorry, bad choice of words." Philip wiped one hand over his mouth, aware now of the faint whiff of oranges mixing in with the bitter odor of burnt plastics. "Get those repair crews moving. Double-check everything they do. We don't know where that enemy agent is, but he or she will be less likely to muck up the computer systems if you're watching."

"I can set trip alarms on key functions. If someone tries, we'll know," Con promised.

"Excellent. Do it. We also need command staff personnel armed at all times." Philip switched his gaze from Welford to Rya as she edged away from the bulkhead.

"We'll need an assessment of personal weapons brought on board," she said. "With your permission, I want to confiscate everything except those carried by bridge, command, and engineering staff."

"Do it."

"I have a personal Mag-Five in my quarters," Welford said. "I believe Commander Adney has one too."

"Her quarters will open to your palm code." Philip pointed to the door. "Use her Mag-Five for now. Then get yours and transfer your stuff into her quarters, once we have the bridge under control."

Nodding, Con pushed himself out of his seat.

"Bennton," Philip said, rising as well, "we're going to need more than a few Mag-Fives and donated L7s.

Come with me. It's time to break out the rest of the arsenal."

And maybe find a spare five-point-two seconds to try to explain the unexplainable to Rya the Rebel. In private. If the cat would let him.

13

The clock was ticking; it was an outdated analogy of time running away. Philip Guthrie had never actually seen a mechanical ticking clock outside of history vids, but he felt the relentless pressure all the same as Rya and the cat trailed him through the main salon of his quarters and into his small bedroom. His closets held more than his personal arsenal. Jodey had sent a small stash from the *Nowicki* on Adney's shuttle. Time and continuing crises had prevented Philip from distributing the weapons until now.

His carpets were soaked, his bed looked soggy. If someone from damage control didn't get in here soon with a quadra-flash evaporator, it would be a long, miserable night. If he ever got to sleep. But at least his closets were dry.

He tapped in his security code, very aware that Rya stood inches behind him. Very aware that at some point—likely much later—he was going to want to drag her into his arms again. A low voice in the back of his mind told the Old Man to get a grip. Another low voice told him it was about goddamned time. It had been over three years since he and Chaz split. More than that since the romance between them died. He ignored both voices and yanked out a square black durocase, dragging it onto the floor. Water squished up around the edges in small foamy bubbles.

Captain Folly pranced by, shaking water from his paws, then leapt up to the less-damp location of Philip's nightstand.

"Four Carver-Tens for distribution to command staff," Philip told Rya, tossing the cases onto the corner of his bed, near where she stood. They landed with a muted thump on the waterlogged mattress. He checked the next pair of sealed cases. "Six Stingers. Security." He tossed those too, one after the other. Rya already had one Carver case open, checking the power pack on the weapon.

"They're rebuilts off the *Nowicki*," he told her. A few he'd worked on himself while Doc Galan had him locked down in the therapy room, poking, prodding, and in general doing nasty things to his damaged hip and leg. "Unless they were tampered with on the shuttle on the way here, they're fine." It was one thing to get the *Folly*'s primaries. It was another to get his personal lock codes.

"You willing to rule that out?" she asked, opening the next case. "Sir?" she added.

Sir. But then, he'd called her Subbie right after kissing her. Signal understood and accepted.

"I rule out nothing. Check them all."

The last case held a trio of L7s. He checked those and the Stingers she hadn't checked yet.

He watched her handle the weapons and saw clear echoes of Captain Cory Bennton in her movements, in her scrutiny. He wondered what Cory would think of his daughter's situation now. He wondered what Cory would do if he knew Philip had kissed her.

"Rya—"

"I'm a grown woman, Philip." She hefted the Carver-10 in her hand and faced him, chin lifting almost in defiance. "The fat little girl you taught to shoot a Carver has been through a lot in the past twenty years. Enough that she—that *I*—have very few illusions about myself. I know what I am. I know what I have to give. And I know what I want. And when you're ready to discuss that in a mature fashion—without guilt or excuses—you know where to find me."

He choked back a laugh. God, she was priceless. If she was ten years older—or he ten years younger—he wouldn't have one qualm about a relationship with her. But she wasn't and he wasn't, and that still made him stop and think, play it more carefully—though he was honestly surprised to find himself "playing" at all. "Rya—"

"In the meantime, as your chief of security, I think this should be mine." She held up the Carver-10.

He studied her. Headstrong? Impulsive? Her former COs didn't know the half of it. "No," he said. He plucked the Carver-10 from her fingers.

Her eyes widened slightly. Her mouth thinned more than slightly. It was all he could do to keep a grin off his own face.

"No," he repeated. "As my chief of security, this should be yours." He pulled the spare Carver-12 from his closet and placed it in her outstretched hand.

Then, grinning, he limped back past her and toward his office before the expression of sheer joy on her face made him give in to his desire to kiss her again. Guilt, excuses, and all.

The clock still ticked. Forty minutes out from the C-6. Damage control was blasting his quarters dry and, if not answers, at least theories were coming in to his office. The ship was on full alert, all crew stationed at general quarters or in their cabins. Rya and her teams were roving, watching. Con came and went several times with weapons status, crew assignments, and more theories. Which was why Philip was in his office and not on the bridge, where, by SOP—Fleet or Alliance—he should be.

His office door was closed. That alone was an indicator of the seriousness of the situation.

Crew and weapons—what little he had of both—were set to engage the enemy. The fighters from Umoran Defense flanking the ship confirmed a go status. He needed those fighters; the *Folly* was still essentially a civilian ship with only lasers as defense. Lasers, two hefty tow fields, and a slightly insane plan from a more than slightly insane admiral. It had required some dogged haranguing from both him and Sparks to convince Con of the plan's viability. That and a bet that revolved around a bottle of very expensive Lashto brandy.

He didn't need Con's approval, but he wanted it. The Great Guthrie and the Tin Man went back more than a few years.

Philip tapped open a blinking databox on his deskscreen and studied the latest inconclusive information: the analysis of the fire in the forward lifts; the analysis of the minor systems malfunction that created the small diversion that sent Martoni to Deck 4; the analysis of the attempt to take over the auxiliary bridge. It amazed him how much his skeleton crew had been able to accomplish. It worried him that his crew was skeleton.

It worried him more that his ship had been infiltrated. That made his gut clench, his trigger finger itch.

It was something neither Rya, Con, nor Martoni could provide answers to. Yet. Dina Adney—his former XO—was also a puzzle. He'd told Jodey as much, along with instructions to update Consul Falkner not only on the *Folly*'s status but the situation with the hospital ship and the C-6. He was waiting to hear back from the *Nowicki*'s captain.

In the meantime, he had traps to lay. And enemies to catch: one here and one out there. The latter was easier. He knew, relatively, what the Farosian ship wanted, what it would do. And he'd put his money on the fact that the Farosians wanted him alive.

He had no idea what motivated his onboard enemy. He didn't even know if the agent was Farosian or Imperial.

His office door chimed, the security code Rya and Sparks had instituted flashing on his deskscreen, confirming that one of his command staff waited on the other side. He keyed the lock off the door and pulled his Carver from where it rested against his hip, just in case. The safety was already off.

Rya stepped in. Fifteen minutes ago she'd shown up with Con. That had been with the last update on the Deck 4 diversion. Now she was alone and with dark smudges on her left cheekbone. He could lie to himself that with all else that was going on, her appearance affected him not in the least—didn't get his heart beating a little faster, didn't make his senses tune that much more finely.

But it would be a lie.

She eyed him, sighing disapproval. "You're too big of a target, Guthrie. I told you—"

"To move out of the direct line of fire when opening the door, yes, I know." He raised his gun. "You were in my direct line. This desk wouldn't stop a Carver."

Pursed lips were his only answer. She slid into the chair on his left as his office door closed and locked. She swiveled so that her back was to the wall and she could keep an eye not only on his office door but on the closed door to his quarters.

Textbook ImpSec SPS.

"I think I have something on the fire," she said.

No "sir." No preliminaries. Pure Rya. He'd learned that in, what, three days with her now? She'd defined herself as his bodyguard without his permission. She'd tranked him without his permission. She'd initiated investigations without his permission.

And she'd invaded his heart without his permission.

Pure Rya the Rebel. If she started flinging forkfuls of peas at him again, it wouldn't surprise him.

And now one of her investigations—authorized or otherwise—had panned out. That explained the smudges. "Tell me it's good news."

"It is if you know where to buy disatone tylethelene. And how to handle it once you've got it."

Disatone ty—

"Disty?" he asked, using the old ammo-head's term for the highly unstable accelerant. "Someone has disty-boom on board?"

"We didn't catch it the first time, because who looks for disty-boom anymore? The Empire ceased production of it thirty or so years ago. But Commander Dennvil, who taught my explosives class at the academy, was a real ammo-head. She'd been around since before disty-boom was banned."

He almost admitted knowing Galacia Dennvil, but that would remind Rya that he, too, had been around since before disty-boom was banned.

"Something about the burn pattern struck me. I showed it to Sparks—"

"Concentric spalling with indistinct demarcation lines," Philip intoned.

Another sigh, but this one was accompanied by the smallest of smiles. "I should have guessed you'd know."

"Us ammo-heads tend to stick together. Sparks confirmed it?"

"He and a couple of techs from science are doing that now. They're going to try to identify source or manufacturer from the residue in the lift. There were only two main chemical firms in the Empire—"

"Regmont-Allen and Synthachem."

"Right. Evidently their formulas were slightly different. Knowing which lab it came from might help pinpoint who our mole is. Or where he came from."

"If we even have time to act on the information." Philip shifted in his seat and checked ship's position on his deskcomp. "We're going to be very busy once we hit the C-Six." Long-range scanners already sought any configuration that could be a Farosian Star-Ripper.

"Will someone try to stop us—again—before then?"

He wondered for a moment if her question signaled the first sign of fear—something he hadn't seen from Rya Bennton to this point. But her tone, her posture, told him otherwise. She was reminding him that the Star-Ripper was but one of many problems.

"Depends which side that someone is on. A Farosian would. An Imperial would hope that Farosians would do the job for him. Or her," he added.

Rya sucked in a hard breath. "I didn't want to mention this, but I have to. Could Commander Adney be behind this? Could her breakdown be a ploy to cover what she's done?"

"I've thought at that." He had, and it troubled him deeply. Because if Adney was a mole, that meant security on the *Nowicki* was compromised. And God only knew where else in the Alliance Fleet.

"She's tranked now, comfortable," he continued. "Locked in sick bay. If that was her best attempt, she failed."

"If her attempt was to reduce the functionality of an already limited crew, she succeeded." She paused, her voice softening. "I wish to hell I'd let my father teach me starship navigation, helm. He tried. I just kept heading for the firing range."

He heard her frustration. He didn't do helpless well either. But she was far from helpless. "I need you exactly where you are, Rya." He let his tone soften to match hers. There was a double meaning to his words, which were all, at the moment, he had to offer her.

His deskscreen pinged, halting whatever she was about to say. He turned away from her, seeing the data he knew was coming. Long-range scanners had picked up something, something big. They weren't close enough yet to make a positive identification.

They didn't need to.

Philip Guthrie knew.

Rya Bennton had two of the three things she most wanted in life: a Carver-12 on her hip and the rank of security chief on a heavy cruiser looking to take down the Empire. The third . . . She angled around and caught Philip's profile as he sat—straight-backed and fully alert—in the command chair in the center of the *Folly*'s bridge. He probably knew she was looking at him. She couldn't for long. There was a Farosian warship out there. And an enemy agent in here, somewhere. The first she could do nothing about. The second had her arming Corvang, Sachi Holton, and

Will Tramer with Stingers. Sachi escorted an emergency repair team, tackling a short list of problems that Philip and Sparks deemed couldn't wait until they hit the safety of jumpspace. Will worked access points on Deck 3.

Welford, Martoni, Mather, and Dillon had Carver-10s. The Mag-5s and L7s—some of which were personal weapons she and Corvang had confiscated earlier—were distributed to Sparks's people and the team in weapons.

On admiral's orders, it was shoot first and ask questions second. And everyone on board knew that.

There was tense chatter on the bridge about the Farosian ship's position—thirty minutes out—and confirmation of orders coming in from Seth's P-33s and a trio of Ratch fighters sent from Umoran. Rya caught that much in the exchanges between Philip, Burnaby Mather at the comm, and Welford, who went from staring over Dillon's shoulder at second helm to standing rigidly at the XO's console on Philip's left.

"We must have just flashed on their screens," Welford said, looking quickly from his console to the forward datascreen and back to his console again. "The Star-Ripper's changing course to intercept."

"Got a reading on her armaments?" Philip asked.

"Working on it, sir."

Rya dragged her gaze away from the large datascreen on the bridge's forward bulkhead. It would be too easy to be distracted by the ship images, green-tinged against the black of the grid, by the flashing yellow icons showing potential targeting points, and by the cascading red, yellow, and green numbers relating distance, speed, and God and Philip Guthrie only knew what else.

The closer they got to the Star-Ripper, the greater the danger that the agent on board would act. Again.

She turned for the corridor and let her fingers close around the grip of the Carver-12 on her hip. It was Philip's. Now it was hers. Like his passionate kisses in the midst of the sprinkler deluge and his veiled references to needing her in his office, the gift of the pistol was something she understood—but didn't. She was his chief of security. She was also his self-indulgence. Both, she knew, could be very temporary positions. He had an empty space to fill. She was available. Replacement crew at Ferrin's could well provide more-experienced, more-appropriate prospects for Admiral Philip Guthrie.

She'd been too forward, too available, and she knew it. Shyness had never been one of her attributes. She wasn't pretty enough to be shy. If she wanted a man, she had to be bold about it. So she knew how to stand and she knew how to stare.

Because it was always JFFS: Just For Fun Sex.

Except it never occurred to her that Philip Guthrie, her long-lost always-forever dream hero, would know how to play the same game. And that the game would no longer be what she wanted to play once she met him.

A loud clang on her left had her swinging around, Carver out. Then another clang, a thunk, and Sachi's voice floated up the stairwell. "Holton with repairs."

She holstered the weapon with a glance at her watch. Right on schedule. "Bennton. Acknowledge!" From the clanks and banging it sounded as if they were accessing the damaged lifts from Deck 2 below.

The noise evidently bothered someone else. A flash of white streaked up the stairs, trotted behind her, then came to a stop at Rya's right ankle. She hunkered down and scratched Captain Folly's mismatched ears, all the while darting glances toward the bridge and back to the stairwell.

"Things could get dangerous," she told the cat. "Wish I had a safety kennel, somewhere you could stay. I'll even loan you my beret to sleep on." She made a mental note to mention it to Sparks or maybe Welford. But, no, not Welford. His attitude since learning she was named chief of security had become chilly, almost disapproving.

He no doubt had noticed she'd been damned near puddling at Philip's feet since they arrived on Seth. He no doubt thought she'd traded some JFFS for the position.

As if she and Philip had time . . . But then the image of Welford's scowling face popped up from memory. She, standing in the open doorway of Philip's quarters, playfully blowing a kiss. And Welford, exiting the lifts . . .

"Hey, Rya." Sachi's voice echoed up the stairs, then her dusky face appeared. Her short braids were pinned against her head with a series of small red clips. "You know that section of bulkhead you and Sparks wanted for testing? A piece just broke off." She halted at the top step and held out a rectangle of sheet metal about seven inches in length. "You want I should run this down to Sparks now or wait until we clear the jumpgate?"

The section contained part of the crazed burn pattern that first lead Rya to suspect the use of distyboom. "Stay with the repair crew." She took the metal piece from Sachi. "I'll stow this in the ready room until—"

Tsst! Tsst! Tsst!

Rapid-fire sneezing erupted from the cat sitting by

her feet. The cat shook his head violently, then started again. *Tsst! Tsst! Tsst!*

"That's strange." Sachi shrugged.

"Yeah. Thanks." Rya watched the cat as Sachi hurried back down the stairwell.

Tsst!

Rya lowered the metal piece closer to the cat. More sneezes erupted. One white paw lifted and scoured eyes and whiskers. Then, with a hard flick of his black tail, Captain Folly bounded down the corridor for the bridge.

No, Rya thought, straightening. *Not strange at all.* Centuries back, before the technology was perfected, arson investigators used a dog's sense of smell to locate and identify traces of accelerants.

That technology didn't currently reside on the *Folly.* Captain Folly, however, did.

Captain Folly was a natural-born disty-boom detector.

Rya had no doubt that there was still some of the chemical on board, very likely in the possession of or in the quarters of the enemy agent.

Captain Folly could find it.

Plans unfolding quickly in her mind, she headed for the ready room to secure the sample. Then she needed three minutes of Philip's undivided attention on the bridge.

"Incoming!"

Here we go. Philip quickly checked the main command screen angled out from his armrest at Welford's terse warning. Chatter around him rose and fell: grunted confirmations from Corvang working both nav and scanners, higher-pitched tones from the female officer, Ensign Jasli, working the ship's meager laser banks along with Martoni.

"Shields at full," Philip announced, knowing his bridge staff was checking, knowing they knew that. But they were shorthanded. His announcement, if redundant, was reassuring.

So was the Farosian's target: not the *Folly* but one of Umoran's Ratch fighters. The small ship angled deftly away as a blast from a P-33 destroyed the torpedo.

"Too easy!" The P-33's captain's laugh sounded through the forward datascreen speakers.

Philip wasn't going to deem things easy yet, but at fifteen minutes out from the C-6 jumpgate, the Farosians *were* playing it cautious. It looked as if they wanted him alive. Any doubts about that dissolved with the Star-Ripper's next volley, again targeting the escort ships.

"Locking on. Got it!" Martoni called out. The *Folly*'s lasers scored a hit on the incoming torpedo. On the forward screen, Philip watched two Ratch fighters roll as a P-33 took out the other one.

The scenario was clear: the Farosians wanted the fighters gone, the *Folly* damaged, and Philip Guthrie under their control.

"Get this damned cat out of here!"

Burnaby Mather's angry tones jerked Philip's attention from the forward datascreen. The large white cat crouched on the edge of the communications console, black tail twitching, head shaking. Mather swung a fist at the hissing cat. No. It was sneezing, Philip realized. Not hissing. Sneezing.

What in hell's fat ass?

Con, standing behind Dillon at the second helm, lunged for Mather's station on his left. He grabbed the cat by the scruff. The beast yowled, claws raking the air.

"Hey!"

Philip twisted in his chair, hearing Rya's voice. She darted onto the bridge from the doorway to the ready room.

He had no time for this. "Lock the cat in my quarters, now!" he ordered her.

Whatever she was about to say was halted by Con's shoving the creature into her arms. "You heard the admiral. Move!"

The cat buried its head in the crook of Rya's arm, suddenly calm and silent.

Con stared. Mather was still swearing. If Philip wasn't so goddamned busy with the Farosians and a hospital ship about to appear in the middle of a firefight, he would have laughed at the beast's sudden transformation. The cat hated men.

Without comment, Rya turned on her heel and hurried off, a long black tail wrapped partly around the weapons belt at her waist.

Philip turned back to the Farosians. There was no communication from the Star-Ripper. He didn't expect any. At least not until the escort ships were destroyed, at which time he felt sure the Farosians would contact him with some offer of surrender.

He had no intention of letting the P-33s and fighters be destroyed. He had no intention of surrendering. He had other plans. He sent a coded transmission to the senior P-33 captain, then raised his gaze from the small screen set into his armrest. Now they knew what Con and Sparks did. Everyone one else on the bridge would find it out piecemeal as he issued his orders. A necessary precaution.

It was time. "Mr. Dillon, Lieutenant Welford will take over main helm now."

"Yes, sir." If Dillon was surprised by Philip's command, his voice didn't show it. Con was already sliding into the seat next to Dillon.

Then that something he couldn't identify told him Rya was back on the bridge, standing guard at her usual place, next to the nonfunctioning security console, with her very functional Carver-12 on her hip.

He needed her there. If there was a Farosian agent on the bridge, his next command might well force him or her to act. He opened intraship to engineering. "Sparks, I need sublights at full. Constantine, adjust course. Let's dead-eye that Star-Ripper."

14

The *Folly*'s sublights kicked to max. With a quick tap, Philip brought up the schematics of the Star-Ripper on his command screen. The Ripper was a small but powerful ship—essentially a 350-ton arsenal ringed by torpedo tubes and crowned with a row of ion cannons. The *Folly* could have used Captain Ellis's Gritter cannon right about now, but she didn't have that.

She did have, however, two very powerful tow fields. And some damned good partners in the escort fighters from Umoran Defense. And a crazy idea Philip had played with in sims but never actually pulled off with real ships.

First time for everything.

A torpedo detonated off the *Folly*'s port side. Screens blinked for a microsecond. An alarm wailed shrilly as shield configurations restructured.

"Kill that!" Philip ordered, then: "Keep us on course, Mr. Welford."

The alarm fell silent along with all chatter on the bridge.

The trio of Ratch fighters pulled into a V-formation,

with the P-33s flanking each side, essentially functioning as the extended scanning and weapons systems the *Folly* had lost at decommission. The escort ships were taking heavy fire, dodging, breaking formation but regrouping, keeping the *Folly*'s path clear. That was essential. He had to get close enough to—

"Martoni, watch those torpedoes, starboard side!"

It was a double volley, coming in on the wake shadow of another torpedo. The *Folly*'s stripped-down tech couldn't see it. Philip caught the movement on his command screen only out of the corner of his eye.

"Sensors locking on!" Ensign Jasli called out, but they didn't, and neither could Martoni manually. The *Folly*'s lasers missed; the P-33 missed. A Ratch fighter dove into the weapon's path, and Philip's gut clenched. He saw the sacrifice coming, recognized the mind-set, but it wrenched him, as it always did. Debris exploded soundlessly on the *Folly*'s forward screen.

Shield alarms wailed, impact sensors flashed frantically. The ship shuddered. Philip grabbed his armrest and jammed one boot against the decking, steadying himself, teeth gritted in aggravation and frustration.

Bodies tumbled around him. One was Rya's—he recognized her breathy "fuck!" behind him. Then officers and crew scrambled to their feet.

"Status!" Philip called out. "Damage report!" But even as he asked, he knew. Data streamed to his command screen. No hull breaches, but starboard shields were down to forty-one percent.

One of the Umoran Ratch fighters was destroyed. A pilot and a gunner wouldn't be going home to their families tonight. The first casualties in a list that— Philip knew with grim certainty—would grow.

"Incoming!" Jasli had them this time, but that was followed by another pair of torpedoes, then the first searing blast from the Ripper's ion cannons. Another minute and they'd be in laser range.

A P-33 suddenly veered sharply away, debris trailing from a hole in its port flank.

"We're hit, but enviro's holding," the P-33's captain reported through the forward screen. "Reconfiguring shields."

One torpedo. Just one. Or an ion cannon. Or a Gritter. Philip's fist clenched as his desire to retaliate warred with his ship's impotence. A goddamned fruit hauler with nothing more than close-range lasers and two tow fields.

And he had no doubt the Farosians knew that.

But he knew something about the incompatibility of Farosian and Imperial technology and something about the design flaws in a Star-Ripper. The latter was rumor, but rumor from some fairly good sources, and it formed the base of what he'd convinced Sparks and Con they had to try.

He was certifiably insane, but there was no other choice. He had to keep that Ripper busy until they reached the jumpgate. Then he had to pray the *Folly*'s powerful tow fields and equally powerful jumpdrives didn't fail. And that her Imperial-based shields would prevent Farosian sensors from learning the truth.

Another explosion. Another Ratch fighter veering off, not destroyed but trailing debris. The damaged P-33 had yet to move back into position. Engine trouble, the security-coded readout on Philip's command screen informed him.

The triple chime of the jumpgate's outer beacon sounded.

Philip swore under his breath. They were so close. But they were down to one P-33 and one fighter, if that other one couldn't recover. That wasn't enough firepower. There was no way. He should have demanded additional escorts from Seth and Umoran. But that would have put thousands of civilians back there at risk, instead of just—

"Admiral, we're being hailed by the Star-Ripper." Mather turned at his station, one hand cupping the comm set against his right ear. "They're sending terms for our surrender. They want . . . Sir, they want you personally to deliver the surrender."

"Over my dead body." Rya's voice sounded tersely behind him.

He glanced over his right shoulder, caught hazel eyes narrowed under a mop of brown curls barely being contained by a dark-blue ImpSec beret. She'd positioned herself between him and the doorway to the corridor.

Oh, Rebel . . . But the Farosians' request didn't surprise him. If anything, he'd expected it ten minutes ago.

"Sir?" Mather prompted.

"Acknowledge acceptance of their terms," Philip said flatly, to a bridge suddenly gone silent. Except for Mather, who was sputtering, half rising out of his seat.

"But, but—"

"*But* do it through text transmission. Tell them our audio systems are dead. Tell them we're launching our shuttle in three minutes with Admiral Philip Guthrie on board. He will, as requested, surrender in person to them on their ship. You understand, Mr. Mather?"

"I—yes, sir." Mather turned to his console.

The silence on the bridge was like a palpable sheet of ice. No one stood, rejoicing, but that didn't mean there wasn't a Farosian operative on his bridge.

"Welford, keep us on course, but take us down to one-half sublight. Martoni, drop aft shields, then raise them. Make it look like we have problems. Big problems. Cool all weapons ports while you're at it."

Martoni stared at him for a long second, then an understanding smile played across his lips. "Yes, sir!"

The ice thawed. Philip chanced another glance at Rya. She was grinning. He wondered if she'd figured out his plan. It wouldn't surprise him if she had.

He punched intraship. "Sparks, get ready to wake up those jumpdrives. I'm going to need power more than pretty."

"Want me to launch the shuttle now, Skipper?" Sparks asked. "Got the shields all rigged."

Philip rechecked the *Folly*'s distance to the Ripper and the jumpgate. They were farther from the gate than he wanted to be. And they were on the wrong axis relative to the Ripper. But beggars—and rebels— couldn't be choosers. He wasn't going to get another chance. He sent a coded message to the senior Umoran captain to stand down. "One minute. Martoni, make our shields go a little crazier."

"Extinguish running lights," Rya intoned.

He glanced at her again with a quick nod. "Cut running lights and go dark on Decks Two Aft, Three, and Four."

"Fifteen-degree list to starboard," she added. "When a Stryker's sublights go bad, that's what she does."

"Fifteen-degree starboard list, Welford," Philip said, hearing echoes of Captain Cory as he brought the tow fields on line. He tapped intraship again. "Sparks, jettison the shuttle." *Hell, it's only money.*

Philip grabbed the small ship with the tow fields the minute it shot from the bay. What could pull could also push. The Ripper slowed, the *Folly* drifting now, shields in disarray, decks dark or flickering. Guiding the rigged shuttle through the empty space between the two ships wasn't the hard part. Dead-eyeing the Ripper's landing bay—just under the row of ion cannons—would be. It had to look as if he was actually coming in to the bay. If he veered off course too soon, the Farosians wouldn't lower their bay shields. They'd fire on the shuttle, destroying it—and Philip's one chance to destroy them.

"Welford, shove her a little. Bring us closer." The tow fields were harder to control at this distance. It was dangerous, damned dangerous, but he had to close the gap between the *Folly* and the Farosian's 350-ton arsenal. And that lethal array of ion cannons on top.

"Admiral," Con's tone was cautious. "That's going to hamper our ability to—"

"Closer, Constantine, or our abilities won't matter."

"Yes, sir."

Sims were so much easier. In sims you could make a mistake and try again. And in the sims, he still had his P-33s and Ratch fighters. He still had options if the Ripper got wise and struck out.

He was out of options. He was also almost out of time. The hospital ship with Alliance wounded and two of Consul Falkner's key aides on board would be coming through the gate in less than forty minutes. Less than thirty, quite likely, as he knew they were desperate to reach help and, if he was that ship's captain, he would have been going flat-out full-bore at that point.

One of the tow fields suddenly stuttered, its power signal cresting, then flattening.

"Welford!" Philip couldn't take his eyes off his command screen as he wrestled the other tow field into position.

"On it!" Con answered.

"On it," came Sparks's reply through intraship.

The shuttle shimmied, jerking. Philip knew with certainty that alarms were raised on the Ripper. There was no way with only one tow field he could control the small ship's movements. The Farosians had to know something was wrong. They'd raise shields at the shuttle bays. He needed those shields down.

A blur of movement on his left. Rya, at the XO's console. "Sending wide-band distress signal through the shuttle," she said.

He had no time to ponder how she knew to do that, except it had Cory Bennton written all over it. It didn't solve his problem, but it legitimized the shuttle's erratic flight and possibly bought them a few more minutes before the Ripper would raise shields and start firing.

"Power's up!" Con called out just as the second tow field's icon lit up on Philip's command screen. He grabbed the shuttle again, but too hard, overcorrecting. It skewed to port—

"Ripper's ion cannons just went hot!" Martoni's voice was tense, strident. "Shields still down."

Philip threw the full power of both tow fields against the shuttle, like two cue sticks pounding a billiard ball. The shuttle lurched, twisting, and for a very long horrible second he knew he'd missed, he knew he was too far way, too off course . . .

Then, impact! Debris spewed from the top of the Ripper, chunks of metal and connecting lattice flying. He tore his gaze from his command screen and watched the destruction on the larger, more-detailed forward datascreen. Someone behind him whooped, someone else shouted. He'd hit the Ripper right between the two shuttle bays, just at the rumored vulnerable point where the ion-cannon array met the outer hull. One cannon twisted, toppling, discharging a blast directly into the Ripper.

The *Folly*'s lasers fired, raking a gash down the side of the Farosian ship. More debris hurtled into space.

He slapped intraship, heart pounding. "Sparks, punch it! Hit the gate, now! All hands, brace!"

Philip slammed against the back of his seat as the *Folly*'s jumpdrives kicked on, hard. Sublights screamed as power flooded the drives. The ship trembled, shaking, and the last thing Philip Guthrie saw before the *Folly* sliced through the gate was the twisted, rolling image of the Farosian Star-Ripper, literally ripping itself apart.

Jump transit was supposed to be the quiet time, the easy time. With no communication possible in or out, and no other ships to deal with or contact, the crew kicked back or attended to minor matters.

Rya leaned her elbows on the desktop in the vacant office at the far end of divisionals on Deck 2 Aft and scrubbed the heels of her hands against her aching eyes. Whoever stated that was a liar. Or had never worked for Tin Man Welford.

It had been four hours since they crossed the C-6 gate, four hours since they left the decimated Star-Ripper behind. Within ten minutes of gate transit, Welford corralled her—"as the new security chief"—into divisionals with a list of things to do that damned near spanned Calth sector. Her requests to speak to Philip were brushed off.

"The admiral's extremely busy," Welford had said tersely, then left before one word of explanation could come out of her mouth. The cat. Disty-boom. The crash of the lifts that had been foretold by the cargo driver before they even left Seth.

She couldn't even send Philip a message. The deskscreen in the small office didn't have that capability even if she knew the clearance codes.

She didn't. Some chief of security she was.

Right now she was vetting the personnel jackets of every officer and crew member waiting at Ferrin's—over one hundred twenty names. She knew it was necessary. It was on her own list of things to do before they hit the exit gate. But it took Commander Adney two days to clear the seventy-eight currently on board the *Folly.* Welford wanted it in hours.

Slagging slave driver. No wonder Captain Folly...

The image of the cat growling and spitting while Welford held him by the scruff surfaced in her mind. Captain Folly didn't like Con Welford at all.

Captain Folly didn't like disty-boom.

Maybe... Her gut tightened. Who else but Tin Man would know how to rig a bomb? Who else but Tin Man would know where to find something as obscure as disty-boom? Maybe it wasn't Welford's size at all that kept him from crawling with her into the maintenance tunnels as the fire raged.

Maybe he didn't want the fire put out.

No. She paged down another screen, scrolling through a crew member's references as part of her mind played good cop to her bad cop. Fact: Philip trusted Con Welford. Fact: Con Welford had been on the *Loviti.* Fact: Con Welford had helped her when Adney didn't believe her about the intruder.

But they never found the intruder. Could Welford have—

"Bennton, you look tired."

Rya glanced up, startled, one hand automatically

flying to the Carver on her hip. The burly form of Burnaby Mather filled the doorway of the office.

"Don't shoot!" He raised his hands. Both contained bottles of water. "Thought you might be thirsty. Don't kill a man for trying to do a good deed, hey?"

She chuckled, releasing her grip on the weapon. He held a bottle out to her.

She stood, leaning over the desk, and grabbed it. "You're a lifesaver."

"Not much else for a commo to do in jump." He pulled the seal off his water bottle. She did the same. "You're stuck up here, just like the rest of the poor slag-heads stuck in their cabins on Three and Four. I hear the rumblings down there are getting louder."

When Sachi and Tramer had stopped by briefly, two hours before, they'd mentioned there were two or three complainers, but nothing as bad as Mather made it sound. "People with too much time on their hands." Rya shrugged. "You know it's necessary."

Mather swiveled a gray metal chair around, then plopped down, angling slightly to accommodate the Carver by his side. "Is it? Come on, Rya, do you really think we have some dangerous enemy agent on board?" He wiggled his eyebrows, then took a long draft of water.

She smiled at his attempt at levity, but it was a thin smile. "Someone set that fire."

"So we're sure it was set? Not just another malfunction?"

Mather didn't know about the presence of disatone tylethelene in the lift shaft. He was command staff, off the *Nowicki*. Philip had given him a Carver. He should have been updated. But Philip hadn't because there hadn't been time for a full update meeting since the fire. Well, there was time now, but Welford had blocked any chance of that happening by stashing her in divisionals. Rya took a mouthful of cool water before answering. "Ever hear of disty-boom?"

"Disty what?"

"An accelerant. Highly flammable, highly illegal, explosive. Banned years ago, so I didn't catch it right away. Neither did Sparks. But it leaves a unique burn pattern. So, yeah, that was no malfunction."

"We've got someone making bombs on this ship? You're kidding, right?"

"We have the confirmed presence of disatone tylethelene at the source of the fire. It doesn't mean whoever put it there is still on board. It doesn't mean they're not. However—"

"Those intruder incidents Tin Man found. You're thinking someone got on board, rigged bombs." Mather's brow furrowed.

"Bomb," she corrected. "Unless you know about another one."

"Me?" He snorted. "I'm just Mather the Commo. Messages in, messages out."

But he'd served on the *Nowicki*, was one of the officers handpicked by Captain Bralford to transfer to the *Folly*. He was part of the *Folly*'s advance team. Which meant he was not only trusted but had experience. "But you'd know if you overheard something that could relate to explosives. Or saw a message that might be suspect."

"On this ship? Rya, my dear, you're damned lucky I could get intraship up and limping. This isn't Fleet. We don't have the equipment to intercept. It took me twenty slagging minutes to get a live link with the *Nowicki* the other day, and it was all shits-and-sticks... Sorry." He grinned sheepishly. "There was a lot of interference."

She grinned back. "I know the expression."

"Anyway, Scruffy—uh, that is, Admiral Guthrie—has all communications locked down, except the bridge and his own. There's nothing to listen to."

"Scruffy?" Rya leaned forward, lips twitching. "Scruffy?"

"You've never heard him called Scruffy Guthrie?"

"I've heard the Great Guthrie."

"And Guth. Those are names he'll admit to. But to most everyone who's served under him, especially once he took over the *Loviti*, he's Scruffy. Even Captain Bralford's called him that. Behind his back." Mather winked.

Rya thought for a moment. "I can't say I've ever seen him the least bit scruffy." Not even when rolling on the station floor, Norlack blasting chunks out of the shuttle counter. And not even when he was soaking wet, standing in the ready room, kissing her in the most self-indulgent manner. There was something innately elegant about Philip Guthrie even when he was thoroughly disheveled.

"That's the whole point." Mather's eyes narrowed. "Daddy's money keeps you looking nice and gets you even nicer assignments on nicer ships."

"Except this one," Rya pointed out, even as she considered the suddenly harsh tone in Mather's voice. He reminded her at that moment of the sneering naked man she'd left in her bed on Calth 9. Whenever he couldn't get his way, Barrister Matthew Crowley turned petulant. Like Mather did now.

Burnaby Mather was likely near Philip's age. But his career had been less stellar, and it bothered him.

"Just goes to prove he's human and, yes, there is a God," Mather quipped. Then he laughed, his expression lightening. "Wow, listen to me. Telling tales about the Great Guthrie to Cory's kid. Yeah, he's had lots of breaks, got the top assignments. But we all know he's one hundred percent devoted to the Alliance. He'll ask you to work long hours, but he'll work even longer ones himself. The Great Guthrie." Mather shook his head, smiling. "If anyone can get this bucket to Ferrin's, he can. Providing, of course, someone doesn't blow us out of the space lanes before we get there with that distoon stuff."

"Disty-boom," Rya corrected. "But don't worry. If there's any more of that on board, I'll find it."

"What, you think someone has a big jar labeled Disty-Boom sitting in the middle of his cabin?"

"Labels aren't required when you have Captain Folly."

Mather frowned again. "Captain—you mean that cat?"

Rya nodded. "I had a piece of the damaged bulkhead from the lift earlier. He went into violent sneezing fits as soon as he came close to it. I'm going to test him later with other sections from the fire. If he keeps sneezing, well, then he's as good as any high-tech sensor the arson guys use."

"Get serious, Rya. You're going to use a sneezing cat as evidence?"

"An animal's sense of smell is beyond a human's range. That's why dogs were used for centuries by arson investigators. It's a valid methodology."

"Sounds crazy to me, but what do I know? I've never even seen the cat sneeze." Mather shrugged, rising. He touched his fingers to his forehead in salute. "Security Chief Bennton, I know you have work to do. But at least you're not as thirsty."

Rya raised the half-empty bottle. "I appreciate it."

"Just doing what I can to make things right." He patted the Carver on his hip and left.

Rya paged up the next prospective crew member's data as Mather's boot steps faded. Then there was the muted thud of the blast doors. She stared at the information on her screen, her eyes seeing but her mind refusing to focus.

Something about Mather's petulance then sudden shift prickled her cop senses. She shook it off. *Just because someone doesn't worship Philip like you do doesn't automatically make him suspect,* she chided herself.

Being skipper of a space bucket wasn't a popularity contest, her father often reminded her. Still . . .

She tapped in her security code and pulled up the current ship's roster, scrolling through until she found *Mather, Burnaby.* She scanned quickly. If Welford came in and caught her not working on Ferrin's clearances, there'd be hell to pay.

Okay. She was right on Mather's age: late forties, a little older than Philip. Graduated from the academy the year before Philip. Mather's most recent posting to the *Nowicki* came three years ago, after a transfer off the *Waldor Rey.* Olefar was the captain. She couldn't remember his first name, only that her father had little respect for the man.

Mather was third commo on the *Rey*, third commo on the *Nowicki*, where he got his COMTAC rating right before the Empire fractured.

He also had several EFS commendations in his file: Exemplary Fleet Service. An EFS was long considered a perfunctory pat on the head, a way to reward someone not good enough to qualify for promotion.

No wonder Mather was bitter. He was the quintessential invisible officer. Never good enough to promote.

Never bad enough to demote. He did his job but never went beyond—

But wait. One of the commendations was an EFS-Gold. Personally approved by Darius Tage, the Emperor's primary adviser. The man who ordered the death of her father.

The commendation came a few months before Mather's transfer to the *Nowicki* but without the usual promotion. It was as if Mather just blended back into the bulkheads again.

Definitely reason to be bitter. But was he bitter against the Empire or against Philip Guthrie personally? He *was* working against the Empire and for the Alliance. *Just doing what I can to make things right,* he'd said.

Made sense.

Didn't it?

15

Philip checked the corner of his deskscreen as his door chimed. Command-staff code. He slipped his Carver from its holster anyway. The Star-Ripper was gone. The *Folly* was in the relative safety of jumpspace. But he had no illusions that they were safe, by any means.

Con Welford stepped in through the opening door, eyes slightly narrowed, gray uniform shirtsleeves rolled up to his elbows, hands empty of his usual datapad. Neither Martoni, Tramer, nor Dillon was with him, as they were in the two earlier meetings. And his second in command looked tired, distracted. Defeated?

Ah. Con's objections to the ploy to use the shuttle surfaced in Philip's mind along with the informal bet: a bottle of rare Lashto brandy. Con had never been a cheerful loser.

And it had taken him almost four hours to come to Philip's office alone to admit it. Granted, they were busy with other things—meetings with Martoni, briefings with Sparks, and in between Philip had stopped in sick bay to check on Adney's progress—but... "You didn't think my plan would work, did you?" he asked jovially as he holstered the Carver. "Where's your faith, Constantine? More than that," he slapped his palm on the top of his desk, "where's my brandy?"

He waited for Con to take a seat. Con remained standing. "I'm glad it did, sir, but it was a risk. A big one."

"The risk is over. You still owe me my brandy," Philip answered.

"I'm concerned about another risk. Sir."

Sir. Philip finally caught it. Far too many "sirs" from a man he'd known for years. And not a threat against the ship or Con wouldn't be so obviously hesitant. This was something Con didn't want to talk about. Philip had a feeling he didn't want to talk about it either. "Sit, Constantine."

Con didn't move. "Requesting permission to speak freely, Admiral."

"Sit." Philip didn't like the sound of this at all. "We've served together a long time. Been through a lot. You want to tell me something, you tell me."

Con sat stiffly and laced his hands together at his knees. "We *have* been through a lot. That's why I'm concerned. I think you're stressed. Pushing yourself too hard."

"Stressed? Hell, yeah, I'm stressed. We're all stressed. This is damned near war—"

"I think it's affecting your decisions. You're still recovering from your injuries. You know Doc Galan released you only because you gave her no other choice."

Affecting his decisions? "My leg and hip were injured, Constantine. Not my mind. Or are you saying that's not working well either?"

"Philip, I've known you a long time. I can think of no one I respect as much as you. But since Raft Thirty, since the problems on Sullivan's ship, you've... changed. I can sense it. Jodey sensed it."

Philip leaned back in his chair and regarded Con through narrowed eyes. He heard echoes of some of the conversations he had with Jodey weeks ago in Con's words. He was touched by their concern. But they hadn't seen what he had. "Death has a way of realigning your priorities."

"So does losing your wife."

Con's words hit him like a slap in the face. Philip willed himself not to flinch. "Chaz? You think I'm sitting in this godforsaken bucket because of Chaz?"

"I think decisions you're making on the *Folly* are partly affected by seeing her with Sullivan—"

"I'm happy as hell for her! That's something you and Jodey can't seem to get through your heads."

"—and partly by what happened at Raft Thirty. I don't know what it would be like to see your officers, your friends executed. But it has to have impact. It *has* had impact."

"Are you accusing me of neglecting my duties, Mr. Welford?" Philip's tone went colder than he ever thought it could when speaking with Con Welford. His longtime officer. His friend.

Con lowered his face and scrubbed his hands over it. "God, no, Philip. It's not that."

"Then what is it?"

Con looked up. "It's your infatuation with Sub-Lieutenant Bennton."

Philip felt as if he'd been blindsided. "Rya?"

"You're her CO. You're twenty years older than she is—"

"Sixteen."

"—and she's an ImpSec-trained assassin with a death wish. No, hear me out," Con said quickly when Philip leaned forward. "She wants to take down the Empire and she doesn't care who she has to walk over, kill, or sleep with to accomplish that task. Believe me, Philip, I know. I've talked to her and to people on Calth Nine who know her. Sachi Holton is right: Rya Bennton is scary. But you're so tied up in knots over Cory Bennton's death and over losing Chaz, you can't see what you're doing here."

Philip realized he was breathing hard. "What exactly is it you think I'm doing?"

"If I didn't respect you so much, I wouldn't be forced to say this. You're making a fool of yourself. I don't want to see that happen. Jodey doesn't want to see that happen. Sparks doesn't want to see that happen."

"Sparks?"

"You really think no one's noticed, don't you?"

"I think," he said, spacing his words carefully, "someone is creating—*imagining*—a problem where there is none. Not with me. Not with Rya Bennton. And if anyone on Calth Nine—who in hell gave you permission to do that?" He blurted the last part out, because Con's admission finally registered: *I've talked to people on Calth Nine who know her.*

"Adney."

Adney? God. "So on the advice of a woman severely deficient in her mental faculties, you go poking around into Rya's past?" He didn't bother to keep the sarcasm out of his voice.

"This was before Adney's collapse. I worked personnel clearances with her before you even made Kirro. Bennton's jacket worried her. It worried me. I checked further and I think," and he hesitated, taking a breath, "my worries are justified. You said it yourself many times: she's ImpSec. Not just ImpSec but Special Protection Service. They're highly, intensely trained. It was ImpSec that hunted down the *Loviti* crew on Corsau."

"You're accusing Rya Bennton of being Tage's agent?"

"I'd worry less if she was, because that would at least keep her in check. No, she's gone rogue. The restraints are off. She prowls around the ship at all hours, with God only knows how many guns and knives on her, on a mission of her own. And she's not above using you and the rest of us to accomplish it."

Rya was about halfway through the list of personnel waiting for the *Folly* on Ferrin's when she heard Sachi Holton call out her name. "Hey, Rya, hungry yet?"

It took two seconds for her brain to confer with her stomach. "Starving." She glanced at her watch. It was well into dinnertime. The bottle of water Mather had brought her was empty.

Sachi appeared in the office doorway and leaned against the jamb. "I'm bored *and* starving. I hate jump transit. Where'd you get the water?"

"Mather came by about an hour ago."

"Commo's a nice man. Always trying to be helpful."

Rya shut down her deskscreen and stood. "Where's dinner, or is the mess hall no longer off limits to bridge crew?"

"We get the royal treatment, don't you know?" Sachi put her hands on her hips, wiggling them saucily as Rya rounded the desk. "Dinner's in the ready room with Constantine Welford himself. I volunteered to fetch you since none of us is supposed to be running around alone here for long."

Welford? Oh, great. Her torturer. But then, she knew Sachi never missed a chance to eye Con Welford. "He can be your date. I'll take—"

A flash of movement behind her had Rya jerk around.

Captain Folly stood on her desk and emitted a raspy meow. He cocked his face to one side, then butted her hand with his broad head when she reached for him.

"Why am I not surprised you show up at the mention of food?" She bundled the large cat into her arms. "As I said, you can have Welford. The captain and I have a date. So, see? I'm not alone."

"That scruffy thing?" Sachi laughed as they headed into the corridor. "I don't know what you see in him."

"Scruffy holds a special place in my heart," Rya replied as lightly as the truth behind the words would allow her.

"Lack of food has made you delusional. I hope Con ordered enough to eat."

It wasn't the menu that was on Rya's mind when they took the stairwell down to Deck 3 then up to 2 Forward but the cat's reaction to Con Welford. If the man had handled disatone tylethelene, then there

would be residue on his clothes. His boots. And
Captain Scruffy Folly was just the one to verify that.

Philip sat for a long time after Con Welford left his office, fingers steepled before his mouth. Once his anger
over Con's accusations faded, past sins and present
foibles—as Captain Cory Bennton used to term
them—paraded through his mind. He'd made mistakes
with Chaz, many of which Con and Jodey were privy
to. He didn't want to repeat them. Not with anyone,
especially Rya. He'd made mistakes in his career, trusting people against his gut instinct. He was working
now more on gut. He could see where that would scare
Constantine Welford and Jodey Bralford. In many
ways he was not the Philip Guthrie they'd known for
almost fifteen years.

Con was wrong about Rya. Philip *knew* Rya Taylor
Bennton. But how and why he knew her so well was
something he couldn't risk trying to explain. Not to
Con. Not without his XO questioning the Old Man's
sanity any more than he already did. Not without putting Rya's reputation and possibly her career in jeop-
ardy.

It started when he pressed that Carver into that annoying child's hands twenty years ago. She was a natural—she'd launched that forkful of peas at him with
unerring accuracy. It exploded when she fondled the
Norlack, when she cried over the loss of her father,
when she told him "hell, no" more than once, his rank,
illustrious family name, and damned exalted service
history notwithstanding.

It solidified when he recognized in her soul a com-
panion to his.

And Chaz wasn't?

Yes, Chaz was. But Chaz's path was different. He knew that long before he ever opened the discussion of divorce. He was important in Chaz Bergren's life for a period of time. But only a short period of time.

He had to go through what he did with Chaz in order to understand, to appreciate Rya Bennton. Chaz was a lesson—not without pain—that he had to learn.

But Rya—he now saw in himself one who could bring tremendous pain into Rya's life. As if killing her father weren't enough.

Con was right about one thing: a chunk of years separated them. Twenty-nine was mere memory to him. But twenty-nine was something she lived daily.

He closed his eyes and let his head fall wearily back against his chair. He'd made a promise to Captain Cory, to keep his only child safe. Maybe it was time for Philip Guthrie to realize that keeping Rya safe didn't also mean keeping her in his arms.

She'd be better off on the *Nowicki*. He'd give her a top recommendation, put her transfer through when they hit Ferrin's. She'd have to work second to Jodey's current security chief, but Philip would make sure Rya Bennton was on the first new ship the Alliance commissioned, with full rank and privileges. She'd do well. Hell, she was Cory's kid. She'd do spectacularly.

He would help her launch her career, make a name for herself. Make her father and "Uncle" Philip—he cringed—proud.

He turned toward his deskscreen and tapped up the databox with the transfer forms, wondering how something so good could make him feel so miserable.

Rya dragged the crust of bread through the remnants of the stew in her bowl as she pondered Sachi's question. "The most afraid I've been in my career? Hell, I don't know." She glanced from Sachi, whose elbow was on the ready-room table, chin on her palm, to Con Welford, lounging back in his chair with Captain Folly—Captain Folly!—snoring in his lap. So much for her theory. Captain Folly hadn't sneezed once. He hadn't even twitched a whisker. He had, however, enjoyed a bowl of stew.

Now they were playing twenty questions, or rather she and Sachi were. Welford seemed content to listen. And seemed a bit less monstrous than he had a few hours before. Whatever had set him on edge had disappeared. "You both have been in Fleet longer than I have."

"Yeah, but you're the one who has to go up against the crazies we only hear about when we hit dock," Sachi said.

"We didn't get all that many crazies on Calth Nine. But SPS stationed me in Port Chalo on Talgarrath for three months. You're talking dirtsiders. All that wide open space and no limits. Lots of crazies. And lots of twilighters." Port Chalo was a sanctuary port. Anybody and anything could land there, no questions asked.

That left it wide open for the illegal drug and arms trade.

Rya chewed the last of her bread. Sachi was still staring wide-eyed at her. Evidently the stories of her hostage-scenario exercises on station weren't enough. "Okay, there was an arms-smuggling ring ImpSec was tasked to take down a couple years ago. It was summer in Chalo. I remember how hot and sticky it was in my tac gear. Orders came down to set up a sting. They needed someone to pose as the money and someone to pose as the ammo-head who could verify the shipment."

"Let me guess," Sachi cut in. "You were the ammo-head."

"Hey!" Rya held her hands outward in mock innocence. "So I know my weapons. Anyway, I knew we were in trouble when the runner insisted we go on board his freighter to make the deal. His territory, no easy exits, you know? My lieutenant—he was the money—made the excuses, but the runner had none of it. At the ramp we were ordered to dump clean—hand over our weapons. I had a low-end Mag-Five." She shot an apologetic glance at Welford, remembering too late that's what he usually carried. "Sorry. I just don't think the weapon can . . . Well, never mind. So I gave them that and they found my L7, but I thought they would. It was when they were scanning me really closely that I began to get nervous. The Lou and I both carried zero-tracs—those are small pistols that read null on scanners, you know—and I had a clearknife in each boot.

"One of their security had a modified Norlack. Not as good as this one," she patted the weapon on the seat next to her, "but an ugly weapon can kill you as dead as a pretty one."

Sachi laughed. Welford only nodded.

"So the most scared I've ever been was probably in that cargo bay. It wasn't like my usual missions, where things happen quickly, you respond, it's over. This was something that unfolded slowly. About ten minutes in, the Lou and I knew we'd been burned. We knew our chances of getting out of there alive were rapidly disintegrating. I think waiting to die has to be the most frightening. I'd rather take a shot, point-blank, to the head. That's the way I always handled my—"

Rya stopped. Welford was no longer nodding. Sachi was staring.

She'd just reminded them there was an ImpSec operative in their midst.

"You're one scary woman," Sachi said after a long moment. "But, hey, you're on our side. So how did you get out?"

Rya shrugged, then laughed softly. Maybe her story wasn't the best dinner conversation, but Sachi was still her friend. "The weapons they had to sell were real. They had a Norlack and a bunch of high-end Carvers but didn't seem worried the Lou and I had a case of hand cannons in reach. Val-Nine Punishers. Bulky things, you know. Powerful, but they can be complicated to fire—unless you know about the emergency kill-point release by the trigger. Most people, even lots of ammo-heads, don't know that. Lets you ratch up and fire like that."

She raised her hand, flicking her thumb quickly over her index finger. "If it makes any difference," and judging from the look of disapproval on Welford's face, it didn't, "they fired first."

Later, sorting through the last of the personnel jackets Ferrin's had sent, she thought of something her father told her: most people in the Empire, civilians or Fleet, hadn't experienced the hard realities of war in over twenty years—longer than that in the secured inner stations and worlds of Aldan sector. They thought enemies never lied at the bargaining tables. They thought criminals and twilighters were simply misunderstood. There was a time for talk, but there was a time for action.

The Admirals' Council had gone soft, he told her. It was all about talk now. About resolutions and committees. The council funded studies when they should be funding new weapons and better ships. They'd forgotten how to take action.

So she changed tracks her first year in the academy and signed on with ImpSec. She never wanted to forget how to take action.

Tage hadn't. He now chose his assassins from ImpSec's ranks. That almost made her regret—made her *ashamed* of—her career choice. Except those same skills Tage now had working for him, she offered to the Alliance. It made Welford's disapproving looks and Adney's suspicions worth it.

But it also made her realize she could never underestimate the opposition.

Rya passed Martoni and Corvang in the stairwell on Deck 3 on her way up to 2 Forward. She hadn't seen Philip since they crossed the C-6, more than seven hours ago. She was officially—or semi-officially, considering the situation—off duty. Maybe he was less busy. Maybe—

"Great shirt, Bennton!" Martoni was laughing.

"What?" She followed his gaze, which was centered on her chest. She knew why most men stared at her chest. This time, however, the reason was different.

"Looks like you and that cat traded uniforms," Corvang said, his low voice holding his own growl of laughter.

It did. Her dark shirt was smeared with white fur. She brushed at it. "He kept me company in divisionals the past few hours."

"Shedding, not sneezing, eh?" Martoni asked.

She'd just stepped past him. She turned. "What?" she said for the second time in as many minutes.

"Sneezing. Didn't you see him on Mather's console

before we hit jump? Cat was sneezing and spitting all over poor Commo. Pissed Mather off. Welford had to grab him. The cat, not Commo. Thought you were there."

Her mind raced. "Yes. Right."

"Lieutenant Bennton, you know you're not supposed to be alone," Corvang reminded her.

"Right," she said again.

Martoni and Corvang trudged past her, heading down the stairs. Rya stood, unmoving, the scene playing over in her mind: Welford grasping the hissing cat by the neck. Philip ordering her to lock the cat in his quarters.

Because Captain Folly had been spitting—and sneezing—all over Burnaby Mather. The same Burnaby Mather who brought her water and who very clearly harbored a grudge against Philip Guthrie. Who so easily drew information out of her—a goddamned rookie, shit-for-brains, slag-headed security chief—about the firebomb. About disty-boom. About Captain Folly's ability to track down the chemical that was their lone lead to the enemy agent on board.

The same Burnaby Mather who denied ever seeing the cat sneeze. Good ol' Commo.

Just doing what I can to make things right, he said when he left her office in divisionals.

God. No.

Heart pounding, she raced up the stairs. She had to find Captain Folly before Mather did.

She slapped the palm pad at the main door to Philip's quarters, waited a few seconds to see if he answered, then tapped in her security override codes, hand shaking. "Guthrie!" she shouted as the door opened. No answer. The main salon was empty.

"Guthrie?" She sprinted to his bedroom. Empty but for a dark jacket thrown on the corner of his bed, white fur striping one corner. Folly had been here, but she didn't know how long ago. The jacket wasn't warm to the touch.

"Folly? Kitty-kitty?" She dropped to her knees, but the bed was on a platform. The cat couldn't fit under there.

"Folly!" Nothing in Philip's clothes closet—the others were locked. Nothing in his lav across the small hallway.

Back in the main salon again. *Think, Rya. Think like a cat.*

She checked under the couch, checked the dining-area chairs. Fur. No Captain Folly.

The door to Philip's office was open. Surely if the cat was in there, he would have come to her call.

Or not. He could be sleeping, curled up under . . .

She dove for Philip's desk, pushing his chair back. No cat. She turned, the glow from his deskscreen catching her eye.

That and her name. For two, three seconds she stared. This was Philip's private deskscreen. The *admiral's* private deskscreen. She had no right to—

Oh, God. He was transferring her off the ship. Immediately. As soon as they made Ferrin's. Her heart plummeted, her throat tightening as disappointment and defeat threatened to choke her.

She pushed away from the desk. There was no time for that now.

To hell with you, Philip Guthrie.

Captain Folly needed her. And she needed to stop Burnaby Mather.

Dillon, at helm, turned when Rya trotted onto the bridge. Jasli was talking to Tramer over at weapons, though the console was dark. Philip's command chair was empty.

"Seen Commo?" she asked as lightly as she could. It occurred to her—her ImpSec training kicking in as she'd raced up the bridge stairs—that Mather might not be working alone. She had to assume he wasn't. ImpSec Rule Number One: trust no one. ImpSec Rule Number Two: trust no one.

She'd already violated that rule by seeing Mather as command staff and trusting him with the information about disty-boom and Captain Folly. *Stupid slag-head.*

"You just missed him," Dillon said. "He came by five minutes ago."

"Yeah, well, I'm late." Her growing annoyance at herself made her sound genuinely grumpy. "Guess he got tired of waiting. Did he say where he was going?"

"No. Sorry. You want to put a shout out on intra-ship?"

"It's not that important." She did not want to warn Mather she was coming. "But if you see him, tell him I'm looking for him, okay?"

"You're not supposed to be wandering around the ship alone. Admiral's orders."

"I wouldn't be alone if I could find Mather!" she called out over her shoulder. She hit the stairs, checked the corridor on Deck 2 Forward again quickly. "Folly? Kitty-kitty?"

No cat. No Commo.

Decks 3 and 4 were under restricted access. That didn't mean Mather wasn't there—he was command staff, he was permitted entry. He could have gone back to his cabin on Deck 4. Philip said all bridge and command staff were to bunk in on 1 and 2. She hadn't had time to retrieve her pillow and blanket yet, but Mather was commo and off duty since they cleared the gate. He'd had plenty of time—

—to move any disatone tylethelene. He wouldn't want it to be found in his quarters. He probably didn't know the cat would smell it anyway. Disty-boom traces stayed around a long time. Odorless, colorless, and damned hard to get rid of.

Unless you put it into another bomb. What did he say just before he left? *Providing someone doesn't blow us out of the space lanes before we get there....* *There* was Ferrin's.

No, there wasn't a lot for a commo to do in jump.

Except build another bomb. And hunt down the cat who could expose him.

Mather wouldn't be in his quarters on Deck 4. He'd be in the maintenance shop on 5. Right where she'd startled him the other day. Right next to the shuttle bays. The vulnerable center of a Stryker-class heavy cruiser.

Philip Guthrie wasn't the only one who knew how to blow up a ship.

It had been a long, painful climb down with no working lifts, but Philip Guthrie was determined. He was not going to raise Sparks on intraship, pull the man out of engineering and up into his office. The admiral's office had the propensity to make people call him "sir." He needed honesty from Sparks, not deference.

Still, trepidation mixed with relief when he eased down into one of the metal-framed chairs in Sparks's small office. It felt so damned good to sit down. He just wasn't sure he was going to like what Sparks had to say.

Not after Con's lecture. Losing Constantine's respect hurt more than Philip thought it would. The younger man made it clear he no longer trusted Philip's judgment.

How in hell's fat ass could he command a ship, let alone a fleet, if his XO didn't trust him?

"Welford chewed me out a few hours ago," Philip said as Sparks closed his office door. "So I sat around thinking unkind thoughts about my new XO, then I sat around thinking rather morose and self-pitying thoughts about myself. Then I decided to come down here and see if you had anything to add to this doddering old fool's long list of failings."

He leaned back, crossing his arms over his chest. The chair creaked. The light scent of oranges drifted over him. He barely noticed it anymore.

Sparks lowered himself into his chair on the other side of the desk. It creaked too. "Doddering old fool, eh? That what Welford called you?"

"Not in so many words. But they teach you to read between the lines in admiral's school."

Sparks shook his head, then puffed out his cheeks with a short laugh. "I imagine Welford was blunt."

"I would have preferred blunt. He kept calling me sir and professing his respect. That immediately got my hackles up. So be blunt with me, Sparks."

The older man leaned back in his chair. It creaked again. "My concerns aren't the same as Welford's. ImpSec makes him skittish. Cory's kid scares the hell out of him. He's too young to remember the wars. He just heard the usual stories about *Ragkiril* monsters and ImpSec assassins. And he can't think of ImpSec without seeing Tage behind it."

Philip nodded. That took some of the sting out of Con's words. Not all, but some. He'd worked through his own prejudices about *Ragkiril* shape-shifters—

Chaz was in love with one. Watching Gabriel Sullivan deal with what he was—a human *Kyi-Ragkiril*—taught Philip much about the terrible price of power and that gifts could also be curses.

Philip also understood other people's reactions to ImpSec operatives, their training, their weapons. Fleet mind-set had long been that the military was a defender. ImpSec was staffed by killers.

And Con had likely never fondled a Norlack nor wanted to. He carried a lowly Mag-5, for God's sake.

"But I am concerned," Sparks continued, "about the situation that seems to be bringing you and Rya Bennton together. And what it could do to both your careers."

"I suppose if I told you there is no 'together' where Rya and I are concerned, you'd not believe me."

"Skipper." Sparks eyed him pointedly. "The paint damned near peels off the bulkheads every time the two of you look at each other."

Well, yeah. There was that. Philip cleared his throat. "That doesn't mean—"

"That you're sleeping with her, which is what Welford believes? No, but something is happening or about to happen. I'm concerned because what's bringing you together isn't a relationship that's grown slowly, where working together develops a mutual respect. This is an explosion. And in my estimation it's fueled by grief. And guilt."

Philip straightened, startled by Sparks's words.

"I saw it a lot during the war," Sparks said. "Proximity to death seems to set off an almost instinctual desire to mate. At least," Sparks added with a wave of one hand, "that's how the psychologists babble about it. That means Cory Bennton's death is the catalyst here. It ties the two of you together, seeking comfort in each other.

"There's nothing wrong with that." Sparks shrugged. "As I said, I saw it a lot during the war. Lots of relationships—intense relationships—started after the loss of crew members, friends. And they dissolved later, when the grief healed."

"I'm a big boy. I think I can handle a little heartache, if it comes to that."

Sparks leaned forward, hands against his desktop. "You're more than a big boy. You're an Alliance admiral. A leader. You are, or will be, highly visible. Everything you do will be scrutinized not just by Falkner's people but by your crew, your officers. A brief fling with a very junior officer could be viewed at the very least as an error in judgment. But more than that, everything you do is being watched by the Empire. The enemy. A brief fling could easily turn out to be a major disaster." He paused. "Darius Tage didn't hesitate to threaten Chaz's life to get at you. And you were no longer even married to her."

Tage did more than threaten. He set up Captain Chaz Bergren on false charges, imprisoned her, and then arrested her brother, Thad. Also Philip's friend. Also a former officer. Former.

Cory Bennton's wasn't the only death on Philip's soul's slate.

It would be a long walk back up five flights of stairs from engineering to the bridge. And painful, Philip knew with grim certainty, in more ways than one.

On Calth 9, she would have called for backup. In Port Chalo, she would have called for backup. But Rya Bennton wasn't on station or in a dirtside port. She was no longer even in ImpSec. She was on a Stryker-class heavy cruiser in the middle of the no-man's-land of jumpspace and there was no one she could fully trust. Or wanted to.

And there was no time.

She hit Deck 5 sucking wind, heart pounding in her ears. Time to start a diet, use the gym. Tomorrow, definitely. If there was a tomorrow. Going after an enemy operative with no backup generally reduced the probability of tomorrows.

She hated dieting anyway.

She flattened herself against the bulkhead at the entrance to the forward stairwell and listened, her heartbeat automatically slowing, the Norlack draped over her back digging into her shoulder blades. If she was lucky, Burnaby Mather sang or whistled while he crafted bombs.

She wasn't that lucky.

Okay, check the maintenance shop first, then the shuttle bays, then the upper cargo area and the auxiliary bridge. Mather or the cat—or both—had to be down here somewhere. For the hundredth time she yearned for a crew-locator system.

And people in hell want ice water.

A clank. Then a soft thud. She froze, then whipped around toward the sound.

Maintenance shop. Finishing what she'd interrupted?

She soft-footed past the shuttle bays, alert now to every creak and groan the ship made. Her hours wandering the corridors stood her in good stead. She knew with fair accuracy ship creaks from nonship creaks. Human sounds.

She considered for a moment powering up the Norlack, but that was a long-range weapon, capable of punching holes in bulkheads if she wasn't careful. Instead, she pulled her Carver out, safety off, power on full. Tiny red and blue dots glowed down the pistol's short barrel. If Mather was who she thought he was, if he was doing what she suspected he was doing, it would be kill or be killed. He had a Carver too. And probably more, just as she did. She doubted Tage or the Justice Wardens would send an operative in with no weapons.

She sprinted quickly across the empty corridor, her back to the portside bulkhead—the same side as the entrance to the maintenance shop, fifteen, twenty feet farther down. She held the Carver in a standard two-handed grip, chest high, and tamped down the urge to run for the door, blast it open. Expertise trumped emotions now. Stealth was everything. She tried not to think of it as time wasted; if Captain Folly was dead, the best revenge would be a cold, concise, exacting one.

But she prayed she'd be in time. Dead humanoids bothered her far less than an innocent pet murdered.

She reached the door, ears straining, eyes noting it no longer sat skewed on its track. It might have been fixed as part of routine maintenance. Or it could be someone's private project. A quick check of the palm pad showed the door was locked. She dropped her left hand off her pistol and keyed in a security code, bringing up recent entries.

A half hour ago, someone had used a command code to enter the shop.

The timing—if it was Mather—was right.

This was the critical moment. Standing, she'd be a target in the open doorway. She had to hit the door pad, drop, and roll through. And hope the attention of whoever was inside would be drawn upward by the movement of the door, the light spilling in from the corridor, and not down to one shit-for-brains security chief on the decking.

She paused for a moment, racking her memory for any other way into the shop. Sections of the *Alric Stockwell*'s schematics flashed into her mind. Ventilation ducts. That was all. There was no other way in or out. A good reason why Mather would have chosen to use the shop. A sole entry meant easy defense and no surprise visitors—not with the door fixed.

He was about to get one anyway.

She secured the Norlack rifle in front of her and sucked in a breath. Three, two . . . now! She punched the palm pad. She dropped to her knees, shoved herself through the opening door onto her hip, then her elbow, as soundlessly as she could, teeth gritted, Carver and rifle tucked against her chest. Shop overhead lights were on. A row of tall duro-hards on her right caught her immediate attention. She lunged for them in a crouch as something crashed to the decking, metal on metal.

Just like last time.

She froze, screened by the large canisters from whoever was in the shop. There were no more noises, and the harsh shadows patterning the decking on her left and right didn't change. She glanced up. Light panels striped the overhead, except where they filtered down through a large cargo security netting suspended near the far bulkhead.

A short snap like a measured footfall. Then darkness. Light panels winked out.

Shit. Low-light targeting was her worst skill. It was a waiting game now. She hated waiting. It was like a slow death. A damned miserable way to die.

Tsst! Tsst!

Rya's heart stuttered. She knew that sound. Captain Folly sneezing.

Tsst!

Fuck. But at least he was still alive.

Something rattled, tinny-sounding and high-pitched. She narrowed her eyes in the darkness, which wasn't as dark as she'd thought. The tiny red dots of power ports glowed from the bulkheads at random intervals. A green emergency lightbar was set over the door. There might be others, but she couldn't see them from her position. So she ignored her eyes and used her ears, listening, letting her mind repeat the sounds. Pinpoint it. That had always been one of her strong suits.

Another rattle. A cage or chain. Lightweight. Behind her on her left. She turned slowly, carefully, putting the sound on her right.

Tsst!

That's where Captain Folly was. The question then became, where was Mather? Was he with the cat, knowing that whoever entered the shop would be drawn to the sound? Or on the opposite axis, ready to shoot her in the back?

Someone had to make the first move. And she hated waiting.

She pushed the Norlack quietly over her back again, then pulled off her ImpSec beret, again studded with its metal service pins, and balled it up in one hand. It was dark and soft, should fly through the air unnoticed until it landed with a *clink* from the pins. Then she'd see who reacted.

She threw it from the left side of the duro-hard, away from where the cat was. One, two...*tinkle, clink*. It hit the decking.

A scuffling sound, weight shifting abruptly, fabric moving. Rya snapped her body into shooting stance, swung out from behind the duro-hard, and fired at the sound. Twice, three times.

Laser energy flared as it hit pylons, worktables, and for the briefest of moments she saw the outlines of a set of servostairs, some stacked shapes that were cargo boxes. And a man's form, short and stocky. Muscular. Lunging for the decking. She'd missed him by mere inches.

She jerked back behind the duro-hards just as he returned fire, dropping to her knees in case his Carver penetrated whatever was in the containers. The duro-hards shook, something sizzled, but nothing punched through.

Well, fancy that. Luck.

She listened again. Nothing. He wasn't going to give away his position again unless she forced him to.

She swung out again and fired overhead, the pistol's

energy causing a small flare as it impacted against the light panel. She used those few seconds to catch Mather's furtive movements on the far side of the shop, heading for Captain Folly. She couldn't let Mather kill him, couldn't let the cat die for her own stupidity.

She fired again. Mather dropped to the floor with a grunt, and for a moment she thought she had him. Then a laser's burning energy grazed her shoulder, only because she heard the sound of the discharge before she saw it and jumped back in time.

Shit! Her shoulder stung, but the fact that it was stinging at all told her it was a minor wound. A direct hit and she'd feel nothing. She might not even know her arm was gone until it hit the decking.

She scrambled behind the duro-hards but kept moving because she heard something now. A low, muffled laugh.

Bastard. Think this is funny? ImpSec assassins never laughed. The only sound they were permitted to make was breathing. And *that* only on occasion.

Then a louder sound. Clinking. The bastard was at Captain Folly's cage. No. She had to stop him now. She inched out, quickly, silently, keeping low, then jerked hard around the corner of the duro-hard, flicking on the laser sights just as she did so. It would give away her position. But it would also insure that this time she wouldn't miss.

The red dot flared against a mass of white. Shit! Not Mather. She checked her fire, swearing silently, hands cramping. Captain Folly was where Mather's chest should be.

A burst of laser energy surged toward her, along with the body of the cat. She rolled, firing low, trying to avoid the white blur coming at her. It hit the ground with a cry and a hiss. God and stars, the cat was alive! *Run, Folly, run!* she urged him silently.

Mather was moving, ducking behind high, dark shapes. She fired again. This time his grunt held real pain. Good, she'd hit the bastard, in the hip or leg, she thought. She heard him stumble, crash into something.

A barrage of shots forced her to scoot quickly to the right to a group of dark shapes. She had leaned against what felt like a table leg, getting her bearings, shoulder throbbing, when Mather fired again and again. He was scared now. She could sense it, feel it.

Light flared into the maintenance shop as the door slid open, a panel sizzling on the bulkhead. For a half second she thought help had arrived, Sachi or Tramer. Hope crested. The sizzling told her otherwise. In his firing frenzy, Mather had hit the door controls.

Good move, Commo. And thanks. This changed the game. He could see her. But she could see him. And hear him. She edged toward the right side of the boxes stacked against the low table. Her shoulder burned, and she could feel thin, warm rivulets running down her chest. Maybe it was a little more than a grazing wound, but she still had her arm. And she'd hit Mather. That was all that mattered. And Captain Folly was free.

More shuffling. Sounded like he was dragging one leg. She dropped to one knee, the Carver in her hands moving unerringly toward the sound. Her eyes were secondary, useful only when—

There! She saw him, a dark, shadowed shape, rising. Time for the kill.

Suddenly she was facedown, something heavy slamming painfully against her back, pinning her arms and legs to the decking. Her lungs burned. The Norlack cut into her spine. She tasted blood, and as footsteps pounded closer she realized that a metal lattice covered her hand, felt the thick bars scrape against her cheek as she inched her face to the right. Her Carver was a foot away, under the same crosshatched grating. She pushed against the grating—the security netting she now remembered hanging from the overhead—and tried to lever up as Mather's boots came into view. She couldn't move it. She was trapped.

"You just don't listen to orders, do you, Bennton?" Mather's voice was low and harsh. A bloody stream darkened one pant leg. "No one's permitted to wander about the ship alone."

Philip was on the third stair tread when something extremely odd made him stop, turn, and stare down the corridor on Deck 5 Aft. An animal, from its loping gait. White. One dark ear. The cat, he realized with a start. But what was that dark thing in front of it? And the brownish streak—

He was off the stairs in a quick move, ignoring the jolt of pain. He lunged forward, closing the distance between the cat and himself. Captain Folly slowed, and Philip could see that brownish streak was a smear of blood down one flank. And the dark thing in its mouth, dangling between its front legs...

God. Rya's dark-blue beret.

His heart stopped. The cat dropped the beret at his boots.

"Where's Rya?" he rasped out, as if the cat could answer.

The cat turned and took off back down the corridor in a dead run.

With a grunt, Philip snatched the beret from the

decking and, teeth gritted, lunged quickly after the beast.

He was almost to the shuttle bays when the sounds reached him: laser fire, then a loud crash. He slowed, shoving Rya's beret through his belt, then drew his Carver. The big ugly cat stopped just short of the open door to the maintenance shop, back arched, fur on end. Hissing.

A male voice filtered out. Then a woman's. He couldn't quite make out the words, but he knew both. Mather and Rya. He edged closer.

"Justice Wardens?" Mather laughed. "They're slag, garbage. Just like your so-called Alliance. You're both destroying the Empire. You—"

Mather's voice halted. He knew someone was there. How could he not? Philip's approach wasn't exactly quiet. He damned himself, his injured leg, and the fact that he'd reacted without thinking, without analyzing. *Sloppy, Guthrie.*

Sloppy could get Rya hurt. Or killed. He didn't know where she was or what she was doing there, but the words *Justice Wardens* and *Empire* told him Rya had somehow found their mole. But he didn't know if Mather held her captive or they were both dead-eyeing each other with their Carvers. He added this ship with its inadequate tech to the list of things to be damned.

Barging through that open doorway could get them both killed.

"Run out of reasons to kill me, Commo?" Rya's voice came through clearly. He listened intently, trying to pinpoint where she was.

"Shut up!" Mather's answer was low, angry.

"Why? Trapping me under this chain-link—"

"Quiet!" It was a harsh, barely audible whisper. "Or you're dead!"

Chain-link. Philip knew exactly where she was—somewhere near the equipment-containment area, a section of decking where small objects that could come loose during transit were confined under a heavy metal netting. And she risked her life to tell him. Mather could kill her easily. Would kill her, if he knew who stood in the corridor outside the maintenance-shop door.

Slowly, Philip backed away. Mather had to wonder if someone was still in the corridor, someone was still waiting for the opportunity to rush in.

But there was another way into the maintenance shop. Jodey had given him the updated schematics before he left the *Nowicki*. Changes were all on Deck 5 in the cargo, shuttle, and maintenance areas, changes he'd confirmed on his walk-through with Welford, days ago. Changes a commercial hauler needed and a warship didn't.

Changes that put a new access tunnel between the shuttle bays and the shop.

Philip prayed Mather didn't know that.

Another ten feet brought him to the shuttle bays. Philip tapped in the code, holding his breath as the wide double doors slid open. If they creaked, rattled, or rumbled, he would scrap this goddamned bucket at Ferrin's.

If they creaked, rattled, or rumbled, Rya was dead.

They slid open with a low rumble. Very low.

It took him less than two minutes to find the new access tunnel that connected the shuttle bay to the shop. It felt like two hours. He pulled back the crosshatched cover—not unlike the larger panel he suspected covered Rya—and tensed for the slightest metallic squeak. He refused to let himself consider that Rya might already be dead.

He'd lied to Sparks. This was a heartache he could not handle.

He rolled his shoulders, pushing out some of the tension, then slipped inside the opening, which was a good six inches shorter than he was. Grateful that the pipes and conduit were down only one side he pressed his back against the outer wall for support. He left his cane in the shuttle bay. All he needed was his walking arsenal, holstered, tucked, or stashed on his body.

And hope.

The narrow tunnel moved on an uphill slant after the first ten feet, light dimming as he left the shuttle bay behind. A small glow guided him ahead. His ears strained for sounds that Rya was still alive. He didn't hear a Carver's distinct whine, but then, knives were silent. And equally deadly.

He slowed as the tunnel's grated cover came into view. The muted light filtering in to the shop from the open doorway was barely enough to let him make out the cover's thin metal bars. He was surprised Mather hadn't closed the doorway to the corridor. He suspected he couldn't. He was more surprised Mather hadn't activated the shop overhead lights. Either they were broken too or he felt he still needed somewhere to hide.

He sank down to his knees and peered cautiously through the grating at an angle. Rya's unmoving form, trapped under the metal grid of a cargo net, was in the upper right corner. Philip's jaw clenched, his throat tightened, and for a dangerous moment his vision blurred. He blinked, clearing his eyes.

Where in hell was Mather? He searched the harsh shadows. Yes. No. He was wrong. That wasn't . . . Yes. It was.

His heart hammered. Not enough room to use a

plasma star. Angle was wrong. It had to be the Carver. One clear shot. That's all he wanted. Not answers, not information, not explanations. He didn't care why Mather was there, who he worked for, what he intended to do. The man held Rya Bennton prisoner. That qualified him for a death sentence in Philip Guthrie's world.

Mather crouched by a row of duro-hards, nervously watching the open doorway but with his Carver clearly trained on Rya. Taking no chances.

But life was all about taking chances, wasn't it?

Philip poked the short barrel of his Carver-12 through the grating. A few inches to the left. That's all he needed for a clear shot. A few short—

A grinding clank, a thump. Mather jerked up, twisting as Rya kicked the soles of her boots hard against the large grating, raising it a few inches, her right hand grasping for the small of her back. Her L7.

"You're dead, Bennton," Mather cried, lunging forward.

Philip fired, an invisible stream of laser energy racing across the wide expanse. Rya twisted on her side, L7 now in her hands, but Philip couldn't tell if she got a shot off, couldn't hear the L7's low hum amid the high whines of two Carvers discharging: his and Mather's.

Philip fired again, then it was Mather who was twisting, stumbling forward, falling. He crashed on top of the grating that covered Rya, his Carver spinning across the decking.

"Rya!" Philip's voice was raw, harsh with wrenching emotion. He kicked the grating out, then shoved himself out of the tunnel, his back aching, his leg screaming in searing pain. None of that mattered. "Rya!"

He caught his hip on the edge of a worktable as he barreled across the shop decking. He stumbled briefly but kept going, shoving empty cargo crates out of his way.

"Guthrie?" Her voice was muffled, weak, but, God and stars above, she was alive.

He staggered to a halt, then dropped to his knees next to Mather's body. He grabbed the man's collar and wrenched him backward. There was no resistance. Mather was either dead or unconscious.

Philip didn't care.

Rya lay on her stomach, the L7 in her left hand, the wide grating once again pinning her to the decking. He lifted one edge but couldn't shove it off her. It jammed against a table and some duro-hards. He swore out loud. "That's as high as it goes. Can you move, scoot over here to me?"

"Yeah," she said, but her voice was thin. He didn't want to think Mather's shot had found its mark.

"I'm going to grab your arm and pull you. Ready?"

"Set. Go." Her voice was a low whisper.

He yanked her out and up against him. The metal gridwork crashed back down to the decking. They fell backward in a tangle of arms and weapons, the barrel of the Norlack strapped across her back grazing his temple. Philip rolled on his side, taking her with him, holding her tightly against his body before releasing her. She was injured. He angled up on one painful elbow, gently sliding her down to the decking, laying her on her back. He needed to see her face, needed to see her eyes open, needed to hear her say—

"Fuck." Her voice was breathy. Her eyes fluttered open. "I hate getting shot."

"Where are you hit? How bad?"

"Right shoulder. Front's just grazed. The back," and

she winced. "Hurts like a bitch. But I don't think anything's severed."

He saw the blood now and the charred edges of her uniform. He ran trembling fingers down the side of her face. "There's an intraship panel by the door. Stay here."

"Why not? View's great," he heard her rasp as he shoved himself to his feet.

He stumbled to the panel and punched at the glowing green icon with the side of his fist. "Guthrie, Code Red! Full medical team. Maintenance shop, Deck Five. Now!" Then he hit the icons for the overhead lights. Only the back and the right side came on, the others probably casualties of the firefight between Mather and Rya. But it was enough for him to see that Burnaby Mather was dead, a large bloody stain on his left thigh and a smaller, more deadly hit to his left temple. The latter was Philip's shot.

But he also more clearly saw the tight lines of pain around Rya's mouth and the labored rise and fall of her chest.

His own chest tightened. He knelt beside her, pulled the L7 from her grasp, then folded her left hand inside both of his. Her skin was cold. Wide hazel eyes studied him under dark slanted brows.

"Rebel—"

"Guthrie!" Sparks, shouting his name, followed by thudding boot steps, then more shouts. Then Con and Sachi Holton and, seconds later, Corvang pushing his tall frame past them all, two med-techs in tow.

Philip rose, releasing Rya to the med-techs and their blinking, beeping instruments, their hushed voices, their concerned frowns. One of the techs tore Rya's shirt at the shoulder, then ripped the lacy strap of her undershirt. The other slapped pale-colored patches on her bare, bruised skin. She stared at Philip through the whole procedure, her gaze wavering only when she blinked.

Words he ached to say stuck in his throat.

An antigrav stretcher appeared from somewhere—the ship had medical supplies on each deck, but if you asked him now, he knew he couldn't locate a one. He could only watch her face, her steady hazel gaze.

Only as they lifted her onto the stretcher did she turn her face away.

And only as they guided her stretcher under the glare of the doorway light did he see the lone tear running down her cheek.

Coward. He accepted his self-damnation without question. *Yes.*

He looked back into the maintenance shop. Con and Tramer had turned Mather's body over. At the far end of the room, Sachi Holton was examining a small cage on a wide worktable, which also held a number of metal canisters and other things Philip couldn't identify from this distance.

Someone pressed his cane into his hand. Sparks. "What happened here, Skipper?"

He met his chief engineer's gaze evenly. "Failure and stupidity." He didn't even try to keep the bitterness out of his voice. "Both mine."

He leaned on his cane and pushed for the corridor. It was going to be a long, painful walk back up to sick bay.

17

It was twenty minutes before Philip was allowed access to her in sick bay. And when he was, he found Rya sitting up on the edge of a diagnostic bed, palms pressed flat against the sheets, a thin pale-blue towel draped around her neck. The corner of a yellow pain patch was visible on the right side of her collarbone. Her shirt and undershirt were missing. Any other time, the thought of Rya half naked would put a broad grin on his face. And generate more interesting reactions in other parts of his anatomy.

Now, perversely, it angered him. "What in hell are you doing sitting up?"

"Where's Welford?" she shot back.

"I tried telling Lieutenant Bennton she needs to rest," came a male voice from an adjoining room behind Rya. Not Welford's voice. One of the med-tech's. Dugan. Philip read his name tag as the meddie walked in, one hand up, two large light-purple anti-infective sticky patches dangling from his fingertips. "She won't listen."

Philip looked back at Rya. "You're confined—"

"Get Welford up here. We need to—" She jerked upright with a yelp. "Slagging mother of God, that stings!"

Dugan grinned at Philip from over Rya's bare shoulder. "Triple dose, Lieutenant. Or else you're not leaving my sick bay."

"Sadist."

Rya's flinching had rearranged the towel, which would not under normal circumstances, Philip noted sagely, have done much to cover her anyway. Now one breast and peaked nipple were exposed. With a self-chastising sigh, he stepped closer and grabbed the edges of the towel with his free hand, bringing them together almost under her chin. He tried not to notice how that action revealed the sides of her breasts.

He glared down at her. She glared up at him.

"If you'll excuse me, Admiral, Lieutenant, I, uh, have other patients to torture." Dugan disappeared.

"You need to stay in sick bay," Philip said, his voice softening.

"You need to get Welford up here. Holton and Sparks too. Mather was an Imperial mole. And one who liked to brag. There's never been anything wrong with the *Folly*'s communications systems. Tage knows everything that's happened on board this ship. And everything that's happened on the *Nowicki*."

It took a heartbeat or two for her words to register. *Tage knows . . .*

Philip released his grasp on her towel, then shoved his cane in her hand. He yanked at the zipper on his gray uniform shirt, stripping down to the black long-sleeved thermal he wore underneath. "Put this on," he said gruffly, pulling the shirtsleeves over his wrists. "We'll discuss it in the ready room."

She was staring at him again with those clear hazel

eyes. Defiantly. Challengingly. He couldn't look away.
He didn't want to look away. He stood there, his shirt
balled up in one hand, very aware of her knees pressed
against his thighs, of the heat generated at their point
of contact. Very aware of heat rising to his face.
Slowly, she pulled the towel from around her neck, one
tantalizing inch at a time, until only rich brown curls
brushed against her bare shoulders and against the yellow and purple med-broches stuck haphazardly on her
skin.

He felt his groin tighten in response, the heat on his
face flashing through his body.

Somewhere, he was sure, paint peeled off the bulkheads.

She was shot, she was bruised, and she was, in
Philip's estimation, beyond beautiful. Incredibly desirable.

She plucked at the shirt in his fingers with a gentle
tug, then another, before his brain kicked in, telling
him what he wanted. She shoved the towel into his
empty hand with a much firmer motion. At that point
he forced himself to look away, because this could not
go where he wanted it to, no matter how much he and
his body wanted it to.

He had a war to wage and a fleet to cobble together.
And Darius Tage knew far, far too much.

Rya leaned back against the ready-room chair, tugging
Philip's shirt more tightly around her. Fifteen minutes
ago, when she pulled it on, it held the warmth of his
body. That warmth was gone but it still smelled like
him, like holster leather and soap and maleness. She
tried to concentrate on that, not on the throbbing
pain in her shoulder or the prickly sting of the slagging

anti-infective patches stuck on her skin like grotesque pastel leeches.

She probably should be in sick bay, but God damn it, she was the one who'd unmasked Mather as an Imperial operative. This was *her* mission, *her* investigation. She would see it through to the end or to the point where Philip tossed her off his ship. Whichever came first.

And she'd take his shirt with her.

And Captain Folly too. The cat snored softly on the chair on her right. The deep scratch on his side that he endured bolting from his cage had been cleaned by the same Dugan the Sadist who'd treated her. Only a lot more gently, she was sure. The captain had claws.

She reached over and scratched his ears as Welford trudged in from the bridge, mouth pursed. He shoved his datapad across the table to where she and Philip sat, waiting for the XO's preliminary analysis on the extent of Mather's subterfuge. And sabotage.

"I took apart everything that's happened at Commo's station since we came on board. He's been transmitting to a datalink here," Welford leaned in front of Philip to jab his finger on the pad's screen, "that in turns feeds everything to three different Imperial drones. Two in Calth, one in Baris. He's been receiving information, probably orders as well. But what he received, I can't tell you."

"Self-destructs?" Philip asked.

"The Empire is nothing if not consistent," Welford answered.

Philip nodded.

"Even self-destructs leave behind something," Rya said.

Welford huffed out a sigh. "With the equipment on Ferrin's, I might be able to do more. But on this ship and in jump transit—hell. I can't even send the code fragments to someone else for analysis."

Which was why they couldn't warn the *Nowicki*. One of the first things they'd discussed. Philip had a top-priority heavily encoded message ready to go the moment they cleared the exit gate. But that was almost two shipdays away.

A lot could happen out there in real time in two shipdays.

Sachi Holton stepped into the ready room from the corridor. Two of her short braids had unraveled. Dark curls hung down the left side of her face, the red hair clips she'd used now secured to the collar of her gray shirt. "Sparks confirmed those containers in the machine shop contained just enough disty-boom to set off another explosion. Probably, as Rya guessed, in the shop or the shuttle bays. Mather had a detonator almost finished on the table down there. Corvang found more parts when we tossed his cabin."

"Any archivers or log feeds?" Rya asked.

Sachi shook her head, making her braids wiggle. "Not that Corvang or I could find."

Philip snorted softly. "You think he was recording his evil deeds for posterity?"

Rya slanted him a glance. "He was an operative in deep cover, out of contact for most of the time with his handlers. He *couldn't* trust his memory to accurately relay what the Empire wanted to know. He had to use some kind of data-storage device like an archiver. Something easily concealed that could be encrypted."

"He could have destroyed it as a precaution," Welford said.

"I didn't get the feeling down there in the machine shop that he thought today was his day to die."

"I'll look again," Sachi offered. "There are a couple

empty cabins down the corridor from his. He might have stashed things in there."

Rya grasped the arms of her chair and pushed herself up. "I'll go with you."

Philip held her chair in place. "Sit, Lieutenant."

"I know what I'm looking for. Sir," she added because she knew her doing so irked him. And she couldn't help herself. Must be the pain meds.

He didn't let go of her chair. "Request denied. Now, sit!"

She sat, but she glared at him.

He glared back at her.

"I'll go check those cabins." Sachi ducked quickly out of the ready room.

"I can and will," Philip said with a soft but insistent tone in his voice, his gaze unwavering, "beat you with my cane."

Welford made a disgusted noise. "I might as well go help Holton." He headed for the corridor. Or at least Rya thought he did. She was still staring at the marvelous blue eyes and wasn't totally sure of what else was happening in the ready room.

Damned pain meds.

Philip turned away abruptly, dragging Welford's datapad in front of him.

She refocused, pushing away her pain, the physical and the emotional.

"Even self-destructs leave behind something," she reiterated, because she knew what bothered him about Welford's report. The same thing that bothered her. The problem was larger than they thought. And their only source of information was dead.

He grunted, scowling.

She leaned to her right and pulled up the closest deskscreen. Her security code brought up the files she'd saved after Commo—Mather left her office. "He transferred off the *Waldor Rey* to the *Nowicki*, about three years ago. That makes sense. A few other things don't, in light of what happened."

Philip angled his face toward her. "Olefar was the *Rey*'s captain."

Olefar. Amazing how much could be transmitted through tone and three syllables. Philip didn't like the man any more than her father had. "I thought he still was."

"He got the *Masling* after Tage—" He stopped, eyes darkening. "He was rewarded for his loyalty."

"Mather wasn't. He got an EFS-Gold and went nowhere. He was still third commo when the *Nowicki* took him." Or did he really go nowhere? Maybe his promotions, unlike his Exemplary Fleet Service commendation, were not the kind normally recorded in a standard personnel jacket.

"What else?"

"Here." She pointed to her deskscreen as he leaned on the arm of her chair. "COMTAC training right after assignment to the *Nowicki*. So they put him on the ship, then send him off to school, then put him back. Not unusual, but not—"

"This is only what Fleet wants us to see, not what really happened. Not who or what Mather really is."

"He was a year ahead of you in the academy. Did you know him?"

Philip pursed his lips, eyes narrowing. "Not that I remember. And that's assuming this," he pointed to her screen, "is even remotely factual. I'm going to take a wild guess and state that Tage put Mather on the *Nowicki* because of me. I'd been," and he sighed, shaking his head, "incredibly naive, and with the promise of an admiralty dangled before me, by Tage, I took to confiding in him all the things I saw wrong with the Empire and the Admirals' Council. He encouraged my 'refreshing honesty,' as he used to call it. All my honesty did was provide him with a list of people he could call traitors."

"Why put Mather on the *Nowicki*? The *Loviti* was your ship."

"Jodey Bralford was my XO on the *Loviti*. And a good friend. Still is. When he took command of the *Nowicki*, it evidently presented Tage with the perfect opportunity to have all my conversations with Jodey recorded and sent to him, especially after the incident on Marker with Chaz and Sullivan."

Incident on Marker? Marker was actually several stations that comprised the main Imperial shipyards in Aldan. "The fire there a few month ago?" she asked, her mind grasping for details.

"Remember the incident on Corsau years ago when a shipment of jukors ... Well, you might not be old enough." Philip cleared his throat.

"I remember. A shipment of those mutant beasts escaped, killing civilians, just like on Umoran recently." Jukors scared the hell out of her. She'd seen one once. She never wanted to see another fanged, razor-winged abomination again.

"There was a breeding facility for them on Marker. Sullivan and Chaz destroyed it and have been hunting down other breeding labs ever since. Corsau was no accident. Neither was Umoran. Thing is, I helped them get off Marker before station cops could find them. I always wondered if Tage somehow suspected. Once Jodey took over the *Nowicki*, and with Mather in position as commo, Tage had his proof. Proof of that and everything else since." He shook his head slowly, his mouth a grim line. "I can see that so goddamned clearly now."

"And when the *Nowicki* came with the Alliance, so did Mather."

"The entire Alliance is at risk, and there's not one goddamned thing I can do about it. Even if I could reach Jodey right now, the damage is already done. Every bit of data that's on that ship is in Tage's hands."

"Found them!" Sachi Holton bounced into the ready room, breathless. Welford appeared behind her. She glanced over her shoulder at him, then held up two thin rectangular objects, triumph in the wide grin on her face.

"Archivers," Rya said softly. Vindication. She was right. *Throw my ass off this ship, will you, Guthrie?*

"I want to use one of these deskscreens to open them," Welford said, pointing to the ready-room table, "but I need to isolate it first. We don't know what fail-safes this contains. A worm that shuts down this ship in the middle of jump transit would not be a good thing."

"I can do that," Rya said. She pushed back her chair and slipped to the decking before Philip could stop her. She'd helped Welford integrate the deskscreens in this room. She could easily help him un-integrate them.

That took about five minutes, during which time Philip left the ready room and Sachi Holton crawled under the table to hold the handbeam while Rya poked and tapped according to Welford's instructions.

Sachi helped her to her feet. Philip was nowhere to be seen, but Alek Dillon leaned on the back of Welford's chair, exchanging "yeah, okay" and "no, try that" with him.

Philip wasn't on the bridge either. "In his office, I think," Corvang offered.

Probably fine-tuning her transfer. Rya sat in one of the chairs at the empty weapons console, fatigue washing over her. Her wristwatch told her it was 2200 hours. Her body told her it was much later than that.

Too late for her and Philip. All the soppy love scenes she'd ever read where the stalwart hero professes his deep love for the injured heroine were shown to be just what they were—pure fiction—down in the maintenance shop. Evidently the self-indulgence that surfaced in response to impending doom happened only when the doom was Philip's. When it was her life on the line, it was business as usual. Even a "please don't die, I might miss you" would have been appreciated.

Nothing. She was just another crew member to him. She wasn't even sure he saw her as a woman, because when he'd handed her his shirt in sick bay, he just stood there, as if her being half naked was no concern. So she made sure she was very half naked, because she had to know...

And he turned away.

Lose thirty pounds...

Even Matt never turned away. But then, she didn't know Matt to ever turn away a woman. Just For Fun Sex was so much easier. Caring hurt.

She stood, wondering how to make herself useful on a ship with no security systems and more than half the crew at battle stations, when a low epithet that sounded very like Welford caught her attention. She turned on her heel and took the few steps back into the ready room.

He looked up at her approach. "Perfect timing, Bennton. Where's Admiral Guthrie?" His tone was grim.

"Corvang said in his office. But I—"

"Get on intraship," Welford ordered, pointing to

the panel on the bulkhead. "Get him up here. We have serious problems."

Philip didn't like the sound of Rya's voice on intraship. He liked even less the looks on Rya's and Con Welford's faces when he came into the ready room.

"Sparks is on his way up, along with Martoni," Con told him. "I'll give you the basics right now but I'll hold up on details until they get here. Close the door, Bennton," he added.

Rya reached the palm pad for the corridor door while Philip was still taking the seat next to Con. She closed the bridge door as he studied the few snippets of sentences on Con's deskscreen. By the time she sat, Philip understood the urgency behind the summons only too well.

He clenched his fists on the tabletop, when pounding them would have felt far more appropriate. "The Empire will have ships waiting for the *Folly* at the C-Six gate."

"All data indicates that, yes," Con said. "They know we left Seth, they know about the encounter with the Star-Ripper. They know that we survived Mather's attempts to disable this ship—the firebomb in the lift, the move in the auxiliary bridge—so that the Imperial strike force tracking you could catch up."

"I noticed Mather wasn't at his console during the fire, but I thought he was helping elsewhere," Philip said.

"He was," Rya put in. "It just wasn't us he was helping."

The corridor door chimed, the command-staff code flashing on the deskscreen on Philip's right and evidently on Rya's too, because she stood. But not without first putting her hand on the Carver. Absently, he noticed she still wore his shirt. She'd tucked it in her pants, but it was large for her and bloused out around her waist. Another time he might have found that amusing, maybe even endearing. But life had turned serious and bordered on dire.

She hit the palm pad. Sparks came in, followed by a frowning Martoni.

"It looks like none of us is going to get any sleep tonight," Sparks said, swiveling a chair around.

Philip waited for the doors to close. "Tell them."

"We found the archivers Mather used," Con said. "Summaries he made of his orders and his reports. The Empire not only knows everything that happened until we hit the gate, it will be waiting for us when we exit."

There was a tight silence, full of anguish and frustration.

"How many ships?" Philip asked. The brief sections of transcribed text he viewed didn't show that data.

"He wasn't given that information, or if he was, he didn't note it," Con answered. "But we won't be far from the Baris border. You'd know better than I would what ships the Empire has been keeping at Starport Six or Talgarrath."

Philip did, and it wasn't an encouraging summation. "What we—what they've kept there may not be what's there now. But it's not unlikely we could face the *Drey,* the *Masling,* or even the *Loviti,* in addition to whatever this strike force is Mather talks about. The plain fact is, all we have are short-range laser banks. We'd have a chance against some P-33s. As long as they weren't leading a pair of cruisers." Maybe.

"So we abort out of jump before the gate." Martoni splayed one hand out, looking from Con to Sparks. "They won't know—"

"You ever been part of an aborted jump, boy?" Sparks asked. "Aborting a jump takes precise, defined data from instruments this ship no longer has. This ain't no captain's pinnace or some tricked-out Imperial fighter. This is an eight-hundred-fifty-ton fruit hauler. Forget what she used to be—and even when she was what she used to be, I don't know if I'd have wanted to chance an aborted jump in her. She predates the technology that made those things only slightly less than fatal."

"Imperial ships at exit are completely fatal," Philip said, understanding Sparks's objections but, like Martoni, wanting options. Needing options. "Is there any chance—"

"Skipper, I'd like nothing more than to make you happy. Especially right now, given all you've been through here. I'm sorry. I can't make you happy."

He could hear it in Sparks's voice. His miracle worker had run out of miracles. Philip turned back to Con. "What else is in those archivers? Give us everything, no matter how insignificant. There has to be something we can use."

Con sighed. "The Empire doesn't know Mather's dead. They don't know that we know they'll be waiting at gate exit. Other than that..."

The XO went through the data on both archivers in chronological order. The first started just before Mather left the *Nowicki* with Adney and her team. If they lived through this, Philip thought, he'd have to tell Jodey to strip Mather's cabin—hell, strip down the whole ship. There might be other archivers and more data the Alliance could use.

If they lived through this—no. He'd add that to the encrypted message to Jodey, send it three different ways as soon as they exited the gate. One of the messages would make it. Even if Philip didn't.

But it wasn't just his own mortality on the horizon. It was his officers, his crew. It was Sparks coming out of retirement. It was Corvang, who'd studied everything the Great Guthrie ever wrote. It was Con Welford, who deserved better than an old fool for a CO.

And it was Rya.

He couldn't let thoughts of her surface, not now. There was too much to do, too much at stake. But, dear God and sweet stars above, there was Rya.

It wasn't that he doubted her abilities to handle this, not as an officer. She was a Bennton; every hour he spent with her, he saw more of Cory's resolve, his dedication. But there was also Rya the woman who fought by his side on Kirro Station, who saved his life on the shuttle, who should be in sick bay and wasn't.

He didn't doubt her. He doubted himself. And that scared the hell out of him.

"One thing I noticed in going over Mather's notes again," Con said, "are some of the technical terms he uses. We thought of him as Commo. I think he was more than that."

"He had ship's primaries and intended to run the ship himself from the auxiliary bridge," Rya pointed out.

"For a short time," Martoni said.

"He still would have to have more knowledge for that than what's reflected in his records," Rya said.

"It's as if he was purposely kept at third-shift commo up until now so no one would notice him," Philip put in. "And in jump transit, no one would care if he wasn't at his post. He wouldn't be expected to be, yet as command staff, he had access to everything."

Rya looked at him. "We need to track down everything he had access to."

"The entire ship," Con said with a broad wave of

his hand. "The admiral said it. Mather was command staff. He had codes. He had the authority."

Philip nodded. "And he was one of the first on board, along with you, Adney, and Corvang. Those first few days, he had total access to this ship. And very few eyes watching him."

"What are you saying?" Con regarded Philip with narrowed eyes.

"I'm saying we've had problems with this ship that we wrote off because she's a Stryker-class bucket. What if the problems aren't the ship but Mather?"

"He knew enough about the communications system to make it malfunction," Rya said.

"That was his job." Martoni leaned forward. "He would know those things."

"But what if he knew more?" Philip persisted.

"He could have known how to build a Stryker from the inside out." Sparks leaned back in his chair, lips pursed. He angled toward Philip. "But, Skipper, that's not going to give us the ability to do an aborted jump. You can alter what's here. You can't add what isn't."

Philip stood, leaning his fists on the table. "We have a little more than one and a half shipdays before we have to face the inevitable on the other side of that jumpgate. Constantine, Sparks, get your best technical people together. If we can't do the impossible, then we need to at least be able to do the unexpected." He took in the faces around the table, seeing rumpled uniforms and shadows under eyes. "Priority right now is getting intraship fully functional and getting all deskscreens linked."

"On it," Martoni and Con said together.

"Then get a few hours' sleep—working exhausted won't help. Next meeting is 0630, this room. Dismissed.

"Oh, and Con," he added as Sparks and Martoni rose, "if the data on those archivers is clean, shoot me over a copy of everything once deskscreens are linked. Fresh eyes never hurt."

If he was going to die, he damned well wanted to understand the man who'd brought him to that point before he did so.

Philip couldn't sleep. He'd stared at the data Con sent for over an hour, his gut clenching, his head pounding, anger clashing with determination. He would not let the Imperials take this ship. There was an answer here somewhere. There had to be.

But his eyesight was also blurring. He'd told his command staff not to work to exhaustion. *Listen to your own advice, Guthrie.*

So he'd trudged, cane in hand, across his main salon and collapsed onto his bed. He left his discarded clothes in a very un-Philip-Guthrie-like pile on the decking next to the bed. *Finally living up to your nickname, eh, Scruffy?*

At one point the cat pattered in and out. At one point the scent of oranges drifted in, then disappeared. His body was exhausted. His mind ached. His heart was torn to pieces.

Sparks's words haunted him. *Darius Tage didn't hesitate to threaten Chaz's life to get at you.*

His family was still in the Empire. His parents' estate was on Sylvadae. Guthrie Global Systems headquarters were there as well, and on Garno, where his youngest brother, Devin, lived. Like Philip, Dev was unmarried. But that didn't mean there weren't lots of other Guthries out there. They were all civilians. Potential targets.

Philip was the only Guthrie who'd veered away from three centuries of Guthrie Global money and followed his heart into the military.

His older brother, Jonathan—Jonathan Macy Guthrie II—had three children: Jonathan Macy Guthrie III, who'd earned the nickname Trippy because he was the third, the triple. First year at college; a smart and personable young man with a damned good hook shot. Trip's sister, Thana, was sixteen. Max was twelve. And those were just Jonathan's and Marguerite's children.

Ethan, forty-one, and his wife, Hannah, had four children: Glynnis, a bit younger than Thana, the twins, Charity Joy and Cherilyn Faith, and little four-year-old Marcus.

Throw in his parents, J. M. and Valerie, who were in their late seventies, and that was enough—more than enough—for Tage's purposes. More than enough for a man who had no qualms about "civilian casualties." More than enough for a man who sent ImpSec assassins after the remaining *Loviti* officers on Corsau Station.

The *Folly* could not survive a firefight with an Imperial cruiser, but Philip had no reason to believe any personal surrender on his part would guarantee the lives of his officers and crew. It was a death sentence either way, quite frankly.

So he would go down fighting.

"Philip."

He jerked awake, though he hadn't been asleep, just lying there with one arm thrown over his eyes. But if he wasn't asleep, why didn't he hear—

"Rya?" He knew her voice immediately, and more than that he knew the outline of her form—all curves and softness, with the slight bulk of the Carver on her hip. The dim decklights from the lav opposite his bedroom limned her softly. "What's wrong?"

He rose up on his elbows, the sheet sliding down his chest.

"Lights, low," she ordered, her voice barely more than a whisper. A diffuse glow filled his room, just enough so that she wasn't completely in shadow. She took two steps—hesitantly—toward his bed.

It occurred to Philip he might be dreaming. Except, in his dreams, she was never hesitant.

"Rya?" he repeated.

She pulled at the zipper of her shirt—*his* shirt. She drew it back over her bare shoulders, then let it slide down her arms, her gaze locked on his. Just like in sick bay. Just like damned near every other time they were within feet of each other.

He could see the med-broches dotting her skin and the faint dark areas that were bruises. But he could more clearly see her breasts—full, nipples peaked. Perfect. Soft.

Her shirt slid to the floor.

His body heated.

She unhooked her weapons belt and, as it dangled in one hand, unfastened her pants. With an agonizingly enticing wiggle, she skimmed them down her hips. Her naked—

Oh, God and heaven. His breath hitched, his body hardening. Paint peeled off the bulkheads.

She stepped out of her pants. Her weapons belt fell on the pile of clothing with a muted *thunk*. "It's that damned impending doom," she said, her voice husky. "It makes me self-indulgent."

18

She almost lost her nerve. Right between unzipping the shirt Philip had given her and unbuckling her weapons belt—why was that always her security blanket?—Rya almost bolted from Philip's quarters. Good thing the lights were low. That masked her shaking fingers, the heat she knew flamed on her face.

It was far from the first time she'd seduced a man. But it was the first time it mattered so damned much.

It took every bit of her ImpSec training—show no emotion, breathe only on command—to get through the striptease she'd run over and over in her mind for the past two hours. She'd read Mather's logs on the now nicely functional deskscreen system. She'd heard Sparks's facts on what the ship could not do. She knew what they faced on the other end of the jump-gate: they would either be destroyed upon exit or be captured.

Either way, she was dead. So was Philip, and she could not—*would* not—let her life end without giving him her all, everything, now, tonight. She never gave much thought to an afterlife, but if there was one, she didn't want to be sitting there without the experience of loving Philip Guthrie as one of her memories.

And if there wasn't an afterlife—if things simply ended—then she wanted things to end this way: making love to her long-lost always-forever dream hero. Who had somehow become a real man with needs and fears, mistakes and triumphs. There was still an element of hero worship when she looked at him; there always would be. But the real Philip Guthrie overshadowed that. She'd made him laugh. She'd felt his desperation, his anguish. She'd shared his joy.

She *connected* with him, and where a few hours ago it angered her that he didn't share that connection, that he was willing to transfer her off his ship, she no longer cared about that.

Life was all about giving. Not about what she would get in return.

She stepped over her pile of clothes and his. He was angled up on his elbows, sheet pooled around his waist, watching her, his expression unreadable except for the brief moment when she shimmied out of her pants. She swore she saw his lips part in surprise. In anticipation.

She hoped that's what it was. Not those damned thirty—

Shut up, Rya. Don't think about that, don't lose your focus. It's now or never. You know you can do things with your hands, your mouth, and he won't care what you weigh . . .

"Rebel, you shouldn't—"

Rebel. He called her Rebel. A small spark of confidence surged. She knelt on the edge of his bed.

"—be here. I, that is, you could—"

She moved toward him on all fours, her hands now on either side of his legs, trapping them under the bedsheet. He stopped speaking and, closer now, she read uncertainty in the way his gaze zigzagged. His lips parted. Another protest about to be launched.

She lowered her face and nipped his bare stomach. His muscles rippled. She circled his navel with her tongue.

He groaned, collapsing back, thrusting his hands in her hair.

She brought one leg over his, her tongue moving lower over his flat abdomen, when he suddenly grabbed her shoulders, quickly releasing her right shoulder—the injured one—to pull her up with his left hand, his right hand now at her waist. There was an insistence in his grip, in his fingers drawing her up but at the same time pushing her against him so she could feel the heat of his body, the coarseness of his chest hair against her breasts, the hard length of his erection against her thigh.

She clearly saw smoky desire in the darkening of his blue eyes, half hooded now.

Then one hand was back in her hair and his mouth found hers, his kiss bruising her lips. She opened her mouth, her tongue tasting his, her fingers desperate and seeking. She clutched his shoulders as his hand pulled out of her hair to caress her back, knead her hip, and hold her more firmly, tighter...

He broke their kiss. "Oh, sweet God. Rya." His words were a hoarse whisper so filled with longing that her heart stuttered, her breath sped up. He rubbed his mouth across her cheek until he reached her ear. He nipped her as she'd nipped him minutes ago. Then he continued downward. She arched her throat, wanting the heat of his mouth everywhere.

He pulled her up farther so she straddled him, his gaze once again intent yet searching. Her hands gripped the hard muscles of his shoulders as he took the tip of one breast into his mouth, his tongue teasing an already hard nipple, creating exquisite sensations that shot straight between her legs.

Eyes closed, she rocked against him, wanting more, wanting everything.

He ran his hands up the column of her neck, threading his fingers into her hair, and brought her face down to his. Her eyes fluttered open, the desire she saw on his face quickening her pulse.

"Slow down, beautiful," he breathed against her lips. "We have a lifetime."

They did. The whole one and a half shipdays that were left of it. And, wonder of wonders, he called her "beautiful." The man was clearly delusional. She intended to keep him that way.

His kiss this time was slower, deeper, a deliberate torture by a man who knew how to heat a woman's soul. A low moan filled her throat; she knew he heard it and felt it, because his body trembled slightly. Then he was ripping the sheet away, the last bit of impediment, and it was all heated skin against heated skin.

He clasped her against him, one arm across her back, one around her waist, moving her easily as if she weighed nothing. He rolled her onto her back, his mouth bruising hers again. Now it was her fingers finding the muscles of his back and shoulders, then up, threading through his short, thick hair.

Hot, wet kisses trailed down the side of her neck, then found her other breast, sucking gently. She arched against him. His hands slid down her hips, cupped her rear, and only as he lifted her slightly did she realize he was the one intent on giving.

No, it was supposed to be *her* seduction of him!

"Philip," she gasped. His answer was a soft, throaty

laugh against her belly. Then a gentle nip on the sensitive flesh of her inner thigh. Then a mouth and tongue that kissed, stroked, and teased until she was gasping for breath, biting back cries of pleasure that could, if she released them, wake the whole damned ship.

She tugged at his hair. Hard. He slid up her body, his kisses once again fierce against her mouth, his breathing as ragged as her own. Then, with damnable perfection, he slowed, his kisses and touches teasing, and she knew that she was prey and he the hunter. He had the experience, he had the patience, and—

God and stars!

—his fingers found every pleasure center on her body with unerring accuracy. She arched into his hand, breathless. And more than ready.

His gaze locked on hers and she sensed possession, need. He slid deeply inside her, still controlled, but now the muscles of his shoulders trembled under her fingers. She moved with his thrusts as he filled her, using every bit of her body to draw him deeper, to offer him everything, to give him all she had. His hand tightened on her hip. She could feel him fighting for control, so she brought her legs up around his waist. Her reward was his hard exhalation of pleasure against her mouth, not quite a gasp, not quite a moan. And a kiss—intense, demanding, and desperate.

"Now, beautiful," he rasped out, shuddering into her, thrusting deeper, heat and pleasure racing through her in response. She clenched her body around his and lost herself in the feel of him, the scent of him, and in the heat generated by their sweat-slickened bodies. In the sound of her name on his lips as he cried out in release. In the feel of his mouth against hers as her passion crested along with his.

Until their breathing slowed, his touched gentled,

and the discordant rumbling of a cat purring was the loudest sound in the room.

Rya's eyelids fluttered open as her brain informed her of her surroundings: bed. Man on one side. Cat on the other. The clock on the nightstand told her it was 0545. It all seemed terribly normal.

Her whole universe was upside down.

The cat and the clock she understood, but the man was Philip Guthrie, and the bed was on a ship that would shortly face Imperial forces intent on its destruction.

She felt wonderful. She felt terrified. She felt confused. She felt—perhaps for the first time in her life—at peace.

And her shoulder hurt like hell.

She should leave, quietly, quickly, before the proverbial heat of passion wilted under the proverbial light of day. Even if that light of day was artificial shiplight. More so because it *was* shiplight, but, damn, Philip had made love to her and, damn, she just wanted a few more self-indulgent minutes—

"You're frowning." A man's deep voice rumbled in her ear. "Was last night so terrible?"

Not just a man. Philip Guthrie.

Warm lips found the side of her neck. Warmer kisses brushed her skin. Hands slid over her hips in a slow, seductive massage. Warmth threatened to turn to heat.

She closed her eyes, trying to still her rapidly beating heart and her screaming brain that said, yes, sweet God, she'd slept with Philip Guthrie. Slept. Not just had sex. She'd had sex with lots of men. She never slept with any of them. Never *woke up* with any of them next to her. When the sex was over—even if it was 0400 hours—she left or he left. Always.

Yet here she was with Philip. And it felt wonderful. Right. But she couldn't explain that without telling him about all the other men....

"My shoulder hurts," she said lamely.

The tantalizing massage stilled. Now he was frowning. "God, Rya. I'm a selfish bastard. I'm sorry." He levered up on one elbow. "Turn over. Let me see if you're bleeding."

His genuine concern tore at her. "I'm not. That is, I'm sure I'm not. It just throbs a bit."

"Turn over, Subbie, or I will beat you with my cane and then you will really hurt." He pinned her with a narrow-eyed gaze, lips twitching.

That made her giggle, uncharacteristically so, but he appeared so comically fierce—and this was Philip "Scruffy" Guthrie. And he was, oh, God, yes, so beautifully naked. Better she not look at him any longer than she had to.

She turned over and, seconds later, strong fingers prodded her back and shoulder. "A little bleeding. Damn it all. I should have never—"

"I'm fine," she said into the pillow. "Honest."

"I'll get one of the meddies down here—"

"Not Dugan the Sadist!" she wailed. "Anything but that." Plus, she didn't want a med-tech finding her in Philip's bed. Even if they only had a day left to live, it was a small ship.

Warm lips once again pressed against the back of her neck. "I'd never hurt you, beautiful. Believe that. But we do need to get you to sick bay and have someone replace those patches."

The sheets rustled, the bed jiggled. Captain Folly let out a raspy meow. "I'll hit the lav first," Philip's voice told her while her face was still buried in the pillow. "Then I'll make coffee—and feed the cat—while you get dressed."

She listened to his uneven steps fade into the lav opposite his bedroom, heard the door close. She rolled over with a sigh.

No, he'd never hurt her. He'd just transfer off his ship and out of his life. If they lived that long.

It was 0610 and Philip found himself in his office, sipping coffee alone, unless Captain Folly counted as company. Rya insisted she'd get herself to sick bay. "I'd rather not have any witnesses when I clock Dugan the Sadist," she'd quipped, finishing her coffee. There was time for only one paint-peeling, coffee-flavored kiss before she headed out the door.

He couldn't discount the truth in her statement, but he was also a little disconcerted—okay, his male ego was bruised—by her abrupt departure. That left him with time to think about what happened last night. He wasn't fully sure analyzing it was the best thing to do right now, and not just because the litany of *Cap'n Cory is going to kick my ass* wouldn't stop.

He had a lot more-pressing problems than why Rya Bennton showed up in his bedroom. Cap'n Cory notwithstanding, Philip should have sent her away. Any other time, Lieutenant Philip Guthrie or Captain Philip Guthrie would have. His relationship with Chaz had developed much more slowly.

But this—Sparks was right. Paint peeled off walls.

The reality was, he could not have sent her away. He wanted her too badly. The question then became: why was she there? Last desperate fling before impending doom? She'd thrown his quip back at him. Trouble was, that might be more fact than quip for her.

If there was one good thing about the Imperial firing squad they'd face coming out of jump, it was that Philip could die believing Rya honestly cared for him. Not that he was some way of atoning for her father's death or that she'd wanted to add an admiral to her list of conquests.

There was, he couldn't forget, a barrister named Matthew Crowley back on Calth 9.

Worry about that after you destroy the Imperial Fleet, Guthrie.

With a snort of self-derision, he pushed himself out of his chair and headed for the bridge. He had a few minutes yet before his meeting in the ready room. He did his best thinking on his feet. Even if that thinking once again raised options he knew his officers wouldn't like.

There was one very clear solution to the problem. It all depended on how badly the Empire wanted Philip Guthrie.

And how fast the *Folly* could run.

Con Welford was leaning over the navigation console when Philip came onto the bridge. Corvang sat helm, Dillon and Tramer at engineering.

"Admiral's on the bridge," Con called out.

"Seats," Philip replied, catching everyone halfway up. Protocol was nice when there was time for it. There was no time for it.

Con remained standing. Philip came up to him, catching what his XO had on the screens. The same thing Philip had in mind: the old trader routes from data from Sullivan's *Boru Karn*. Routes and jumpgates the Empire didn't have. If the *Folly* could lose Imperial ships long enough to get to one, the Empire would not only *not* know where she went, but they'd not know where she'd come out. It would delay their arrival at Ferrin's, but at least they'd have a chance to get there.

"Great minds," Philip intoned over Con's shoulder, then moved away, stopping behind Corvang for a moment before passing the empty station at communications where Mather used to sit. A new commo would take that seat as soon as they neared the gate. Then he stood at the XO's console for a few minutes, right next to the command chair, and stared at ship's data flowing across the multitude of screens, most of which the day before—because of Mather's interference—were incomplete or blank. Now the *Folly* was awake, alive, moving, functioning. God willing, she should keep doing so. With or without Admiral Guthrie.

At least for a while. There was always the chance Philip could escape from wherever the Empire imprisoned him before they decided to execute him. He felt fairly certain Chaz would be behind some rescue scheme. If she and Sullivan found out in time.

Then again, maybe Sparks had unearthed a miracle. Philip glanced at the time stamp on the closest deskscreen. "Ready room, Mr. Welford."

He hit the palm pad, not surprised to find Rya and Sparks already there, heads together, talking quietly. He waved one hand, indicating they should keep their seats, though his gaze stayed on Rya a lot longer than it should have.

"How's the shoulder?" he asked her. "Moreover, is my sick bay still in one piece?"

Her small smile warmed him. It was an innocent enough question. Her injuries were common knowledge. But only she and Philip knew he'd kissed those same injuries.

"Dugan's still among the living," she said. She no longer wore his shirt. Evidently she did more than just visit sick bay. Martoni came in from the corridor just as Philip sat.

"Sorry," he said, sounding a bit breathless. "I was running some sims in divisionals and lost track of time."

"You have slept, haven't you, Mr. Martoni?"

"Yes, sir. Couple hours."

A couple technically meant two. Not enough, but then, Philip hadn't had all that much sleep himself. He wasn't going to challenge the younger man on the point.

Con closed the door to the bridge, then sat.

"We have twenty-six hours, a little more than a shipday," Philip said. "We need all ideas and options on the table now."

"The biggest thing in our favor," Martoni said after a short nod from Con, "is whoever is waiting for us at the gate doesn't know that Mather's dead or that we know what Mather's done. Lieutenant Bennton and I went over a few scenarios after our last meeting. She feels—if Welford can duplicate the codes—we might be able to fake a message from Mather to the waiting ships. We—as Mather—could tell them he's just about in control of this ship, but they need to delay, back off until he gives them a signal."

"The closest trader's jumpgate is about two hours away at top speeds," Con said. "But top speeds might look too much like we're running—which we would be. They'd get suspicious."

"They might get suspicious before that," Philip put in. "You're assuming Mather wasn't expendable. My gut feeling is he was. Yes, the Empire wants to put me on trial for treason. But Tage is not going to shed a tear if my execution—and the execution of everyone else on board this ship—comes first. You're dealing with someone who's already authorized civilian casualties. None of you is a civilian to him."

"If we only knew where these ships will be positioned." Sparks folded his hands on the tabletop, lips pursed thoughtfully. "Ten minutes out is different than an hour out. Are we talking a visual ident on the *Folly* or a long-range sensor sweep? There are ways," and he looked around the table, one bushy eyebrow arched, "to falsify a ship's ident. Ways that even an Imperial cruiser won't be able to break."

"Sullivan does it all the time," Philip murmured.

"We could appear to be an Englarian hospital ship or missionary ship." Rya sounded excited. Hopeful. "The Empire wouldn't dare touch us."

An Englarian mercy ship would be an excellent cover. The Empire had a hands-off policy on its religious factions, which included the Englarians. It still worked in Tage's favor to do so. Most of the Takans—who formed the bulk of the Imperial physical labor and security work forces—were Englarians. "Unless they're in visual range," Philip said. "Then they're looking for a Stryker-class heavy cruiser, and that's what we are. Then they'd know it was a ploy, that Mather was in custody or dead. But," he continued, as expressions darkened, "I think it's an option we have to implement. One of the options." And it could work, if the Imperial ships were far enough away. He returned Sparks's arched-eyebrow glance. "I won't ask how you came upon that knowledge, Commander Sparkington."

"You'd be surprised what you can learn on Dock Five, Skipper," Sparks said. "Or maybe not."

"One thing we can't forget: we have no ability to successfully attack whatever ships are waiting for us," Con said. "All we can do is use whatever deceptions we can and then hit one of the old traders' gates that Captain Chaz Bergren's contacts supplied us. That will delay our arrival in Ferrin's by two to as much as five days. But as far as we know, the Empire doesn't have these gates and won't know, once we hit jumpspace, where we've gone or where we'll come out. Unless they blockade Ferrin's, we should make it."

"I have one more option—the only option we have if Imperial ships are within visual range when we clear the gate," Philip said. "In visual range, muddying our ident will have no effect. And if they're in visual range, making a run for it will get us shot to hell and back. I cannot—*will not*—sentence everyone on board this ship to death."

He raised his hand to stop Con from speaking, because Con was leaning forward, brows down, very probably knowing exactly what Philip was about to say and not liking it one bit. "Constantine has been with me a long time. He knows my feelings on that matter. I will not sacrifice ship and crew when there are options. And, as I said, there is one more option."

He glanced around the ready-room table and tried not to let the fear he saw in Rya's eyes affect him. "This ship no longer has a shuttle, but it has escape pods on Decks Two, Three, and Five. Using the idea that Commander Martoni and Lieutenant Bennton worked on, if Imperial ships are in visual range, we

send a message from Mather to the ships. We tell
them he's in control of the *Folly* and has placed
Admiral Philip Guthrie's unconscious body in an escape pod and is sending Guthrie to them. This will
likely delay attempts to board this ship and take control of it. At least for a time. And time is something
you'll need."

"We could send an empty pod," Rya put in quickly.

"No, we can't. This is Imperial ship to Imperial
ship. Not like with the Farosian Star-Ripper, which
couldn't be positive if its scans of an Imperial ship were
accurate. And the shuttle we used in that ploy had
shields. Pods don't. Those Imperials will scan a pod
and if they don't read out a living breathing human—
so, no, Subbie, we cannot use Mather's body—they'll
know it's a ploy. The Imperials want me, badly. Badly
enough, I believe, to focus on me in a pod and less on
the *Folly*. That could let the *Folly* get far enough out of
their range to be able to make a run for a gate we know
is there and they don't. And when they bring me on
board, I can cause enough problems—and, believe me,
I can—to give this ship, all of you, more time." He expected the stunned silence that followed. He didn't expect Rya bolting half out of her seat, hands fisted
against the tabletop.

"Philip, send me."

Philip stared at her. He knew she'd be upset, but it
never occurred to him she'd counter his plans. Or use
his first name in front of Con, Sparks, and Martoni.
That made his mind stutter just long enough that she
kept talking.

"Put me in that pod. I'm expendable. You're not.
The Alliance needs you, needs what you know, needs
what you can do—"

The emotion in her voice ripped through his heart. "You have no idea what these people would do—"

"I know exactly what they'd do. I'm an ImpSec assassin. Ask your XO. He's made inquiries. He knows what I am. And what I am is what I'll be facing on board whatever ships they send. The same ships they probably sent to Corsau. Who better to fight an assassin than another assassin?"

"No." He didn't shout out the word, but the emphasis was there. Nor did he look at Con. They'd already had their discussion on Rya's former career. "The matter is closed."

"She's right," Con said.

This time he did look at Con, and it was through narrowed eyes. "I said—"

"They might not kill me right away," Rya continued as if neither he nor Con had spoken. "I can convince them I know things, things they want. I can convince them to take me to Tage." Determination lit up her face. Determination and something primal, feral. Like a predator scenting blood. "I could—"

"No!" This time he shouted, one hand slamming flat against the tabletop. Con jerked back in his seat.

Philip couldn't remember the last time he'd lost his temper in front of Con. But Con knew how Philip felt about Rya. He could almost hear the accusations forming in his XO's mind. "Don't start on me, Constantine," Philip warned.

But it was Sparks who spoke up. "I don't like the idea, Skipper, but the two of you would have a much better chance than just one."

"And how do we explain their sensors reading two life forms in the pod?" Philip asked Sparks tersely.

"I'm Mather," Rya said. "But the point is, you

shouldn't be going at all. You're the admiral. And you're injured."

"My Carver's not."

"You can't run."

"I can when I have to. Or have you forgotten Kirro? Plus, I can have Dugan build a brace for my leg. It's something Doc Galan and I toyed with. I opted for the cane because it's less cumbersome and wouldn't constantly require readjustments. But with a brace I can function decently for about two hours. That's all we should need. It's all duck and shoot on a ship, anyway. Running won't keep you alive."

"Dillon or Tramer," Rya persisted. "Hell, send Corvang with me. Not you."

"The matter, Lieutenant Bennton, is closed." He shoved himself to his feet, cane already in hand. "Sparks, set up some alternate idents. An Englarian ship is a good one. We also have the old docs showing us as a cargo hauler. Martoni, work with Welford on the Imperial codes Mather used. Bennton, you say one more word and you're in the brig." He glared at her, anger fusing with desperation.

She lifted her chin but kept her mouth shut.

His jaw hurt from clenching it, he had a headache starting right between his eyes, and his hip throbbed in painful surges. How convenient. "I'll be in sick bay getting a brace constructed. We'll meet back here for an update at 1530 hours."

He headed for the corridor, very aware that Rya's mouth being shut in no way stopped her brain from working. That made him halt at the door before he hit the palm pad. "Bennton."

She rose from her seat, chin still tilted in defiance. "Sir?"

"The Norlack." He motioned to the weapon slung

across her back, then held his hand out, palm up.
"Now." He'd need it when the Imperials opened his
pod.

For a long second, she didn't move. For a long second, her eyes widened, her lips parted infinitesimally.
She paled, then color flared on her cheeks and those
widened eyes narrowed.

Slowly, she lifted the strap over her head, careful of
her dark-blue beret. Her grip on the gun was tight—
her knuckles whitening—as she passed it to him.

The look in her eyes was almost as lethal as the
weapon. And far more dangerous.

He may have to lock her in the brig yet.

Dugan had Doc Galan's files on the makeshift brace on
sick bay's deskscreen. "I'll need ten, fifteen minutes to
review her notes, sir."

Philip peered over the meddie's shoulder. Damned
thing looked like the schematics for a bizarre, torpedo-
like ship. He could use one of those, especially if it had
weapons. "Do we have the parts?"

"One of the things I'll need to find out, sir. If you
want to check back—"

"Is Dina Adney up to receiving visitors?" Philip
had spoken briefly with her yesterday, but she'd still
been sedated. He knew Jodey would be worried
about her; *he* was worried about her. There had been
no indication that she couldn't handle stress, other
than, yes, she was known to be a stickler for rules.
But rules were yet another thing a rebel fleet had in
short supply.

"She did two hours of cogno-therapy on the med
unit earlier. If she seems tired, I suggest keeping the

visit short. Stressing her right now could set us back a bit."

"Understood. She's still in Three?"

"Yes, sir."

Philip angled around, careful of his hip and its persistent twinges, and headed for the small room that was now Dina Adney's existence. A glass panel showed she was sitting in the reclining chair next to the narrow bed, the screen of a reader glowing dimly on the armrest. He knocked twice. She looked up quickly, seeing his face through the panel.

She nodded, then moved as if to rise when he entered. He waved her down. Her eyes were clearer, livelier than yesterday. But her fingers still trembled. She tucked them under her thighs as he leaned against the end of her bed.

"Dugan says you're feeling better," Philip said.

"I am feeling very ashamed, sir. I should never have accepted this posting. I realize that now. I regret that my actions endangered people."

"This hasn't been an easy time for anyone, Dina."

"And I made it worse. I don't think . . . I'm sorry, sir, but I don't think I belong in a combat situation. I have excellent organizational skills. I know I can be useful. But this . . ." And she looked away from him and toward the viewport, artificially darkened now in jumpspace, her voice trailing off.

"We'll talk again when we get to Ferrin's," he told her.

She turned back to him. "You will get us to Ferrin's, won't you?"

"I'll do everything in my power to get this ship to Ferrin's. That's a promise."

She held his gaze for a long moment, then returned her attention to the reader, humming softly.

Only as he stepped into sick bay's corridor did he recognize the tune—a hymn from his childhood. *The stars protect those who have faith and hope* was the only line he could remember.

Hope he had. But he doubted any of the verses also mentioned a subbie called Rebel and a cat named Folly.

19

Philip fully expected to find Rya waiting for him when he came out of sick bay, almost two hours later.

But the short wide corridor was empty, and none of the faces he saw at the various working—working!—consoles in divisionals was topped by a dark-blue beret or glared daggers at him.

Although, with Rya, plasma stars might be more appropriate. He touched the small of his back. Still there, a hand's width from the Norlack.

With any other woman, he'd interpret her absence as sulking. But this was Rya Bennton. She wasn't sulking. She was scheming. He knew it. He could feel it.

He was just going to have to outscheme her.

He stopped in the XO's office on his way out of divisionals and leaned against the doorjamb. The office was small, utilitarian, with its gray bulkheads and a gray metal desk that looked as if it'd had an unhappy encounter with a freightloader at some point, with a large dent in the left side panel and a few smaller ones in front.

Not unlike its occupant, whose bent nose and scars

were his trademark. Con looked up, his fingers still curled around a mug of coffee. Philip sniffed. Not coffee. Tea.

"Anything new from Mather's data?"

"He was a lot smarter than we gave him credit for."

"Not that smart. He's dead."

"He had more technical abilities than we realized."

"I assumed that. He handled disty-boom like a pro."

"But he was linear. Sabotaging the *Folly* was his job. When the Farosians came into play with their Star-Ripper, he was at a loss." Con tapped one finger on his screen. "He had to help save the very ship he was ordered to hinder. It put him in an uncomfortable position. He was betting the fire on board would make us return to Seth. Then you gave the order to continue on for the C-Six—"

"I guess he never served under a lunatic skipper before."

"—which forced him to try to take control through the aux bridge. When that failed, it appears he alerted the Empire to pick us up on the other side, with the assurance he'd have this ship in his control by then."

"Cocky bastard."

"What if he has a time-delay bomb in this ship somewhere? Something keyed to the jumpdrives? He had time to plant one, once we hit jump. It detonates upon arrival into realspace, and all the Empire has to do is lock tows on us and drag our smoking carcass to Tage."

"An intelligent, cocky bastard, then, with a very devious mind. Good thing you're just as devious."

"It's not my mind that works that way, Admiral. It's Bennton's, word for word. I'm surprised you didn't recognize her phrasing. She and Dillon are looking for that bomb now."

That explained the lack of her presence. It still didn't mean she wasn't scheming something. Only now she could enlist Dillon's help.

"You can't turn yourself over to the Imperials, if it comes to that," Con said.

Sounded like she had Con's help too.

Philip grunted. "Think they'll find out something from me they didn't already learn from Mather? He was on the *Nowicki*."

"It's more than that."

"I'm tired of running, Constantine. Maybe it's time Tage and I had a face to face." He'd thought about that, long and hard. That's when his trigger finger itched the worse.

"That's Falkner's job. You're a soldier, not a diplomat. Besides, the only face to face you'll get is with one of his assassins."

"Better me than my family. Or those I care about." Philip's voice rose harshly. "He killed Thad Bergren to get at Chaz. Do you think for one minute he won't come after my brothers, their wives, their children? My seventy-six-year-old mother? They're in Aldan, right in the heart of the Empire. Right within Tage's grasp. They have better-than-average security at the estate, at their offices, but even better-than-average isn't going to stop Tage."

"He'll come after them anyway," Rya's voice said softly behind him.

He spun around. He hadn't heard her approach, but then he realized he rarely did unless she wanted him to.

"It's what we do, how we operate," she continued. "Get the main target, create a confession that incriminates a wider base, then go after them. He'll take your family's funds, property, everything. Until there's nothing left." She shrugged. "He took my parents' apartment. Locked down their accounts. Voided my father's will. I never even got a chance to go back there, get my things. It's all evidence, you know."

Her words struck him. But her dispassionate tone struck him more. "Rya, I'm sorry. I didn't—"

"If you let the Imperials get you, Guthrie, you're just making it easy for him. As long as you're out there, he'll be focused more on you and less on them. Which is why I'll be in that pod, not you. My parents are dead. Our property's gone. I'm all that's left of the Benntons. I have nothing to lose. He can't hurt us anymore."

She angled around him and nodded at Con. "Ship swept clean, sir. I'm going to meet Dillon back on the bridge. We're going to try to get that security console operational."

She disappeared down the stairwell as quietly as she'd appeared.

He felt the urge to go after her, but Con was watching. He turned back to his XO.

"I don't agree with her reasoning," Con said, "but she's right. We need you alive and kicking. Not being paraded around by Tage as a warning."

"I don't see we have a lot of choices. It's either they get me or they get this entire ship, crew *and* me."

"You're assuming they'll be waiting at the gate."

"I've spent my adult life with the Imperial Fleet, so, yes, they will be. They have nothing to fear from a decommissioned Stryker with close-range lasers as her only defense. Reverse the situation, Constantine. We're in the *Loviti* with orders to pick up or take down, if need be, a freighter. Where would I put us? Right outside the reach of the freighter's lasers but well within the zone of attack for our cannons, our torpedoes. One shot, maybe two if the freighter's shields are strong. Take out her sublights, lock a tow on her, and, yes, drag her smoking carcass to Tage."

"They still have to get us off the ship. We could fight—"

"They'll cut enviro. You know how we handle that. Or flood the ship with gas, because Fleet doesn't have a real Admirals' Council to act as its conscience anymore."

"And ImpSec's not kind to traitors from its own ranks," Con added, his voice low now. "That's also what's behind this, isn't it?"

"I told you before. Don't start on me, Constantine." Philip pushed away from the door and headed for his office. He had things to do, private, personal. And final.

The security console kicked on far too quickly and too easily for Rya's liking. Well, those components in place did. A crew-locator module was still missing. But the six security cams that one of Martoni's tech teams had hooked up earlier winked on without a flicker. The data-integration module signaled ready.

Too quick. Too easy. She needed something—*problems* to keep her busy. She didn't want to think about what would happen when they came out of jump. She didn't want to think about Philip. She couldn't stop thinking about either.

And she really needed that Norlack back.

"Looks good, eh?" Dillon asked her. He was on the other side of the square console, elbows on its edge.

Rya realized she was staring at one of the screens filled with orange and yellow data yet seeing nothing.

"A work of beauty," she said, forcing a smile. "You're totally apex, Dillon."

He grinned back. "I'll run a check through the XO's console, then the ready room."

Alek Dillon had a nice smile—and an even nicer ass, Rya noted as he crossed behind the empty command chair. But it wasn't Philip's smile. And it wasn't Philip's ass. Dillon smiled too much at her. Philip smiled but he also scowled, and she loved that, because she knew she made him think.

He made her scowl too. But he also left her breathless.

Damn him.

This was not the time to think about that. She tapped in her acknowledgment of Dillon's query on her screen.

"Ready room," he called.

She waved him on, noting Corvang was at helm, Jasli at engineering, and two other crew whose names she couldn't come up with right now were synching a datapad to the scanner console.

The darker woman was Kagdan, one of Sparks's people. The name came to her as Dillon's query popped on her screen. The ready room and the security console were linking nicely.

Amazing. This ship gets up and running just in time for the Imperials to blow her out of the space lanes.

Don't think about that. Think about the fact that this ship up and running can run fast enough to keep Philip alive.

She really needed that Norlack.

Her security-console screen pinged. She glanced down, expecting a message from Dillon. But the ident was sick bay's, and the message was signed by Dugan:

Saw your station just come online. Thought I'd remind you it's time for a patch change.

Her fingers halted over the screen. She was about to tell him she was too busy, but something Philip said came into mind. *Polite, professional, and prepared to puncture.*

Sick bay could hold an answer to her problem. She'd make time for Dugan.

Several hours later, when she arrived at the ready room for the 1530 meeting, not only did her shoulder feel better but she'd helped get another security camera online, synched another station, and felt significantly more confident in her plans to thwart Philip's plans. She followed Martoni in. They were the last to arrive, or rather, it appeared that Sparks, Welford, and Philip—a trio in gray uniform shirts—had arrived early. A change of schedule and she wasn't informed?

Not surprising. And it didn't matter. He could play all the games he wanted behind her back. She had *her* plans.

"Update us, Mr. Welford," Philip said as soon as she took a seat beside Martoni.

"Burnaby Mather's position as part of the advance team allowed him unquestioned access to this ship's systems and the time, before Admiral Guthrie and the rest of the crew arrived, to reroute or subroute just about anything he wanted. We all worked alone and unquestioned for hours on end those first few ship-days. We were also working under time constraints. If someone offered to help—and Mather did, a lot—no one turned down the offer. Whenever something went wrong, Mather was right there, helping. Learning what we all did and also making sure his sabotage wasn't uncovered or fixed."

Rya nodded, remembering the first time the lights

went out on board. Mather was over Welford's shoulders. Helping.

And when a reset was needed through the aux bridge, it was Mather who went down there. Helping.

"He either programmed or hardwired problems into almost every major system on board, many of which he controlled through his communications console on the bridge. Others he carried on this archiver," Welford held up the rectangular unit, "which he could key from any deskscreen because, yes, they all worked. For him.

"Since our last meeting, we've managed to bring the *Folly* back to what I'd say is ninety percent of what she was when the fruit-transport company sold her to the Alliance. Captain Bralford probably needs to apologize for any complaints he'd made to Mr. Pavyer's people. Yes, she's an old Stryker and she's been stripped down, but she's far sturdier and far more reliable than we thought." Welford glanced around the table. "Questions?"

"I'll voice the one you all want to know." Sparks raised one knobby finger in the air. "Can we survive an encounter with an Imperial ship? I've just been telling Admiral Guthrie. There are ways to increase a laser's range. But what we gain in distance, we'll lose in accuracy and power. Conversely, I can work on increasing our weapons' kick. Let them get close enough, then punch 'em good. But if there's more than one ship on us, or if our punch isn't strong enough, or they retaliate quickly . . . the odds aren't good."

Martoni leaned forward. "I still say we bluff them. We send them a message as Mather stating that he'll have control of the ship in two and a half hours. By the time they start wondering, we'll be at the gate. And gone."

Welford splayed one hand outward. "The minute they see our jumpdrives come online, they'll fire."

"Unless we give them something else to keep their interest," Philip said.

Sparks frowned. "Skipper, we've been over that."

"He's not listening to me either." Welford shrugged, then jerked his chin toward Rya. "Or to Bennton."

That's why, Rya knew, her plan was the best option.

"I'm going to reset the lasers," Sparks said. "So you tell me. Distance or power?"

"Distance," Philip answered quickly. Welford was nodding. "They won't expect that. And if they pursue, you'll want to be able to make them back off."

"You got it, Skipper."

"Good. Now tell me about shields, best- and worst-case scenarios."

Rya didn't miss how Philip said "you" not "we." He had every intention of leaving the ship, sacrificing himself once they cleared the gate. She understood his fears about his family, but that was the very reason he needed to keep fighting. And that was one of her jobs as chief of security, wasn't it? Keeping the commanding officer alive.

The talk turned to the sublight engines and the jumpdrives—the one area Mather hadn't been able to effect. Either he had no knowledge there or knew Sparks would catch on. There was no way of knowing.

"Barring someone putting a torpedo through my engine room," Sparks said, leaning back in his chair, "we're fine."

Philip turned those marvelous blue eyes on her. "Lieutenant Bennton. You've been quiet."

She met his gaze evenly. "Brig, sir."

She watched his eyes narrow. She was being impu-

dent and knew it. But he expected that. She needed to
do the expected, in case he suspected...

"What can you tell us that will not require my tossing you in the brig?"

"We have six security cameras now functioning."
She outlined their locations and decks. "The bridge
console links to the XO's station, the ready room,
damage control, the aux bridge, and the secondary security station in divisionals. There are two additional
substations, evidently added by the fruit-transport
company—one in cargo and one in the shuttle bay. We
should have those functioning within the hour. There's
still no crew-locator system, but the slots are all
there—it appears they were removed at decommission
and the transport company never replaced them.
They'll link in nicely with whatever standard locator
system Ferrin's provides us. No ittle-doos. Sir."

She saw his mouth twitch on the "ittle-doo" refer-
ence. Then it was gone. He looked quickly away from
her but not before she caught a dark hint of pain in his
eyes.

She knew the feeling.

"Then we have a few hours left," Philip said, "to get
this ship and her crew as ready as she can be for whatever we find when we exit jump. Double-check all critical systems. We'll have one final meeting at 0545
tomorrow, after which I'll make a general announcement to the crew as to what to expect. In the meantime, if you find any problems or positives, since we
now have a fully working intraship and communications system, don't hesitate to send anything and everything to the deskscreen in my office. Dismissed."

She swiveled her chair but so did Martoni, his long
legs blocking her, and she had to wait for him to stand
before she could. Sparks was already at the door. She

leaned back as Con Welford passed by her, then she shoved herself to her feet.

She had things to do, not the least of which was checking on those secondary security stations on Deck 5.

"Lieutenant Bennton." Philip's voice stopped her just short of the door to the corridor.

Damn it. Not now. She blanked her face of emotion and turned.

He was standing, his lack of expression holding no clue to his thoughts. "My office. Five minutes. You too, Mr. Welford. I need to check something on the bridge. I'll meet you both there."

Welford? Rya glanced to her right. Welford was frowning, looking as confused as she felt. The summons wasn't expected.

"I know that look on the Old Man's face," Welford said under his breath as they headed down the corridor for the stairwell. "We're in trouble."

"Likely me, not you," Rya told him. "You're just there to escort me to the brig."

"I take it you have some sort of plan to keep him from sacrificing himself to the Imperials?"

"I'd tell you, Welford, but then I'd have to kill you. It's an ImpSec tradition, you know."

"So you think he knows you're planning something?"

"I don't see how he could, other than we tend to think alike."

"I've noticed."

They trudged the rest of the way in silence, Rya's mind working. The only way Philip would know what she planned was if Dugan had taken inventory right after she left. That didn't seem logical or likely. If he did, she'd kill the sadist meddie. Right after she escaped from the brig.

Rya leaned against the bulkhead at Philip's office door. Welford stood in the corridor, feet apart, hands locked behind his back. They didn't have long to wait. The lift doors opened. Philip pointed his cane at Welford.

"Hit the palm pad, Constantine. It's not locked."

Rya stood behind the chair on the right side of Philip's desk. Welford positioned himself at the other. Philip came in, closing his office door behind him. He didn't sit, as she expected, but tapped up his deskscreen while standing. Nor did he tell them to sit.

His glance, when it finally fell on her, was quick, nervous.

Nervous? Philip Guthrie?

"Ship's record, on," he said. "Philip Guthrie, Admiral, Alliance First Fleet." He recited the date and shiptime. "Be it known on this date I am naming Lieutenant Commander Constantine Welford as acting captain of *Hope's Folly*—"

Beside her, Welford straightened in surprise.

But Rya wasn't, and as Philip recited the rest of the orders, her heart filled with grief. It was real. It was final. This wasn't a promotion as much as it was a bequest. The *Folly* would lose her commanding officer at the exit of the C-6 jumpgate. Philip's action simply insured that there would be someone on board to guide the ship to Ferrin's.

If it got that far.

But Welford was a good choice. In spite of their differences—and she knew his feelings about ImpSec—Welford was an intelligent, resourceful, and dedicated officer. And, she knew, Philip's friend.

It was a shame he'd never get a chance to really be in

command. Security Chief Rya Taylor Bennton had no intention of letting Philip get in that pod. And, thanks to sick bay, she knew she would succeed.

"Captain Welford." Philip looked directly at Welford. "Do you accept the responsibilities and commission offered?"

"Yes, sir, I do. Thank you, sir."

But there was no joy in Welford's voice. He knew what Rya knew and why Philip was doing this.

"Pause ship's record." Philip glanced at his deskscreen and tapped something in the corner.

That should be it, then. She was witness to Welford's promotion. The brig no longer beckoned. "Congratulations," she said to Welford.

"We're not through yet, Bennton." Philip looked back at her, then at Welford. "Captain Welford, I'm sure you're aware of Imperial Regulation Fifty-seven A, paragraphs A and B? It's a long-standing tradition, one that dates back to the days when fleets were relegated to the seas, not space. The Alliance Fleet hasn't yet finalized its regulations, but I think I can say with assurance this isn't one that would be rescinded. And if it is, then I stand on historical maritime tradition and law. Are you following me, Captain Welford?"

Rya racked her brain for Imperial Regulation 57 A, any of the paragraphs, but she didn't know Fleet regs like she did ImpSec ones. And maritime law—*law*. The brig suddenly loomed large again.

Maybe they'd just confine her to her cabin. She could probably hack into that lock.

"Fifty-seven A, sir? No. Unless you mean..." Welford's mouth opened, then closed quickly. He swallowed, hard. "You can't be serious. Sir."

Rya stared at Acting Captain Welford. God and stars. They were going to make her walk the plank. Or whatever the deep-space equivalent of that was. Jettison her out a cargo hatch?

"I'm dead serious." Philip held out his hand toward her. "Rya."

Her own flew to the Carver at her side. Dugan had taken inventory, told Philip the trank was missing. Now they were going to strip her of her weapons and space her. They probably thought she meant to kill him. God, no. Just knock him out for a little while, long enough to get through the gate, long enough so he couldn't sacrifice himself.

Wasn't she at least entitled to a trial first?

"Rya," Philip repeated. "Over here. Now."

Name, rank, serial number. Name, rank, serial number. Say nothing incriminating. Name, rank, serial number.

She stepped toward him, raising her hands slowly out from her sides.

Philip frowned, head tilted slightly.

Behind her, Welford snorted out a laugh. "She doesn't know Fleet regs, Admiral. She thinks we're going to arrest her."

Philip's eyebrows moved upward as he took a step toward her. He grabbed her hand, his strong fingers tightening around hers, and as she tensed, waiting for him to slap the restraints on her wrists, he said, "God, no, Rya. We're getting married."

Rya froze in place.

We're getting married.

The words paraded through her mind but she couldn't grasp them yet, even though Philip was holding on to her hand, the warmth of him seeping into her skin as he stepped closer.

We're getting married.

She stared at him. He was staring at her.

"Imperial Regulation Fifty-seven A," Welford's voice penetrated her shock, "pertains to the authority of the captain of a vessel to perform a legally binding marriage between two consenting adults."

"Marry me, Rya," Philip said softly. He'd propped his cane against the edge of his desk and enclosed her hand completely in both of his. He regarded her through eyes half hooded.

"You're insane." She breathed out the words.

There was a slight twitch of his mouth, but it was a smile born of sadness. "That's arguable. But not the question here. Marry me, Rya. I have the money, the family, and the name to give you everything your father wanted you to have but Tage took away. I have assets already in Alliance space. Captain Bralford knows, Consul Falkner's people know. But there's also a substantial amount in the midst of transfer that could get delayed or confiscated. As my wife, they'll go to you unquestioned and quickly. I know you'll use them wisely. I know you'll carry on the fight."

Inexplicably, her throat tightened. He was talking about money. He'd said nothing about love. She'd be his beneficiary, not his wife. But the look in his eyes, the way his gaze searched her face, spoke of something else. Something she wanted to know but couldn't stand the pain of knowing.

And not this way. Not under these circumstances.

Besides, she was the one whose life would be risked tomorrow, not his. But if she admitted that, if she said, *You're wasting your time, Philip Guthrie. You don't need to bequeath anything to anyone ... because you're not the one going to die ...* he'd know.

He'd try to stop her. He'd lock her in the brig. She knew that.

She sucked in a hard breath as her options narrowed

to the only one that would save his life. "You *are* insane. But if that's what you feel is best to do for the Alliance"—and, damn it, her voice was shaking!—"then, okay, we'll get married." She lifted her chin and tried like hell to pin him with her most defiant stare.

Damn the man, he was grinning, triumphant. "Captain Welford, you'll find the ceremony and the vows on my deskscreen. Rebel, your part is easy. Just say 'I do.' Ship's record, on."

20

Philip was still holding her hand. The door closed as Welford left, muttering something about checking on Martoni, and Philip was still holding her hand. Rya couldn't look at him, hadn't looked at him for most of the brief ceremony. Only when she'd said, "I do," and then she had to look quickly away because she felt her face heating, her heart racing, and her mouth going dry.

She was married to Philip Guthrie, her long-lost always-forever dream hero—because he needed someone to accept transfer of his financial accounts. If it wasn't so damned sensible, so very Philip Guthrie, she would have thought it was a joke. Or that he had some bizarre ulterior motive.

But it was sensible. Her parents—her last ties to the Empire—were dead. She was an Alliance citizen, unquestionably. But Philip was a Guthrie—they were an old Imperial family with lots of old Imperial money. Money that, upon Philip's death, would go back to his family in the Empire.

The only way to ensure those funds stayed in the Alliance was to establish an Alliance family. A legal tie.

Her. Mrs. Rya Guthrie.

Holy slagging mother of God. She was married.

The room suddenly seemed a little too bright. She swayed, her head spinning.

"Rya?" He released her hand and grabbed her shoulders, concern written in the downward angle of his brows.

"It's okay. It's just, I just..." She sucked in a long breath, then another. *Breathe, idiot. It's just a stress reaction.*

He murmured something unintelligible and leaned back against his desk, pulling her into his arms, tucking her head under his chin.

No, no, this is not where she wanted this to go, this is not what she wanted to do right now. She had to get those security consoles working. Then she had to trank him and take the Norlack back. And that plasma star while she was at it. That would come in handy, if she could figure out how to use it. Maybe there was time for him to teach her...

"Better now?" His mouth brushed her ear.

She closed her eyes with a sigh, letting his warmth envelop her. He smelled good. He felt good. He was her—

No. Don't think that. Don't think the H-word.

He was her commanding officer. She was doing her duty. Part of a mission to stop Tage. That's all.

She angled back as far as his embrace let her. "Yes, sir. Fine, sir. I need to get back to work." She chanced a glance at him, panicked, and chose to stare over his shoulder at his deskscreen. A text transcript of the ship's record filled the screen, delineating a marriage ceremony, Acting Captain Constantine Welford presiding.

He put his fingers under her chin, lifting her face back to his. "It's that damned impending doom," he whispered. His mouth closed over hers, his kiss gentle, searching, but he was not going to give up and—*damn him, damn him*—she didn't want him to.

She returned his kiss, the hands she'd fisted against his chest opening, moving to his shoulders. Then her arms encircled his neck, because she wanted the decadent luxury of kissing him, tasting him, opening herself to him, now.

He was insane. She was insane. But for the next few minutes, she didn't want to care about that. She didn't want to think about anything other than the sensations that erupted in her body because Philip was kissing her, touching her.

His deskscreen pinged.

He broke their kiss with a low growl. She stepped back, chilled, but with reality coming in hard at the same time. That she and Philip could have any kind of functional romantic relationship was pure fantasy. That they'd even live beyond the next full shipday was questionable.

He slid into his seat, the fingers of his left hand loosely threaded through hers as he tapped on the screen. He gave an absent tug, pulling her closer, but she took her hand out of his. This wasn't the time. And there wasn't time. She felt more awkward than she had since she was a small child, and just as confused.

He glanced over his shoulder. She was already backing up. "You have work to do. So do I."

"Rya—"

"Send whatever account numbers, whatever I need to know, to my cabin deskscreen. A copy to Welford might be a good idea too." She was almost to the door. "He can encrypt them."

She hit the palm pad, then fled into the corridor before her body—insane traitor that it was—let her change her mind.

The pinging on Philip's deskscreen was a summons to engineering. Sparks wanted to show him an idea he had about reconfiguring the lasers. So Philip took the lift down to Deck 5, still tasting Rya's kisses on his lips and knowing that if he hadn't lost his sanity, he had seriously misplaced it. There were, obviously, other legal ways to ensure the security of funds in transit to him in the Alliance other than by marrying Rya Bennton and designating her as his legal heir. But none of those ways was so immediately available—or so eminently desirable. Or seemed so right, such an easy way to do something for someone who'd lost so much. Because of Philip.

Setting up a complex trust structure—which admittedly he should have done weeks ago, when he worked with Sullivan and Chaz on the financial issues—could have been another option, but there wasn't a barrister on board now. Of course, he probably could ask Rya's boyfriend . . . what was his name—

Rya's boyfriend. Her sudden panic, her obvious discomfort, replayed before his eyes.

Having sex with her commanding officer was one thing. Marrying him was another. Especially when she'd been living with Matthew whatever-his-name-was for almost two years.

Damn, he'd forgotten about that.

You really are a galactic-class ass, Guthrie.

But she crawled into your bed easily enough.

Impending doom. A shipboard fling. Happens all the time. Well, he didn't have them, but he knew lots of officers and crew who did. *She could lie about sleeping with her CO. She can't lie to Boyfriend the Barrister when she's accepting funds in the name of her late husband.*

He stepped through the doors of engineering, feeling very much the fool. And angry at himself for hurting Rya. Again.

"Skipper! Take a look." Sparks waved him over to a far console in engineering.

Philip pushed harder against his cane as he crossed the gray decking, but the exertion did little to dampen his growing foul mood. He nodded to Vange, one of Sparks's top techs, but others working at consoles or tapping data into the large hologrid boards suspended in front of the sublight drives were familiar faces with unknown names. There hadn't been time to get to know his crew as he should have. As he wanted to.

He already knew Rya far too well.

"Think I can get us a little more range and a little more power," Sparks said.

Philip leaned on the edge of the console, pushed the problem of Rya Bennton from his mind, and studied the data. He owed Sparks his full attention.

"Only the portside laser banks," Sparks was saying, "but that's good, in a way. We fire on 'em first with the starboard banks, showing how short our range is. So then they're not afraid to move in closer. And, bang, we hit 'em when they're not even expecting it."

"If they don't ram a torpedo down our throat first," Philip said, but the data was encouraging. "We're only going to get one good chance. After that, they'll retreat and return fire."

"We have to try, Skipper." Sparks lowered his voice. "I'm not letting you get in that pod. Chaz would kill me."

Philip patted the shorter man on the shoulder. "You're a good man, Commander Sparkington. Let's hope it won't come to that."

"It won't come to that," Sparks repeated. "But, look, maybe if we adjust this amplification factor a little more..."

An hour later, once again amazed at the miracles Sparks could work—even if he didn't think this one could save them—Philip trudged down the corridor to the lifts. He stopped, seeing the stairwell in the distance and knowing beyond that was the machine shop where Mather and Rya had fought. But no cat came running this time, a familiar dark-blue beret in its mouth.

And there was no Rya who needed rescuing.

Truth was, Rya didn't need him at all.

But, selfishly, he needed her. There were others on board he knew better than he knew Rya, and there were others on board he'd known longer. But there wasn't anyone on board he *connected* with as he connected with Rya.

He exited the lift on Deck 3. It was main-shift dinnertime. She might be in her cabin or she might be in the mess. Either way, he thought a wedding-night dinner was in order. He might be able to find out more about Barrister Boyfriend. Allay any fears she had that he meant in any way to upset her life.

Truth was, he just needed to be with her right now. Tomorrow was coming up much too quickly. And life seemed colder than the frosty temperatures that haunted this deck as if space itself leaked in through unseen fissures in the bulkhead.

Her cabin number was 8, another gray door in a series of gray doors. He tapped the palm pad, then once again, but there was no answer. Crew passed him by, saluting, some adding, "Sir." He thought of Rya. When she said "sir" was when the trouble started.

He headed for the mess hall and, when he didn't see her beret or brown curls, sought out a deskscreen. It wasn't a crew-locator system, but it was something. He tapped in a message—*Come find me for dinner . . . PG*—then amended it to add *I'm buying,* because it seemed less an order, more friendly. He sent it to her cabin screen and her security console on the bridge. She did say she had work to do.

But she wasn't on the bridge or in divisionals. She never came to his office.

And he wasn't going to chase her down any further. There was work to be done.

He just would have preferred to do some of it with her by his side.

He ended up pulling a bowl of soup from the processor in his quarters' small galley and sharing it with the cat.

Helluva last meal.

He realized it quite likely was.

It wasn't any specific sound that woke Philip hours later. If anything, it was the absence of sound where it should have been. There was the slightest movement of air, which should have been the result of something that caused a sound.

There was no sound.

Suddenly he knew why.

He grabbed the wrist coming toward him. No hesitation, no thought. Just instinct. Survival. A hand at his throat meant death. He could return the favor.

He yanked, twisting, using his weight and the weight of his attacker. Knee up, one leg kicking out. A body tumbled over his, landing hard in the middle of the bed with the first sound he heard: a pained exhalation. A heartbeat later Philip had the attacker's arms up and pinned at the wrists. A knee in the gut made sure escape was not an option.

"Lights on," he barked, narrowing his eyes because the initial flare could be painful.

But not half as painful as the anger now blazing at him from a pair of hazel eyes. Her breathing was rapid and harsh, her face was flushed. He could see her jaw clenching. He'd made stronger, larger men gasp in pain from his counterattacks.

She just glared at him, brown curls in disarray against his light-gray blanket.

He moved his knee quickly off her abdomen, straddling her. He didn't release her wrists. There was a hypo in her fingers. Conflicting emotions surged through him.

"You're late, Mrs. Guthrie," he told her, noticing how her breasts strained against the front of her uniform shirt and her lips thinned. God, he wanted to kiss her even now. Even if she was trying to kill him. "You missed dinner."

She glared at him a moment longer, then her gaze flicked down his naked body and up again. "The mess hall has a dress code." Her voice was breathy, but he doubted it was his undressed state that caused that.

He chuckled harshly. "I was thinking of eating in. With you as dessert." He raked her with the same thorough appraisal she'd used on him. Then he jerked his chin up toward the cylinder in her right hand. "I take it that's not whipped cream?"

The defiant look left her face and she closed her eyes briefly. "I was positive you were asleep—"

"I was."

"Then how did you hear me?"

"Rya." His voice was a low growl of frustration. "I wrote the damned training manual."

She frowned slightly. "Where did I screw up?"

"Tell me what's in the hypo. Then I'll be glad to critique your technique."

"Oh, that. Same thing I shot you full of in the shuttle. Generic trank. Just enough to make you sleep through the jumpgate."

So that Imperial agents could take over this ship? She'd have to trank out more than just him. Or so that he couldn't use his personal surrender as a diversion? He leaned harder against her wrists. "Why should I believe you?"

"You shouldn't. If I were your security chief, I'd insist you have it tested."

"You are my security chief."

"Only until you transfer me to the *Nowicki*."

Her transfer. Maybe nothing to do with the Imperials at all. "How did you—"

"Folly-cat was missing. I had to find him before Mather did." She arched her back slightly as she spoke. It was clear she didn't like being pinned, arms over her head. He liked it just fine, but her wriggling was causing a reaction in his anatomy. "Your office was one of the first places I looked. My transfer was on your deskscreen."

"Puncturing me is your revenge?"

She snorted softly. "That would really convince you to rescind the transfer." She lowered the pitch of her voice. "Thanks for knocking me out cold, Subbie. Please stay."

"Your impersonation skills are severely lacking." But her other skills weren't. She was wriggling again and his body was responding again. He tightened his grip on her wrists, very aware of her Carver at his knee. And God only knew what else in various places on her body.

"Relax, Mrs. Guthrie," he ordered through gritted teeth, because the thought of various places on her body wasn't relaxing his at all.

"My right shoulder is about to explode. Admiral Guthrie. Sir."

He imagined it was. She'd been shot twice. Yesterday. Being cruel wasn't like him. But being cautious definitely was, though it meant hurting her a bit longer. He yanked her wrists tightly together, locking them with one hand as he plucked the hypo from her right. He tossed it into the bedroom hallway. Even left-handed, his aim was good. He heard it *clink* against the tile in the lav.

Then he reached for the Carver at her side, pulling the weapon from her holster while he kept his gaze on hers. He knew she was in pain, but she didn't flinch. Nor did she struggle, although if she intended to fight back, this was her best chance to do so.

But she was ImpSec-trained. ImpSec agents didn't use the best chance, the most obvious chances. They just made sure the chance they took was the one that worked.

He considered holding her at gunpoint, but keeping her immobile seemed the wiser option. He tossed the Carver onto his nightstand—ostensibly within her reach, but he'd get to it first. And part of him wanted to see if she'd try. Then he shoved his hand under her waist and down the back of her pants, leaning closer to her as he felt for her L7 stunner.

"Having fun?" Her voice was definitely breathy. She tilted her face back slightly and watched him through slitted eyes.

"You have no idea." No, the way his body pressed against hers, likely she did. He felt the outlines of the small stunner but took a moment to let his fingers travel farther and caress a handful of her magnificent ass. Then he reluctantly retrieved the stunner. It, too, went on his nightstand.

He reclaimed her left wrist, separating her hands just enough to relieve the worst of the pressure on her injured shoulder. He felt some of the stiffness leach from her body. Shame he couldn't say the same for his.

"What else?" he asked her.

"Knife in my boot."

"Left, inside?"

"We read the same training manual."

They had, and he'd given her several chances to make a move. She hadn't. He was beginning to suspect that if—*when*—he had that hypo tested, it would be exactly what she said it was. Generic trank, enough to make him sleep for a few hours. The motive, then, was not killing him. Not that he ever thought it was. ImpSec doesn't bother tranking you if they want you dead. "I guess I'll just have to trust you not to slit my throat. Anything else?"

She thought, brows lowering. "I could bite you."

"You did, several times last night. It was memorable."

Her lashes dipped briefly. "Yes, it was." Her voice went soft.

He sighed and, still clasping her wrists, drew her arms down even with her shoulders. That should cause her no pain at all. His heart held enough for both of them. Last night had been more than memorable.

"Better, Mrs. Guthrie?"

"Much."

"So who put you up to this? Constantine?"

She sputtered. "The Tin Man? He'd have you tranking *me* out until I could be dumped on the *Nowicki*. He thinks I'm dangerous."

Philip couldn't argue with that.

"Sparks, then." Chaz's ire was something to be reckoned with. And neither Sparks nor Con was happy with his plan to act as decoy with the Imperials.

She gave him a disbelieving look, mouth pursed. "No."

"Who wants me out of commission?"

"I don't want you out of commission, Guthrie." Some of the fire flickered back into her eyes. "I want you alive, scowling and limping all over the goddamned Alliance. I want you hunting down Tage and kicking his pompous ass to hell and back. And I want you to dead-eye Olefar in the *Masling* and tell him he has no right"—she stopped, her voice catching, her lower lip suddenly trembling—"no *right* to sit his unworthy carcass in my father's command chair!" She turned her face away, her left cheek against his blanket, a tear sliding down her right. "Damn you," she whispered. Then, even softer: "I can't lose you both."

His heart constricted, her pain washing over him. He never really thought she was trying to kill him. She was trying to save his life—and would try again, through her tears, through her pain.

She wouldn't be his rebel if she didn't.

He released her hands, then laced his fingers through hers. Leaning on his elbows, he touched his lips to the tears on her face, tasting the salt that was there because of him. "I'm always making you cry, beautiful. I'm sorry."

She turned a watery gaze to him, blinking, then she angled her face, her lips seeking his, her kiss searing, demanding. Her fingers squeezed his as if she held on to him for dear life.

A tremor rippled through his body. He answered her kiss with one equally demanding. Wanting her was his only focus. Loving her was his only goal.

He slipped one hand from hers and fumbled for the zipper on her shirt, ready to tear the damned thing, but he found it and yanked it down. She was pulling her shirt off as quickly as he was, breaking their kiss only to toss her shirt and then her thin lace undershirt somewhere across the room.

She pulled him down on top of her, their mouths fusing as her hands explored his body with an expert insistence. He rolled onto his side, bringing her with him, then, in the small space between their bodies, found her breast, letting its soft weight fill his hand before tracing a hard nipple with his thumb.

Her breath hitched in his mouth. He deepened his kiss, his heart pounding, his body throbbing. She clung to him. His hand skimmed down her waist, over the swell of her hip. He tugged on her pants.

"Off," he rasped against her lips.

Her answer was a breathless "Yes, sir," and a rapid unfastening of pants, then bootstraps. She sat up to pull them off. He moved behind her, filling both hands with her breasts. He nipped the back of her neck, gently. Her boots hit the decking with a thud, then she was arching against him because his fingers slid through the moist heat between her legs, teasing her, making himself crazy with need.

He pushed her back down on the bed, his mouth finishing what his fingers had started, until she was panting, gasping, and he was at the edge of his control. This was no slow seduction. There were no more lifetimes. This was everything. This was now.

He moved up her body, tasting every inch of her. He had to see her face. He claimed her mouth again. Her hands clasped his shoulders as he thrust his fingers in her hair, not letting her break the kiss.

She locked her legs around his hips. He rolled over. He wanted her straddling him, heat against heat. She rocked against him, stroking.

He needed to be in her. Now.

"Wait," she whispered.

Wait?

A soft laugh, more than a little wicked, then a coolness where her body's warmth had been. She nipped his abdomen. A wet tongue circled his navel, then her mouth took him all in, her tongue licking, teasing, her fingers knowing just where to caress...

Head thrown back, Philip knotted the bedsheets into his hands, his mind praying for control, his body damned near delirious with pleasure.

"Rya," he pleaded finally, reaching blindly for her because control was seconds from losing the battle.

She slid up his body, and this time, when she straddled him, he thrust into her, claiming her, branding her. Her breath stuttered, her fingers tightened on his shoulders. All coherent thought fled, replaced by passion and desire, wanting and needing. And the knowing, as the heat of pleasure roared through him, that this was the only lifetime that mattered.

She collapsed against him, her heart pounding as hard as his, her skin slick beneath his fingers. He nuzzled her face until his lips found hers. He kissed her with a passion he knew would never be spent, a passion that went beyond words.

He had words. He just didn't know what she'd do if he said them. She hadn't been overly thrilled to be his wife.

And there was her boyfriend the barrister.

So he kissed her because that was something she accepted, interpreted in her own way. It let him say what he wanted. It kept her in his arms, where, at least until tomorrow, she was safe.

And she was his.

The sound of a holster's thumb snap snicking into place woke her. Her eyes flew open, body tensing as she took rapid inventory in the dim light filtering in from the lav: bed, cat, Philip.

Philip. Fully dressed, fully armed, including her Norlack across his back.

She sat up quickly, sheet falling to her waist. "Lights, half. Just where do you think you're going?"

He turned away from the closet, silently. He could move like she could. Obviously, because he'd managed to slip out of bed and get dressed without her knowing.

Except for the click of a holster. That sound always drew her. Like a sea predator to blood in the water.

He gave her a knowing half smile. "I need to check on a few things before the action starts."

She knew what those few things were: an escape pod. And the ones on Deck 5 that were the only ones—

because of tech incompatibilities—not yet integrated into the bridge systems. Launching a pod from there set off no alarms on the bridge. "No, you don't."

"Rya—"

"I didn't risk life, limb, career, and sanity to have you stuff yourself in an escape pod when we clear the gate. I will chase you down and trank you right on the bridge, in front of Welford and everybody, if I have to."

"You're so beautiful when you're angry. I know it's a cheap and overused phrase. But in your case, it's true. You really *are* beautiful when you're angry." The half smile widened. He stepped to her side of the bed. "And naked."

"You leave this cabin, it will take me two minutes, less, to get dressed and come after you."

He leaned over and kissed her, hard, making her pulse jump and her heart flutter. "You have to find your clothes first," he whispered against her lips.

Then, with a low chuckle, he grabbed his cane from where it rested against the bedside table and headed for the door.

Find her clothes? "Lights, full!" She kicked off the sheet, pushing herself out of bed. Captain Folly jumped out of her way and bolted from the room. She looked left, right, everywhere. There was nothing on the decking. Nothing. "Damn you, Philip Guthrie, get back here!" She ripped the sheet off the bed. She yanked open the bedside-table drawers. Nothing. Empty.

"Philip!" She pulled on his closet doors. Locked. Damn him!

She strode into his main room, hands fisted. Folly-cat sat on the galley counter, lapping a bowl of cream. Philip was gone.

Biting back a scream of rage, she lunged for the bedroom. Not only were her clothes gone, so were her weapons. She pounded on a closet door with the flat of her hand. Goddamned slagging son of a bitch!

He'd outsmarted her.

She'd find him, oh, she would. But those first precious minutes would be lost. He was doing something to one of the Deck 5 escape pods, and she had no way of knowing what or which one. It would take her a lot longer than two minutes to get dressed.

She glanced at the bedside clock. 0450. Sachi Holton was going to kill her—once she stopped asking what Rya was doing, naked, in the admiral's quarters. She trudged back to Philip's galley and hit intraship, tapping in the code for Sachi's cabin. "Sach? It's Rya. Look, I'm sorry to wake you, but I have a bit of a problem...."

21

Sheet wrapped around her, Rya unlocked Philip's door for Sachi Holton. Sachi's braids were embellished with purple clips today. She was yawning. Her dark eyes widened as Rya stepped aside, letting her in. She craned her neck, shoving the stack of clothing in Rya's direction.

"He's not here?"

"No."

Sachi turned those still-wide eyes on her. "And he left you with nothing but a bedsheet?"

"Yes."

"Why did he hide your clothes?"

Rya headed for the bedroom, trying not to trip on the edge of the sheet. "Because he's a slag-headed over-bearing sneaky bastard."

"Oh," Sachi said, stopping at the galley counter to scratch Captain Folly's ears. Rya continued on into the bedroom.

"Is he any good?" Sachi called after her.

Rya tossed the clothes on the mattress and let the sheet slip to the floor. Was he any good? Her body heated in spite of her nakedness.

"For a slag-headed overbearing sneaky bastard, yes. He is."

She quickly pulled on her underclothes, her shirt, then her pants. She shoved her feet into her boots—they were her spare pair and not her favorite, damn him. And damn him, she still felt naked. She didn't have any weapons. She couldn't remember the last time she didn't have at least a stunner somewhere on her body. Or a knife. At least within reach.

Matt used to gripe that she'd shower with her Stinger in her holster if it wouldn't ruin the leather.

Sachi was rubbing the underside of Captain Folly's chin and crooning nonsense at him when Rya trudged into the main room. "Thanks, Sach. I owe you."

"So, was this just a onetime thing?" Sachi asked, clearly curious as she followed Rya to the door. And clearly unsure how to phrase her questions about Admiral Philip Guthrie. "Or is he, like, your boyfriend?"

Philip had to know she'd contact Sachi to bring her some clothes. And the story of her being naked in his quarters would likely get out. A fling would be a boost to his ego—or maybe, as he saw it, his legacy. Unless it was made clear that it wasn't a fling.

"Boyfriend? Hell, no, he's not my boyfriend." Rya hit the palm pad for the door and faced Sachi squarely. "He's my husband."

She left Sachi standing in the corridor, eyes wide, mouth open, and headed for the lifts.

Three hours to gate exit.

The pods on Deck 5 were not far from the auxiliary bridge. More than a half hour had passed; Rya doubted she'd find him there. And inspecting each pod would be time-consuming—if he'd even left them open. Knowing Philip—and she felt she did—he'd lock several, keyed to a code only he knew. One would be his. The rest would be decoys.

It was time for drastic measures. She had to see if there was a way she could prevent the pods from launching. Or launching only if her command code was entered as well. She'd hate to strand the crew if there was a real emergency.

She took the lift all the way down to Deck 6, to the bowels of the ship, where the lower cargo bays, storage lockers, and power and purification plants were linked by crisscrossing maintenance tunnels. At the point where she'd be standing under the aux bridge, there'd be triple-plated bulkheading overhead. The pods and their launching mechanisms shouldn't be too far aft of that.

She had a basic expertise in things mechanical and no real background in engineering. But you didn't grow up on a station, you didn't work security on a station, without knowing how to wrestle with docking clamps and launching rigs. There were always manual overrides to the clamps so a ship on fire or in danger of exploding could be released from its berth at a station. And there were always manual overrides to launching rigs, so a shuttle could be jettisoned from a bay under the same circumstances.

All she had to do, she told herself as she squeezed past the hatchway into the dimly lit and dirty tunnel, was the opposite. Keep the clamps on the pods. Lock down the launch rig.

Easy.

But she had to find the damned things first. Without her utility belt. Without her handbeam.

Thank you, Philip Guthrie.

She brought the ship's schematics to mind and

headed through the first two intersecting tunnels, confident of her destination. She wasn't far enough aft yet. There was no triple-plating overhead. Lots of grime and lots of grimy pipes and conduits and tubing. Several broken light panels. And the delightful scent of oranges.

But at the third intersecting tunnel she stopped. It went off at an odd angle that made no sense based on the schematics she'd seen and was narrower on her left than on her right. She kept going. The next tunnel was sealed off. And the one after that...

She wiped her sleeve over her face. It was hot as hell down here. Sweat beaded at her hairline, trickled down her neck. And she no longer had a clear idea of where she was in relation to the deck above. She should have brought Dillon with her, though he didn't know Strykers. Corvang wouldn't fit. Maybe Sparks... But Philip would notice his chief engineer's absence, and they were all supposed to be in the ready room for a meeting....

She pulled back her sleeve. Shit. She had no idea. Philip had her watch.

She pushed on, the ship pinging and clanking and whooshing around her. She was hot, she was hungry, and she was mad as hell at Philip Guthrie. Her long-lost always-forever dream hero. Her husband.

How absolutely insane and absolutely heartbreaking was that? He had no idea what it did to her to hear him call her "Mrs. Guthrie." It made her ache so badly inside that she didn't know if she wanted to punch him in the face or strip his clothes off and make wild, frantic love to him.

She hadn't lied to Sachi. He was incredible in bed—a tender, giving, passionate lover.

Why did he have to be such a slag-headed bastard

outside the bedroom? Why couldn't that caring man actually care? And care about her and not just for sex.

She ducked under a low-hanging conduit and laughed at her thoughts.

Not just for sex. Every guy in her life up until now had been only for sex. Just For Fun Sex. Those were her rules. It's what she wanted.

Until now.

And now...

Now she'd walked too far. She somehow had missed the aux bridge. She was past engineering, the whine of the jumpdrives clearly behind her. Damn it!

She pulled her shirt out of the waistband of her pants and wiped the bottom over her face. There was a short side tunnel on her left with a yellow-striped maintenance hatch at the end. If memory served her, it went to an enviro substation about the size of a small storage bay. Well, it would be cooler out there and she might be able to get her bearings. Or at least find a deskscreen and contact Dillon. Or Sparks.

She lifted the handle on the hatch and pushed it open. Cooler air hit her immediately as she climbed into the room. It was dark, with only green emergency light panels glowing over the doorways.

"Lights," she said, not even sure the system would respond down here, but it did, though admittedly not with any great effort. Two of the six panels winked on overhead.

Contact Sparks, definitely, she decided, looking around. He didn't have to come with her—just tell her where the pod clamps were. Then he could be at the meeting, which—

Shit. An intraship panel on the bulkhead read out the time: 0552. She was late. And there was no way she was going to contact Sparks in the ready room. Philip was there. Defeat and frustration washing over her, she trudged away from the bulkhead and sagged against the edge of an enviro converter.

And realized this converter wasn't vibrating, wasn't giving off the typical high-pitched whooshing whine they all did. But it should be. It had to be. An enviro malfunction was a serious threat to a station or a ship. She turned and touched the ones on the left and right. Vibrating. Whining. But this one . . .

She took a few steps back and stared at it. Suddenly she knew what she was looking at. A brand-new, pristine GRT-10 plasma cannon power unit.

She blinked.

A Gritter. A goddamned slagging Gritter, right here on the *Folly,* tucked in between two larger enviro converters. The base power unit was about ten feet in length and six or so wide and came up to her shoulders. It even looked like an enviro converter—the same dull metal plating and a similar row of lighted power indicators on the lower left. But it was a Gritter. If there was one thing ImpSec taught all its officers, it was how to recognize one of the most common and illegal weapons that traders and pirates used. Plus, the plasma coils on the right gave it away.

She ran one hand over its housing, her heart pounding.

Then it sank. Maybe it didn't work. Maybe it wasn't installed. This was the *Folly.* Maybe . . .

Maybe she should stop standing here like a slag-headed idiot and contact Philip Guthrie. Before the *Folly* cleared the gate. Before the Imperials attacked. Before Philip died.

Before she lost the chance to tell her long-lost always-forever dream hero that she loved him.

She lunged for the bulkhead and slapped intraship,

tapping in the code for the ready room as soon as the panel showed ready.

The panel went out. And the overhead lights died. The enviro converters continued to whine quietly behind her.

Shit. She'd broken Philip's ship. But it was probably a faulty panel. Just this room. She yanked on the door handle and shoved the door sideways.

The corridor beyond was dark.

Fuck.

Maybe it was just this section, this deck. She headed for the dim green glow of the emergency lights marking the stairwell, her gut tensing when she passed the lifts and saw their lights out too.

It was six long flights to the ready room.

She hit the stairs running.

Rya was late. She was likely also extremely angry, and that, Philip knew, might cause her to want to keep him waiting. It wasn't that she didn't have clothes. He'd stopped in his quarters on the way to the ready room. She was gone, sheets and blanket on the floor with Captain Folly snoozing in the middle of them.

With fair certainty, he knew who'd fetched her clothes. Sachi Holton was giving him odd looks—admiration with a tinge of conspiracy. At least, he hoped it was admiration.

But now Rya was late, fifteen minutes late. That went beyond the personal and now bordered on the professional. Unless she thought he still intended to transfer her. Then she might no longer care about her career.

Unless . . .

"Constantine, hit intraship and see if Lieutenant Bennton is scheming down in engineering."

Con stood and tapped at the panel.

The lights went out, plunging the ready room into green-tinged darkness.

Philip's pulse rate spiked. His hand flew to the Carver on his hip. Exclamations sounded through the open door to the bridge behind him. Lights from hand-beams crisscrossed bulkheads.

Sparks was already rising. "On it, Skipper."

Philip swiveled in his chair. "Welford, go with him. Martoni, secure the bridge." He grabbed his cane, looping the Norlack over his shoulder as he stood. "I don't like this, gentlemen," he called out. And if Rya had anything to do with this, if this was some kind of game or scheme, he would bust her down to ensign, put her on galley duty and any other thing he could think of. Rebel, indeed.

Not that he didn't deserve some kind of retaliation. Locking her clothes and weapons away was a particularly nasty trick. Especially her weapons. He knew that would bother her a lot more than her missing clothes, and he didn't doubt she was capable of showing up on the bridge in nothing but his bedsheet and her Carver. But if this was revenge, the timing was bad.

And if this wasn't because of Rya ... He headed for the XO's console, relieved to see some lights dancing across its surface. "How bad is it?" he asked Tramer, who worked the station when Con wasn't there.

"Good news, sir? Main bridge computers, drives, enviro, emergency lights are all on. Bad news is, secondary systems, intraship, lights, lifts are out."

"Scanners are out, sensors are down," Sparks called out.

Scanners and sensors were linked to the primary

computer systems. If that was on, they should be on. They weren't. This looked less and less like Rya's doing and more and more like something he didn't want to consider.

Mather hadn't worked alone.

And Rya was missing. Now his gut really clenched. Now worried thoughts spun through his head. Mather had tried to kill her and failed.

Someone else stalked her, and he'd taken her goddamned weapons away. He might as well have put a target on her back.

Rapid bootsteps in the corridor had him turning, hope mixing with dread. But it was the slender young ensign, Jasli, handbeam guiding her way.

"Divisionals is down," she said, looking around quickly. She headed for Con.

"Whole ship's down," Con said.

"We figured that, sir. One of the lieutenants is securing divisionals. I volunteered to play messenger. I'm a pretty good runner."

Philip strode toward her. "Is Lieutenant Bennton in divisionals?" *Please say yes. Please tell me she's safe and being efficient as usual.*

"Bennton? No, sir. I haven't seen her this shift."

"Get down to engineering," Sparks told Jasli as he came up on Con's left. "Tell Dillon you're our runner, get his report, and come back up."

"Yes, sir!" She sprinted off, light shining ahead of her. Her rapid bootsteps faded into the dark corridor.

He watched her go. When he turned back, Sparks was looking at him. "Rya's probably got whoever's responsible for this at gunpoint."

"You don't understand." Philip's tone was grim. "She's unarmed. I...played a little joke on her this morning. All her weapons are locked in my closet."

Con stared at him. Sparks was shaking his head. "That's a damned strange joke to play on the woman you love."

Now it was Philip's turn to stare. At Sparks. He hadn't realized his feelings were so easy to read. But then, Con had probably told Sparks about the wedding. And Sparks knew Philip. "It's a damned stupid thing to do to the woman I love," he admitted, then turned away and headed back for the command chair. But he didn't sit. It made him feel helpless. And hopeless. Rya was missing. And they were stuck on a blind, defenseless ship less than two hours from an exit gate. With an Imperial strike force on the other side, waiting to dead-eye them.

"Philip!"

He spun toward the corridor, heart in his throat, hip protesting in pain. He ignored the pain, because he knew her voice. His name had never sounded so wonderful.

A familiar curvy shape moved out of the darkness.

"Rya! Where in hell have you been?" His voice was rough, strained.

She rushed onto the bridge, shirttails flying, and, as she came closer, he could see she was sweaty and dirt-streaked. He reached for her but she looked away from him, peering through the green-tinged gloom and columns of light from handbeams on consoles and chairs. "Welford, Sparks, we need a team, we need techs—" She was gulping for air. He grabbed her arm, steadying her. She may have ignored his hand moments ago, but, damn it, he had to touch her, he had to know she was safe and unharmed.

"We need techs," she repeated. "Deck Six aft."

"That's where the power outage is?" Con asked, handbeam glowing at his side.

"I don't know a damned thing about this power outage," she replied, her breathing still choppy. "But that's where our Gritter is."

"Gritter?" Shock poured through Philip. "Are you—"

"I know a GRT-Ten when I see one." She shot him a look of annoyance, eyes narrowed. "ImpSec pulls them off ships all the time. And this one was tucked down with the enviro converters. If I hadn't almost tripped over it, I wouldn't have seen it."

"Welford and I have been over this ship's weapons systems a dozen times," Sparks said. "There is nothing on the weapons console or in engineering for arming a Gritter."

"Maybe the fruit guy never had time to install it," Rya said. "That's why someone has to get down there, take a look. But maybe—and I thought about this the whole six flights up—maybe it's working." She sucked in a long breath. "Stop thinking like Fleet. Start thinking like a pirate, or a trader afraid of both Fleet and pirates. How would you configure it?"

"Someplace easy to get to but not on the weapons console," Philip said.

Sparks ran a hand over his wide face. "Skipper, we've got no scanners, no sensors. Even if that Gritter is working, we can't target anything. And we're hitting that gate exit in less than two hours."

"Get those scanners and sensors up. I don't care how you do it. Forget lights, intraship, lifts." He plucked the handbeam off a nearby console and gave it to her. "Rya and I, and any other ammo-heads I can find, will head down to Six and take a look at that Gritter."

But first he had to stop in his quarters.

He tucked his hand in hers and pulled her out of the stairwell when they hit Deck 2.

"What are you doing?" she asked.

"Atoning for my sins."

He hit the palm pad on the door and led her inside the darkened main salon. The light from her beam swept across the decking. "I'm a complete and total idiot. Of course, that's probably no news to you," he said to her. "Or you," he told the cat, sprawled on his galley counter, the emergency overheads turning the white parts of his fur green. "But this ship is not safe. No place is really safe, especially not with the Alliance so new. And Tage so intent on destroying us. And so, knowing that, what do I do? I let you loose on this ship without a means to defend yourself."

The puzzlement on her face changed to triumph. "I have a mean bite," she said.

"Yes, but I'm the only one you're allowed to use it on." He headed for the bedroom, Rya still in tow. She played the beam around the room. Green lights glowed along the edge of the decking. He tapped in the code on his locked closet, reading off the numbers as he did so.

"Got it?" he asked her.

She nodded.

"Repeat it back to me."

She did without hesitation.

"One error corrected," he said. He released her hand to pull out her weapons belt, Carver, and L7. Her clothes he tossed on the bed, along with her boot knife. He found her handbeam and turned it on, setting it on its side on the top shelf of the closet. A second cone of light cut through the room.

When he turned, she'd put her beam down on his bed and was strapping on her holster. The L7 had already disappeared down the back of her pants. He envied its view. She had a terrific ass.

She picked up the knife and bent over, boot on the edge of the bed as she secured it under her pant leg. Left, inside.

"I owe you an apology," he said. "I put you at risk. I never, ever meant to do that."

"And I shouldn't have tried to trank you," she answered. "But I can't . . ." and she hesitated. "I told you. I won't lose you. Not that way."

He heard the pain and fear in her voice clearly. He reached for her face, cupping her cheek with his hand. "You're not going to lose me, beautiful." He wished the cabin had more light, because he wanted desperately to read something in her eyes, her face. And he couldn't. And he desperately wanted to tell her what was in his heart. And he couldn't. There was no time.

So he drew her into his arms and kissed her, hoping she understood. And praying to God and stars above for just a little more time.

They ran into Ensign Jasli in the forward stairwell between Decks 3 and 4. Rya was ahead of him, Carver in one hand, beam in the other. He was, by necessity, bringing up the rear. It wasn't a position he usually took, but the view was definite compensation.

"Dillon said he and Captain Welford must have missed one of Mather's sabotage programs," he heard Jasli say. "He said the pattern is familiar." She raised the datapad in her hand. "I have a copy. Sparks and Captain Welford should be able to break it down."

"Go, Ensign." There wasn't much time. "Good work," he called after her.

"Thank you, sir!" floated back down over the hammering of her boots.

"The ghost of Burnaby Mather?" Rya moved ahead.

"Or the specter of ittle-doos. But to be fair"—and, damn, if going down these stairs was this painful, how in hell was he going to get back up?—"we've all been working on far too many problems with far too little time and resources." He saw her slow. "Don't wait for me. See what ammo-heads Dillon can spare from engineering. I'll catch up with you on Six."

"Philip—"

"Go!" He waved his handbeam at her.

She clambered down the stairs, curls bouncing.

He hoped to hell Dillon had some ammo-heads he could spare. It had been a long time since Philip had had to hook up a weapon into a ship's systems. His specialty was hand-held weapons like Val-9s, Norlacks, and Surgers. He didn't know if he could rig a Gritter in the time they had.

He didn't know if he had much of a choice.

When he reached Deck 6, Rya was waiting, two men by her side. He was surprised to see Martoni but more surprised to see Dillon, who was tapping something into a small hand-held. He knew how much Sparks valued Dillon and hoped the fact that this was the admiral's project hadn't pulled Dillon away from what needed to be done in engineering.

"Sparks can spare you?" Philip asked, leaning a little more heavily on his cane than he wanted to. It made him feel older, weaker, and that was something his ego didn't like dwelling on around Rya.

"Kagdan's handling everything," Dillon answered. "She's almost as much of a miracle worker as Sparks."

Miracle workers were good. A flock of angels would come in handy right about now.

"Didn't know you were an ammo-head, Martoni," Philip said as they proceeded down the corridor.

The younger man cleared his throat. "I, uh, had an aunt who had a freighter business, sir. Operated out of Dock Five. During school breaks, I spent lots of time…That is, I got to know Gritters pretty well. Then my parents divorced and after that we lost touch with that side of the family. It never appeared on my transcripts or my jacket. Fleet wouldn't have approved. Sir."

He heard Rya snort softly.

"This admiral approves, Mr. Martoni."

"Thank you, sir. It's a relief to know that."

"Here," Rya said, training her handbeam on an open doorway.

Philip followed them in, watched in silence as Martoni and Dillon inspected the housing and then removed a side panel. Definitely a Gritter, and one helluva nice unit too.

But there was one huge problem, and he saw it just as Dillon, squatting next to the unit, spoke out: "It's not hooked up yet. It needs to be installed to the weapons system, calibrated and tested."

In under two hours.

Rya was behind Dillon, holding her handbeam over the engineer's dark head. Philip tapped her leg with the edge of his cane. "Scoot over, Rebel. Let me take a look."

Dillon was right. The unit was brand-new. A gift from the gods, perhaps, but unwrapping this present could take more time than they had.

"Hot-patch it in," he said finally. He could do one

in fifteen minutes. Ten, if pressed and he had the right tools.

Dillon frowned up at him. "Sir, that's—"

"Risky? Damned right it's risky." A hot patch was dangerous, dirty, and—if it failed—could blow out a huge chunk of bulkheading. Right amidships, aft. Right next to engineering. Sparks had more to worry about than an Imperial torpedo.

"Give me another option, Mr. Dillon."

"I might be able to work her through the starboard laser banks, trick the system into accepting her."

He studied the unit again. Possible... "But we'd lose starboard lasers."

"Yes, sir, we would."

Helluva choice: hole in his ship's hull or half of her meager defenses dead. And they were still standing in the dark. That meant sensors and scanners were also down.

Tage shouldn't have bothered sending a strike force to stop the *Folly*. The ship was going to fall apart of its own accord as soon as it cleared the gate.

"Disconnect starboard lasers and run the Gritter through there. You have forty-five minutes, Mr. Dillon. If we can't get her functional by that time, I'm hot-patching her in."

"Understand, sir." Dillon unhooked the utility belt and put it on the floor next to him, then pushed up his gray coverall sleeves.

Philip lowered himself to the decking next to Dillon with an ungraceful thud. "Martoni, aim that beam over here." He rolled up his sleeves as he spoke. "Rya, scour those tool lockers. Bring me everything you find."

He had no idea if there'd be anything useful. But his words to Jodey Bralford back on the *Nowicki* were now a constant in his mind: *beggars—rebels, in this case—can't be choosers*. If he was lucky, he just might invent the first ittle-doo that actually did. And get to live long enough to take his new wife to dinner.

He'd happily provide her with a fork and a supply of peas.

22

Rifling through storage lockers in the dark took Rya back to one of the earlier raids she'd worked as a novice ImpSec agent. The freighter's captain had deliberately blown the power core, hoping to buy some time, to slow down the seizure of his ship. But very few things slowed down Lieutenant Kat "Kick Down the Door" Andrico. Rya had learned a lot from the woman, including don't assume, don't overlook, and don't second-guess. And deal with what you have, which right now was no lights, no time, and . . . No, she couldn't say no hope.

She didn't want to believe that. For all its awkward and uncertain beginnings, the *Folly* and her crew were coming solidly together. There had to be some divine intervention that put Martoni, Dillon, and the Gritter on the same ship. And Sparks and Welford. Their talents meshed. Where one was weak, the other was strong.

And Philip. She'd never known of any other admiral to be on the decking, shirtsleeves pushed up, sweating and swearing like some crusty rim-station dockhand. No mere pretty boy, her pretty boy.

Her...but, oh, there was that H-word, and, oh, how it frightened her. It could mean far too much if she let it. That was where her hope died, in spite of that fact he'd called her "beautiful."

She'd also called him a slag-headed bastard. It didn't mean she really felt that way.

Most of the time.

She put the next tray of components she found on the decking between Philip and Dillon, holding her handbeam over it. Martoni was one deck up in engineering, finishing the disconnect of the starboard laser banks.

"Ah, Dillon, look at this!" Philip sounded gleeful as he plucked a large square something from the tray that was all wires and crystal parts.

Dillon took it from Philip, held it up in the light. "Totally apex! Uh, sir."

Rya made a mental note to introduce Dillon to Lyza, if Matt was bored with her by then. Or, more likely, if Lyza was bored with Matt.

Philip laughed. "That just saved us fifteen minutes of aggravation."

But would it be enough? They were a little more than an hour from gate exit.

Boot steps in the corridor had her fingers grasping her Carver, but it was Martoni, returning.

"Done," he said, meaning the starboard laser banks.

"Good. Cory, give me a hand with this." Dillon waved him over. "Look what Rya found."

Somewhere in the process of installing the Gritter, Martoni became Cory, Dillon was Alek, and she was no longer Bennton but Rya. Except for Philip, who was still "sir." The fact that Martoni shared a name with her father didn't bother her. If anything, she clung to it as a positive omen. If Cap'n Cory were here, he'd definitely be in the thick of things, helping.

Martoni and Dillon moved to a panel on the bulkhead and began what seemed to be a delicate process of attaching whatever it was she'd found. Philip was still on his back, knees bent, next to the Gritter's main power unit. He angled up on his elbows. "Over here."

She squatted down next to him and directed her beam where she thought he wanted it.

His hand snaked around her neck and, the next thing she knew, she was against his chest and he was kissing her. She almost dropped the handbeam as she returned his kiss, matching the passion and desperation she could feel in the pressure of his fingers at the nape of her neck, his lips on hers.

He pulled back. "It's not like I have time to waste," he said, his voice deep, rasping, "but that was not time wasted."

"We'll make it." She wasn't sure she believed that, but she had to say it.

He studied her for a heartbeat longer with those magnificent blue eyes, sending her pulse racing. Then Dillon called out, "Admiral Guthrie?"

He released his hold on her with obvious reluctance. "What do you have?"

"Your oranges."

"What?"

Rya straightened, surprised.

"Well, not quite," Dillon continued. "What I am seeing and feeling on a section of this access panel is evidence of corrosion. There's a secondary cargo hold above us. Regular cargo, not plated with anticorrosives for perishables. The fruit may be gone but the oils, the acids, never left. They're part of the bulkheading wherever the previous owner stored fruit, because a Stryker normally doesn't have that kind of anti-corrosive plating."

Philip barked out a short laugh. "Does it affect the Gritter?"

"Not in the least."

One mystery solved, a dozen problems to go. Warmed by Philip's kiss and laughter, Rya returned to pilfering lockers, running parts and tools back and forth, and adjusting handbeams.

The overhead lights flared on.

For a moment, there was silence. For a moment, everyone froze in place—Martoni and Philip by a secondary power panel a few feet from the Gritter, and Dillon at the Gritter's main unit with Rya seated on the decking next to him, linking two components together under Dillon's verbal guidance.

Dillon pumped his fist in the air. "Yes! Sparks, thank you!" Martoni let out a whoop. Rya had turned toward Martoni and Philip, grin widening on her face, when someone grabbed her shoulders. Before she knew what was happening, Dillon kissed her.

She pushed against him, surprise widening her eyes, confusion flooding her mind.

"Sorry," he breathed, but one hand was still on her shoulder and he was staring at her.

She didn't have to look to her left to know Philip was too.

She wrapped her fingers around his wrist and removed his hand. "It's okay. Things are a little crazy right now." It wasn't okay, but this was so unexpected. She didn't want to *assume*—Andrico had taught her as much—but she didn't want to hurt. Or encourage. Not at all. Philip—

"We never did get to that card game," Dillon said.

"Do we know what systems are operational?" she

asked, turning away from him to look at Philip and Martoni. Her breath caught, and only her ImpSec training kept her emotions in check at the pain she saw on Philip's face.

Then it was gone. He looked down at whatever he had in his hands, which was obviously more important than looking at her so she could mouth an apology. Something. Anything. A look that would say, *You're all I want. Not him. You.*

But he wouldn't look at her.

Martoni lunged away from the panel. "I'll try intra-ship."

Intraship was on. Lights were on. Sensors and scanners were moments from coming on. Lifts were even operational.

"Ghost of Burnaby Mather," Welford's voice said over intraship.

"We're almost done here," Martoni told him.

"Good. Forty-five to gate exit. Tell me when we have a plasma cannon to blast holes in the Imperials and I'll be a happy man. Welford out."

Philip finally looked at her, his face expressionless. "When you're finished with Dillon, Bennton, get back to the bridge. Security systems should be back up. Keep an eye on things. We don't need surprises." He looked away.

Bennton. Not Rya. Not Rebel. Not even Subbie. Bennton. Her father's treasured name sounded like a curse.

When you're finished with Dillon...

She was more than finished with Dillon, with Guthrie—anything male.

Fuck you all. She shoved herself to her feet, and only as she crossed the doorway to the corridor did she halt and angle back toward him. "Yes, sir!"

She headed for the lifts with a determined gait and clenched teeth.

Philip didn't know what bothered him more: the pain or the stupidity. Both were his. *Galactic-class ass* didn't even cover it.

But his nerves and his patience were stretched to the breaking point with the ship about to cross the jumpgate and the Gritter not yet operational—and then Alek Dillon kissed Rya. Philip felt sucker-punched, gut seizing, air forced from his lungs. He had been worried about Matthew the Barrister Boyfriend. He should have been watching Alek Dillon.

Dillon was putting moves on his wife.

Dillon doesn't know she's your wife.

Granted, Rya hadn't seemed remotely thrilled by those moves, but during the few moments Dillon's mouth was on hers, rational thought wasn't one of Philip's strong points. So he had acted on instinct— separate them. Like two feuding crew members, or two crew members who couldn't keep their hands off each other, ignoring propriety and professionalism.

Yeah, like you thought of that when you kissed her.

That was different. He was the admiral. And a galactic-class ass.

"Linkage confirmations coming through now," Dillon announced, watching his hand-held closely. "Cory, get whoever is sitting weapons on the bridge to tell me they're seeing what I'm seeing."

Philip stepped away from the secondary power panel and watched the data flash onto Dillon's small screen. By hell's fat ass, it was working. Signals from the Gritter were dancing down the starboard laser bank's datafeeds as easily as if they'd belonged there all along.

He heard Martoni raise the bridge and, after a few moments, heard Sparks's enthusiastic confirmation.

The Gritter was online.

Philip couldn't help it. He'd been raised in a strong faith family, though for him, it had been years. But he closed his eyes and bowed his head, just for a few seconds, in humble acknowledgement of prayers answered, of wisdom bestowed at the right time, of things coming together in divine order—not on his timetable but by unseen hands that were infinitely wiser than he was.

And weren't, as he was, galactic-class asses.

The glowing numbers on the intraship panel told him they had thirty-five minutes to gate exit. He could already hear the difference in the jumpdrives. Sparks was warming up the sublights.

"Gentlemen, excellent work," he told Dillon and Martoni. "Now seal it up, pack it up, and get ready to unload our little surprise on our welcoming committee."

When Philip came onto the bridge—a much easier trip, thanks to working lifts—Rya was bent over the security station, tapping something on one of the screens.

"Admiral's on the bridge," Tramer called out, which had Philip responding with, "Seats!" before Tramer's final syllables faded. When he had a real working ship and a real working fleet, he'd indulge in protocols. Not now.

Con was halfway out of the command chair. Philip waved him back in. Standing or pacing suited him better. He chose to stand next to Rya.

"We have only minutes before all hell breaks loose,"

he said under his breath and in her right ear because she wouldn't look at him, though she did glower at him briefly before concentrating on her console again. "Rebel, I'm sorry. When we hit Ferrin's, I think I'll have that phrase tattooed on my ass. Then you can rightfully kick it whenever I do something stupid again. As I likely will."

She choked back a laugh.

He felt two hundred percent better, her small smile warming him.

Three chimes sounded on the bridge. Outer edge of the exit gate.

"Eight minutes to realspace," Con called out. Martoni hustled onto the bridge, replacing Tramer at the XO's console. He hit intraship and repeated the information with the requisite "stow and secure" warning.

Despite all his years in space, Philip found his heart rate speeding up. It wasn't the transition to realspace but what lay beyond that. An Imperial strike force to blast through. And the rest of his life with Rya the Rebel by his side.

Sparks was at the engineering console, verifying the sublight engines' increasing levels with Dillon, now back down on Deck 5. Corvang was at helm, long fingers tapping commands into both jumpspace- and realspace-guidance screens. He caught the young Takan hesitate only long enough to roll his wide shoulders, then continue working.

Other officers sat at nav, communications, and weapons. Faces he knew. Names he'd yet to memorize.

Rya's concentration was on her security cameras, scanning decks for anything or anyone where they shouldn't be. Another screen she watched segued to damage control, monitoring everything from enviro inside to hull integrity outside.

Philip left her to her work and headed for Sparks at the engineering console. To the left of him was Tramer, working scanners and sensors.

The decking under his boots trembled in a familiar pattern. Five minutes to realspace.

Sparks nodded at him. "Unless they've got the entire Fleet out there, that Gritter should get us where we need to be, Skipper."

That Gritter, the element of surprise, and an old trader's gate a mere two short hours away.

Gate chimes sounded. He planted his cane firmly on the decking and used his free hand to brace himself against the back of Sparks's chair. There was no reason the *Folly* shouldn't handle a gate transit smoothly, but there were times that sublights shimmied for no reason. He'd seen captains and crew caught unawares and knocked to their asses. So he braced and he watched sublight data on Sparks's console on his right and the beginnings of scanner data forming on his left.

"Exiting gate," Con said, more calmly than Philip knew any of them felt. "Ready bogey check. Sending transmits to the *Nowicki*."

The forward screens blanked, then flashed back on, a velvet black starfield coming into focus. Philip realized he was holding his breath. He let it out slowly. They were through the gate. And anything and everything Jodey needed to know was on its way.

"Initiating bogey check," Tramer confirmed. "Bogey check sweep one. Clear."

"Sublights at full," Sparks said. "Jumpdrives off line. All systems normal."

"Sweep two. Clear."

Could Tage have changed his mind? Or had someone—the *Nowicki* or some Alliance strike force formed while they were in jump—already cleared their path? Could—

"Sweep three. We have bogeys."

Philip's adrenaline spiked.

"Confirming range and position now," Tramer continued.

Con opened intraship. "Battle stations!"

Chatter on the bridge doubled as shields charged to maximum, sublights were fine-tuned, and critical bulkhead doors groaned into position.

He chanced a quick glance at Rya. She had one hand on her Carver and one tapping out commands on her console. No time now...He turned back to Tramer, leaning over the man's shoulder, reading the same data he knew Con and Sparks had on their screens.

Tage hadn't given up. And no one from the Alliance was here to save them. Two P-75s and a 400-ton Imperial Arrow-class destroyer were coming in from their starboard axis and were fifteen minutes out.

He looked over his shoulder at Con, not surprised to meet his gaze. "That gives us a little room."

Con nodded. "Agreed. The closer we can get to the next gate, the better."

Philip turned back. "Punch it, Sparks. Let's not let them know we can fight back. Yet."

"Aye, Skipper. Captain," Sparks responded without taking his gaze off his console. He was increasing power to the sublights even as Philip spoke to him.

"Patrol ships kicking hot, destroyer following," Tramer said.

"Any ident on the destroyer yet?" Philip wasn't concerned about the P-75s. But knowing who the captain of the destroyer was could make things easier. The ships had to come in from Baris, probably Talgarrath or Starport 6. He knew most of the captains—or did. Things had changed a lot in the past six months.

"Working on it," Tramer replied.

Breathing down the kid's neck isn't going to help any, Guthrie. They're a good crew. You've got Constantine. You've got Sparks.

He stepped over to the command chair and leaned one hand on the back. Con was used to Philip breathing down his neck.

"Bets on who's in the chair?" Con angled his head toward Philip.

"You still haven't paid me the bottle of Lashto you owe me."

"Double or nothing."

"Double or nothing it is. Who's in the chair?"

"Confirmation on the destroyer coming in," Tramer called out. "Reads as the *Padrin Drey.*"

"Willa Hillarston," Philip said. "Unless Rayburn's moved people around." Knowing the predicament the fracturing of Fleet had placed Admiral Weston Rayburn in, that wasn't unlikely. "Hillarston doesn't like to waste time and she won't play games. Those are her strong points. Her weak one is she relies too much on computer scenarios for her tactics and targeting."

"Message incoming from the *Drey,*" Martoni said. "Captain Hillarston is demanding we kill sublights and prepare to be boarded."

"That's two bottles you owe me, Constantine."

"We'll argue that later, Admiral. Martoni, inform Captain Hillarston that *Hope's Folly* will not comply with her demand. Tell her we're an unarmed vessel in transit to a depot and any aggression on the *Drey*'s part will be taken as an act of piracy."

It was all rhetoric. Philip knew that, as did Con and every officer on the bridge. But they were going to make it to Ferrin's. They *were*. And a record of what the Empire was doing and where had value. As well as confirmation that, yes, Hillarston was still in the chair on the *Drey*.

"Eleven minutes and closing," Tramer said.

Then from Martoni: "Hillarston's requesting ship's documents and the captain's certificate. Sending the Pavyer Fruit Transport Services file."

That would, Philip knew, keep Hillarston busy for only a short time. She had to be confirming through her scanners even now that they were a Stryker-class ship. And if Mather's information had gotten through, that was exactly the class ship the Empire was looking for.

"*Drey* at ten minutes."

Con tapped a screen. "One hour forty-five minutes to gate."

Sparks, the miracle worker, was pushing his engines beyond spec. They'd shaved a few minutes off their time. Every few minutes more—

"Patrol ships firing. Torpedoes incoming!"

"Arming lasers," said a pale-haired man, one of the officers at weapons. "Tracking, targeting..."

This was only a warning shot, Philip knew. A deadly one, because they had only one working laser bank. The *Drey* would see that, as would the patrol ships. If they were stupid—and he prayed they were—they'd try to come at the *Folly* on what they believed was her weak side, her starboard side.

The side that held a plasma cannon they didn't know about.

But the portside lasers were short-range, even with all that Sparks had been able to do to them. He intensely disliked torpedoes coming that close.

So did Con. "Stand by for emergency evasive action, Mr. Corvang."

"Standing by, sir."

A short flash of color on the forward screen.

"Bogey one, direct hit," Tramer called out. "Bogey two . . . gone! Direct hit."

"Willarston is telling her bridge officers that this will be easy." Philip walked behind Con's chair, heading for the XO's console. "She'll have the patrol ships throw a few more birds at us just to be sure all we have is one lousy bank of lasers. They'll come closer and closer." He moved past Martoni and headed for the helm, nodding to Sachi Holton as she hurried by. "The big question is, do they want us dead or just disabled? I'm guessing disabled, or they'd be unloading a lot more firepower on us. What we have as defenses wouldn't matter if they wanted us dead."

"A request for surrender, sir. Hillarston's specifically demanding we turn you over to her. She guarantees that no action will be taken against the *Folly*'s officers or crew."

Philip glanced back at Martoni. This was the point he'd known would come. The point where the life of one could save the lives of many. He could feel Rya's gaze on him. He could feel Con's, Sparks's.

There may yet be a day, a situation so dire that that was an action he'd have to take.

But today wasn't that day.

He held up one hand. "Don't answer her yet, Martoni. Let her think we're thinking about it." He turned farther around, to Rya. "We're not. So put that trank back in your pocket, Subbie."

He didn't know if she had one, but the wide-eyed look on her face and the frown on Con's when he glanced in his direction was worth the jibe.

His good humor was short-lived. A patrol ship threw another bird at them, changing the angle of attack, moving more toward the starboard so the *Folly* had to angle as well to counter. Two more birds exploded under the *Folly*'s laser. The next came too close, detonating short of the *Folly*'s hull but close enough to put her starboard shields in disarray and send tremors through the decking.

"Return fire!" Con ordered, and the *Folly* laid down a barrage. The patrol ships backed off, regrouping.

Philip's trigger finger itched. *C'mon, Hillarston. Just a little closer. You know we're running. You know we're helpless. We're not going to listen to your P-75s. You need to bring the big guns out.*

"The *Drey*'s moving in, weapons ports hot," Tramer said.

Thank you, Hillarston. He was a much better game player than Captain Hillarston, but he still didn't like it. And this was a game where all the odds except one were on her side. He had his surprise, a Gritter, and a little-known gate, now only an hour and a half away.

He braced himself against the XO's console and watched the destroyer's icon move toward theirs on the screen.

"Now, Admiral?" Con asked.

"Now, Captain Welford."

Con gave the order. "Arm the Gritter."

Philip brought up a pattern of attack honing in on the destroyer's weak spots and sent it to weapons. "But keep those lasers on the patrol ships!"

"Got it, sir! Gritter online and—"

Philip saw the malfunction signal flash on the screen just as Sparks did. His gut clenched, breath catching in his throat.

"Dillon, get down to Six!" Anger and panic mixed in Sparks's voice as he shouted into intraship. "Gritter's gone dead."

No, the Gritter wasn't dead. They were. Two P-75s and an Arrow-class destroyer, minutes out, with weapons ports hot. Coming right for the *Folly*. He'd let them get too close. He'd miscalculated the risks.

"Fire lasers!" Con ordered.

They had only minutes...

A hot patch. He had to try. "I'm on it," Philip told Con as he lunged away from the console and headed for the corridor in a painful, limping run, praying the lifts still worked.

He pushed through the lift doors before they fully opened and was turning, reaching for the panel, when Rya shoved herself next to him, one hand grabbing his arm.

Her mouth was a thin line, her brows drawn.

"Trank me and we'll never get that thing online," he growled at her, hitting the button for Deck 6.

"You don't know why the Gritter went off line," she said tersely as the lift doors closed. "Someone could be down there. You said it yourself: this ship still isn't a safe place."

He knew that but in his shock and anger had forgotten that option was still very real.

"Let's hope Mather's ghost just flipped the off switch. If it's more than that, we have problems." And no time to solve them.

"Dillon might have answers."

The lift doors opened. Philip strode out, cane digging into the decking, Rya at his side, Carver in hand. The ship shook again. Another torpedo, detonating too close. They couldn't take much more of this.

Dillon had the housing off and the main power panel open when Philip lunged through the doorway.

"It's not the primary feed, it's the secondary," Dillon said before Philip could ask. He was crouched on the unit's right side, datapad in hand. "It can't handle the—"

"Hot-patch it. Now. Don't argue." He dropped to his knees next to Dillon. "Rya, that red toolbox. Bring it here." He turned back to Dillon again, wondering how many corners he could cut without having the thing blow up in their faces. "Have you hot-patched a plasma cannon before?"

"Only in the lab, in the academy."

"This will be ten times more dangerous. Do what I tell you, but for God's sake, if you're not sure, ask." He pulled the toolbox between them. "Power's off?"

"Off," Dillon confirmed. He wiped his sleeve over his damp brow. The room was too warm and held that grimy, oily smell common to maintenance shops and power plants.

"Rya, I need ten feet of D-93 optic conduit. There's a stack—"

Her boots were already moving. "Saw it before."

Philip plucked out two small laser knives from the toolbox and handed one to Dillon. "We need to cut the feeds here, here, and here." He put his hand inside the Gritter, pointing. "In that order. Then the same thing on the other side. Then—"

The ship shook violently, lights dimming. "Five minutes, Constantine. Give me five minutes!"

"Conduit." Rya was back, a large coil in her hand.

"Can you splice?"

"Yes."

"Three sections. This end only. Dillon, cut the feeds." Philip flicked on his knife and made his slices, then the next set, Dillon mirroring his movements. He concentrated fully on the Gritter, on the patch. Rya was no longer Rya but someone who followed orders, who brought this, spliced that. He had to forget she was Rya, because if he remembered then he had to face the fact that what he was doing would likely kill her. A patch like this could fail.

If Imperial torpedoes didn't blow a hole in their hull, their own weapon would.

The ship shook again, this time setting alarms wailing.

"This end on the power panel?" Dillon shouted over the noise.

"Exactly." Philip shoved himself awkwardly to his feet. He'd think about his throbbing hip later. He prayed there was a later.

Rya had his arm, then she shoved his cane into his hand.

"This way?" Dillon asked, holding the conduit in front of a row of blinking connectors.

"No!" He lurched forward, shirt sticking to his back. "You have it backward."

Dillon corrected his mistake in the few seconds it took Philip to reach him. Philip leaned against the bulkhead on the other side of the power panel and interlaced the rest of the conduit, sweat dripping down his face. Time; they were running out of time.

"Rya," he called out over his shoulder. "Get the laser-bank program up on the main console." This was critical. Once he started the recoding—redirecting the laser banks' commands and inserting the Gritter's—a power fluctuation would wipe everything out.

Give me a miracle, Sparks.

"Program's up!"

"Dillon, I'll finish here. You get that recoding started. Delete all safety overrides. Go!"

But Dillon was already going. Then the tapping and beeping of the screen and the low snap of the last pieces of conduit were the only sounds other than the harsh breathing of three people on a race against time. The alarm had shut off—Philip couldn't say when. But it was quiet again, the ship's sublights a constant vibration.

"Almost there," Dillon called.

"Tell me when." Philip threaded his way around the enviro converters, back to the Gritter. He shoved open the small access panel and checked the spliced feeds. They looked good. "Then get up to engineering. If there's a second failure, you'll see it start there before I will down here. Cut all power to the unit if that happens."

"Almost . . . yes. Done!"

"Engineering, now." Philip hit the Gritter's manual reset. Power indicators blinked on, then a low hum vibrated from the Gritter. He glanced quickly at the bulkhead power panel. No sparking overloads. Everything was holding. He let out a long breath.

Rya stepped toward him.

The room plunged into darkness, the ship lurching hard to port. He fell against a converter. Teeth gritted in pain and anger, he grabbed frantically for an edge to keep his balance. He heard a thump, heard Rya swear, then alarms wailed again as green emergency lights winked on overhead.

"Rya!"

"I'm all right."

He glanced at the indicator lights on the Gritter. The patch was holding. For now.

A handbeam flashed on in his direction. He couldn't

see her but she could see him. Another hard lurch. He dropped to his knees, swearing under his breath. She was already crawling toward him.

He grabbed her arm. "Get out of here. This thing blows, it's taking this whole section with it."

"You coming?"

Two lights on the Gritter went from green to yellow.

"Fuck." The feeds had come loose. But there hadn't been time to link the conduit, to solder connections. He slid quickly over to the unit and shoved the access hatch aside with one hand, feeling in the toolbox for the laser knife with the other.

Rya pressed it into his hand.

"Rya, out. Now."

"I've got the other knife." She wedged the hand-beam into a vent in the Gritter's housing, illuminating the feeds. "I watched what Dillon did. Tell me what you need done."

"This unit's live. You're not touching a damned thing."

"And you are?"

"I know what I'm doing." He held his breath, angling the knife in carefully, bracing his right hand with his left. If he touched the wrong feed or brushed against one, he was dead. It was like threading a needle in a rocking chair. His body swayed, sweat dripping into his eyes.

His first try missed. He yanked his hand out quickly, swearing.

His second try shoved the thin feed line snugly back into position. For now. Until Hillarston threw a torpedo at them again.

"One green light's back on."

"Lieutenant Bennton, you have two seconds to get your ass out of here or you will be an ensign."

The ship shuddered. If that shudder had been ten seconds earlier, while his hands were in the unit, he'd be dead. Hand on her arm, he gave her a push toward the door.

She pushed back. "If you lean your arm on my shoulder when you fix the other one, it'll steady you."

It would, but that wasn't the point. The ship was vibrating, lurching. They were under attack. "*Ensign* Bennton."

"You're wasting time, Guthrie. Here." She scooted under his arm, her back against the unit's housing.

"Rya." His voice was strained. He was tired, he was angry. He was scared. "If I touch the wrong feed, we'll both die."

She tilted her chin up in a familiar defiant move. "Cheaper than a divorce."

"Divorce?"

"You tell me to leave one more time and, yes, I'm filing for a divorce. Now, are you going to fix that goddamned thing or not?"

He exhaled harshly. "Hold still." But just as he said that, the ship bucked again. She grabbed a handful of his shirt.

"That's it! Get out—"

"They're firing. That shimmy is a Gritter firing. And misfiring, because that thing in there is loose." She stared at him, hard. "Now, are you fixing it or are we going to divorce court?"

The ship's odd shimmy *was* from the Gritter. He'd never experienced it down on a power-converter deck before. Always on the bridge in a ship with properly installed plasma cannons. Not a desperately patched-in Gritter.

He sucked in a breath, steadying himself against her shoulder, and slid the knife toward the ruptured feed.

He could kill them both in the next few seconds. Emotions churned inside him. He had to let them out. "Why would you," he asked, one eye squinted shut as he stared at the cluster of feeds and not at her face, "divorce a man who loves you?"

"Why would you send away a woman who loves you?" she asked quietly.

He drew another long breath, chancing a glance at her face in the harsh light of the handbeam. The defiance was absent. There was only softness and a mouth that pleaded for kisses.

There was no time. He wrenched his gaze off her face and stared at the feeds, at the tip of his laser knife, concentrating harder than he ever had before in his life. Her words were the only things keeping him focused in this hell down in the bowels of this ship. He tapped the loose feed with the edge of the knife. Shit! It swung too far to the left, the ship's vibration throwing him off target. Tension cramped the muscles of his arms, his calves, his lower back. If Con fired the Gritter now, if it misfired—

No. Nudge the feed back. Just...a...little... nudge.

It wiggled. It fell into place.

Gods and stars. Keep it there. Please.

His arm was shaking when he pulled it out. But all lights on the unit were green. He looked at Rya, his mind still clinging to what she'd said. *A woman who loves you.*

"I keep sending you away, beautiful, because I'm trying to keep you alive. Long enough," and he hesitated, "that we'll have a chance. That you'll forget that guy back on Calth Nine."

She frowned, puzzled, then she shook her head slowly. "There's no guy worth remembering back on

Calth Nine. The only guy I want is right here with me now."

His breath caught, his heart stuttering. "Rya—"

A shimmy wrenched the decking—a big one. She grabbed his shirt again. He dragged her away from the unit. Con was firing the Gritter. But the hot patch was not going to hold much longer.

He used the side of the enviro converter to lever himself up. "Get the handbeam."

"Not without—"

"I'm coming! We have to take this thing off line from engineering. It's got only a few more shots left before it blows." A disconnect at the unit, with the hot patch so erratic, would only hasten the process.

She was on her feet, grabbing the handbeam. He put his hand on her back. "Go! I'm right behind you."

She moved, he lunged, but he took one last look back at the indicator lights. Still green. If the lights turned red before he and Rya reached engineering, they were dead.

23

Philip ran up the dark stairs after her, using the railing to pull himself up each step. The pain in his leg wouldn't matter if he was dead. The pain in his heart—if he lost Rya—would never end.

She grabbed his arm, half-dragging him into the stairwell and under the green glow of the emergency overheads. The ship shimmied, lurching to port again. The Gritter, firing. There was still thirty, forty feet of corridor. One more shot could set it off, shearing away decks.

"Tell Dillon to start a shutdown!" He shoved her away.

She broke into a run, boots pounding, the light from her handbeam zigzagging through the corridor.

He limped quickly after her, praying Dillon didn't panic, praying he initiated the shutdown in the right sequence. Praying ... just praying.

Suddenly the corridor lights flickered on brightly but, before his eyes could adjust, went out again, plunging him into darkness. A good sign or a ship in the throes of death? He didn't know.

He careened into engineering, raking his gaze over the forms silhouetted by console screens. Screens were on. That meant primary computers were on. The bridge was working. The bridge had to be working.

"Philip!"

He saw her next to the taller, ponytailed Dillon at a line of consoles on the left. "Off line yet?" he gasped out as he headed for them.

"Captain Welford needs a little more time," Dillon answered.

"We don't have any more damned time. If that Gritter blows, it's taking this whole section with it." He came to a halt at Dillon's console and realized Ensign Jasli was next to Rya. Intraship was definitely out.

"You just come from the bridge?" he asked her.

"Yes, sir—"

"Status!"

"Both P-75s are destroyed. The *Drey*'s hit bad, but, sir, so are we. Deck Three Aft and the starboard shuttle bay."

He'd felt that one. That was probably what sent him and Rya to their knees. But the patrol ships, gone. A small taste of victory. "What else?"

"Shields are down to sixty percent port, forty-three starboard. At least they were a few minutes ago. Captain Welford said that Gritter is our only hope."

He wanted to ask about casualties, how many injured, how many dead. No time. "Dillon, let me at that program. There might be one more thing we can try."

"A Taison loop?"

"You can do one?"

"Already started."

He almost forgave the man for kissing Rya, right then and there. The loop was a temporary stabilization program that could regulate the pulses of energy surging through the Gritter, dovetailing one into the next. It would be one less thing jostling the feeds out of position. But it, too, would eventually fail as the energy surges piled up, coming faster than the loop could handle them.

But it could buy them twenty, thirty minutes. Maybe.

He nodded to Jasli. "Tell Captain Welford he has twenty minutes. Go!"

She bolted for the corridor.

"How did we lose power?" he asked Dillon.

"Jasli said Sparks did that. He's using the power from the lights, lifts, and intraship and rerouting it to the shields. Or they'd be gone."

Miracle worker. "Stay on that program. If you see a rupture coming, shut down the Gritter, even if it's five minutes from now. I'm not going to help the Imperials by blowing a hole in our own hull.

"Rya." Philip put his hand on her shoulder. "Bridge."

It would be a long climb. But he wanted to be there if the *Folly* destroyed the *Drey*. And he had to be there if the Gritter failed and the *Drey* put that fatal shot into the *Folly*.

"Lean on me," Rya said. They'd reached Deck 3, and she could tell Philip was in pain by his harsh breathing. And the occasional bitter epithet he said under his breath and thought she couldn't hear.

She heard them all. But the most important words were the ones said on Deck 6: *a man who loves you.* Her throat tightened even now as she replayed those words in her mind, hearing emotions roughen his voice.

"The Old Man will make it," Philip said.

"You damned well better. I'm already picking out that tattoo parlor."

He answered with a harsh laugh, but he let her put her arm around his waist.

At the stairwell for 2 Forward he stopped, pulling her back.

"Rya." Her name was a low rumble in his chest and then she was against his chest, her back to the stairwell bulkhead, his mouth searing hers with a kiss she was sure would make the Gritter's detonation look like the weak flare of a match. She shoved the handbeam into her utility belt, then ran her hands up the hard planes of his back, feeling muscles bunched in pain, feeling the dampness of his shirt. She clung to him, kissing him with a blinding desperation. If the Gritter blew, if the *Drey*'s torpedo found that last target, then this is where she wanted to be, in Philip's arms.

He pulled back, cupping her face with his hands. He brushed his thumb over her lips. "Okay, Mrs. Guthrie," he said softly. "Now we can go on."

Something bumped against her leg. She glanced down quickly, saw the white cat now greenish in the emergency lights.

"Captain Folly too," Philip said as she picked up the cat, holding him against her chest. He butted her chin with his soft head.

The ship rumbled, lurching, voices from the bridge suddenly spilling down the stairs.

"This is it." Philip's voice went tight. "We need to be on the bridge. Now."

Fear and hope clashed somewhere in the middle of Rya's chest. She held Captain Folly more tightly against her and moved quickly up the final set of stairs, Philip just behind her.

"Shields down to twenty, sector four-seventeen!"

"Starboard side, incoming. Fire!"

"Helm, execute—"

The ship lurched. Rya stumbled against the bridge door. She felt Philip's hand on her back, then he lunged past her, heading for the command chair, staring at the forward screens.

She stared too, her breath catching. The Imperial Arrow-class destroyer looked massive, spiky with weapons jutting from aft and forward ports as it revolved slowly through the black starfield. Gaping holes charred its hull, debris spewing left and right. Entire sections of hull had no lights. Only a few were still lit on its narrow bridge, which rose amidships on a short column.

Con Welford turned as Philip's hand found his chair. Rya caught up with him and braced herself against the XO's console on the left. Con had a gash on his forehead, a thin line of blood trickling down his cheek.

She looked around quickly, saw Corvang, Sparks, Sachi. Others with their backs to her. She knew there were injuries, but she couldn't tell in the dim lighting who were at their posts and who were replacements.

"We've almost got her, Guthrie," Con said. "I need one more good shot...Sparks!" Con jerked to his right.

"Gritter's powering up. But she's overloading fast. This could be the last one. It could take her out. It could blow us apart."

Voices hushed on the bridge.

"Dillon has a Taison loop running," Philip said. "But that's no guarantee."

"*Drey*'s powering her ion cannons." Martoni at weapons. Rya recognized his voice.

"It's us or them," Philip said quietly. He held his arm out toward her. She lunged into his embrace, bundling the cat between them. He brushed her forehead with a kiss. "I love you, Rya."

"And I love you, Philip," she whispered against his neck. Then she raised her face and stared at the hulking Imperial destroyer on the forward screen.

"Admiral?" Con's face clearly held the desperation they all felt.

Philip nodded. "Fire."

The ship shuddered, bucking. Philip's grip on Rya tightened. For three, four heartbeats there wasn't a sound on the bridge. Then a flash of light on the screen and a million jagged bolts of lightning seemed to race across the *Drey*'s hull.

"Direct hit," Martoni called out, voice shaking. "She's—"

The destroyer fractured, her bridge shearing off, sections of bulkhead wheeling away into the darkness.

"Gone," Con said.

The *Padrin Drey* was gone.

"Sparks, disarm the Gritter!" Philip bellowed, turning away from Rya but not letting her go.

She realized she was shaking, adrenaline coursing through her body.

"Disarming," Sparks called back. "Dillon's mirroring the program up here to my screens. He's on it, Skipper. Power surges are backing down. No ruptures yet. She's holding. She's holding. She's—"

Rya could see the older man's shoulders trembling, even in the dim lighting. He wiped one hand over his face, clearing his throat noisily. Was something wrong? The Gritter could still explode, take out engineering, kill dozens, strand the ship. Panic seized her for a moment, then—

"She's off line. Disarmed." His voice cracked. "We'll make it, Skipper."

She felt Philip shudder out a breath, then he straightened forcefully, as if drawing energy from his reserves. "Constantine, how far to the gate?"

"Forty-five minutes, sir."

"Sparks, get us moving. Martoni, keep an eye out for more bogies. They'll send someone after us once they realize the *Drey* is gone. But I sincerely doubt they're going to get anyone out here in the next forty-five minutes."

"Aye, sir."

Philip stepped forward, bringing her with him. She could feel his heart pounding, his grip on her still tight. He drew in a deep breath and, for a long moment, made sure everyone on the bridge felt his gaze.

"I could tell you all that you're magnificent, but that would be an understatement." His voice was firm and clear, in spite of the pounding of his heart. "Your dedication and your courage will not be forgotten. I know we've suffered losses. I know we have repairs to do. Right now there will be no time for either celebrations or grieving. Those things will come. Your tears will be mine. So will your joys. But we have done the impossible, and that is something to be very, very proud of. And I am very, very proud of all of you." He paused, turning slightly. "Now, Captain Welford—"

"Damage control is already working," Con said.

"Sublights have a bit of a shimmy, but the jump-drives are fine," Sparks called out.

"Now, Captain Welford, if I can have one more moment of the bridge's attention?"

"Sir?"

Philip plucked the cat from Rya's arms and handed him to Con, along with his cane.

"Ladies and gentlemen, I have one bit of good news to share. Sub-Lieutenant Bennton is no longer just your chief of security." He drew her around, hands on her shoulders. Rya felt heat rising rapidly to her face, her heart hammering in her chest. She dipped her chin, but he brought her face back up with the slight pressure of two fingers.

"She's also now my wife. Rya Bennton Guthrie. You've all not only helped me do the impossible but you've brought the most incredible woman into my life. And for that, I'm very grateful."

And with those words, her long-lost always-forever dream hero kissed her. Right in front of Con Welford and everybody.

24

Philip didn't know what was the more beautiful sight framed by the wide viewports of the Officers' Club on Ferrin's Station: *Hope's Folly*, tethered to the end of the shipyard's long repair dock, the starfield twinkling around her, or his wife, Rya, across the table from him in the most incredible dark-green dress that put golden shimmers in her hazel eyes and clung oh-so-enticingly to the curves of her body. When she was standing. Right now she was sitting, so he couldn't see all the curves, but even so, yes, she was definitely the more beautiful sight.

She took a sip of her wine, watching him over the rim of her glass.

"So, how's our second week of dating going so far?" he asked. Most people dated first, then got married, but that wasn't how their life had worked out. Marrying her had been an impulsive move. But it was a move he wanted to be permanent.

So did Rya. The fact that she now had her M-R-S degree, as she called it, was no guarantee of permanency. A real marriage took work. Commitment. Patience and respect.

And that took time.

So now they were dating. Married but dating. Philip rather liked the idea.

She grinned. "You're too well behaved. I'm getting suspicious. So is Captain Folly. You're being far too nice to him."

"You're thinking I mean to seduce you."

"You're never mean when you seduce me," she said, her voice low and sexy.

"Dinner, sir?" The black-clad waiter arrived, anti-grav tray at his side. Which was just as well, because their conversation was about to make Philip suggest they have dessert first.

"Thank you." Philip leaned back in his seat as the waiter put the silver-domed dish in front of him. The Officers' Club had better than decent fare. Not as good as his own cooking, which was why the galley on board the *Folly* was getting a major overhaul. But the club offered the pomp of the elegantly attired waiters, candlelight dining, and, of course, an attendant behind each chair when dinner was served, ready to whisk away the domed covers in one well-timed move.

He'd grown up eating in restaurants like this all the time with his parents. It didn't mean that much to him. But this was their two-week anniversary.

"And for Mrs. Guthrie, this evening's special."

Rya's dish appeared, then white-gloved hands reached around. Covers raised. Too late, he saw there was a fork already in her hand. And a large pile of peas on the left side of her plate.

He ducked out of the way, laughing, when the first forkful went flying.

But Rya the Rebel got him neatly in the chest with her second.

Right in the heart.

ABOUT THE AUTHOR

Winner of the prestigious national book award the RITA, science fiction romance author **Linnea Sinclair** has become a name synonymous with high-action, emotionally intense, character-driven novels. Reviewers note that Sinclair's novels "have the 'wow!' factor in spades," earning her accolades from both the science fiction and the romance communities. A former news reporter and retired private detective, Sinclair resides in Naples, Florida, in the winter and Columbus, Ohio, in the summer with her husband, Robert Bernadino, and their two thoroughly spoiled cats. Readers can find her perched on the third barstool from the left in her Intergalactic Bar and Grille at www.linneasinclair.com.